To S

Jeremiah 1:4-5

yours sister Love you both
Sheila

The Redemption of Madelyne

A Novel by

Sheila K. Milam

WestBow Press
A DIVISION OF THOMAS NELSON
& ZONDERVAN

Copyright © 2016 Sheila K. Milam.

All rights reserved. No part of this book may be used or reproduced by any means, graphic, electronic, or mechanical, including photocopying, recording, taping or by any information storage retrieval system without the written permission of the author except in the case of brief quotations embodied in critical articles and reviews.

This is a work of fiction. All of the characters, names, incidents, organizations, and dialogue in this novel are either the products of the author's imagination or are used fictitiously.

Scripture taken from the Holy Bible, NEW INTERNATIONAL VERSION®. Copyright © 1973, 1978, 1984, 2011 by Biblica, Inc. All rights reserved worldwide. Used by permission. NEW INTERNATIONAL VERSION® and NIV® are registered trademarks of Biblica, Inc. Use of either trademark for the offering of goods or services requires the prior written consent of Biblica US, Inc.

WestBow Press books may be ordered through booksellers or by contacting:

WestBow Press
A Division of Thomas Nelson & Zondervan
1663 Liberty Drive
Bloomington, IN 47403
www.westbowpress.com
1 (866) 928-1240

Because of the dynamic nature of the Internet, any web addresses or links contained in this book may have changed since publication and may no longer be valid. The views expressed in this work are solely those of the author and do not necessarily reflect the views of the publisher, and the publisher hereby disclaims any responsibility for them.

Any people depicted in stock imagery provided by Thinkstock are models, and such images are being used for illustrative purposes only. Certain stock imagery © Thinkstock.

ISBN: 978-1-5127-5428-5 (sc)
ISBN: 978-1-5127-5429-2 (hc)
ISBN: 978-1-5127-5427-8 (e)

Library of Congress Control Number: 2016913780

Print information available on the last page.

WestBow Press rev. date: 08/24/2016

Author's message to all who read this book

*And hope does not disappoint us, because God has poured out his love
into our hearts by the Holy Spirit, whom he has given us.
You see, at just the right time, when we were still powerless,
Christ died for the ungodly. . .. God demonstrated his own love
for us in this: While we were still sinners, Christ died for us.*
Rom 5:5-8

Always know that Jesus Loves and Cares for You!

Acknowledgements

I wish to personally thank the following people for their contributions to my inspiration and knowledge in the writing of this book:

Del, my husband, for his encouragement to move forward regardless of the odds against. Lori Schoonmaker, Director of HOPE Pregnancy Resource Center located in Kellogg, Idaho, for the books borrowed, and the information shared. She provides encouragement, education, and positive options for girl's facing unplanned pregnancies. Her steadfast faith and love of Jesus is an inspiration. A special thanks for Beth Otto and Shirley Lyle—HOPE volunteers who shared kind words mingled with laughter.

For
Baby Ray
In my arms but a moment,
In my heart forever.

Chapter One

Nicole paused for a moment to watch the frantic pace of the backstage crew as they completed the final setup for the evening's program. Overwhelmed at her surroundings, she was unable to remain still for long; nervous energy kept her on the move. Pacing off the only floor space free of trailing cords, wires, and coaxial cable, she tried to remember why she'd come and what she was supposed to say. She had spoken in front of audiences before, but never one of such size. A peek through the curtains reassured her that Micah was still there. He was just a speck standing next to another speck at the far end of the auditorium. How could she possibly keep the attention of an audience of this magnitude for over two hours? She must have been out of her mind to accept the invitation from the Women's Advisory Board. When she dared to look through the slit in the curtains once more, a flock of birds took flight in her stomach. Fighting nausea, she wondered if she would be sick right there in front of everyone. Falling into a chair, she tried to convince her stomach to stay where it belonged, and almost fainted when a hand clasped her shoulder.

"Are you ready? We're getting quite a crowd and the bulk of them haven't taken their seats yet. They're still grouped out in the foyer trying to decide if balcony seating is preferable to the main floor."

"Micah, you scared me to death." Micah, her husband, stood before her grinning with excitement. From her seated position he seemed taller than usual; she had to tilt her head back to look at him. "Never come up on a woman from behind when she's scared witless. You don't know what she might do, and to answer your question, no, I'm not ready. I feel sick--and--well, maybe we should call the whole thing off." Peeking at him out of the corner of her eye, she almost hoped he'd take her seriously.

"Call it off," he chuckled as he looked from the wings out on the auditorium. "We couldn't call this off even if we wanted to." He turned to her and grinned encouragingly. "You're just nervous, and rightly so. But you'll be fine as soon as you step out on that stage." Kneeling, he took both her hands to hold them in his. "Remember why we're here and who made it all possible. The Lord wouldn't have brought us this far just to see you fall on your face. Don't forget that we'll be praying for you the whole time. Matthew has been in prayer all day, and I know our church family back home is on their knees right at this moment."

"I'm aware of all that, but what if they," she nodded toward the auditorium, "don't want to hear what I have to say? What if...?"

"There's no room for ifs, Nicole. This is what the Lord has been leading you to do your entire life. Now take a deep breath, because in just a few minutes I'll be introducing you. So what if a few of them leave?" he shrugged. "Even if your message only reaches one or two, that's two minds changed, and hopefully, two lives saved. Man, your hands are like ice," he said as he massaged warmth back in her fingertips. Kissing her cheek, he bowed his head and began to pray. She prayed with him, as was their custom, before speaking to any gathering no matter how large or small. He thanked the Lord for His guidance and asked for strength and inner peace for her. She prayed that her message would be well received, and that her words would have enough impact to change hearts. At the "Amen," he gave her a wink and another peck on the forehead. Smoothing his gray-streaked hair unnecessarily, the only indication of his own nervousness, he turned with an inquiring look.

She stepped to his side to straighten his already impeccable tie. A sense of total calm quieted her quaking heart. "You look wonderful, in fact, you've never looked better. Now go out there and knock 'em dead." From the sidelines she reassured him with a wink, and admired the line of his shoulders and handsome profile as he stepped to the microphone. Her stomach tightened as she waited for her husband to finish the introductions.

The Redemption of Madelyne

The audience of several hundred quieted as Micah made his way across the stage. Looking completely at-ease, he smiled as if every one of them were close, personal friends. Tension filled the air as they prepared to listen-settling into their seats.

"My name is Micah Anderson and I have the honor and privilege to introduce your guest speaker. When we were first invited to come here, we had reservations about whether to accept. We took it to the Lord in prayer. He said, "Go!" We trusted Him to provide the means for us to be here with you folks tonight. So it's with great pride that I introduce my wife, Nicci."

Her heels clicked rapidly across the stage as she moved to join her husband at the podium. Smiling across the vast auditorium into a sea of faces, she was surprised when certain ones became more distinct. Were these the women the Lord had sent her to speak to? Forgetting the size of the room, she focused on the message God had sent her to share. Lifting a hand, she gave a little wave of greeting, "How do you, do? My name is Nicole Anderson and I'm not here to teach or to entertain, but to tell a story. Before I begin, it's only fair to warn you that some of my story deals with sensitive issues." Pausing to scan the audience with a practiced eye, she wondered how many seats would be empty after her announcement. "I'm speaking tonight about the long term effect of abortion." A slight murmuring and restless shuffling of feet was the only response to her announcement.

Silent, grateful prayer filled her heart. Micah gave her hand a supportive squeeze as he left the stage. She paid little attention, focusing on the task at-hand.

Drawing a deep, steadying breath she launched into the story she'd come to tell. "I'm against abortion, and before you pass judgment, hear me out. I encourage anyone that may be toying with the idea to think about it long and hard. The repercussions of such a decision are devastating, and only a woman who's been through it knows the heartache it brings. Hear my story and try to understand why I hope and pray it creates a change in thinking." She stepped away from the podium, moving downstage to be closer to the audience.

"I want you to meet someone," she confided. Behind her, a theatre sized screen rolled down and clicked into place. The beautiful face of a young woman with cinnamon, waist-length hair was pictured there. One hand was raised to her temple to hold wind-swept hair away from her face. Several wolf whistles echoed throughout the auditorium.

"Pretty, isn't she? This is my friend Madelyne and she was twenty years old. Now, look at another picture taken within just a few days of the first." A second photo flashed across the screen showing the smiling faces of two young women. The beautiful face of the first was easily recognized. The second girl was pretty, but lacked the same striking features. The redhead was taller, curvaceous and long-legged. She looked out on the audience with a bemused expression that curved her lush, full lips into a slight smile. An apple-blossom complexion complemented mink-brown eyes surrounded by a fringe of thick, black lashes. She would be noticed even in a crowd. The second girl, although blonde and blue-eyed with a tanned, comely face, paled in comparison.

"Does the girl on the right look familiar? In case you're not sure, it's me. I know I look different now, but time has a way of shifting things. The force of gravity is irreversible," she laughed. "I'm older, a little heavier, and a whole lot wiser, and for that I thank God. Madelyne and I had just moved into our first apartment and thought we were so grown-up. We were young, foolish, and self-centered as many young people are. Even though we were wise in worldly pursuits, we lacked wisdom. We were naïve enough to believe that if we stayed within socially acceptable boundaries then nothing we did was wrong. But, I'm getting ahead of myself. I need to back up a little bit to the end of our senior year. For some of you, life hadn't even begun, but for us, life was just starting and promised to be a great adventure. . .

Chapter Two

It was our final year of school and graduation was over with. I was looking forward to a typical summer of sleeping in, tanning in my backyard, and trying to figure out what to do with the rest of my life. Madelyne wanted to find a summer job, and when my dad heard us talking about it one day, thought it was a great idea. Since neither one of us had plans to attend college, he didn't want us to waste what education we had doing nothing. "You need some direction in your life" was a frequent lecture. He rushed home from work one evening to tell me exactly what direction he thought was best.

"You go to town tomorrow and buy some practical dress shoes instead of those flimsy things you usually wear," he said as he regarded my sandals with distaste. "Two straps and a thin piece of leather won't hold up for long." Seated on the couch beside my mother, he stretched out his long legs on the coffee table and loosened his tie.

"Why?" I asked. "These shoes are almost new and besides, I like them. They make my legs look good, don't they mom?" My mother nodded in agreement, and leaned forward to second my opinion when she noticed the scowl on my father's face. She shut her mouth and a slight frown furrowed between her delicate brows.

"Your father's right, Nicole, those sandals aren't adequate footwear. You'd better get some shoes that are more, well, . . . um, more substantial."

"Why the attention to my choice in footwear all of a sudden? Did your company buy out a shoe store or something?"

"Save the sarcasm." He leveled me with a stony glare until I dropped my eyes and looked away. "Never mind," he grinned, "I've got great news and want to share it with you. Our daughter," he said pointedly, "won't spend another summer sleeping or lying around on the beach. It's time she does something to better herself, so I got her a job with the company. You start Monday, which leaves you three more days to goof off." He sat back in his chair with a great smile of satisfaction--beaming at us both.

"Work," I exploded, "what about my summer? Did you even think I might have plans of my own?" My father was not a patient man and didn't tolerate back talk. He was considered handsome, with dark hair thinning around the forehead, and deep brown eyes flecked with gold. Not bad, except for the stern expression he always wore. His stony visage, however, didn't come close to the rigid, forbidding personality hidden under his suit jacket. When he came out of his chair like it was spring-loaded and crossed over to me, my heart leaped into my throat. I feared he might strike me, but knew better. Dad never hit-he didn't have to. My mother turned to face the wall--her usual response to his intimidating behavior. If she ignored it, then it didn't happen.

"You will go to work on Monday and start earning your keep. Remember, miss-high-and-mighty, who made the decision not to go to college and make something of herself. You've only got a few things going for you. It's up to me as your father to see that you take advantage of what natural talent you were born with. For one, you're pretty, but that won't last. For two, you know how to type. If we're lucky, maybe you'll catch the eye of one of the young exec's and get married. One thing's for certain, you aren't going to lie around for an entire summer doing nothing. Work starts at nine, be there at eight-thirty, got it?"

"Yes, Daddy," I answered obediently. Feeling more depressed than when I missed the ninth grade dance due to strep throat, I ran to my bedroom to have a good cry. Later, Dad knocked on my door. "By the way, Madelyne will be working for the company, too. She also starts on Monday." That little piece of news cheered me, and I even looked forward to my first day of work.

On Saturday, Maddie and I went to town. We bought new shoes, and clothes more appropriate for an office than a day at the beach. "What are you going to wear the first day?" she asked as she flopped down on my bed after our day of shopping.

The Redemption of Madelyne

I pulled a light green suit from my closet that I thought looked professional. "My mom thought this would be a good choice. What do you think?"

"Ugh, that's what I think. You're not going to a funeral and you're not eighty years old. You could wear the skirt, but get rid of the jacket." She selected a silky blouse with a scoop neckline, and the sash from another outfit for a belt. "Put the blouse on with the skirt and let me see how it looks," she ordered. She adjusted the neckline of the blouse, and tied the sash around my waist. When she finished, the effect was casually professional, but also sexy. "Much better," she advised, "but raise the hem at least an inch or so, unless you want to remain in the typing pool. In this day and age, a girl's got to look better than average and be good at what she does in order to move up the ladder; so nimble up those fingers and give yourself a good manicure before Monday. If you need to talk, call me," she said as she went out the door. Smoothing her hair back, she gave a little toss of her head. She could have been posing for a magazine cover. Her face was flawless, her makeup perfect, and style of dress suited to her model's figure. If I were the envious type, I would have hated her, but didn't. I loved her like a sister.

"I'm wearing a prim, lady-like black skirt with a slit clear up to here." Her fingertips grazed her thigh, as she gave me a parting wink. "I plan to work my way up the ladder as quickly as possible. See ya', there." She waggled her fingers as she closed the door. I had no doubt that whatever Madelyne chose to wear would be subtle, but stunning enough to catch the boss's eye.

Our first day of work wasn't as frightening as I thought it would be, and I was surprised when lunch break came around so quickly. It was exciting to enter the employee cafeteria and investigate other doors marked, "Staff Only." Since I was the daughter of the 'Director of Personnel', I was allowed to explore as much as I wanted as long as work wasn't interrupted. At first, it was a blast to take the elevator to the top floor to sneak into the Executive Boardroom, but the novelty soon wore off. Madelyne swore she'd be part of the staff on the eighth floor before the end of summer. I rolled my eyes in disbelief. It wasn't that I doubted she'd eventually be there because Madelyne usually accomplished her goals. It was the end of summer part that I found unbelievable.

By the end of the first week, we discovered only "nerds" ate in the cafeteria. Staff members of the twenty-five and under group took their breaks on the back patio. Neither of us wanted to be different, so we followed suit. One block away was an affordable deli where we purchased tall lattes', which was the preferred beverage if you wanted to appear sophisticated and grown-up.

Madelyne was moved from the typing pool to a receptionist's position at the end of our second week. We met every day at the deli and then would run, breathless, to the patio to catch up on company gossip. Our first month passed uneventfully, and the money we earned spent freely on clothes or whatever struck our fancy. But, Madelyne had dreams of becoming a model and wasn't satisfied with sitting behind a desk. She had a lot more going for her than just a pretty face and a great pair of legs.

"Your friend is one smart young lady," my father commented at dinner one night. "She's been helping my staff complete some comparison analyses on sales according to store location and doing very well. I've tried to talk her into taking some night classes, but college seems to be out of the question. She wants nothing to do with the idea. I offered to pay for it all, and she laughed as if my suggestion was hilariously funny. She's determined to be a model. Well, with looks like hers, and brains to match, I suppose she can be a success in that field, too. It's a shame to waste a mathematical mind like hers, but if modeling is her goal then I'll help in any way I can. I've contacted a few people and now we'll wait and see."

"Wait and see," I yelled, "I don't remember any offers like that. What about me, Dad? I don't want to be stuck in the typing pool for the rest of my life. How could you do more for my best friend than you do for me . . .your own daughter?"

"Don't be having a hissie-fit," he warned. "If you want to quit work and go to college, I'll pay for your books and tuition. In fact, I'll pay for the whole kit-and-caboodle if you'll stick to it; graduate, and do something intelligent with your life. But remember this, I won't foot the bill for you to use college as an excuse to waste another four years learning nothing except make-up and the latest dress styles. In high school you refused to take any of the classes I suggested, and look where you are.

While you majored in choir, dance, and drama, Madelyne took classes in calculus, statistics, and accounting. It isn't hard to figure out who used their head and who didn't." Taking my clenched fist in his, he smoothed out my fingers and patted me on the head. "There's no point in arguing. You have a pretty face, but an empty head just like your mother."

Mom flashed him a dirty look, but didn't interrupt. She had taken a few night classes once, but he'd made her quit because her schedule didn't coincide with his. My mother was blonde, blue-eyed, petite, pretty, and silently resentful. She took care of the house, played tennis, faithfully went to the gym, and spent a lot of money shopping. I resembled her with one exception; I still knew how to smile.

"You won't be in the typing pool forever. When you've learned a little more about the company, maybe you'll work into a secretary's position."

"Oh great--a secretary. What an exciting career," I complained. Snatching my hand away from his, I stormed to my room and called Madelyne. It wasn't the first time she and I argued, but she understood. Later, we went to the movies and pigged out on popcorn. I was standing at the refreshment counter deciding what brand of soda to order when a masculine voice interrupted my concentration.

"I know this sounds corny, but haven't I seen you somewhere before?" I turned to gaze into a pair of the sexiest, chocolate-brown eyes that I'd ever seen. For a moment I was tongue-tied, and didn't know what to say. He was one handsome guy, and all I could do was stand there and blush. Dark, brown hair covered his head in a mass of soft waves, and I had the most embarrassing desire to run my hands through it just to see if it was as soft as it appeared. Thick, black lashes surrounded eyes I could have looked into for the rest of my life. He regarded me thoughtfully--a sincere smile curving his sensuous, full lips. Snapping his fingers, recognition flooded his face. "Of course! You work for The Corporation, don't you?"

I nodded and asked, "How did you know? It's not like I advertise or anything. Do you work there, too? It's funny because I don't remember seeing you."

"You probably wouldn't. My office is three floors above yours, that is, if you still work on the first. By the way, my name's Richard and I'd love to take you for coffee or something." We shook hands, and I was just about to accept his invitation when Madelyne stepped out of the lady's room and came over to join us.

"Wow! Would you introduce me?" Richard asked. As I made the necessary introductions, Richard's friend Keith joined us, making our group a foursome. Tall and angular, with straight blonde hair and light blue eyes, Keith was okay, but nothing when compared to Richard's muscular body and dynamite good looks. Madelyne and Keith hit it off immediately, so if Richard had any ideas about Maddie, they were quickly shelved. Hiding his disappointment, he devoted all attention to me when we left the theatre and headed to a popular nightclub. Maddie didn't bat an eye at being in a bar for the first time, but I gawked at everything. I was flattered such a handsome, worldly man found me attractive. I'm afraid I drank too much and made a complete idiot of myself by giggling like a little girl at everything he said. It didn't put him off though. In fact, it was the first of many dates to come. Madelyne and Keith's relationship didn't move along as quickly or as smoothly. They hit a few rocks along the way, and she found her prince not so charming.

Richard and I had been dating a while when it came to my father's attention. He came home one night, and grabbed me around the waist to swing me around as he had when I was a child. "And I thought my little girl wasn't so smart. It does my heart good to know you'll be well taken care of."

"Dad," I protested, beginning to laugh with him, "what are you talking about? What did I do that makes you so happy?" Putting me down, he beamed like I'd just won the Pulitzer or something.

"As if you didn't know," he said. "How long were you going to keep it secret that you're dating the boss's son."

"The boss's son," I gasped, "I'm not dating, . . . wait, do you mean Richard? Is Richard the boss's son?"

"Well, of course," he said, "how many families do you know with the same last name? It isn't everyone that can call themselves Richard James Franklin IV." At my shocked expression, a look of disgust stole over his face. "It would figure. You've been dating this guy for over two weeks and never had sense enough to put two and two together. Hasn't he ever mentioned his parents, or talked about himself?"

"Well, yeah, once in a while. He said his mother's name was Gwen and that he was named after his dad."

"His mom's name is Gwen," he mocked. "She's Gwendolyn Franklin III and she's always in the society pages for something-or-other. She's quite a philanthropist. Everybody's heard of her, and she prefers to be called Gwen instead of her given name." His snort of sarcasm was aimed at my stupidity.

"It never occurred to me to make the connection." I grinned to myself. Richard's value as a prospective husband just went up a couple notches.

"Girl, you play your cards right and by this time next year, you'll be Mrs. Richard James Franklin the Fourth." Dad touched my chin with his knuckles and then went off in search of my mother. He couldn't wait to tell her the good news. Later, when Richard came to pick me up for our date, my welcome was intentionally warmer than it had ever been before. Running to greet him, I threw myself into his arms and kissed him passionately. He showed his pleasure by pulling me across the plush seat of his Mercedes and keeping his free hand on my knee. I couldn't wait to introduce him to all my friends. Maddie already knew who he was and approved not only of him, but his money, his good looks, impeccable grooming, taste in cars, and did I mention his money? I liked those things, too, but wasn't so sure I always liked Richard.

At the end of summer many of our high school friends were going off to college. We were invited to several going away parties, but accepted only one. It was held on a Friday night at the beach and was the perfect opportunity to introduce Keith and Richard. We wanted to show-off our prospects to friends we might never see again. The girls were jealous beyond words and the guys envious of his nice car. Richard was on his best behavior as we roasted hot dogs, danced in the sand, and toasted each other with hot chocolate while sitting by the campfire.

"It was sure nice of you to extend your invitation to include me," Richard said as he shook hands with our host. "I've enjoyed meeting you, but it's getting late and time to get Nicole home." I looked at Richard with surprise. He frequently worked for a few hours on Saturday mornings so Friday night dates sometimes ended early, but he hadn't mentioned anything before. It looked like I'd be home and in bed before twelve. Helping me to my feet, we laughed at the flurry of sand he brushed from the seat of my pants. Richard didn't have so much as a grain anywhere, including his shoes. We said our good-byes and drove off, but not toward town. He took a side road that led into the woods on the north end of town.

"Where are you headed?"

"We're taking a little side trip. I've been a good boy for all your friends and now I expect some extra attention as a reward." Reaching behind the seat, he pulled out a bottle of whiskey and unscrewed the top. "Under your seat is a couple glasses. Dig them out and pour me a drink." I filled a glass about halfway and he drank it down in one swallow. "Whew, that's good stuff. Pour me another and one for you, too."

"I don't want a drink and you should know by now I don't like the taste of whiskey unless it's mixed with something."

He grinned devilishly as he reached under the seat to pull out a can of cola from his hidden stash. "Drink up," he commanded, "the party's just begun." I didn't argue. When he parked the car in a little clearing, one or two drinks ended up being five or six; and a friendly little kiss led to heavy petting.

"Stop, I don't want to do this." Pulling away, I leaned against the door panel to catch my breath. My cheeks were hot and I desperately needed some fresh air.

"Why not?" he asked. Grabbing me around the waist with one arm, he explored my body with the other. The more I struggled, the more excited he seemed to get. "Maybe you need another drink so you can relax. I don't know what you're so uptight about," he said with contempt. "I just want a sample of what to expect after we're married." His whiskey breath nauseated me and for a moment, I almost hated him.

"Married," I said with equal contempt, "I don't remember anybody mentioning marriage, and I certainly don't remember being asked. Now please--let me go." I tried to squirm away, but he only gripped me tighter. His kisses were demanding, bruising my lips, bringing a rush of fear to my throat. I'd fooled myself into believing a man like Richard would respect me enough to wait. Afraid of losing him if I said no, I stopped resisting and allowed the inevitable to happen. When it was over, I stumbled from the car and became violently sick. One sleeve of my blouse caught on the door handle and ripped. Tears ran down my cheeks. He got out of the car and wrapped his arms around me.

"Don't worry," he said as he wiped away my tears, "we'll be married as soon as possible. I've already spoke to your parents and they think it's a wonderful idea. All you need to do is set the date."

"You asked my parents before you asked me," I asked incredulously? "But, what if I don't really love you? What if marriage isn't what I want to do right now?"

"Who said anything about love? People don't get married because they love each other," he scoffed, "they marry because it's a profitable outcome of the male/female relationship. Love isn't a necessary component for a successful marriage. Your father is a good business man and looks out for your best interests. He knows I'll take good care of you. I'll provide everything you could possibly want or need so quit acting like a martyr and dry your eyes. We're going to get married because it's a good arrangement for both of us. I want an attractive wife, and you want a husband with money to burn. We both win," he shrugged.

I sniffled all the way home. When he stopped the car, I ran into the house before he had a chance to follow. Slamming the door behind me, my shaking knees collapsed, and I fell into a heap on the kitchen floor. My mother found me, sobbing out my grief for a loss I didn't quite understand. Throwing myself into her arms, I expected outrage, sympathy, or anger, but didn't get either one.

Fingering my torn blouse, she regarded me cynically, "It isn't fun being a woman sometimes, but you've got to expect that a man will be a man. You've been playing a fool's game. You expected a guy like Richard to act like one of your high school boyfriends. He's not a boy, Nicole," she hissed, "and you found that out tonight. You can't keep a man dangling and expect him to keep his hands off while you're parading around in skirts too short, and shirts that barely cover anything." Bringing her face close to mine, she delivered the final blow. "Grow up and stop acting like a wounded debutante. At least you know what to expect after you get married. Now go upstairs, take a shower, and clean yourself up because unless you have plans to refuse his offer, we have a wedding to arrange."

"But, Mom, don't you realize what happened tonight?" I thought I would be sick all over again when she grabbed both my arms and shook me hard.

"Of course I know. But did you resist him? I don't see any damage except a slightly torn sleeve. Do you want to see a doctor? Is there reason to believe he raped you? Would you really want to accuse him of something that could have been avoided?" Her blue eyes pierced mine, searching out the truth. I shook my head and stared at her as if she were a stranger. My soft-spoken mother had never talked to me like this before. "I didn't think so," she sighed with regret. "You'd rather take the abuse than to stand up for yourself. Everything your father said is true, Nicole. You're a weak woman looking for an easy way out."

"Are you talking about me, or yourself?" I accused. Ignoring the question, her eyes flicked over me with disgust.

"I always wanted better for you than what I've got, but you'll marry a man you don't love rather than wait for a poorer one that would love and cherish you with all his heart. Maybe you're smarter than we ever gave you credit for. Richard will provide you with every comfort imaginable and his requirements will be minimal. Is that what you want?"

"I guess so," I mumbled. The idea of pressing charges was out of the question and if marriage was the best solution, then why make waves? I was as much a part of the problem as he was. "Women are supposed to be the weaker sex," I told myself. Blaming Richard for something I could have stopped, I allowed him to use me and then wrapped myself in a blanket of self-pity. And to make the package complete, I decided right then and there that if I had to get married, then it was going to cost somebody plenty.

Chapter Three

I'd always dreamed of a storybook wedding and for once, Daddy gave full rein with the checkbook. He told me to get the best wedding money could buy, and instructed my mother to rent the largest ballroom at the Hilton. He even bragged to co-workers about the amount of money we were spending.

"Another couple hundred on flowers? No, problem," he grinned to one of his salesmen as he handed me the checkbook, "there's nothing too good for my little girl." Throwing an arm around my shoulders, he hugged me in a rare show of affection. I played along, smiling as expected, even though I thought it a charade performed to impress Richard's parents who just happened to employ us all.

The irony of the situation was ludicrous. I'd always scorned people of wealth and figured they were boorish and terribly conceited. My ideas changed, however, when the realization dawned that wealth had always been a fact of my life and taken for granted. I tried not to show surprise at the extravagant amount ledgered in the checkbook register. Each number was written in my mother's neat hand. With so much money at my disposal, it was a pleasure to walk into the most exclusive shops to buy whatever I wanted. Madelyne's eyes grew round with undisguised shock when she spied the price tag for my wedding dress and veil.

"Three thousand dollars? You're spending almost as much for your dress as I make in two months, and that includes my raise." She dropped the sales slip, and carefully removed tissue paper from the delicate hairpiece ordered special to hold my trailing veil. "It is pretty," she admitted as she adjusted the filmy netting onto it, "and you'll look like an absolute dream. But, aren't you spending an awful lot? Your veil cost twice that and it doesn't include the under slip or shoes. She punched numbers into a calculator as her eyebrows peaked in astonishment. "Wow, I sure hope he's worth it." She studied my expression for a moment, searching for signs of doubt.

"Don't look at me like that, you know it makes me nervous," I snapped. "Of course he's worth it. Why else would I go to all this trouble? Everybody knows he's good-looking, rich, and will someday own the company. What more could I possibly want?"

"Plenty," she answered with her usual frankness. "What about love? I've never heard you say you love him or that he loves you." She knelt down on one knee to rearrange the veil around me. From her position on the floor, she cocked her head, allowing her cinnamon hair to cascade over a shoulder where it spread around her in a red waterfall. Sunlight cast a hazy glow, catching her in its illumination. Dreamy-eyed, she rocked back with one knee pulled to her chest.

"I hope you find the same kind of love that Keith and I share. We'll get married someday, too, but ours will be for all the right reasons. I could care less how much money we have as long as he loves me," she said with a theatric flick of her wrist. For a fraction of a second, a wistful expression crossed her face as she gazed at my dress.

Shoving the white gown back in my closet, I grew impatient with myself. I'd always tried to please others by doing what they expected me to do, but this time uncertainty about the future kept my emotions in turmoil. "I do care about him," I said defensively. Tears stung my eyes and my throat tightened. Madelyne jumped to her feet and came over to wrap her arms around me.

"Of course you do," she soothed, "and I didn't mean to sound so self-righteous. You have such a soft heart, it's no wonder he wants to marry you. If he doesn't love you now, he'll learn to and be absolutely crazy about you. Just wait and see." Remorse filled her beautiful, brown eyes and her lower lip trembled.

"Look at you," I said, "talk about someone with a soft heart. You really are the icing on the cake." Shaking my head, I gazed at her fondly. "You're such a good friend," I said earnestly as I tucked a strand of hair behind her ear, "I hope our friendship goes on forever because life would be empty without you. I'm looking forward to old age when we'll sit in our rocking chairs sharing stories about our grandchildren."

"Grandchildren?" she scoffed, "and rocking chairs? Let's not rush things. Neither of us is married yet, and when the time comes, don't you think it would be better to share grandparent stories with Richard?" One eyebrow lifted quizzically as she looked at me with arms folded across her chest. Her lips tilted, smiling with amused pleasure at my reaction.

"You know what I mean," I fumed. "Why do you always take things so seriously? Can't we enjoy a little pipe dream? Does everything have to revolve around Richard?" I knew the answer before it was asked.

She nodded her head and laughed, "From the moment you say I do, your life will no longer be your own." She sobered for a moment and regarded me with sympathy as she stroked my cheek. "Your life has never been your own, has it? You've always done what they wanted you to do and not once have you disappointed them."

Uncomfortable with the serious direction of our conversation, I snatched the headpiece and veil from my head and threw it on the floor. "How do you do it, Madelyne? We've been in this hot, stuffy room for over two hours and I've got sweat running down my armpits like Niagara. You look like you just stepped off the cover of Vogue. It's disgusting and I hate you for it."

"Well, you might as well know there's only one thing that sets my blood to boiling." Throwing herself down on the bed, she stretched luxuriously and grinned like a Cheshire cat, "and his name is Keith."

"Are you saying that you and Keith have, well, you know?" This time it was my turn to scrutinize her. A secretive smile touched her lips as she whispered, "Ssshhh, I'm not telling. A lady never talks about the personal side of her romantic relationships." A rosy flush tinted her cheeks. "You know, it is warm. A tall glass of ice water would taste really good right now."

"Ice water," I said derisively, "an icy glass of cola would taste better."

"You'd better stick with water," she warned as she pinched my side with two fingers, "Richard won't like it if you can pinch-more-than-an-inch and even one or two pounds will make a difference on the fit of your gown."

Fear clutched my heart as I whirled to face the mirror. Leaning close, I inspected my face and body until satisfied with the trim figure reflected there. "Don't scare me like that. I've dropped ten pounds since starting to date Richard and I don't want to find them again. Maybe water would be a better choice," I agreed. "Besides, it's good for me and my complexion." We went down the stairs arm in arm. I was grateful for her honesty, but wished it didn't include my diet.

The next few weeks flew by at an exhausting pace as arrangements were finalized. Decorations for the ballroom were completed, and the menu for the reception approved. Wedding rehearsals were scheduled and then invitations for my bridal showers accepted. First, my Mother's sister threw me a shower because she thought she should. As gifts, I received towels, sheets, and other linens. It was great fun opening all the packages marked, "Bride and Groom," and the party was nice. Then, my mother held a shower for me because she had to outdo her sister. I opened packages containing dishes, pots and pans, and other accessories for a kitchen. The party was a great success and I enjoyed myself immensely. Richard's mother held the third bridal shower because she wanted to outdo my mother. There were so many guests in attendance I couldn't keep track of them all. Most came because it was expected knowing I would never lay eyes on them again. The gifts were extravagant. We wouldn't need to buy much to complete the furnishings of our future home, and I regretted that the house would be decorated with someone else's taste in mind. Several items were absolutely hideous, but Richard loved the gift-giver, and refused to part with them. He planned to display them prominently in the living room or den. I, on the other-hand, thought a nice corner of the garage would be perfect.

After opening so many packages, the idea of another shower complete with punch, cake, and guests with ribbon bedecked gifts gave me a migraine. My hand shook with dread when Madelyne delivered her invitation. After opening the pink envelope, I grinned from ear-to-ear. This was not the atypical invitation. It was on plain notebook paper and written in Maddie's characteristic scrawl. It was so like her to know exactly what I needed and when. Her letter was short and to the point:

Nicole, I'm giving a shower for you on Saturday at the park. It starts at ten and gets over whenever. All our friends have been invited, but expect only a few to attend. Remember it's at ten o'clock on Saturday. Be there!

P.S. Bring your bicycle and I'm wearing shorts and a halter-top.

Whatever she had in mind would be fun and a welcome change... something to look forward to. When I returned home from work Tuesday evening, my mother was on the phone with my father. He wouldn't be home until late and she wasn't to hold dinner or wait up. It was the third night in a row of such calls, and I marveled she took the news so calmly. Her voice remained level with only a slight stiffening of the spine to hint of her displeasure.

"Mom," I chided, "why don't you just tell him off. For as long as I can remember, you've never raised your voice or told him what you really think. You can't continue to let him use you for a door mat." I shook my head, and with hands on hips, criticized her for the way she handled her marriage. "I can tell you one thing for certain, I'll never allow Richard to treat me the way dad does you. There's absolutely no way I'll tolerate him being gone night after night. Do you know, I can't remember one uninterrupted weekend or vacation when dad put us before work? Why do you do it?"

Mom regarded me with an odd expression, and then her lips curved into the same practiced smile she often gave Dad. "So you think things will be different for you? I sincerely doubt it." All of a sudden her shoulders slumped, and within the depths of her steady gaze was a sadness I'd never noticed before. "If you marry a man like Richard, count on it because it will happen and often." Her right hand flew to her lips and uncertainty clouded her eyes. She straightened her shoulders and gave me a tight hug. "Daughter, it's time you had your first lesson in being the wife of an executive. Tomorrow morning, bright and early, we're going shopping." I started to protest, but she wouldn't listen to any argument. "I know you're tired, but think of it as necessary education for a successful marriage."

The following morning, she kept up a steady stream of chatter as we drove to town. It was barely past eight and her grooming was perfect. I wondered if I'd ever have the same flawlessness that she wore so effortlessly. We were driving by a local discount store when my education began.

"This is as good a place as any," she said as she turned into the parking lot.

"You're not really going in there are you? Mom, you have trouble buying anything without a brand name, and the more exclusive the better. I didn't think you even knew this side of town." I stared at her in amazement.

She flashed a secretive smile as she switched off the ignition. "Listen, watch, and learn. Look at all the cars in this parking lot. How many do you think there are?"

"Oh, maybe a hundred or so." Looking around, I did a rapid estimate. Already I was learning new things about my mother. "What does a parking lot have to do with marriage?"

She laughed girlishly; enjoying a secret joke. "You'll find out," she said mysteriously. Getting out of the car, she motioned for me to follow. Inside the store, she whispered, "we're going to take our time, so don't be in a hurry." We must have walked down every aisle in the place and if heads turned as she walked by, she didn't notice. Stopping to browse through a display of newly arrived fall sweaters--my jaw dropped to the floor when she selected one and then found her place at one of the checkout stands. As we waited to pay, she asked in a voice kept intentionally low.

"Okay, we've been from one end of the store to the other. Give me a good guesstimate of the ratio of men to women shoppers."

"Why?"

"Humor me, would you? What do you think?"

Shrugging my shoulders, I did some rough calculations. "I'd say there were approximately four women for every man. But, I wasn't counting and what does it matter?"

Sighing in the same exasperated way my Algebra teacher used to, she explained in terms even I could understand. "You've got the numbers right, but I'd better enlighten you before we go further. Statistically speaking, about eight-two percent were women and the rest men. Some of the women are just browsing to pass the time, but the rest won't leave until they've found something to buy whether they need it or not. Now, we're going to my side of town. Let's see if you notice a difference." We wandered in and out of several shops where my mother was well known. Most of the stores on this side of town had fancy names with pricey merchandise on their shelves. She bought a few more items with the most expensive being a dinner ring costing more than last year's groceries. As we left the last store, a smile of satisfaction tilted the corners of her mouth as she admired the ring on her finger. "Well, did you notice? Comparing one side of town to the other, which had more early morning shoppers?"

I nodded, "It was about the same and I'm surprised we're even having this conversation. None of it makes any sense."

She dropped the discount store sweater into a donation box then crossed the street to a popular sidewalk café. We took our latte's to a little table and sipped at them delicately as we watched the traffic go by. Placing a hand over mine, she explained. "Last night I was upset your father wasn't coming home. Men like your father, and that includes Richard, won't be bothered with emotional tantrums or angry outbursts from overly sensitive wives. Our job is to keep their lives running smoothly, and not to make waves. They expect you to look well-groomed at all times, and to keep their home neat and tidy. You don't know when they might invite someone for an impromptu dinner party or evening cocktail."

"That all sounds so archaic, so old-fashioned. Mom, this is not the dark ages. Women are free to do and be whatever they want," I scoffed. She grabbed my wrist in a painful grip, staring me down with a stony gaze.

"You'd better listen to me, girl, and listen good. . . Richard is no different than your father. Don't think you can change him after your married because it won't happen. You've already had a glimpse of how much he respects you," she sneered, "and after what he did, you can only expect more. A man will want, even demand, you be promiscuous in his bed, but you'd better look and act like a lady come the light of day."

"Mother," I gasped, shocked not only at her words, but at her passion. "I don't believe it, I can't. Madelyne's question echoed in my ears and I heard myself asking the same thing. "What about love?"

"Love," she scoffed. "I had ideas like that once, but time wiped them away long ago." The pain in her voice brought tears to my eyes. For a second, I could see the beautiful, vulnerable young woman she had once been. "When you're feeling down, or hurt, or sick or any of a hundred different emotions you're going to be plagued with, never let him see it. He'll run away if you show such weakness and remember there are plenty of women willing to share their. . .I mean, his bed. Why, your father has never seen me across the table at morning coffee looking any less than perfect. I'm not bragging, just stating a fact. When you're hurting, go shopping. Most of the women you've seen today aren't shopping because they need anything. They'll buy themselves some little thing, a trinket or bauble," she glanced at the ring on her finger, "to boost their moral and help themselves feel good enough to go back and face their husbands again. Whatever you buy won't stop the pain, but it'll make you feel better for a little while."

"Did you and Dad ever love each other? Has your entire marriage been like this?"

"I think we held mutual admiration for one another, but never love. Your father and I have been married long enough that he no longer cares what I buy as long as I don't make waves. We actually have a very solid marriage. I don't do anything to disrupt his life and he can no longer disturb mine." She gazed off into the distance for a moment and for once, I felt close to her. I understood why she seemed so unemotional at stressful times during my growing up. She had learned to hide her pain behind this perfect wife façade.

I received a valuable education that day, and took the first steps in understanding what it meant to be a woman. I've never forgotten, and even though it was the only time she ever opened up to me, it was enough to shed a little insight into the woman behind the mask.

When I called Maddie late that afternoon, she wasn't surprised at the things my mother had said. "You're such a pampered pet," she said affectionately, "and you've always been sheltered from the harshness of the world. Your mother, on the other hand, has been on the front lines paving the way. It's about time you recognize what she's sacrificed in order to keep your world together. But, then, she wouldn't have been strong enough to take a different route because work wasn't part of her lifestyle. Even though my parents divorced, and my mother has worked ever since I can remember, I don't think she led a life any lonelier than your mother's has been."

"I suppose you're right, but then you usually are."

"Of course I'm right," she chuckled. We chatted for a few minutes longer then rang off. She had a date with Keith, and I wanted a long, hot bubble bath before turning in. Richard had plans of his own for the evening, and I looked forward to a quiet night to myself without the usual wrestling match in the backseat of his car. I wondered if Keith subjected Madelyne to the same treatment at the end of one of their dates? Nah, she wouldn't have allowed it! She was always so ladylike it was hard to imagine her being treated otherwise. Besides, he loved her and would have respect enough to keep his hands to himself, wouldn't he? I knew they were intimately involved, but figured their relationship had to be different because they loved each other.

I arrived at the park on Saturday morning promptly at ten and was surprised to see so many of our high school friends gathered around Maddie. When I pulled up, they each held a section of banner decorated in crayon that said, "Congratulations Nicole." They had all signed it, and their handwritten messages brought tears to my eyes. Most of the attendees were friends from our graduating class with the exception of one. Diane graduated two years ahead of us, and I hadn't seen her since the party we'd held for her at the lake. There had been quite a few changes in her life over the last couple years. I figured she'd go off to some fancy college, and become a doctor or professor of something or other because she was such a brain. She hadn't done either one, but had been busy just the same. Motherhood had curved out her boyish figure and where a rather plain girl had been a pretty woman took her place. Twin baby girls blinked at us from the dual carriage she pulled behind her bicycle. I'd seen cute before, but they were adorable.

After spending a suitable length of time admiring and playing with the twins, we took a nice leisurely ride around the park. If we followed the bike path from beginning to end, it would be about ten miles. Diane didn't object when Madelyne suggested it.

"Isn't that an awful long way to pull that contraption?" I asked with a nod toward the carriage. "We don't have to ride quite so far, in fact, the shorter path might be better."

"Are you kidding," Diane laughed as she sped away. "How do you think I maintain my figure? The girls and I go riding almost every day and enjoy it immensely." She was definitely in good shape, accustomed to riding, and put most of us to shame in the fitness department. I found myself gasping for breath just trying to keep up even though the pace was slow and leisurely with frequent stops for drinks of water, chit-chat, and trips to the potty. At the end of the ride I was exhausted. Throwing myself down on a blanket spread out on the grass, I was grateful our little workout had come to an end.

Some of the others were equally tired and complained of sore muscles and leg cramps. Suddenly, I didn't feel quite so bad. It was the most exercise I'd had in over a year. After resting for a bit, Madelyne moved us to a shaded area near a small flower garden. It was cooler in the leafy alcove, close to drinking fountains and restrooms, but secluded enough to give a feeling of isolation. A picnic table was already setup and lunch was quickly laid out. All the girls contributed something, and our simple little luncheon could have rivaled any fine restaurant. Everyone, except me, had been instructed to bring foods they loved, but rarely ate because of preparation time, expense, or calorie content. As we prepared to fill our plates, Diane bowed her head.

"What are you doing?" I asked in a whisper.

"Why, I'm giving thanks," she said matter-of-factly. "My husband and I make it a habit to thank the good Lord for His faithfulness before every meal."

Madelyne gazed at her with undisguised amusement. "You're thanking God for this?" she indicated the food and wrappings. "He didn't have anything to do with it. I stuffed those mushrooms myself, and not once did I see Him in my kitchen." She started to laugh, but cut it short. Diane wasn't laughing; her expression serene and unruffled.

"You may not have seen Him, but He was there just the same," she said with sincerity.

"My apologies," Madelyne whispered in surprise. "You honestly believe that stuff, don't you? Sorry, I didn't mean to make fun." She touched Diane's arm in silent, self-reproach as guilt colored her face.

"He is the unseen guest at every meal and has been here with us today, too," Diane explained as she squeezed Maddie's hand. Her warm, steady gaze didn't blame or find fault, but swept over each of us with open affection.

My jaw dropped in astonishment when a flush of embarrassment tinted Maddie's cheeks a rosy-red. I knew she'd never deliberately say or do anything to humiliate anyone. She felt bad for making fun of Diane's faith, and rarely showed such obvious embarrassment. Not another word was said as Diane finished her prayer. A moment of uncomfortable silence passed before she grabbed the paper plates and shoved them into our hands.

"Let's eat," she invited, "I'm starved." Furtive looks passed between us, and we gladly turned the topic of conversation in another direction.

We pigged out on stuffed mushrooms, Caesar salad, marinated artichokes, chocolate covered cherries, veggie sandwiches made with paper thin French bread, cantaloupe slices, and for dessert—chocolate cream pie from my favorite bakery. Madelyne thought of everything. Diane's contribution was a thermos of hot coffee. By the time our hunger was satiated, there wasn't a crumb or morsel of food left and the thermos was dry.

"What a great day this has been," I said as I leaned against a tree to finish the last few swallows of my coffee. "How can I ever thank you for such a wonderful memory? No prospective bride ever had a better shower than you've given me." Sniffing back a few tears, I couldn't help wishing for a camera. I wanted to capture their sunburned faces on film so I'd never forget the moment. Madelyne, always prepared, whipped a camera out of her purse and snapped a few pictures for my photo album.

"Don't take any more pictures," one complained with a groan. "If my boyfriend sees the way I look," she brushed a few crumbs off her shirt and wiped sweat from her nose, "he'll turn around and run."

"Don't underestimate him," Diane admonished, "maybe he'd like seeing the real you. Besides, I think you look great--healthy, sunburned and sweaty--but beautiful. Sooner or later he's going to see you looking less than perfect so why worry about it?" Pulling her blouse away from her underarms, she unashamedly allowed the air to dry the damp circles hidden there. "You have to admit," she grinned, "it was a hot day for a bike ride. I always sweat like a pig."

"It's okay to let your husband see the real you after you're married," the girl sniffed, "but the rest of us are still trying to talk our guys into taking the plunge. They expect a cover girl image and until they realize the difference, I'll oblige," the one retorted with a grimace of distaste at her own wet underarms.

"We look like we spent the day outdoors and it's been hot," I commented as I inspected a recent insect bite on my leg. Glancing toward Maddie, I snorted contemptuously. "Except you," I accused, the rest of us look like we just stepped out of a sauna and you're not even flushed. How do you do it?"

She stretched out in the grass, and turned to her side with a smug expression on her face. "I already told you. The one who lights my fire is named Keith and he's not anywhere around."

Diane came to her feet and grabbed the camera. "Everyone stand up and move in close." Snapping the shutter a couple of times, she laughed at the contrast between Maddie and the rest of us. She was the only one without sunburned cheeks and a sweaty, red nose. One photo was a close-up of her that would be viewed by many in years to come.

The twins woke from a short nap, and we took turns holding them as she dug a few toys from the huge canvas tote she carried. Holding one of them on my lap, I cuddled her close, enjoying the sweet, baby scent of her. I hadn't thought seriously about motherhood before, but after holding that little body against mine, I began to look forward to it.

"How long have you been married?" I asked. "You were always such a brain. Everybody thought you'd go to college, lead a busy, but fulfilling life saving souls or some other prestigious thing, but instead you got married. Why?"

"If you think being a wife and mother isn't fulfilling--then you've got a lot to learn." She laughed and shook her head. The same dreamy expression I'd frequently seen on Madelyne's face softened her expression. "In answer to your question, I got married because I was in love. I met Paul my first semester in college, and we married in the spring. I dropped out with the intention to work and support him while he completed a degree for the ministry. But, the Lord changed our plans. Paul is still going to school, but works nights."

"It must be nice, not having to get up every day and go to work."

"Being the wife of a prospective minister and mother of twins is work," Diane argued. "Our day begins when they wake," she gave a nod toward the two girls and chuckled indulgently, "which is often before daylight." Glancing at her watch, she gasped in surprise. "It's almost four o'clock and we've got youth group tonight. I'm sorry to break up this little party, but I've got to leave. Before I go, isn't there something we're forgetting?" Everyone glanced at Maddie with brows raised in question?

"It's definitely time," she agreed. Giggling like schoolgirls, they rushed to Maddie's car to pull several packages from the backseat. Their eyes shone with excited anticipation as they handed them to me.

Tearing into the first, we laughed together as the wrapping fell away. An old, battered, rolling pin with several scratches marring its sides dropped into my lap.

"It's from me," Madelyne grinned, "and don't forget the picture that goes along with it." I searched through the torn wrappings until finding a neatly folded picture. A cartoon of a woman chasing her husband with a rolling pin made us all laugh. All the packages contained similar gag gifts with little handwritten notes enclosed. They were the best wedding gifts I received and were proudly displayed in my home. Each one was cherished more than other costlier items.

There were three packages remaining, and Madelyne explained as she handed them to me. "These are the real thing. We," she indicated all of them, "figured you had everything a bride could want, except for. . .well, you'll see."

A beautiful negligee', nestled in tissue paper, was found in the first package. It wasn't quite see-through, but was soft, ivory satin with tiny pearl beadwork across the bodice. Princess styling gathered under the bust then fell to the floor in thick, full folds. The fabric was clingy enough to show every curve. A matching chiffon robe with a ruffled hem completed the ensemble. It was the most beautiful thing I'd ever seen. Awestruck, I held the gown against me just to enjoy the silky feel of it.

"Do you like it?" they asked as one.

"Who wouldn't? I've never owned anything so beautiful. It's prettier than my wedding gown, and it's an original from Paris." The other two gifts were totally unexpected. Carefully opening the next package, I found two blouses that were cute, but obviously not my size. "Aren't they just a little large?" I asked as I held them up.

Madelyne laughed at the expression on my face. "They aren't for now, silly, they're for later." I didn't understand her meaning until she made a rounded motion over her abdomen. The light came on, and my cheeks filled with heat. Stuffing the maternity smocks back in their wrappings, I glared in mock anger. "I'm not married yet, so don't rush things."

The last package was much smaller, and book shaped. Tearing off the ribbon and colorful paper I was surprised to find a leather bound Bible. In the right-hand corner of the cover was my name etched in gold ink. I leafed through it politely, but wasn't sure how to respond to such an unwelcome gift.

"It's my personal contribution to your marriage," Diane said, "and look, I've marked several verses that may comfort you when you're down or feeling stressed. My favorites are found in the Psalms. Do you like them, too?" The book lay open in my lap and I looked at her speechlessly. "Yeah, I guess," was all I could think of to say. Red-faced, I stuffed the book back in its box. "What nerve," I thought as we packed the trunk of my car. I threw the Bible onto the backseat and forgot about it for the time being.

We all helped pack up the leftovers from our party and hugged each other repeatedly as we said our good-byes. Each of us promised to stay in touch, and I couldn't help but brush away a few tears. A deep sense of loss swept over me. I was afraid of what the future might bring, and feared I'd never see them again. Their bright, youthful faces were so beautiful and full of life; I regretted that our lives would never be so carefree again. Diane pedaled off on her bike, pulling the carriage behind her. The sun glinted off her blonde hair as she turned to wave.

"Don't forget to read your Bible and don't forget ME. Read *Psalms 20*, I underlined it in red," and with that, she turned a corner and was gone.

Madelyne helped load my bike, and then I helped load hers. We were double dating that night for the last time before my wedding, and we both needed a nap and a shower. I was getting married the following Saturday and should have been ecstatic, but was suddenly very depressed.

"You'd better get home and wash that look off your face before tonight. If Richard sees you looking so unhappy, he might call the whole thing off." Maddie wiped a tear from her own cheek as she closed the car door. "Hang it," she said angrily, "why do women get so emotional over such little things? Look at me, I'm crying because you are." Giving me a sisterly hug, she asked, "You will be happy after you're married, won't you?" Her soft, brown eyes darkened with worry as she studied my expression.

"Of course," I promised. Twirling around to my own car, I grinned and waved as I drove off.

Chapter Four

When I arrived home, my future mother-in-law's car was parked in the driveway. Wanting to avoid a scene and prying questions, I sneaked in the back way, and tiptoed up the stairs to my room. Grabbing a box of Kleenex off the dresser, I allowed myself a good cry before wiping away the last tear and blowing my nose with an unladylike blast. After an hour's nap and a long, hot shower, I felt better. It was almost six and Richard would be here at seven so it was a mad rush to get ready. Selecting a pair of hip huggers and a mid-riff top he was especially fond of, I ignored my mother's knock on the door and disappeared into the bathroom. For the next hour, I put on make-up and curled the ends of my hair so the weight of it would swing across my bare shoulders provocatively. When he arrived promptly at seven, I was ready and looking forward to the evening.

"Richard," I squealed as I ran down the stairs into his waiting arms. When he pulled me into a close embrace, I buried my head against his shoulder just to enjoy the protective feel of his arms around me.

"Maybe I should be busy more often," he chuckled as he kissed me on the mouth. "If an absence of one day makes you this eager, you'll be an absolute tiger by the end of next week." My welcoming smile froze in place as I angrily pulled away. This was the first I'd heard that he planned to be out of town for the entire week before our wedding. Throwing an arm around my shoulders, he waved at my dad then led me out the door. His grip on my arm was so tight it made me wince.

"Don't throw a tantrum just because I have to be gone next week," he warned. "Dad is taking me out of town on business, and it has nothing to do with you so get over it. Besides, it won't be the first or the last time. Just because we're getting married doesn't mean I have to rearrange my schedule just to accommodate your little insecurities." Opening the car door, he motioned for me to get in. The lines of displeasure left his face as he admired my figure. "You look great. Did I tell you that already?" Grinning boyishly, he ducked his head and gave me a sheepish look. "I'm sorry about the trip next week, but it's important. I would have mentioned it before, but dad told me about it only today. Do you forgive me?"

How could anyone stay angry when gazing into a face like his? A lock of naturally wavy hair fell across his forehead softening his professional appearance. Even though the style of the day was long, his hair was cut modestly short. The style suited his tanned, chiseled features and drew attention to his dark, brown eyes. His handsome face drew the attention of many women, both single and married. I was lucky to be his fiancé'.

Sliding across the seat, I snuggled close against his side. "You're forgiven, and I promise not to mention it again." Smiling to show my sincerity, I gave him a peck on the cheek. "Are we picking up Keith and Maddie or will they meet us somewhere?" Flashing a bland smile, I hoped my innocent expression would not betray the conflict going on within me. I was angry, but didn't dare show it or be faced with an evening of stony silences and deliberate sarcastic remarks. It was a shock when I realized my mother had been doing the same thing for years.

Keith and Maddie met us in the parking lot of a nearby grocery store. Richard invited them to ride with us, and we all piled into his sports car. "Where have you lovely ladies decided to go tonight? Are we going out for dinner, dancing, or what? I'm ready for just about anything as long as we eat sometime tonight." Richard looked from one to the other of us questioningly.

"Well," Maddie said with a meaningful look at Keith. "How about going back to the theater where we all met? We can watch the movie, and then have dinner at the same coffee shop." She gazed at Keith dreamy-eyed, "It would be so romantic to spend your last date before the wedding at the same place where it all started."

"You're not going to get all sentimental and cry all over my best shirt are you?" Keith asked as he pulled her against him to nuzzle her neck.

"I may not cry, but don't be surprised if I sniffle now and then." We laughed as she dabbed her eyes with a tissue.

"You're such an old softie," I teased. "I'm supposed to be the sentimental one, not you. After all, I'm the one who's getting married next week."

"I know," she wailed.

"Oh boy," Keith said disgustedly, "we'd better get going or she's going to have a real crying jag." Handing her a handkerchief, he made a face when she blew her nose and handed it back. "No thanks, you keep it," he told her.

At the theater we watched a horror flick that was so ridiculously corny, we laughed and made jokes all the way through it. Several times we were asked to quiet down, and we finally had to step out in the lobby. The guys couldn't choke back their loud guffaws any longer; or the explosion of rude snickers and hoarse chuckling when a poorly constructed papier-mache' head went flying across the screen. We kept trying to hush them for fear the manager would throw us out for disrupting the movie.

"Would you quit?" Madelyne reproached, "you're going to get us thrown out." She shook Keith by the arm, but he paid little attention. Chuckling, she excused herself and headed for the bathroom where once inside the safety of the women's rest room, the sound of her laughter drifted back to us.

Richard and I stepped over to order popcorn--leaving Keith to wait for Maddie. It was hard not to hear the comments of the boy behind the counter.

"Who's that girl with the red hair? Man, is she ever pretty. Is she your girl? What I wouldn't give to get a date with a girl like that." Peeking over Richard's shoulder to get a closer look, I smiled at the freckle, faced teenager. He was staring after Madelyne with obvious admiration. A glance toward Keith was enough to know he wasn't equally amused. There was a glint of anger in his eyes, which he directed at Maddie as soon as she exited the ladies room.

"Hey woman," he shouted, "get your skinny butt over here. You've got an admirer I want to introduce you to." She looked confused for a minute, and then turned crimson with embarrassment when she

The Redemption of Madelyne

realized Keith was speaking to her and not someone else. She turned back into the bathroom, but he grabbed her by the wrist to yank her over to him. "Hey, you! Kid behind the counter," he said as he pushed her forward. "You think she's pretty?" he smirked as he held her almost nose-to-nose with the boy.

"Hey man, don't do that. Can't you see you're scaring her?" Keith grabbed the boy by the throat, choking off further objections.

"Shut your mouth before I shut it for you. Take a good look at her because that's all you're getting. She's mine, boy, all mine, and don't you ever forget it."

"Please Keith," she whimpered as she struggled to free herself. Movie-goers were leaving the theater, and stopped with mouths agape at the little drama unfolding. The show in the lobby was more interesting than the one on the screen. "Let me go, please let me go." Tears rolled down her cheeks. Her eyes wide, like the proverbial deer in a car's headlights.

Jumping into the fray, I hit his arm, breaking his hold on the counter boy. "Let go of her, are you crazy or something? Richard," I screamed, "stop him before he hurts her." It wasn't until I screamed that Richard moved in Madelyne's defense.

"All right, Keith, show's over. Let go of her. Say your apologies and make nice-nice with the kid here," he jerked a thumb toward the counter boy, "and then we'll go have a nice quiet dinner and forget the whole thing."

"Sure," he said, "but I better not catch her flirting again. Did you see the way she was swinging her hips, trying to draw attention to herself? She was acting pretty fast and loose and needed to be taught a lesson."

"Yeah, I saw," Richard told him. "Now, let's get out of here before someone calls the cops. Madelyne, quit bawling and dry your eyes," he commanded as he shoved a napkin into her hands. Humiliated beyond words, she kept her head down, using her hair as a shield against the curious stares of the audience that accumulated when Keith's shouting caught their attention. She made her way to the door.

"Richard," I accused, "How can you take his side? You know she didn't do anything and he," I pointed at Keith, "should be horse-whipped for what he did to her." I was so angry, every muscle in my body quivered.

Keith underestimated the counter boy, and grunted with pain when a fist smashed into his face. "If I ever see you around here again, you're a dead man," the boy hissed as he leaped from behind the counter. He stood over Keith with fists clenched, ready to hit him again. Glancing in my direction, the boy motioned for me to follow Maddie. I didn't think twice about it, but hurried out the door to find her. She was a short distance up the street standing in an alcove crying her eyes out. I wrapped my arms around her as we stood there together, rocking back and forth. Richard caught up a few minutes later.

"Come on, it's over now," he said as he hugged us. "I think Keith is learning a good lesson from that kid and will think seriously before talking like that to you, or anyone else, again."

I reeled with astonishment when Maddie, in a moment of panic, threw herself at Richard beating him on the chest repeatedly. "Where's Keith?" she cried, "is he all right?" She almost fainted in relief when he rounded the corner.

"He'll nurse a shiner for a few days, but otherwise will be just fine," Richard assured her with a chuckle. Rushing to Keith, she threw her arms around his neck pleading for his forgiveness.

"You're asking for his forgiveness?" I yelled incredulously, "he should be down on his knees begging for yours." Looking to Richard for moral support, I was surprised to find a mocking smile on his lips. He was totally unperturbed by the whole evening's fiasco and seemed amused by the whole thing.

"Anybody hungry yet," he asked, "I'm starved." Taking my arm, he walked me up the street toward the restaurant. "Let's leave the lovebirds to kiss and make-up," he said sarcastically as he put a finger to my lips, halting any objections.

"How can you think about eating?" I sputtered. "Why didn't you try to stop him? You're just as bad as he is." Pulling away, I crossed my arms over my chest and glared at him in silent accusation.

His smile turned cold as he grabbed my elbow and pulled me close against him to whisper in my ear. "I can think about eating because I'm hungry, and I didn't do anything because a man doesn't get involved in another man's business. Now unless you want to be left here to find your own way home, quit making a scene and come along. I've had about all the foolishness I can take for one evening." With that said he dropped my arm and headed down the street. My jaw dropped in surprise as Keith and Maddie hurried after him. By the time I recovered they were a full block ahead, and I ran to catch up.

We shared a silent meal where I had a hard time meeting Richard's gaze. Madelyne remained in her corner of the table unable to eat. Keith was talkative, even apologetic, and tried to engage her in conversation. He made jokes to get her to laugh, and when that failed his antics grew more desperate. Grabbing a handful of napkins from the dispenser on the table, he threw himself down on the floor. On his knees, he wailed and sobbed pitifully, begging for her forgiveness. Startled, she glanced around to see the restaurant's patrons all staring at them with amused delight. When he peeked around a handful of napkins to catch her response, even I had to smile. A mischievous twinkle from his one good eye hinted at what a naughty little boy he must have been as a child. When he lifted her hand and kissed her palm, you could hear our fellow diner's say, "Aaahhhh." Squinting at her through his black eye, he looked vulnerable and contrite.

"I'm sorry, I truly am. It wouldn't have happened if the guy hadn't made comments about wanting a date with you." Grinning like a five-year-old with his hand caught in the cookie jar, he melted her heart with three words. "I was jealous." The line didn't have a truthful ring to it, and even Richard's brows raised in skepticism.

"Guess we'll be the next ones to get married," he said as he snuggled in close to her. "Would you like that?"

Madelyne nodded, smiling for the first time since walking into the restaurant. Jubilant at her acceptance, he stood up, and announced to the entire restaurant that he'd proposed and she'd accepted. He bought a round of drinks for everyone, and we toasted the jubilant couple. A flush of happiness tinted her cheeks pink as her lips curved in a bittersweet smile. Madelyne had always been a good actress, but not so good as to fool someone who had known her since kindergarten. My heart cried for her, and I secretly hoped she'd dump him at the first opportunity. He wasn't worth the ground she walked on.

Richard left the next morning on the business trip with his dad. They would be gone all week, but he promised to call every night so I wouldn't get lonely. We wouldn't see each other again until I walked down the aisle. I spent the last six days of single life rearranging my prospective new home, and deciding color schemes for the bedroom and master bath. Friday night, after a long gossip session with Maddie, I unplugged my phone and prepared for bed. It was strange, knowing it was the last time I would sleep in this room because by the same time tomorrow, I'd be married. I looked around at the ruffled curtains at the window, the pictures on the wall and the jumbled mess on top of my dresser. Would I miss it? Maybe later—much, much later. I didn't have the expected night-before jitters, but had trouble sleeping just the same. After tossing around until the bed sheets were tangled into a wad, I jumped out of bed to find something to read. Sometimes reading helped me relax so I could sleep. The only book I hadn't already read was the Bible Diane had given me for a shower gift. Sighing, I sat cross-legged in the middle of my bed with the Bible on my lap. It fell open, and my eyes came to rest on the following verses-

> *Husbands, love your wives just as Christ*
> *loved the church and gave himself up for her*
> *to make her holy, cleansing her by washing*
> *with water through the word. . .present*
> *her to himself without stain or wrinkle. . .*
> *(Eph. 5:25-27)*

I slammed the book shut and tossed it across the room where it hit the wall with a loud smack. The verse condemned me, and I felt the burn of shame. It wasn't my fault Richard had forced himself on me, was it? A tiny niggling fear burrowed its way into my thoughts. How long would he want me around after the new wore off? After all, I was far from being holy. What did it mean Christ gave Himself for the church? Deciding the entire passage was gibberish, and made no sense, I turned off the light and lay down. But sleep wouldn't come even though my eyes were heavy. Rising from my bed, I padded over on bare feet to retrieve the book from the floor. Opening my closet, I stuffed it into a far recess on the upper shelf. When I returned to bed and pulled the covers up to my chin, I slept undisturbed until bright morning sunlight filtered through the curtains.

As soon as my feet hit the floor, my mother rushed me off to a salon where my make-up was applied and my hair perfectly coifed to hold the delicate hairpiece and heavier trailing veil. Walking down the long aisle of the church on the arm of my father, I knew I'd never looked better. It was difficult not to be flattered at the admiring glances of all the guests. Richard's eyes lit up when he saw me and for once, his glance never strayed from mine. Everybody said it was the perfect wedding, and I basked in the glory of it. After the reception, Madelyne helped me out of my gown and into my traveling suit.

"Wow, a honeymoon in Hawaii," she said as she admired the glossy travel folder lying on my dresser. "You're going to have an absolutely wonderful time." Smoothing a few flyaway strands of hair, she made me turn a complete circle before totally satisfied with my appearance. "You're beautiful and I'll miss you." Giving me a quick hug, she shoved me towards the door. "You'd better hurry because Richard was ready to leave over an hour ago. Your luggage is already at the airport, and all that's left is for you and Richard to get there on time. Don't worry about a thing, I'll make sure all your stuff is moved to your new place. I'll even put it away as if you'd lived there forever."

"Have I ever told you how much I love you? You're such a great friend," I told her. "You'll be the first one called when we get home." Rushing out the door, I ran down the stairs to Richard. Holding hands, we ran to the waiting car through a rain of white confetti. When I turned to wave good-bye, Madelyne stood alone at the edge of the crowd. Keith had pulled another one of his disappearing acts and left right after playing best man.

We had a wonderful honeymoon lasting seven, glorious days. We returned on a Saturday, and even though we weren't due back until the following Monday, it was obvious our early morning walks and romantic candlelit dinners were over. Rushing me home from the airport, he showered, changed, and headed for the office. I wouldn't see or hear from Richard again until late night. Deciding to make use of the time, I began to unpack and arrange our dresser drawers with underwear in the top drawer, socks in the next, and so on. When the phone rang, I ran to answer thinking it was probably Madelyne, but the low, sexy voice was not hers.

"Is Richard there?" asked the voice.

"No, he's out and won't be back until later. Can I take a message?"

"That won't be necessary. Did he go to the office? If he did, I can catch him there."

I don't know why I felt compelled to lie, but there was something about the woman's voice that made me suspicious. "Actually, he didn't. He mentioned something about racquetball, so maybe he's at the club." I had no idea whether he'd ever been a member of a health club, but she didn't have to know that.

My heart did a nosedive when she chuckled. "The Richard I know doesn't get his exercise at health clubs." Even I understood the intended meaning, and my cheeks grew hot with embarrassment. She seemed to know what to say to humiliate me and added, "If you don't know where he went, all you had to do was say so."

"Who is this?" I demanded. "How dare you call here and insinuate. . ."

"I don't have to insinuate, honey," she said with a sense of bored sarcasm. "I've known Richard for a real, long time and I know what he likes. We have a very close relationship--if you understand my meaning," and then she was gone with a click as the line went dead.

I sat on the edge of the bed with the phone in my hands and didn't realize I was crying until it rang again. Grabbing the receiver, I screamed into the mouthpiece. "Don't call here again and stay away from my husband."

"Is that any way to speak to your best friend?" Madelyne asked with a chuckle. After listening for a few moments to my choked sobs and hysterical rantings she interrupted. "I'll be right over," she promised. "Wipe your eyes and make a pot of coffee. We have a lot to talk about."

Afraid the woman might call back; I stayed right where I was with one hand holding the receiver. When Madelyne arrived she made the coffee herself, and then made a quick search of the house to find me in the bedroom. Wrapping her arms around me as if I were a child, she let me cry until the tears eased and I was more in control. Eventually the storm of emotion quieted enough to explain what had happened. She didn't take the news very seriously.

"I think Richard has a girlfriend," I cried. "She knows our phone number and called to speak directly to him."

"So, if I understand you correctly, a woman with a sexy voice called and asked for Richard. Did you tell her who you are? Did you explain that he's married, and not available for any," she giggled, "extra-curricular activities?"

"No, I guess I forgot to mention about being his wife." I admitted. "Do you suppose she was just an old girlfriend who didn't know he'd gotten married?" That thought brightened my day and suddenly, I was laughing along with Madelyne. "She probably assumed I was just passing through, you know, another one of his conquests," I laughed. We joked about it later as we poured coffee from my new pot, and sipped the hot beverage from new china.

"Okay, you've solved my problem now tell me about you and Keith. Is everything okay? Are you still planning to get married?" My question cast a shadow over our little reunion. She dropped her eyes to hide the sadness in them.

"Keith and I broke off two days ago. He says we can remain friends, but nothing serious for a while. He wants to date other women, and encouraged me to date other men. I'm sorry," she sniffed as she wiped her nose, "I didn't want to get into this right now, but I miss him," she wailed. This time it was my turn to comfort her. By the time she went home, we were both smiling again. Our afternoon was spent consoling one another just as we had done since junior high.

"Are you coming back to work on Monday?" she asked as I walked her to the door.

"Bright and early," I responded, "so save one of those maple bars for me." I waved as she drove off then went inside to finish unpacking. Madelyne always looked at the logical side of things except when it came to Keith. I shook my head as I thought about all she'd told me. What she saw in him I couldn't for the life of me understand, but until she could see for herself how worthless he was, I didn't dare interfere.

Later that evening as Richard and I were preparing for bed, I finally had the opportunity to tell him about the phone call. His response wasn't what I expected.

"When did she call?" he asked.

"I already told you," I explained for the second time, "right after you left for the office. Who is she, Richard? Were you seeing her at the same time we were dating?"

"What's the big deal? She's an old friend and we often get together for a drink and to share a few laughs."

"But, your married now," I stammered. "The only one you're supposed to be laughing with is me." I stood on the opposite side of the bed with hands on hips trying to look angry and imposing. But, I'd never been a good actress and inside I was afraid, very, very afraid. Surely he didn't expect to keep seeing his old girlfriends. I studied the indifferent expression on his face as if seeing it for the first time.

"She's a friend. I've got lots of friends, and I don't plan on cutting them out of my life. You might be my wife, but you don't own me. Just because I signed a piece of paper and stood in front of a preacher, it doesn't make me your private property. I've known most of my friends since long before you came into the picture, and sometimes we get together for an evening or a weekend. Don't worry, I won't ignore you, but don't expect me to wear a collar and a leash either."

"What does that mean?" I asked with dread in my heart.

His back stiffened and the frown on his face could have soured buttermilk. "Don't play games, Nicole. You know exactly what it means. A man needs a little variety in his life or he stagnates. I might get bored with the same old stuff," he looked me up and then down suggestively, "so every now and then I'll need a little spice just to keep life interesting."

It was the first night of many that bitter tears dampened my pillow. Life's lessons were hard to swallow. I learned to hide behind the same practiced smile my mother always wore.

Chapter Five

Over the next few weeks, Richard proved to be an attentive husband, and true to his word. He spent most evenings and weekends with me. We spent a great deal of time exploring the intimate part of married life, and learned a lot about the daily routine kind of stuff that comprises a person's day. Richard remained grumpy and out-of-sorts until he'd showered and had a first cup of coffee. I learned to leave him alone until he'd had both. He learned to tolerate the light from my reading lamp on nights I read myself to sleep. He also learned not to push me beyond the boundaries of modesty and moral decency that I set for myself. We both learned about tolerance.

He squeezed the toothpaste at the top and sometimes left the lid off. I squeezed from the bottom and was meticulous about leaving the tube neatly on the side of the sink with the lid intact. He thought nothing about coming out of the shower with nothing on but a smile. Modesty didn't allow me such freedom. I wore a robe or dressed entirely before exiting the bathroom. In a show of thoughtfulness, he mounted a bracket on the bathroom door to hang my robe while I showered. There were a million things for us to learn about each other in order to live compatibly. Learning to tolerate those little things about your mate that can drive you crazy requires time, patience, and a lot of love. I'm not sure we had enough patience, definitely not enough love, nor the inclination to learn.

Richard liked giving parties for wealthy clients he wanted to impress. It was fun learning how to give dinner parties and being the perfect hostess. For once, my mother and I had something in common. She taught me all I needed to know about table settings, décor', seating arrangements, and whether to serve buffet', or formal. Her lessons on the nuances of correct party conversation saved me from embarrassment many times. I loved the parties, and enjoyed myself immensely as I moved through our guests with a tray of hors d'oeuvres. Richard grew tired of the hip huggers and mini-skirts I usually wore and purchased me an entirely new wardrobe. My closet was full of sophisticated suits, slacks with matching silk blouses, and slinky dresses for evening wear. Our marriage was off to a great start. There were only a few slight flaws that showed up now and again.

Things remained pretty much the same at work, with the exception of a few co-workers. My status as wife of the owner's son intimidated some, and they either avoided me or spoke only when I addressed them first. It didn't bother me like it once would have, but when Madelyne began avoiding me, too, it broke my heart. I couldn't figure out why she was never around at lunch break. Why was she rushing out after work without stopping to say hello?

Unable to tolerate her avoidance any longer, I gathered my courage and marched upstairs to her office. I breathed a sigh of relief. She was alone and her boss was nowhere in sight.

"What is up with you?" I demanded as I dropped into a chair still puffing from climbing the stairs instead of riding the elevator.

"Good morning to you, too," she admonished, "and to answer your question, nothing." Grabbing a ream of paper, she placed it in the printer's paper tray and rammed it into place. She was trying hard to ignore me, but not succeeding. "I'm sorry, Nicci. I haven't deliberately avoided you, but something important is about to happen that will change my life. I've been afraid to say anything for fear of jinxing the whole thing."

"Is Keith involved?" I asked with a knowing wink. She shook her head and looked at me with pleading eyes. "I'm about busting out with wanting to tell you, but since your marriage and Richard being the new CEO and all, I've been afraid to. I don't want word leaked to my boss until I'm ready to tell him."

"Madelyne," I said as I choked back tears of hurt. "How could you possibly think I'd tell anybody your secrets? We've always shared everything and my marriage won't change our friendship." Crying real tears, I reached for a tissue and blew my nose loudly, "You're my best friend and I miss you," I sniffled.

Jumping from her chair she ran around the desk and we hugged as if we hadn't seen each other in years. Both of us were crying and talking all at once when her boss walked in. When he saw the tears rolling down my cheeks he looked to Madelyne for explanation. But, her face was also wet with tears, and her upper lip trembled with the threat of more to come.

"Women," he grumbled. "I don't know what the problem is, but my office is not the place for it. Go for lunch and don't come back until it's settled." Chuckling, he gazed at Maddie with fondness. "I've got four daughters, so I'm used to this kind of thing. Go on! Get out of here the both of you." Madelyne started to argue, but he put up a hand to stop her. "I won't be listening to any excuses. You've earned a few hours to yourself, with pay, so enjoy it while you can." Grinning, he shooed us out the door then locked it behind us.

"Well, what do you think about that?" she asked as she stared at the closed door. Indignation was written all over her face. "I guess we'd better leave because he won't unlock it until we do." We hadn't gone two steps when a fit of giggles overcame her. "Can you imagine how it must have looked when he opened the door? I'll bet he thought we'd had a fight."

Sobering at the idea, I grabbed her arm. "Be serious for a minute. We aren't, are we? I mean, we aren't going to have a disagreement are we?"

"Of course not. I just can't talk about my new job while still on company property. Let's go to that little café on the corner, and then I'll bare my soul and tell you everything."

It seemed a long two blocks before we reached the restaurant. We found a quiet booth in the back where the light was dim, and few patrons. Madelyne didn't speak a word until we were seated. I burned with curiosity and my imagination went wild. What could be so terrible that she couldn't discuss it at work? After placing our orders, we settled ourselves for a long talk.

"Okay, I've been good and haven't pried or asked a single question..."

"But, you just have to know what this is all about, right?" She really wasn't asking a question. My curiosity was at fever pitch and she knew me well enough to know it. Smiling indulgently, she glanced both ways and then asked just like we had when we were kids, "Promise? You can't tell a single soul or your nose will grow like Pinocchio." We laughed together; remembering how often secrets had been shared after coercing the other into repeating the childish vow. Nodding in agreement, I solemnly placed a hand over my heart, anxious to hear the news.

"I'm quitting The Corporation," she whispered with a furtive glance toward a far table where two employees from the mailroom lingered over their coffee, "I'm turning in my resignation tomorrow."

"You're quitting?" I gasped with surprise. It wasn't what I expected and something told me there was more. Keith had to be somewhere in the background. "If you quit, how will you live, or pay for that new car? And what about me? Who will I have lunch with? You must have something else up your sleeve or it wouldn't be such a big deal." Eyeing her suspiciously, I tried to figure out the best tactic to pry the rest out of her. Deciding on a direct route, I demanded without further delay, "Fess up, Maddie. I want the why, when, and how, and don't leave out a thing." Taking a sip of coffee and replacing the cup in its saucer with a clatter, I leaned forward with elbows on the table. The day was young with plenty of time to kill, and if she wanted to draw out the action, then 'Patience' was my name.

"Wow," she said with approval in her voice, "that was definitely not like the old you who wouldn't say scat to a mouse." Shaking her head, she looked at me with a sad smile that was quickly hid behind a wide grin. "Just don't change so fast that there's nothing left of the girl we all know and love," she laughed. Her comment bothered me. I thought everything about my new lifestyle made me worldly and sophisticated. I wasn't either one, but was a plastic imitation of my mother. She was a replica of the wealthy, boring women she fraternized with at the club while I was still that girl in high school trying too hard to impress.

"Well, are you ready to hear my earth shaking announcement or are you going to sit there daydreaming?" Maddie interrupted my private reverie and brought me back to the question-at-hand.

"Okay, quit stalling, and I promise not to get off track again. Tell me all about it."

Reaching into her purse, she extracted a small business card and placed it in front of me. A conspiratorial smile crossed her face as she waited for my reaction.

"Gemstone Modeling Agency," I read. Puzzled, I handed the card back to her, "are you quitting The Corporation to work for them? I didn't think they were big enough to hire anybody. Will you be a bookkeeper or something?"

"Bookkeeper," Maddie repeated as if I'd uttered something vulgar. "Don't you get it? I'm not office help, Nicole. Come on girl, get a clue. What have I wanted to do all of my life?"

Instantly, the light came on. I screeched so loud heads turned. "Are you kidding?" Embarrassed at being the object of attention, I lowered my voice. "Is that where you've been spending all your free time for the past few weeks? This is so cool, and I thought you were mad at me or something. . . What will you be doing? Will you model clothes or. . .?"

"Hold on a minute--slow down. I can only answer one question at a time," she said as she signaled a time-out. Taking a deep breath, she smiled archly. "Are you ready for this?" Glancing from left to right, she leaned across the table and whispered, "I'll be the spokesperson for a local car company. I'll also do a commercial for women's bras." Sitting back in her seat, she allowed time for her news to be absorbed before continuing. "Kurt's New and Used Cars needs a spokesman for their commercials and they selected me from a photo I sent to the agency. The agency hired me on the spot and contracted me for both commercials. And that isn't even the best part. I'll be on TV!" she screeched. "They're teaching me to smile," she flashed an affected grin, "and walk seductively, leading with my hips," she parroted, "and sit on the hood of a car as if I'm an ornament. In the women's bra commercial, you won't see my face, but the torso will be mine," she added as if the absence of her face made the commercial less important. "Both ads will air locally where there's a chance a more exclusive agency may see them. The last model was hired by a place in New York City." Her expressive eyes rounded at the wonder of working in such a prestigious place, "It's not a big job, but it's a start." Satisfied that I was shocked and impressed all at the same time, she eyed me over the rim of her coffee cup--grinning like a pirate.

"Does Keith know?" I asked. "What does your mother think about having a TV celebrity for a daughter?"

The curve of her lips turned downward for a moment, and she looked away as if collecting her thoughts. "Keith doesn't know and probably won't care. He's got a new girlfriend. Mom's afraid the job won't last and my paychecks will be scarce. I don't know how many times she's reminded me that beauty doesn't last, but money in the bank with the right investments lasts a lifetime. She doesn't understand why I chose modeling as a career and I don't understand why she chose alcohol." She shrugged, as if it didn't matter. Glancing across the room, she noticed the admiring gaze of a nearby coffee drinker. With a flirtatious smile, she lifted her cup to him in salute. My face burned crimson at her boldness.

Grabbing her hand, I pulled her to her feet. Leaving enough money to pay our tab plus a healthy tip, I pushed her out the door before the guy got the wrong idea. "Don't practice smiling for strangers. You have no idea how powerful a weapon you've got there so wait until the cameras are rolling," I warned. "Your news is too exciting to ignore. Let's take the afternoon and do something fun to celebrate."

"Like what did you have in mind?"

"How about the zoo and afterwards, hot fudge sundaes?"

She didn't have to think twice. We had always celebrated special occasions by spending a day at the zoo. Afterwards, we wandered through a nearby mall admiring the displays as we ate huge sundaes with plenty of hot fudge, marshmallow, and peanuts. "What are you doing for Thanksgiving?" I asked.

"The usual--I'll cook a big dinner, mom will sit in front of the TV, my brother will come over, and the two of them will get politely soused while enjoying their turkey and mashed potatoes."

"You could come to my house," I suggested, "You're always welcome."

"No, I don't think so. Holidays should be spent with family, even if they aren't desirable dinner guests. They're the only family I've got, and I figure it's good training for when I have a family of my own." Her eyes grew dreamy, lost in her own reverie. "My husband and kids, we'll all eat together around a big oak table and then play board games after dinner. We'll be just like <u>The Walton's</u>." We laughed at the idea as we parted. The afternoon had sped away and it was nearing five o'clock; time for both of us Cinderella's to return to the here and now. We planned a day of Christmas shopping for the day after Thanksgiving. . .'Black Friday'. The biggest shopping day of the year.

Thanksgiving dinner was to be held at our house and I was anxious to show off my cooking skills. Richard purchased a large screen TV for the den so the guys could watch the football game in style. I purchased a cookbook and practiced several new recipes. My garbage disposal really got a workout and my diet was ruined. Someone had to be the taste-tester and I nominated myself.

The day started off perfectly. It was cold, but not freezing, and the sun shone brilliantly. The turkey browned to perfection, potatoes whipped to creamy smoothness, and my pumpkin pies looked like pictures from a magazine. Candlelight reflected a shimmery pool of light around wine-filled, gold goblets placed precisely one inch to the left of each place setting. Our guests were my parents, his parents, a couple of cousins, two business associates, and an uncle. They complimented my attractive table and then began to eat. There was little conversation except for an occasional comment about the game. I was disappointed the meal I'd worked so hard to prepare was over so quickly. Afterward, the men retired to the den to watch another game. My mother and mother-in-law poured themselves another glass of wine, snapped in a movie, and promptly fell asleep.

After cleaning the dining room, loading the dishwasher, and tidying the kitchen, I sat down with a cup of coffee. Richard came up behind me and wrapped his arms around my waist.

"That was an excellent meal, even Uncle Will said so." I knew there was something else he wanted because the compliment was left hanging, as if there were more to come. "The four of us are going to play some poker after the game. How about making us some turkey sandwiches?" Poking his nose into the refrigerator to find what other leftovers looked appetizing, he snitched an olive and popped it into his mouth. Glancing over his shoulder at me, he whispered, "Don't wake them," he thumbed toward the front room where both our mothers snored in front of the

TV, "and knock before you come in. I wouldn't want your sensitive ears to be burned by Uncle Will's rough talk," he teased.

His uncle had flown in unexpectedly for the holiday and must have been the black sheep of their family because he didn't possess the refinement or educated speech of his brother. I figured most of his time was spent in backstreet bars because his vocabulary wouldn't be accepted any place else. He toned it down in front of "the girls" as he put it, but still phrased every comment with colorful expletives that colored my cheeks pink.

"I'll bring enough snacks to keep you guys busy all night," I promised. "Maybe if you eat enough, you won't come to bed reeking of whiskey." Smiling sweetly, I took another sip of coffee and looked at him innocently over the rim.

The intended jab sent him storming out of the kitchen. He frequently enjoyed a drink before bed and sometimes two or three. I hated the smell of it and told him so. He'd been drinking all day and was weaving slightly, showing signs of drunkenness. Richard wasn't nice when under the influence.

"Don't forget those sandwiches and how much I drink is no business of yours," he said when he stepped back into the kitchen to pull me to my feet. He kissed me hard, pushing his tongue into my mouth. My throat constricted at the painful intrusion and when the taste of him spread through my mouth, I gagged. Releasing me, a sardonic grin spread over his face. "Don't forget who wears the pants around here," he ordered. With that said, he returned to the den.

Running to the bathroom, I rinsed my mouth repeatedly and brushed my teeth to rid the taste of him from my tongue. Spitefully, I ignored his request and wandered into the front room instead. My mother and mother-in-law were waking and after pouring themselves another glass of wine settled down to watch another movie. It was a thriller and I forgot about Richard and his sandwiches until the credits rolled across the screen. Snapping off the DVD, I went to the kitchen and loaded a tray with enough food for an army. Juggling the overloaded tray, pot of coffee, paper plates, napkins, and cups, I was prepared to set everything on a nearby end table in order to open the door, but found I didn't have to. The door was slightly ajar so all I had to do was nudge

The Redemption of Madelyne

it open with the toe of my shoe. I hesitated though, because my ears pricked to attention when my name was mentioned.

"Nicole doesn't know about our little business trip does she?" my father-in-law's deep bass asked.

"No, she doesn't and I'm not going to tell her. What I did before we married doesn't concern her. As long as I take care of my husbandly duties and keep her happy, what's done on my own time isn't any of her business either," Richard explained. "Man, wasn't she something though? I didn't know you took so many pictures."

His Dad chuckled, "I didn't know they grew 'em like that. I had to take a few pictures or nobody would have believed me."

"Wow," Uncle Will whistled, "with a figure like that...mmmmmm, she was something."

"Yeah, she must have been. Richard was with her over twenty-four hours before coming up for air. That was one long business meeting; they didn't even come out to eat," Richard's father chuckled. My ears burned at the sound of their lecherous laughter. "Look at this one," he invited.

"OOOHHHweee," Uncle Will shouted, "Now that's my kind of woman. He didn't get a chance to say more because I stormed into the room, breaking in on their secret conversation.

"What do you think you're doing, coming in here without knocking?" My father-in-law scolded as he scooped several pictures back into an envelope. My eyes widened in disbelief. They weren't just photographs, but 8 X 10 glossies of my husband with a woman of obvious bad character. She posed on his lap with a huge mug of beer held over his head. The next photo showed her hugging him tightly around the waist as they both drank from the same goblet. They grinned drunkenly into the camera. I had to swallow hard, twice, before speaking and when I did, it came out in a very unladylike bellow.

"What is this? Who is that woman? Is this the important business trip you just had to attend the week before we got married?" My voice raised in pitch as I fought a surge of anger rising in my throat. I stared at my father as if seeing him for the first time. Tears filled my eyes and my voice shook. "How could you, my own father? How can you look at those pictures and not say anything? Are you condoning his infidelity? Dad, he's been cheating on me," I screeched as I pointed at Richard with a condemning finger, "and you don't even care." Blubbering loudly, I screamed at them, "You're all sick, that's what. I've read about men like you, men that get turned on by looking at dirty pictures. I never figured my father was one or that I'd marry one of the sicko's." My mind was a blur of red as I screamed every obscenity I knew. I called them every insulting term I'd ever heard, aiming every barb at Richard and my father. My mother's smack across the face brought me back to earth.

"Nicole, what do you think you're doing screeching like a banshee?" she chastised. Shaking me none too gently, she admonished, "Get yourself under control and apologize this instant. They were only looking at the pictures taken during Richard's bachelor party."

"You mean," my jaw dropped in surprise, "you've seen them?"

"No, we haven't seen them," my mother-in-law interjected with a yawn, "but it's no big deal. He married you didn't he?" Casting a condemning look toward my mother, she returned to the front room to finish reading the newspaper.

"You'd better get your daughter under control, or she may not be married for long," Richard advised. He was so furious a muscle throbbed in his jaw.

"Oh, that does it," I raged. "My husband cheats and even brings home pictures of his exploits and I'm supposed to just shrug it off? Fat chance!" Mortified not only at my own behavior, but at the unconcerned attitude of my parents, I ran from the room, up the stairs, and to our bedroom. From behind, I heard the irritated mumbling of men's voices as my mother tried to smooth things over.

Taking a suitcase from a storage closet, I threw it onto the bed and started emptying dresser drawers. I wasn't going to spend another night under the same roof with a cheating husband. My thought was to leave—immediately--until I spied my mother in the open doorway silently watching. I collapsed into an ocean of tears, incoherent for several minutes. She waited patiently for my tears to stop. When I was finally in control of myself, she wiped my face while delivering a stern lecture.

"Where do you think you're going? Are you going to just pack up and move out after four months of marriage? You'd better think twice about what you're doing, girl, because if you do, you'll walk out with nothing."

"I don't care," I sniffled. "I'll move back home until the divorce is final and then I"ll. . ."

"Divorce? Move back home? I think not," she said hotly. "You're a married woman with a home of your own. You can't move out until I'm satisfied you've given your marriage an honest effort. So what if the guys go out and have a little fun now and then," she shrugged, "it's what men do. Now dry your eyes, wash your face, fix your make-up, and stop acting like a spoiled brat. If you don't want your husband to fool around, then you'd better make sure he has something worth coming home to. You owe him an apology, Nicole, you've embarrassed him in front of his father and father-in-law."

"Embarrassed him," I sputtered, "what about me? What about what he's done to me?"

"Forget it," she snapped. "There will be no divorce so don't even think about it," she ordered, "and your old bedroom is being remodeled into a second guest room. You can't come home again," she repeated, emphasizing each word with painful clarity. Smiling, she showed the first compassion I'd seen all evening by putting an arm around my shoulders. "It can't be so bad, now can it? After all, he treats you well doesn't he?"

"Well, yes, but he. . ."

"Now, Nicole, don't over dramatize," she interjected. "Has he ever lifted a hand to you?" I shook my head and her smile grew more encouraging. "See, it isn't terrible. I mean, just a few weeks ago you were telling me how good Richard was to you and how much you enjoyed being with him. Why ruin things? You're still newlyweds--give yourself a little more time to adjust."

My thoughts reeled from everything she said when something within me rebelled. In the course of an evening I'd seen evidence of my husband's illicit affairs, been told I couldn't return home again, and that I was to accept it all and not make a scene. An involuntary shiver tingled down my spine as icy fingers worked their way through the flesh, muscle, and bone to my heart. Something changed, making me less caring and unable to trust those closest to me. My hurt and disappointment went deep and no one seemed to care or see how much my sense of wellbeing depended on a stable marriage. I was totally disillusioned with living a lie. How long was a woman expected to look the other way while her husband played the field? My mother had played that game all of her married life and if that was the kind of marriage Richard wanted then I'd stick to his rules no matter the cost. Locking a plastic smile on my lips, I performed an Oscar-winning imitation of my mother, and dutifully responded in my nastiest voice, "I guess since you have such a perfect marriage, that you know best." Turning on my heel, I went into the bathroom to repair the damage. Locking the door behind me, I stared at my reflection, and didn't like the image reflected there. My lips were turned down in a sullen pout, and a furrow of worry wrinkled the space between my brows. I wasn't seeing myself, but an image of my mother as she might have looked before turning into my father's shadow. I refused to follow in her footsteps and vowed to breakout of the mold before becoming an ice queen just like her. I splashed my face with cold water and carefully applied fresh make-up. By the time I finished, all the heartbreak of my evening had been erased. Coming slowly down the stairs, I smiled at Richard and his father.

"I'm sorry for upsetting your evening," I said with such sweetness, my stomach turned, "it will never happen again." Glancing at Richard from beneath lowered lashes, I could tell I'd said exactly the right thing.

"Well, it must have been a shock, seeing those pictures for the first time, but it was my bachelor party," he said as if that explained it all. "Is everything okay," he studied me momentarily, looking for a lingering sign of anger. Satisfied, he pecked me on the cheek and then the four of them returned to the den to finish their poker game.

"I'm glad you've come to your senses, Nicole," my mother-in-law, Gwen, said. "You should be proud of your husband for providing you with such a beautiful home, and plenty of money to spend if you want it. There are plenty of envious, young ladies that would give just about anything to change places with you."

"Yes, I suppose you're right," I agreed.

Finding herself with no one to argue with, she looked to my mother. "I don't know what you said to her, but I want to congratulate you. She's finally making sense."

"Yes," my mother replied, "Nicole was always a dutiful daughter." Pasting a sticky smile on her face, she glanced at my mother-in-law with distaste. "It's too bad your son isn't as amenable as my Nicole." The two glared at each other for a fraction of a second and then pasted on their usual perfect expressions. Spreading the newspaper open on the table, she pointed to a full-page ad. "Look at this, several stores are having big sales and are open 'til midnight." Grabbing her purse, she turned to me with a wink, "Who wants to go shopping?"

"I do," Gwen piped up as she placed her purse over her shoulder and threw on a coat. Both women glanced at me expectantly.

"Count me out," I told them. "I've had all the excitement I can handle. Battling a crowd of over-stuffed, ill-tempered women isn't my idea of a good time. I think I'll go to bed and watch an old movie. Have fun and I'll see you later." Waving them off, I climbed the stairs with a heavy heart. Safe in my room, I buried my face in a pillow and screamed out my frustration where no one could hear. I was just working myself up for another good cry when the phone rang.

"Hi, what are you doing? Am I interrupting some big family gathering or anything?" The sorrowful tone of Madelyne's voice came through loud and clear. She was crying, and trying not to let me hear her sniffling.

"Are you okay?"

"Yeah, I'm fine, but . . .I . . .this day has been absolutely awful," she wailed. "I cooked a great meal and they were so drunk, all they did was fight and then. . ." she blew her nose, "they bought another bottle and now they're all passed out in front of the TV." She sniffled; and I heard all that she was not saying.

"Do you want to go do something? Let's go somewhere where there are lots of people. Someplace where we can talk, and no one knows who we are." Getting lost in a crowd of strangers sounded like a wonderful idea.

Brightening, I could hear the excitement catch in her voice. "I know just the thing. They're having a Christmas parade on the far side of town. There's supposed to be floats, lights, glitz, and Santa. What more could two lonely girls want? I'll fix my face and be over in ten minutes." Our conversation ended abruptly when she hung up the phone. I found myself giggling with anticipation as I pulled on jeans and a sweater. It had been a long time since I'd sat on Santa's lap or enjoyed a parade. At last, something to look forward to.

Chapter Six

As soon as Maddie pulled into the driveway, I hopped into the passenger seat motioning for her to get going. While driving the short distance across town, we shared our stories of a woeful Thanksgiving. We vowed to find something to be thankful for before the night was over. A great number of cars lined the streets, and we had to find parking quite a distance from the parade's route. Figuring a walk would do us good, we parked under a bright neon sign in a grocery store parking lot that advertised Christmas turkeys at thirty-nine cents a pound.

"Wouldn't you just figure?" Madelyne grumbled as she gazed up at the dazzling display. "Thanksgiving isn't over yet, and they're already advertising Christmas. You'd think they could at least wait until tomorrow." An unladylike snort of condemnation matched her frown when she stuck out her tongue in annoyance--just like a little kid. Giggling, we zipped our jackets against the cold, and followed other parade goers to the corner of 4th and Valley where the parade route turned. We were close enough to the announcer's box to hear every word.

As we waited for the parade to begin, we had fun studying the crowd. Across the street was a man and his wife trying to calm three rambunctious kids. Each child had enough energy for ten as they ran circles around their parents. They darted into the street to search impatiently for the parade's beginning, and then ran back again. All the while, they chanted, "We want Santa." Another family stood silently watching the antics with undisguised disgust. It was clear they would not tolerate such shenanigans from their children. Several older couples stood whispering to each other, but watched as eagerly as children for the parade to begin. We wondered if our faces reflected the same excited anticipation seen in those around us.

A vender selling cola's strolled down the street wheeling a cart. We each bought a soda to sip while we waited. The pop was icy cold and sizzled in the throat, just the way I liked it. The parade began with the boom of a cannon that startled everyone. The event kicked off with a reenactment of Washington crossing the Delaware. We gave a startled jump when the cannon went off with a blast of black powder. Several floats were decorated with Christmas lights, tinsel, and other finery, appearing elegant and beautiful under the bluish cast of the streetlights. There were clowns, horse drawn wagons, high school bands, drill teams, and the usual end of parade assortment of cars, walkers, and sign carriers. The float drawing the most attention was the last. It was decorated like Santa's toyshop with several elves busily working to fill Santa's sleigh. Atop a raised throne sat the big man himself, waving and throwing candy. Santa Claus welcomed everyone to a local department store with realistic, "Ho, ho, ho's," and "Merry Christmas. Come to Hutton's Department store after the parade and meet my elves. See you there, ho, ho, ho." We applauded with great enthusiasm.

As the float passed, followed by a brass band, we were shocked to see a familiar figure riding a bicycle and pulling a double carriage. We hadn't seen or heard from Diane since my bridal shower. A small group, all on bikes, accompanied her. At her side rode a handsome young man with longish hair that we assumed was her husband, Paul. They threw flyers into the crowd, and yelled about lost souls needing God's plan. They sounded as if they were hawking wares at a carnival.

"Hurry up, I don't want her to see us," I whispered to Madelyne as we tried to disappear into the crowd.

"Ssshhhh, what are they saying? Oh, this is downright embarrassing," she said with a nasty little snicker. Placing her hand along the side of her face, she hid behind it as we broke into hysterical giggles.

"Save the children," they shouted. "Every life is God's gift. Children are the hope of the world." Their voices dimmed as they turned the corner, following the tail end of the parade. There were several disparaging remarks about Diane's little group as the crowd broke up to follow the parade route down the street. Maddie stooped down and picked up a couple flyers. Glancing at the picture on the front, her eyes rounded before she stuffed one into my purse. The other, she folded and placed in her pants pocket.

"What are you doing," I asked with a roll of my eyes. "You aren't seriously going to read that trash are you?"

"I'm just curious," she explained, "and figure I'm doing my part for the "Keep America Clean" campaign by picking up a few of them." Turning, she wandered off in the direction of the car.

Trailing behind, I asked, "Well, what now? It's too early to go home and I'm still too stuffed to want to eat. Do you have any suggestions?"

"Actually," she yawned as she raked her fingers through her hair, smoothing it away from her face, "I'm out of suggestions. It's been a long, tiring day and I'm exhausted all of a sudden. What sounds good right now is a long hot bath, a good movie, and a cup of hot chocolate."

"You know, that does sound good, especially the hot chocolate part. I think I'll do the same thing when I get home. I've watched <u>It's a Wonderful Life</u> at least ten times and I'll watch it again tonight. But, what about tomorrow? Are you working, or are you free?"

"I'm free as a bird until Monday," she said tiredly and then as if hit with sudden inspiration, her eyes twinkled as her face lit up with excitement. "How about meeting at the coffee shop," she suggested, "like at seven or so? We'll have breakfast then go for some serious Christmas shopping." I covered my mouth with a yawn.

"Breakfast will be my treat," she tempted.

"You're on," I agreed, "but only if dinner is mine. It will be so much fun. We haven't been shopping together for a long time. Let's hit the fudge shop, the mall, the park, and then we can go to. . .."

"Hold on a minute," she interrupted with a good-natured chuckle, "we've only got the day, not a week." Driving home in companionable silence, we promised to meet at our favorite cafe for coffee the following morning.

Richard and the others played cards all night, and he didn't come to bed until I was brushing my teeth the following morning. He mumbled something about six o'clock, but was out as soon as his head hit the pillow. Pulling his shoes off, I tucked the blankets in around him before leaving the room. Dressed warmly for a long day of shopping, I selected a pair of comfortable boots. Snow was falling in huge flakes, which only added to my anticipation, when I opened the garage door.

Madelyne was seated in our favorite booth at the coffee shop and had a cup waiting for me. Just as I took a seat across from her, the waitress brought two gigantic cinnamon rolls with thick frosting, bubbling and warm straight from the oven. Grinning, Maddie plunged her fork into one and popped a generous portion into her mouth. Closing her eyes in ecstasy, she savored the bite and then complimented the cook, "MMMMmmmm, is that ever good. Tell him he could make a fortune if he ever wanted to mass-produce these things. Sell them on the open market, and I volunteer to be his personal spokesperson." She offered a bright smile and seductive raise of a shoulder. "I'd better not," she sighed, "I'd end up eating all the profits." We laughed, but I couldn't help scolding her for ordering the rich desserts.

"Madelyne, what are you thinking? I can't eat these diet busters without feeling the sugar all day. I don't burn off extra calories like you do," I complained.

"I'll make sure you burn off every morsel, now eat and when you're finished, tell me you didn't enjoy it." She made a face at me as she popped another bite into her mouth. We ate every crumb and licked our fingers with relish. It was great not to count calories every now and then.

Finishing our coffee, we planned our shopping to take advantage of all the fifty per cent off sales.

"I have to go to the men's shop to buy Richard a new suit jacket. His mother bought the one he wears most of the time, and I absolutely hate it."

"Great, while you're taking care of that, I can get something for Keith."

"Are you seeing him again?" I grimaced while digging in my purse for my share of the tip.

"Nothing steady, just now and then." She rolled her eyes and crossed her fingers, "but I keep hoping he'll be ready for a serious relationship someday, and when he is, I'll be waiting."

Grabbing her by the arm, we rushed out of the café into the snow with all the enthusiasm of youth. We didn't want to dampen our holiday spirit and were eager to spend the money burning in our pockets. Opening my mouth, I caught snowflakes on my tongue and twirled around like a little girl. The beauty of it immediately captivated Maddie; she turned her face to the sky, allowing her cheeks to be moistened by the falling flakes. Giggling crazily, we rushed off to join the mad rush for the perfect Christmas gift.

We were in and out of more stores in a few hours than most people are in over a year. At first, we moved briskly down the aisles, examining each item carefully before making our purchases. But, as morning led to afternoon and our arms grew leaden from carrying our packages, we decided to take a break. Shopping was one thing, but when it became work, the fun was gone.

"Let's take this stuff to the car. We can stop for a quick cup of something hot, take a little R&R, and then hit the stores again," Maddie suggested. Shuffling the weight of her packages from one arm to the other, she set them down to rest her aching back. Stretching and twisting one way and then another, she lifted them again and set off down the sidewalk.

We each carried an assortment of different sized sacks and boxes. Some were gift-wrapped and others were not, but each had been chosen with care. "Agreed," I said with relief, "and a nice foot massage would go nicely with our coffee."

Taking a shortcut across the parking lot of a major department store, we soon found ourselves out of the shopping district, and closer to the residential area where we parked the car. Our arms were so tired we kept shifting the weight of our purchases from one side to the other. My shoulders felt like they were being pulled out of socket.

"I hope it isn't much farther." I groaned as one of my packages fell to the ground. Kneeling to retrieve it, I dropped everything on the sidewalk not caring if the gaily wrapped packages got wet in the snow.

"It's just around the next corner," Maddie encouraged as she placed her stuff on the back of someone's car. Flashing her most practiced smile at the face watching from a window, she waved as the face blossomed into a wide grin of recognition. The car commercial had already been aired on some stations and all day people had pointed and stared. She took the attention graciously, and returned their curious looks with her new million-dollar smile. I received the same attention because I was in her company. People must have assumed we were both models. The admiring glance of several handsome men had been hard to ignore, but we managed to walk casually by as if the looks cast our way were expected.

Hefting our stuff one last time, we turned the corner and spotted the grocery store where we'd parked the car. With groans of relief, we stepped up our pace and sloshed through the slushy snow to the car. Before we crossed the street to the parking lot, we noticed a large gathering around a cinder block building at the end of the next street over.

"What do you suppose that's all about?" Maddie wondered.

"I don't know and right now, I don't care. All I want to do is rest my aching arms. Come on, Miss Curiosity, we'll stash this stuff and then investigate." Without slowing my steps, I hurried right along to the car before dropping everything into a snowdrift. I was puffing big white clouds by the time everything was stowed safely in the trunk and the car locked. "Man, that worked up a sweat," I panted. I wiped beads of perspiration from my forehead with a coat sleeve.

"Yeah, me too," Maddie said as she flipped open the lapels of her coat. "I think it's warming up. Come on, there are a few more things I need to buy. I still wonder what's going on around the corner?"

As soon as we turned down the sidewalk, we realized the crowd was there for a purpose. Some carried placards while others carried hand painted posters. They circled the cinder block building shouting to all passersby. Our feet slowed to a stop, and our chins dropped when we realized what we'd stumbled onto.

"Do you know where we are?" Maddie asked in a breathless whisper. When I shrugged, gesturing I didn't, she frowned. "Don't you read the paper?" She didn't wait for a response but went on to explain. "This must be the clinic that new doctor opened."

"A clinic? What's so important about a doctor's office?" I asked naively. "What did he do to upset so many people?"

"It's not what he did, it's what he does," she said mysteriously. Lowering her voice to a whisper, she sneered, "He performs abortions." At my blank look, she explained in simpler terms. "You know, where girls go to remove a little problem."

"Let's get out of here. They're picketing and if things get out of hand, I want to be as far away from here as possible." We took a hesitant step backward, prepared to make tracks when as luck would have it, I slipped on the ice. Fighting to maintain balance, I drew the attention of an old man in a wheelchair. As he advanced on us, we froze to the spot.

Gray hair hung to his shoulders like a wispy cobweb, and his clothes were filthy and tobacco stained; his shoes mismatched. The dirt-streaked lines in his face made him appear dark skinned, but where his neck showed above his collar, the skin was light. In his eyes was a fanatical gleam that grew intense as he bore down upon us. All the while, he shouted obscenities and cursed the doctor hiding within the walls of the clinic.

"Beware worshipers of Molech. The disciples of Molech take the children and sacrifice them to their god. They take the innocent—the unborn--the infant and sacrifice them on the altars of Molech," he screeched. We'd never seen anything like it. I wanted to run, but my feet had turned to lead. Morbid curiosity told me to stay. Wheeling close to Madelyne, he stared at her as if to strip away every barrier. Feverish, jaundiced eyes pierced her skin, seeing at a glance all the secrets hidden in her heart. She placed a hand over her mouth as if holding back a scream of intense pain. "I've seen you," he yelled as he pointed at her with a misshapen finger, "and I know your thoughts. You can't escape your destiny. You have been chosen—you are the next disciple of Molech. Will you scream out his name? Will you beg for mercy when the blood of your own drips from his fingers?"

When he turned his threats to me, my knees turned to water. "Jeez-Louise—let's get out of here. The guy is crazy," I screamed. Taking Maddie's hand, I tried to pull her away; but she stood like a stone statue, eyes fixed in fascinated horror.

"Beware--disciples of Molech, one comes who destroys. Are you the one?" he asked in a frenzied scream. Shaking my head, he threw back his head and laughed maniacally then turned his attention back to Maddie. "He's a viper, a murderer, a baby killer. He'll touch you here," he poked Madelyne on the inside of her hip so hard she sucked in air with a hiss. Frightened tears sprang to her eyes, and we leaned toward each other shaking like two leaves. "He'll rip out your unborn for a sacrifice to his god. Look," he pointed to the building, "see the flame of the altar reflected in the eyes of Molech." It was another stroke of bad luck because sunlight filtered through the clouds with a bright intensity, glinting off the windows like twin tongues of flame. That sent a message to my feet—RUN-- don't look back. Turning at the same time, our flight was blocked by the bulk of a man standing behind us. Madelyne screamed and for a minute I thought she might faint.

"Was that old man bothering you? Don't mind him, he's short a few marbles if you get my drift. Are you okay?" asked a burly police officer dressed in a leather coat. He ushered us off in the direction of the nearest department store then turned to speak to the old man. The guy had disappeared, fading into the crowd that dissolved when the officer came on the scene. Maddie and I decided we'd done enough shopping and hurried to the car. Neither of us breathed until locked safely inside.

"Can you believe it?" Maddie panted. Her eyes were as big as saucers as she checked the rear view mirror to be sure we weren't followed. Driving as fast as the speed limit allowed, she didn't relax until we were several blocks away.

A nervous giggle escaped her as we turned onto Eatery Avenue, a street boasting a restaurant on every corner. "I thought that old man was going to poke a hole right through me." She rubbed her side and winced at a tender spot. "I'll bet there's a bruise as big as a fifty cent piece." Shaking her head, she glanced at me and grinned, "Well, what do you think about having a nice cup of coffee to help frazzle my nerves a little bit more. My hands are shaking so bad... if I don't pull over I'm afraid I'll lose control on these slick roads."

"A cup of coffee suits me just fine. In fact, a nice stiff drink might be exactly what we need, but I'll settle for coffee. I can't imagine the nerve of that old man," I fumed. "Do you suppose he's allowed to roam the streets harassing everyone or does he just pick on women? Look at me! I'm still shaking. He gave me the creeps and admit it, Maddie, you were scared to death. We should have had him arrested."

"Arrested for what? Speaking his mind and standing up for something he believes in? There would be more trouble in writing out a complaint than its worth. Just be glad the officer came along when he did and we were able to get away. I've read newspaper articles where other women weren't so fortunate. A few have been threatened by lunatics just like him, and I don't mind admitting that he scared me, too." Parking alongside the restaurant, she grabbed her purse and motioned for me to follow. "Come on, I need to eat and calm my nerves."

After taking our seats, I opened a menu and studied the selections. I hadn't realized I was hungry until my stomach growled, tempted by the delicious aromas drifting from the kitchen. "I hope their food is as good as it smells. I'm hungry all of a sudden. Why don't we have dinner instead of a sandwich," I glanced at my watch to check the time, "it's certainly late enough." We agreed and both ordered steak dinners with baked potatoes, salad, and pie for dessert. After the waitress took our order and filled coffee cups, Madelyne pulled the flyer she'd picked up the night before from her purse. Spreading it open in front of us, she pointed to a grotesque picture of a monster more horrible than anything I'd ever imagined even in my worst nightmares. It held a knife, poised at the body of a faceless infant. "Molech," she needlessly explained as she pointed at the picture. "Gross, isn't he?"

My lips curled back in disgust, and my stomach rolled. The picture was quite vivid and there was no misinterpreting the meaning. "Is this one of the flyers Diane tossed?" At her nod, I grabbed the scrap of paper and wadded it up, "Don't do that," she ordered. Tearing it out of my hands she smoothed out the wrinkles, "I want to keep it," she said.

"Why?" I argued. "It's disgusting." My mouth twisted in revulsion. Whoever had drawn the picture must have been sick-minded because the figure standing over the baby looked demonic with realistic human features. You could almost hear the infant's terrified screams. I looked away until the paper was stowed safely in Maddie's purse.

"I don't want it for myself." Her expression turned sad. "I want it for a girl I know that's contemplating an abortion. Maybe if she reads the flyer, she'll think it over and change her mind. She really wants her baby, but is afraid of what her parents might say. I've advised her to take a chance, tell them and have faith that after the initial shock, they'll be understanding and help her out. I don't want her to do something she'll regret for the rest of her life."

Patting her hand, I was moved with compassion for the girl, but even more for the grief I saw in Maddie. Her expressive eyes reflected sorrow for the plight of this unborn child. "Maddie," I chided, and patting her hand, searched for a tissue in my purse. "I don't know why you have such a heart for people, but you do. I can understand you being upset about this girl and all, but those flyers are connected to the crazies' we saw at that clinic, and to the old man that assaulted you. How can you keep such a thing? That old man is evil and so are these flyers."

"He wasn't evil," she chuckled, "misguided maybe, a little crazy almost certain, but only trying to stop the murder of innocent babies. The poor guy is probably homeless and hungry, but still has enough heart to voice an opinion. Did you notice the size of his arms? Thin, too thin, he hasn't eaten a good meal in a very long time. I thought he was grand; scary--but grand."

Conversation broke off when our food was served, but picked up when the waitress left. "Grand? You thought he was grand?" I asked in a choked voice. "How grand do you think he would have been to that pregnant friend you told me about. Somehow, I don't think he'd have treated her very grandly, but would have marked her for wanton and scared the poor baby right out of her. Honestly Maddie," I said with disgust, "sometimes you have the strangest notions. Now, let's put the whole thing behind us so we can enjoy our supper. I don't want my appetite ruined by a sadistic old man, and some ancient god called Molech."

Talk between us quieted as we ate. After satisfying our hunger, we sat back to enjoy a last swallow of coffee with our pie. With stomach's full, and the sound of people's conversation falling gently on our ears, a sense of normalcy returned to our day.

"Friends?" she asked with fingers flying in our own personal sign language we'd used since we were kids.

"Always," I said sincerely. Snow was beginning to fall making icy roads slick as we left the restaurant. Driving cautiously to my house, she parked in the driveway. "I'll help carry your stuff in and then I'm gone. I want to get home before the roads get worse. Call me later, okay?"

"When the phone rings at nine, it'll be me," I promised. Waving her off, I lugged the remainder of my packages inside before they got soaked. Hearing no voices, I figured no one was home. Shrugging out of my coat, I about jumped out of my skin when Richard spoke from behind me.

"Did you have a good time?" he asked. Twirling around, I was surprised to find him seated in a big armchair in the dark room, blowing smoke rings with a cigar.

"Oh, you startled me," I said. Placing a hand over my heart to still it's rapid beating; I peered at him in the semi-dark. I could feel his anger clear across the room. "Maddie and I went Christmas shopping." A trickle of fear skittered down my spine; I pointed needlessly to the many packages scattered on the floor. I needed to move so hung my coat in the hall closet, and removed my wet shoes. "The stores were sure crowded. We tried to buy all we needed, but..." I didn't get any further. Richard came out of his chair and was at my side in one move.

"Needed?" he hissed. Grabbing one arm, I was pushed against the wall and pinned there, unable to get away. He towered over me, holding me tightly with one arm while the other twisted my hair painfully behind me. "I needed you here at six o'clock," he thundered, "and you weren't here. We had guests invited for dinner and to watch the game afterwards. I expected you to be here, to show the same courtesy to my friends they have shown to you. Sandwiches would have been sufficient, but you were too busy thinking about yourself—having fun spending my money to think about my needs."

"But, I didn't know you'd invited anyone over," I pleaded. "Richard, I swear, I didn't know anyone was coming for dinner. You didn't tell me." My hair was twisted a little bit tighter and several strands were pulled from my head. His breath was overpowering with the smell of whiskey as he shouted into my face.

"I did tell you," he roared, "this morning, before I went to bed I told you. Now, our guests are gone, and I was able to explain your absence, but it better not happen again," he warned.

Sobbing with fear, I could hardly speak. "I promise. It won't happen again," I quavered.

Releasing a length of hair, he wrapped his arms about my waist, and held me in a tight embrace. I was forced to gaze into his eyes where a gleam of threat hid behind the slight smile grazing his lips. "I'm sorry, I didn't mean to lose my temper. But it's after eight o'clock, and I've been worried sick. Don't do this to me again, Nicole, or I won't be responsible for what might happen. A man has a right to know the whereabouts of his wife."

Wiping the tears from my face with the edge of his thumb, he kissed me gently then abruptly let me go. Stretching out on the couch, he poured himself another drink and eyed me over the rim of his glass. "Okay, quit staring like a scared rabbit. It's over now, so forget it." Taking another sip, he sat up, and gestured toward the mishmash of packages on the floor. "Show me what I bought today," he ordered. Before I emptied the first sack, he fell over in a drunken stupor. He slept the night where he fell with nothing to cover him except a light throw used to cover the back of the couch.

By morning he was apologetic, and couldn't do enough to make amends. We went out for breakfast, and had friends over in the afternoon. When Sunday evening rolled around, we were both in good spirits and reluctant for the hectic pace of our work week to begin. I was getting ready to take a bath when the phone rang. Richard's voice dropped to a whisper when he answered, and shortly afterward came to tell me he was going out. He had an important appointment that would take most of the evening. Grabbing his coat from the hall closet, he waved as he stepped out the door. I had no doubt his appointment would take all night, and I was almost relieved.

After several days off for the Thanksgiving holiday there was a pile of work stacked on my desk. I was still in the typing pool, and even though I'd been offered something more official, more fitting my status as the owner's daughter-in-law, I was happy where I was. In order to complete some paperwork needed by my boss, I gladly worked a few extra hours now and then. It was five o'clock on Wednesday when Mr. Kent placed three letters on my desk.

"I hate to ask, but I need these answered right away. Would you mind. . .?" He looked at me hopefully with brows raised in question.

"No problem," I assured him. "It won't take long, and when I'm finished I'll place them on your desk for your approval and signature." I turned to my computer and went to work. It was after six when the phone rang. The display indicated an unknown caller.

"Why aren't you on your way home?" Richard asked in a tight voice.

"I'm almost there," I promised. "Just one letter left to finish and then I'll be on my way. I should be there within thirty minutes."

"That'll be too late," he said angrily. "You know the guys come over on Wednesday for a game of poker. You promised to make sandwiches and bring home the beer," he reminded. His voice dropped to a singsong as he sneered, "There's nothing in the fridge except left-over turkey. I'm sick of leftovers," he yelled. "Get home and I don't mean later, and don't forget to pick up my beer." He yelled so loud, I had to hold the phone far away from my ear.

A braver person would've slammed the phone down and screamed, "Get it yourself." Instead, I quickly finished up, and obediently did exactly what was expected. After stopping at the store for a case of beer, I hurried home to make sandwiches and snacks for Richard's poker game. He was in a pretty good mood by the time everything was laid out on the table, and kissed me passionately before I went upstairs to bed.

"I'll see you later," he promised. "Having you for a wife is the best thing that's ever happened to me." My heart warmed to the compliment, and I returned a smile of affection. "I wouldn't have got a spread like this ready in time for the game. You do this stuff without any effort at all. You're really something, Nicole, and I love ya' for it." My smile froze. His flattery had nothing to do with loving me.

"I could do more if given some warning about you're plans," I offered. I'd have promised anything, just to keep the smile on his face. My arm was still tender from his last temper-tantrum and I preferred not to initiate another angry outburst. I should have kept my mouth shut.

The next morning, he made coffee and kissed my cheek as he went out the door. "See you later," he said with conspiratorial grin.

"Yeah," I said, staring at the cup in my hand as if I'd never seen one before. "I'll see you after work." After he'd gone, I finished my coffee, dressed, and hurried off to work. When I walked into the typing pool the other girls were mysteriously busy. Not one of them returned my morning greeting. A stranger was seated at my desk finishing some documents I'd started the day before.

"What's going on here?" I asked one of the girls. She shrugged and turned back to her desk. All of a sudden, I was invisible. Not one of them would meet my questioning gaze. Turning to the woman seated at my desk, I asked again--only louder--as if she couldn't hear, "What are you doing at my desk and where are my things?" Opening a desk drawer, I found it emptied of all my personal belongings.

"Hey, what are you doing? This is my desk, and that's my purse. You'd better talk to the boss and get this straightened out," the girl informed me. Her eyes flitted nervously toward Mr. Kent's office door and it was obvious she knew what was going on. When he heard my voice, his door swung open.

"Come in, Nicole, we need to talk." He motioned me into his office, and sat behind his desk. A shudder of dread shot through me because it was something he rarely did. "Something's come up and I'm afraid I have to let you go. Your job's been given to Miss Capps and your things are here," he said as he pushed a shoebox full of my personal items toward me.

"But, what have I done? Why are you firing me? What did I do wrong?" Tears filled my eyes, and spilled down my cheeks.

He handed me a Kleenex, and became very interested in straightening all the papers on his desk. "You'll have to take it up with your father-in-law, Nicole. If it were left to me, you'd still be employed, but word came down that if we want to remain employed, we do as the big boss says. When Mr. Richard Franklin III speaks, we jump."

Grabbing the shoebox, I stormed to the top floor, and entered my father-in-law's office unannounced. Angry and frustrated, I plopped down in a chair and burst into tears.

"Why?" I asked, "what did I do that made you want to fire me?" Dabbing at my eyes, I cleared my vision enough to see him clearly as he stood before me with hands clasped behind his back.

"Now Nicole, you've got to understand this isn't about you. Richard feels you're needed more at home and, well, it's not like you need the money or anything." He smiled the same phony paste-up he used on clients he wanted to get rid of. With a placating gesture, he spoke sympathetically as he gazed at me with an amused expression. "Richard will own this company someday and what he says goes. Go home, go shopping, join the country club, have some fun," he said jovially, "but be sure to keep him happy because if you don't, there'll be the devil to pay." His voice was colder than blue steel as he ushered me out the door. When he told me again to go home it wasn't a request--it was an order. What other choice did I have?

Chapter Seven

For two solid weeks I pounded the pavement looking for work, but it seemed Mr. Richard Franklin IV was always one step ahead of me. At most places the employer explained as tactfully as possible that my father-in-law had advised them against hiring me. One oddball believed I was a bad omen and would bring bad luck to his company. So, as a last resort, I tried the country club scene to find a place to fill the empty hours. Most the patrons were affluent, comfortable with their station in life, and more bored than I was. Shopping soon lost its appeal, and you can only clean so many cupboards. I wandered around and felt quite useless. Occasionally Madelyne and I lunched together, but she was busy filming her next commercial and not always available. Feeling more at odds with myself than usual, I went to visit my parents to voice my complaints.

"There's absolutely nothing for me to do," I told my mother. "I need to feel useful. How can a person feel like they're worth anything when all they do is sit around? I want to work."

Wiping tears of frustration from my eyes, "Richard's dad really fixed that for me," I said bitterly. "There isn't a place in town willing to take me on." Breaking down, I allowed myself a good cry.

After a while, my mother handed me a tissue and in a show of compassion, placed a hand on my head and stroked my hair. "Feeling better?" she asked.

A tiny smile curved her lips as she gazed at me. For a minute I felt like she really cared about what I was feeling, and then the moment was gone. "Wipe those tears and start acting like a woman instead of a spoiled, little girl. If you're that bored do volunteer work, have a baby,

The Redemption of Madelyne

find something to make yourself feel better. I tried to tell you what it would be like before the two of you married, but you wouldn't listen. Now, it's time to pay the piper, and you're not liking it. You should have thought about the consequences before you agreed to marry him." Her stern look evaporated as she wrapped her arms around me. "I know it's hard, Nicole," she whispered. "It's hard to be a woman, and even harder to be married to a man like Richard, but you've got to make the most of it." She hugged me tight in a rare display of sympathy. "Feeling better?" she asked.

"Feeling better about what?" asked my father. He stood in the doorway with a perturbed expression on his face. He looked from one to the other of us suspiciously. "I hope you're not telling her she can come home, because I won't allow it. She's married and lives in a finer home than we do, and she's not happy? What more do you want?" he demanded.

"I don't want anything except to be treated like I'm more than a piece of property."

"You are property," he yelled. "You're owned lock, stock and barrel by the richest family in this area and don't you forget it! You made the choice, young lady, and now you're going to live with it. I will not jeopardize my job and livelihood by allowing you to come back here. Richard provides you with a wonderful home that you obviously don't appreciate. If he doesn't show he cares, then be woman enough to make him want to—and I don't think you need a picture drawn to know what I mean. You've got everything any healthy, red-blooded, American woman could want, and I won't let you throw it away."

"Dad, he cheats on me, and he's abusive," I argued.

"Has Richard hit you?" asked my mother. The concern in her face was sincere and for the second time, she placed a comforting arm around my shoulders.

"Not exactly, but he grabbed my arm and I know it was because I came home late, but he also pulled my hair and . . .this all sounds crazy, but, mom, I'm afraid of him sometimes." She looked at me with understanding and as our eyes met, I knew she felt the same way about my father.

"Ted, maybe if she came and spent the night. What could one night hurt? It's not like Richard isn't away, and frequently I might add." The ironic sarcasm in her voice was unmistakable and it didn't set well.

"Don't even entertain the idea, Joanna," he warned. "Having her here could hurt, and a lot. How can I face Mr. Franklin and tell him my daughter isn't woman enough to face up to married life, so she turned tail and ran home? No sir, I won't have it." When he spoke in that tone with that look on his face, there was no use arguing or pursuing further discussion. Taking my coat from the hall closet, he handed it to me signaling an end to my visit. Holding my mother's elbow, he stopped her from escorting me to the door. Flashing a fatherly smile, his final advice was not encouraging, "Go, and make that house a home. Look at your mother, she may not be the happiest woman on earth, but you never hear her complain. She has a full life, and has made this place something we're both proud of. Follow her example." Her sorrowful expression burned into my memory as the door shut behind me.

After the visit to my parents, I decided the best way to deal with a sense of isolation was to get up and go somewhere—anywhere--every day. So as soon as Richard was out the door, I slipped on a coat and gloves and walked uptown. I liked the exercise, enjoyed window shopping, and smiled at passers-by inviting conversation. There was a coffee shop I frequented so often they called me by name. I was enjoying a latte' and a muffin one morning when an idea began to take form. A young woman and her mother came in and sat at a table across from me. The young woman carried a bundle in her arms, and the two of them laughed together as blankets were removed from the wriggling body she carried. A little head was revealed and tiny little hands that waved about excitedly. Two bright little eyes peeked at me over her mother's shoulder. The child looked around the café and then grinned toothlessly at her grandma before hiding her face in her mother's shoulder. The answer to my problem was crystal clear. What better way to make our house a home than to have Richard's baby? Hadn't he mentioned wanting a son to take over the business someday? I went directly home and flushed my birth control pills down the toilet.

Sometimes we make spur-of-the-moment decisions when we're unsure of what we really want. It's the worst kind of decision-making and usually ends in disaster. Richard was never consulted because I was sure he was anxious to take on fatherhood; willing to accept the consequences that would drastically change our lives. I didn't think--I only wanted; and not out of need, but desperation.

The birth control pills were flushed a few days after Christmas and when my cycle came around on schedule in January, I was disappointed and relieved at the same time. Life was settling into a routine that was bearable, and I wasn't sure a baby was really what I wanted. Richard seemed happier and his nights out were spent in the den playing cards or watching football on TV. We were content, if not happy, and except for a few rough edges, life was good. March brought the beginning of spring and warmer weather. As the days grew longer, Richard became restless about spending so much time inside. He paced the house like one of the caged lions at the zoo. In order to appease his need for action, I arranged a picnic at the beach with some friends. It wasn't warm enough to water ski, but great for a boat ride. Afterward some volleyball or four-wheeling would round out the day. He looked forward to Saturday, and bought himself a new swimsuit for the occasion vowing he'd go snorkeling no matter how cold the water. When he woke, he smacked my backside to wake me then jumped out of bed as fresh as a daisy.

"Breakfast will be ready in an hour. I feel like an omelet, how about you?" He looked so cute standing there in his briefs with his hair plastered to his head on one side and sticking straight up on the other. I loved him very much at that moment. Lifting my arms in invitation, he reciprocated with a swift peck on my cheek. He was impatient to start the day.

"I love you," I told him.

Pulling away, he laughed and threw the covers off onto the floor. "Come on, get up. Time's a-wastin' as they used to say." Pulling on long pants and then an undershirt, he padded barefoot to the door. "Do you want an omelet or not?" he asked. "Don't answer. I'll make two ham and cheese omelets with toast, coffee and hash browns if we have any potatoes. Now get up my lovely wife and how about wearing that cute shorts outfit I like so well? You can get an early start on a tan."

"Don't you think it will be a little cold for shorts?"

"So wear a sweater," he suggested with a shrug. When I heard the sound of pots and pans banging in the kitchen I got out of bed and headed for the bathroom. I dug the outfit he liked so well from my stash of summer clothes, and shook out the wrinkles. After fixing my hair in a French braid and applying make-up, I was pleased with the results. What a shock when I slipped the top over my head. It pulled across my chest and was uncomfortably tight. The shorts fit over my hips, but the button refused to meet the buttonhole. Shocked, I stepped on the scale expecting to see the needle soar, but it showed a loss in weight, not a gain. Disgusted with myself for indulging in so many lattes' over the winter, I shoved the outfit into the back of my closet and the scales into the garbage can. They obviously weren't working. I wore jeans and a midi top I'd bought at a sale a few weeks before and was surprised that it too was tighter than when I'd bought it.

When I entered the kitchen, Richard whistled in honest admiration. My spirits lifted as he complimented me on the sexy top I wore.

"Wow, when did this happen?" he asked as he held me at arm's length. Shaking his head, he gave a wolf whistle. "All of a sudden my skinny little wife has developed a chest and more curves than a roller coaster. Wear a sweater," he ordered with a point at my newly acquired cleavage, "and keep that covered up. I wouldn't want any of the guys to look too hard because then I'd have to clobber one of them."

"Oh, for heaven's sake, Richard, nothing's changed. I'm the same skinny girl, and why the attention all of a sudden?" I giggled.

One of the pans on the stove began to sizzle and he quickly lifted the lid to turn a thick slice of ham. "Look at that. Don't it look good?" He blinked with surprise at my unexpected reaction. My stomach rolled, and clasping a hand to my mouth, I ran to the sink and was immediately sick. When I finally quit retching and sank to the floor, I placed a damp dishcloth over my forehead. I tried to focus on Richard, but he seemed to run all together as if he were melting. He still held the slice of ham suspended on a fork as he gaped at me with a shocked expression.

"That was certainly gross," he accused. A muscle twitched in his cheek and his pallor was slightly green. Swallowing convulsively, he dropped the ham back into the pan. Turning on the cold water, he doused his head in the sink and then handed me another damp towel for my head. "Are you sick or something? Why didn't you tell me you were feeling bad? I could have made a few calls and canceled. It's too late now, several of them are already on their way." Helping me to my feet, he placed a hand on my forehead.

"Just give me a minute. My head is still swimming," I cautioned. Taking a deep, steadying breath, I stepped over to the stove and turned the heat down under the ham. The sick feeling left as suddenly as it had come leaving me empty and ravenous. "I'm feeling better, now, really," I assured him as I set the table and tasted a corner of the omelet. After salting the eggs, the pan was set on to the side to finish cooking. I ate a huge breakfast and felt absolutely terrific all day. It wasn't until we were preparing for bed that Richard brought it up again.

"Still feeling okay?" he asked as he toweled off after a shower.

"Sure. Why do you ask?" Glancing up from my magazine, it took a minute to remember why he asked the question. "Oh, that," I said, "it was nothing. I must have stood up too fast or something because whatever it was, it's gone now. I feel great. Tired," I yawned, "but great." Snuggling down into the covers, I rolled over and was immediately asleep.

The bouts of sickness reoccurred, and didn't confine themselves to mornings. Richard became concerned when a friend commented on my pale face and drastic weight loss. He demanded I see a doctor and at once. I refused to see the family doctor and went to one across town. After a complete and thorough exam, he confirmed what I had only suspicioned. I was almost three months pregnant. When I left his office with prescriptions for vitamins and relief of morning sickness, I went straight to the nearest maternity shop. It was hard to keep the smile from my lips as I looked through piles of tiny socks, nighties, receiving blankets, bibs, and hats. Selecting a sweet little sailor outfit with tiny little socks to match, I bought it and two maternity smocks. After making my purchases, I rushed home to unthaw two steaks and start preparations for dinner. I wrapped the baby outfit and tied a perfect bow around it. Everything was primed for Richard's arrival except me. Eyeing myself in the mirror, I took a quick shower, fixed my hair and put on my prettiest dress. When he walked in the door, I was ready for him, posed on the couch with a drink in my hand.

"What's this all about?" he asked with brows raised in surprise. "Did you win the lottery or something?" Brushing past, he placed his briefcase on the couch and gulped down the drink. "What's for dinner, I'm starved?" Poking his nose into the oven, he grinned with delight. "You must be a mind reader. I was thinking about a thick New York steak with baked potato on my way home. By the way," he turned to hang his coat in the closet, "I might have to go out later tonight," and then glancing back at my provocative pose said, "but, maybe not."

It wasn't easy to maintain a charade of secrecy throughout dinner and then his after dinner cocktail. When I handed him the wrapped package, I couldn't help but grin like the proverbial "cat who caught the canary."

"What's this?" he asked. I shrugged, suddenly embarrassed. What if he wasn't as excited as I was? As he tore the bow off the wrapping and then ripped away the paper, he sat holding the little outfit in his hands with the funniest expression on his face. It was unreadable, and a cold finger of doubt sent a chill through me as he continued to sit there staring at the blue and white fabric.

"Is this some kind of joke?" he finally asked, "because I'm not laughing. "What does this mean, Nicole, and don't lie to me."

Clasping my hands in front of me to still my excitement, I knelt at his feet and touched the little sailor suit lovingly. "You have made me very happy." He didn't smile or even blink. His expression was cold, filled with displeasure.

"Explain what you mean and get to the point."

"We're going to have a baby," I blurted out. "That's why I've been so sick lately. I'm pregnant--almost three months' worth. Oh Richard, we're going to be parents. Aren't you happy?"

Throwing the outfit onto the floor, he stared at it as if it had bit him. Rising slowly, a spasm of irritation crossed his face. "I warned you, Nicole, not to surprise me. No wonder you've been getting fat." Giving me the once-over, he stated with icy indifference. "We are not having a baby because I never said I wanted one. There are places to fix these kinds of problems, and you'd better get it taken care of before it goes much further."

"But, I want this baby," I objected, "this is our child. Richard, how could you possibly want to destroy our child?"

Savagely, he dug his fingers into the soft skin of my shoulder, "I'm warning you, either get rid of it, or you'll have it alone. I'll be hanged if I'm going to be saddled with a snot-nosed little brat whining and bawling in my ear. It's bad enough I've got you, but a kid, too? No way! That wasn't part of the bargain."

Grabbing his coat and briefcase, he stalked to the door. Gripping the door handle, he spoke with cool indifference, "I'll stay with a friend until you call the office to tell me it's taken care of. Until then, don't expect me home. I'll put money in the account to see to your needs." With that said he left, slamming the door angrily behind him.

I didn't hear or see much of him after that, but heard through the grapevine he was drinking and partying more than ever. Everyone seemed to think he was happy, and content to leave things between us as they were. The idea of an abortion did cross my mind, but I couldn't justify taking the life growing inside me to save a marriage that was dead. I even went so far as to make an appointment to discuss an abortion with my doctor. However, when I searched in my purse for my keys one day, I found the flyer Madelyne had tucked into it the night of the parade. Cautiously, I unfolded it to read the bold printed lines. When I turned it over to scan the back, my eyes focused on the horrible picture of the figure standing over the helpless infant. The figure became an old man with gray, wispy hair and eyes that burned with an all-consuming fire. I heard the child's screams, and felt the mother's pain as the infant was ripped from her body.

The drawing terrified me. Suddenly, there was a searing, radiating pain deep in my pelvis. Doubling over, I screamed in refusal to do such a thing to my own child, but the screaming wouldn't stop. Somehow, I managed to call Maddie. She rushed me to the hospital, and saved my child's life. The doctor impressed upon us both that if I wanted a healthy baby, I'd need bed rest until after he or she was born. Madelyne accepted the job and moved in without a moment's hesitation. She proved to be a better friend than I'd ever imagined.

The day I went into labor she called Richard's office, and was told he couldn't be reached. She was seeing Keith on a regular basis, and after a quick call to cancel their date, rushed me to the hospital. Keith was waiting for us when we arrived. Madelyne didn't take time to talk to him, but donned a surgical mask, gown, and slippers to go into the delivery room with me. There was no hurry, however, because my labor continued for another fifteen hours. Finally, the nurse said I was ready and wheeled me from the labor room.

"Come on, Nicole, one more time. Breathe and then push," Madelyne encouraged for the tenth time. My strength was running out and I was exhausted. Why wouldn't they let me rest? Another pain gripped my insides and when it passed, I took a deep breath and pushed as hard as I could. Little Matthew David Franklin was born on September the fourth. I knew true love the first time I gazed into his little face. Madelyne left the delivery room with tears in her eyes, and told me later about her conversation with Keith. It went something like this.

"She's finally had the baby, a beautiful baby boy. Keith, I know you're Richard's friend, but Nicole needs him right now. Where is he?"

"I don't know where he is. Do you think I'm my brother's keeper or something?"

"You're not his keeper, but you know where he is. Now you either call him yourself or I'll have the police find him and we both know he wouldn't like that."

"You're a hard woman, Madelyne Hall, do you know that?"

"Only when I have to be. Now get him on the phone and get him here fast. I'm going to call her parents and his. Maybe between them, at least one will be happy about the baby she almost gave her life for."

★ ★ ★

Richard made an appearance at the same time as his parents. I was seated in a wheelchair at the nursery window gaping at my in-laws in astonishment. Both sets of parents made quite a fuss over the baby goo-gooing and coo-cooing at him through the nursery window. I was glad Matthew slept through the entire thing because he could've been frightened by their ridiculous faces. Richard wheeled me back to my room and looked as disgusted as I felt.

"Can you believe them?" he asked. "You'd think they were in their second childhood the way they're makin' over that kid." With a sheepish smile he helped me back to bed. "Sorry about not being here for the kid and all, but I'm not the fatherly type. You might just as well know I won't be coming home. The kid has my name and will have my money someday, but that's all."

"I never expected more," I told him with a sense of boldness I was far from feeling. The nurse poked her head in the door as soon as both sets of grandparents crowded into my room.

"Shall I bring the little fellow in now? Isn't it about time dad got to hold his son?" She didn't wait for an answer figuring Richard was eager to see his son. Such was not the case, and when she placed the baby in his arms, Richard immediately handed him to his mother.

"Ooohhh, wook atta wittle man," she cooed shaking a rattle above his head.

"Give me a gander at the kid," my father-in-law complained. After taking the baby, he gazed into the tiny, innocent face and then raved, "Look at that, he's got Richard's nose. Yes, sir, he's a Franklin all right--Richard Franklin the Fifth. Look at your son, Richard. He looks just like you."

Taking the child from his father, he grinned when the baby clasped his finger in a tiny hand. "Hey, maybe he'll learn to play baseball or something. Yeah, Richard Franklin, you'll be a chip off the ole' block. When you're old enough, I'll teach you everything you need to know about women and before you know it. . . ."

"His name isn't Richard," I interrupted. "His name is Matthew David Franklin." Silence greeted this announcement as all eyes stared at me as if I'd repeated something foul.

"What kind of name is that?" asked Richard. "No one in my family is named Matthew, and it sure isn't your father's name." My dad shook his head in agreement. Indignation glinted in Dad's eyes; he definitely sided with Richard about the naming of the newest addition to the family.

"I read it or heard it somewhere; it doesn't matter where it came from because his name is Matthew David and that's final." Reaching out, I took my baby and held him to my breast to protect him from the world Richard offered. "His name is Matthew," I repeated as I gazed into my son's face.

"Matthew," my father-in-law intoned, "it's a good solid name." For once he didn't argue, but played peacemaker to thwart any verbal attack. You can name this one, but the next one's ours. Isn't that right, son?" He looked towards Richard and clapped him on the shoulder and then back at me. The feral glint in their eyes reminded me of a pack of hungry wolves waiting to destroy my son. They would change his sweet nature into the same ugliness as their own. Holding him protectively, I vowed he'd never know his father's world. There had to be a way to protect him from the very thing I was unable to keep away from myself.

Chapter Eight

Four days after Matthew was born, we went home. Before signing release papers, the doctor gave a final word of caution.

"Don't overdo and get some help in caring for the baby until you're feeling stronger. You had a hard delivery and it will take time for you to recuperate. Get your strength back and then worry about all the other stuff because if you don't, you could end up back here with problems that'll take more than bed rest to cure."

"I promise," I said with a Boy Scout salute. "Besides, even if I wanted to do more I don't think she'd let me." I pointed toward Madelyne who stood patiently by as the doctor gave last minute instructions. Her smile didn't hide the concerned look in her eyes.

"She'll stay in bed if I have to tie her to it," she said emphatically. With a prim shake of her head, she grabbed the handles of the wheelchair and pushed me to the waiting elevator. A nurse stood by and placed the baby in my arms. We were finally going home, and I was anxious to have my son all to myself. It was time to get properly acquainted.

Madelyne was definitely in the wrong profession. She made a great model, but an even better nurse. While I lay in bed, or on the couch allowing my body to heal and regain strength, she cleaned the house, prepared nourishing meals, and cared for Matthew. I almost envied her as she rocked the baby and sang him to sleep. She did a thousand other tasks to help not once asking for anything in return. And when I was finally able to get out of bed and take over the care of my son, she gracefully stepped aside.

"Are you sure you'll be okay? I can take another day off if you think you need me." She stood poised at the door, with one hand on the knob. I knew she was eager to get back to what she loved and her expression proved it. Her eyes glowed with an inner intensity that enhanced an aura of excitement about her that was contagious. She was so antsy, her feet made little dancing steps of impatience as she waited for my response.

Shifting the baby from arm to shoulder, I patted his back. "We'll be fine, Maddie." "My word, it's not like you're going away forever." Giving a little wave, I made as if to push her out the door. "You've already made my lunch, and dinner will be a snap. I'll throw a couple of steaks on the grill and bake a couple of potatoes. Go and don't worry about us. It's time I took over the care of my son without your help."

Plopping a hat on her head she gave a parting wave, blew a kiss to the baby and left. I could almost see her shoulders lift as the staccato click-click of her steps made a rapid retreat. Commercial number three was in the making and she was so excited, she talked about it all the time. In the next one, she'd be seated on a bar stool wearing a glittery evening gown as she sipped a drink. Even though the ad was for a particular brand of whiskey, she thought it put her in a more glamorous light than the other two. "This commercial will certainly catch the attention of Hollywood," she declared. "It's the best I've done so far and very seductive. It really shows off my most attractive assets," she said with a giggle as she raised one shoulder and posed with a silly grin on her face. I laughed as I finished burping Matthew. "You're Aunt Madelyne is quite a lady," I told him as I changed his diaper. "She's very beautiful, not conceited, and becoming quite famous. We should feel honored because she put her busy schedule on hold to take care of us. I guess that makes us pretty special." When the full impact of her compassion hit me, my eyes misted. "Yes sir, little Matt, we can count ourselves privileged to be loved by Madelyne Hall. She's one in a million." Carrying my son to the bedroom for his nap, I stepped carefully, trying to see through a veil of grateful tears.

At two months, Matthew was sleeping through the night, and growing like a weed. He slept less during the day and liked to be talked to for long periods of time. Both sets of grandparents came to visit occasionally and made quite a fuss over him, but never offered to baby sit. One day out of desperation, I called Richard. I couldn't expect

Madelyne to baby-sit every time I needed to go out and since Richard was his father, I figured it was time he took responsibility.

"I want you to come over after work and watch the baby while I go to the grocery store."

"I've got a better idea, why don't you tell me what you need, and I'll pick it up on my way home."

"Pick up my groceries on your way home?" I spit, "how could you possibly do that? You live in a condo clear across town."

"So maybe I'll move out and come home. I still own the house and should start making use of it. There are still empty bedrooms aren't there?"

"Of course. But wouldn't living at home and acting like a husband and father cramp your style?" I didn't hide the sneer in my voice, and hoped the little dig hit him where he lived.

"I never said anything about playing the family-man," he said with smooth directness. "Why should I pay rent when I own a perfectly good house just a few blocks away from work?" Pausing long enough for the impact of his words to come through loud and clear, he added, "I promise not to bring any of my well, uh. . should I say friends home with me?"

He moved into one of the empty bedrooms and did not give so much as a second look at his son. The one and only time I left the baby in his care while I ran to the store, I returned home to find Matthew screaming at the top of his lungs. Richard was passed out on the couch while the baby was left alone in the nursery swaying back-and-forth in an electric swing. I learned a hard lesson. Richard couldn't be trusted to care for his own son. I never left Matthew with him again.

I confronted him on the issue, but he refused to listen to my concerns. The more I talked, the angrier he became. "You could have waited until I got home to start drinking," I accused. "What if something serious happened to the baby? You were so drunk, he could have been hurt and you wouldn't have known."

"He wasn't hurt and I don't know what the big deal is all about. I had a little drink and took a nap. The kid started bawling so I put him in the other room until he shut up."

"You don't leave a baby in a dark room and expect him to shut up," I screamed angrily. My body shook with the intensity of my outrage.

My hands itched to claw his face, to hit, slap, kick, anything to cause him the same pain he caused me and his son.

"Don't raise your voice to me, Nicole, or. . ."

"Or what?" I spit. "Are you going to threaten me or hit me? Better me than him," I said with a nod toward the sleeping baby. "I used to think you were something special. Now I see you for what you really are and you're a pathetic little nothing that can't see beyond the bottom of a bottle." The tone of my voice surprised even me as I bated him into taking some kind of action. "I want you to leave, Richard, and don't come back unless you're sober."

"My, the little mouse has turned into quite a tiger," he sneered. "Since when do you give me orders in my own house? I'll leave, but will be back and don't be surprised if I tell you I want a divorce and you know what that means don't you? No more credit cards, or charge accounts, or extra money deposited in your bank account. I'll cut you off with nothing more than the minimum in child support and won't bat an eye doing it. You mean nothing more to me than a cheap roll in the hay, and a poor one at that I might add. Treat me right, Nicole, or you'll be out on the street with no turning back. But then maybe I need to take advantage of a husband's rights," he purred as his fingers trailed up my arm to my shoulder where they stroked the side of my neck.

Jerking away, I crossed my arms defensively over my chest. "Don't even think about it," I retorted. Gesturing toward the door with furious indignation, I shot him a look of contempt. "Get out, and don't come back."

"You look good all puffed up like an angry peacock."

Pulling me against him, he whispered in my ear so Madelyne couldn't hear. "This new side of you really turns me on so don't be surprised if you wake up some night and find me there beside you. You're still my wife, Nicole," he warned with brutal detachment, "and I have rights that I can legally take advantage of whether you're willing or not." Menace tinged his voice as he gazed into my eyes, "There isn't a court anywhere that won't defend a man's right to have sex with his wife." Pushing away, his gaze raked me over one last time.

Something inside shivered involuntarily as I took a fearful step backward. Grinning with pleasure, he stepped to the door. "I'll be back," he said as a parting shot, "so don't get too comfortable." Closing the door softly, he turned and waved through the glass. The smirk on his lips sent an icy shudder up my spine. The battle lines were drawn and I knew from experience that Richard played to win.

When his car pulled from the driveway, Madelyne rushed into the kitchen. Throwing her arms around my shoulders, I clung to her for a moment as we stood trembling by the door. Suddenly, my legs were rubber and I stumbled to the nearest chair. The aftereffect of Richard's words hit me hard; my insides shook and it was hard to catch my breath. Putting my head down on the table, I wanted to cry, but tears didn't come as easily as they used to. The only emotion left was exhaustion, and I sighed heavily with the full weight of it on my shoulders.

"Do you think he'll be back tonight?" Maddie asked as she peered out the window. Turning the lock, she closed the curtains even though it was still full light. "Nicole, you were magnificent," she said with an ear-to-ear grin. "How did you ever get the courage to face up to him like that?" Pouring each of us a cup of coffee, she sat down and patted my hand. "My hero," she said as she lifted her cup in salute. Taking a sip, her brow wrinkled with concern as her finger traced the rim of her cup. "What will you do if he comes back to make good on his promise?" Her luminous eyes studied me with grave deliberation. I knew she was as afraid as I was, but would staunchly stand with me no matter what.

"I'm not sure about what to do or how to do it, but I'll handle it because I have to," I said. Rising, I lifted the baby from the playpen where he slept. Cuddling him close against me, I added, "He's innocent and has no one to protect him except me. I'll do whatever needs to be done to ensure his safety and happiness. The first thing is to find a job. I can't depend on Richard's money forever because it can be cut off without a moment's notice. For now, however, I need to hold my baby, feed him his bottle, and give him a bath. There'll be time enough tomorrow to worry about what to do next."

For the next month I visited almost every business listed in the phone book with no luck. After exhausting the addresses in the yellow pages, I pounded the pavement and applied to places I was almost embarrassed to be seen going into. As a last resort, I swallowed my pride and approached my father-in-law hoping he would relent and remove his word of censure. He wasn't exactly congenial, and his tone reflected the same attitude as his son.

"Well young lady, it's about time you came to your senses. Admit it, you need your husband and want him to return home. He would, you know, and all he needs is an encouraging word. I can't imagine why you threw him out to begin with. He's been a good provider hasn't he?"

"Yes, but,. . ."

"He'll do what I tell him to do. If you're willing to forget this nonsense and allow him some time to get used to the idea of being a father, maybe your marriage can be saved."

"What if I don't want to save my marriage?" Rising to my feet, I clutched my handbag with icy fingers. How dare he insinuate the problem was all mine. He might be my son's grandfather, but at the moment was acting like a pompous horse's behind. "It takes two people working together to make a good marriage and Richard isn't willing to put in the time. We've been over this argument before, and there's no sense in going over it again. If you won't talk to some of your business friends, will you at least offer me a job? I'm willing to do just about anything. I don't want to live off Richard's money; I want to earn my own way."

"I will not go over my son's head, and if you're so obstinate that you won't listen to reason then you'd best go home and stew in your own juice. My grandson will never go hungry, but as far you're concerned you can go straight to the devil." Opening his office door, he ordered me out with lips pursed in fury.

That night, I cried as I prepared dinner. Placing a casserole of macaroni-and-cheese in the oven, I slumped into a chair. "I've been everywhere and still can't find a job. Is there something wrong that people won't hire me or am I just plain stupid?" Tears of frustration rolled down my cheeks and dripped off my nose. Madelyne regarded me compassionately and placed a box of tissues within easy reach.

"I wish there was something I could do, but I don't know what it would be. There is a job opening where I work, but it's demeaning and doesn't pay much. I haven't mentioned it because you wouldn't earn enough to keep a bird alive. But if you're serious, it's a start."

Sniffling loudly, I sat straight up in my chair. Why had she kept this information from me? "Consider that job filled and where do I apply?"

"Are you sure? It isn't much and like I said, . . .it doesn't pay. . ."

"I don't care what it pays because it's more than I'm making now. Where do I apply and who do I talk to?"

"If you're sure, I'll make a call and let you talk to Jerry. Jerry Amsdale is the office manager and he's the one to make the decision." Handing her the phone, I hung over her until the call was made. Dinner was a festive occasion, because he hired me after asking a few questions, and I was to report for work the next morning. He even mentioned an opportunity to work additional hours at a second job if I wanted to make more money. He didn't mention what the job entailed and I didn't ask. At the end of my first shift, he approached with a bucket, rag, cleaner, and disinfectant.

"Ready for some extra duty? It will add to your paycheck, but nothing to a resume'," he joked. I followed him to the bathrooms where he handed me the bucket. "It pays two dollars more an hour and should take about three hours two or three times a week and don't forget the bathrooms on the other side of the building. Put up the "Closed for Cleaning" sign before entering the men's room and be sure to disinfect the drinking fountains." Tipping back on his heels, he hooked his hands in his suspenders as he waited expectantly for my reaction. I didn't blink an eye. Placing the bucket over one arm and the cleaning rag over the other, I entered the ladies room with a smile. I was determined to make sure every toilet gleamed and each chrome fixture left shining. Doing some quick figuring in my head, I already knew what the extra money would buy. Christmas was just around the corner, and Matthew was outgrowing most of his newborn sizes. Providing for my sons every need was a priority because it was certain his father never would.

As I grew accustomed to the routine of going to work and then rushing home to care for Matthew, I became aware of how shallow my previous life had been. (Previous meant before Matthew). Just a few short months ago, many blissful hours were spent wandering through stores buying whatever I wanted. A lot of time was wasted making myself, and my home look good. Now, I was lucky to spend ten minutes on hair and make-up before rushing out the door to run the baby to the sitter and then myself to work. At night I fell into bed, exhausted, but satisfied with the day's activity. I was living the life of a single mom and finding true happiness for the first time in my life. I was making my own decisions and even if I wasn't always right; I wasn't always wrong either. As my baby grew and his personality developed, my sense of independence developed at the same time. It was a wonderful feeling, and for a short time, I felt invincible--as if anything could be accomplished. Then the walls came crashing down.

"Nicole, you'd better get up." Madelyne tapped on my bedroom door early one morning and the urgent tone in her voice called me from sleep to instant wakefulness.

"What? Is something wrong with the baby? Is he sick or something?" Pulling on a robe, I was halfway to his room before she caught up with me.

"Hold on," she said as she grabbed my shoulders to turn me around, "the baby's fine, but your baby-sitter just called and sounded terrible. She's sick and can't take kids today. I thought you'd want to know so you could make other arrangements for Matthew. You'd better call your mother or something," she said with a yawn as she wandered down the hall to the bathroom. I heard water running and then she poked her head out with a toothbrush stuck in her mouth. "Don't forget, we both promised to come in early for the next couple days while the night crew finish painting the lobby. That means, I've got one hour 'til I'm due at work and you've got an hour and a half. Don't be late." With that said, she ducked back into the bathroom to don make-up and fix her hair. Why did she bother with make-up because they always did it over again when she went in front of the cameras?

Shrugging, I shuffled off to the kitchen to make coffee. I definitely needed a strong cup of something hot to get my brain working. Waiting for it to brew, I rehearsed how to approach my mother to ask for any baby-sitting privileges she might offer. The request sounded simple enough, and it should have been the easiest thing in the world. All I had to do was pick-up the phone and place the call, but something held me back. My stomach began to quiver and felt like it was doing handstands every time I lifted the receiver. Scolding myself for being a coward, I shut my eyes and dialed. When she answered I breathed a sigh of relief, because if it had been my father, I probably would have hung up.

"Hi, Mom," I said brightly, "how are you doing?" The cheerful tone in my voice sounded phony even to my ears. Holding an arm across my stomach to calm its nervous fluttering, I clenched my teeth. It was important to keep the tone light, and not come across sounding like I needed anything. If I sounded anxious or worried, she wouldn't talk to me, but would immediately call Richard.

"How do you expect me to be at such an ungodly hour?" she asked. The irritation in her voice grated against my ears like chalk on a chalkboard. I immediately wanted to apologize for calling, but stopped myself before I did. I was a big girl now and didn't need to react to her tone of voice.

"It isn't that early, Mother. I'm usually up before now and enjoy the quiet of morning. You really ought to try it. You'd be surprised how relaxing it can be to drink a first cup of coffee while the rest of the world still sleeps."

"Yeah, right," she said sarcastically. "What time is it anyway? Why are you calling me before eight in the morning? Have you been drinking, Nicole?"

"Of course I haven't been drinking," I denied vehemently. "Can't a person call their mother without getting the third degree?" This time it was my turn to sound irritated. The muscles in my shoulders tightened and the first warning tingle of a migraine danced across the top of my head and down my neck. Taking a deep breath, I decided to take the plunge and get it over with. It was ridiculous to get so worked up over a simple phone call.

"Mom, there's a reason I'm calling so early."

"Oh, really," she snarled, "did you think I hadn't already guessed that?"

"Come on Mom; have a little concern would you? I need a baby-sitter, but just for today," I assured her. "My regular sitter is sick and I've got to get to work. Can you help me out?"

"Really, Nicole, you can't expect me to just drop everything and come a-running every time you have a little problem. We both know you wouldn't be having these little situations if you hadn't kicked Richard out. I don't know why I should help you because if you were any kind of wife, you'd get on the phone and beg him to come back."

"Beg him to come back," I shouted, "are you crazy? And for your information, I didn't kick him out--he left all by himself. Mom, when are you going to face facts? Richard doesn't want his son or me; now why should I want him?" My stomach knotted into a tight ball as an angry, red flame began to flicker behind my eyes.

Wanting to screech at the top of my lungs, I forced myself to speak in a calm, business-like voice. "Will you baby-sit for me or not?"

"When asking for favors," she responded coldly, "it's best to use a polite tone. Don't call and start yelling at me, young lady, because I don't have to do anything for you at all. In fact, Richard has asked us not to help until you come to your senses and resume your marital responsibilities. But," she sniffed condescendingly, "you are my daughter, no matter how wrong you are. I'll take care of the baby today. I wasn't planning anything anyway, and it will give me something to do. Don't forget to bring enough diapers and be here to pick him up before your father gets home. He won't like this. It might look like we're siding with you over your husband and that could cause problems. We made a good deal when your father signed the contract for the software he developed, and we don't want anything to come between any future contracts that may arise."

"Contract? What contract? How is that related to taking care of your own grandchild?" Rubbing at an ache that throbbed in my temple, I definitely regretted calling her in the first place.

"What contract?" she asked as if I should know all about it. "I'm talking about the one signed between your father and The Corporation the day before you got married. It was agreed that after your marriage, the company would buy all future software developed by your father. He received a big bonus, a new office, and a better position. He's second in command, under Richard of course," she added. The smug tone in her voice came across the telephone wires loud and clear. She was proud of their social standing, and dad's official title at work only made them look better. The significance of what she said went over my head for the time being, but would become clear later. For now, I had a sitter and that was my primary concern. Making an excuse, I hung up and hurried to get the baby and myself ready to go. How could I expect mom to understand my position when she refused to take responsibility for her own?

After dropping off the baby, I lead-footed it to work. In trying to make-up for lost time, my foot was a little heavy on the gas and as luck would have it, I was pulled over and cited for going ten miles over the posted limit. Tears of frustration formed at the back of my eyes as I drove a more sedate speed the rest of the way to work. It was the last thing I needed after arguing with my mother. I was busy most of the morning and didn't have time to call and check on Matthew. It was close to four-thirty when Mr. Amsdale found me at the copy machine.

"Can you work a few extra hours tonight? There's some paperwork I need done, and the restrooms on the other side of the building need a good cleaning," he explained.

"I'm sorry, but I can't. My regular sitter is sick and I've got a stand-in for today. I've got to leave in the next ten minutes to pick up my baby." Turning to the machine, I punched the buttons to make fifty more copies.

"This isn't a request, Nicole," he said with a scowl. Glancing sharply at him, I was taken aback at his tone and the look on his face. I'd never seen this side of him, and my surprise must have been evident.

"But," I tried to explain.

"No buts," he interrupted. "You knew the requirements when you accepted the job. I told you at the time that extra hours would be expected occasionally, and that they came without warning. Now, I need this paperwork completed and the bathrooms are a mess. Are you going to do the job or do I need to start looking for a replacement?"

"No, sir," I sighed miserably, "I'll stay. I've got to call my mother and let her know I'll be a little late. Place the paperwork on my desk, and I'll get to it as soon as I've finished making copies."

"That's a girl," he said with a smile. Placing a hand on my shoulder, he patted my back as if rewarding an obedient dog. "I knew you'd put things into proper perspective. It'd be a shame to replace you just because you didn't plan ahead for proper childcare. See you in the morning."

Gritting my teeth, I choked back a defiant retort and smiled instead. The extra work would put me behind by at least three hours and the last thing I needed was another lecture from my mother. I dreaded making the call, but figured putting it off wouldn't make it any easier. I contacted her first and was surprised she took the news so calmly. Her only response was, "Hurry home and the baby's fine." After talking to my mother, my spirits lifted momentarily as I went to find Maddie. Maybe she could pick up Matthew on her way home.

"Of course I'll get him," she assured me. "I should be on my way by five, so see you when you get there. By the way, we need some milk, will you pick some up on your way home?" She looked at my reflection in her make-up mirror as she brushed on mascara and applied fresh lipstick. She'd been filming all day by the look of it and was just cleaning up. As usual, her flawless perfection made me look dowdy in comparison.

"Yeah, sure. Anything else?"

"Nope. See you later and dinner will be ready when you walk in the door. You look beat, is everything okay?"

"Just fine and dandy," I said sourly. Closing the door, I settled myself in front of the computer. If I hurried, I'd be on my way home before seven.

By the time I left the office, a throbbing ache had settled between my shoulder blades, and it only became more intense when I pulled into the grocery store parking lot. It was jam-packed. I had to drive around the lot three times before finding a place to park. After buying milk and a few other items, I headed home relieved the day was through. The feeling was short-lived. My heart pounded with trepidation as I pulled into the driveway to find Richard's car in my usual parking space.

Lugging the heavy grocery bags into the kitchen, I listened intently for the sound of voices. The deep rumble of Richard's laughter reached my ears at the same time I heard Madelyne cry out. I followed the sound to the den. Richard had his arms wrapped around her and she was struggling to get away. The sleeve of her dress was ripped and her tear-stained face was pasty-white.

"Let me go, please let me go," she begged. Squirming to get away, he tightened his grip and held her firmly, grinding his hips against her.

"Come on, relax. You know you want me. I've noticed you giving me the eye for quite a while. Why not enjoy it?" he asked drunkenly. The terror in her face only seemed to excite him more. When he forced her to kiss him, she screamed. It was deja'vu, and for a moment, I saw myself as I might have looked that long ago night before we married.

"Leave her be," I thundered. When he spun around I slapped him hard on both cheeks. I'm not sure how the lamp got into my hand, but

I found myself threatening to bash him in the face with it if he didn't leave the house at once. Maddie grabbed Matthew from his crib and ran from the room sobbing hysterically. I heard the slam of the bathroom door when she locked it behind her.

"What do you think you're doing," he roared. Coming at me with murder in his eyes and his fists clenched, I raised the lamp in defense. It had a heavy, metal base and hit him right between the eyes. He toppled like a child's set of building blocks. "Richard," I screamed. Kneeling beside him, I wiped his face with a damp cloth terrified that I'd killed him. He eventually came around and lunged for me again. When I darted away, he swayed dizzily with the cloth held against a fresh cut on his forehead.

"She was coming on to me," he stammered. "You should have been here and seen it for yourself. What's a man to do when a piece of trash like her is makin' eyes and struttin' around half-naked? Look at the way she dresses with hemlines clear up to here," he held his hand to his waist. "Makes a guy wonder what's hidden between them long legs of hers."

He tried to defend his actions, but the more he said, the worse he sounded. I knew he was capable of horrible things, but he'd hit an all-time low. For the first time, I noticed a thickening along his jowlline and the broken, red veins alongside his nose. He had every sign of alcoholism, and I could almost see the way he would look in another ten or twelve years. The sight of him was sickening and there was no turning back. I wanted him out of my life... permanently.

"Get out," I said with a point to the door, "and this time don't come back until I'm gone. I'm filing for divorce and afterwards I hope to never see you again. And as far as trash is concerned, I'm looking at it every time I look at you and in fact, you aren't just trash, you're scum. How does it feel Richard, knowing that every time you look in the mirror you're seeing the worst life has to offer?"

"I won't give you a divorce. There's never been a divorce in this family and it's not going to start with me."

"We'll just see about that," I said with arms folded smugly across my chest. "Now get out, before I have you arrested for attempted rape."

Stumbling to the door, he left with a roar of his engine. I visited an attorney the very next day. After Madelyne told the story of how

The Redemption of Madelyne

Richard snuck into the house and attacked her, the attorney called Richard's father. Between the two of them, they kept everything hush-hush to protect the family name. The papers were drawn and signed without a court appearance. Mr. Richard Franklin III's orders were to have the divorce papers recorded privately so nothing appeared in the newspaper. It was all handled very efficiently without undue emotion, and if anyone was upset about the disintegration of a marriage, I never heard about it. The main concern revolved around damage to the Franklin family name. After all, gossip surrounding a divorce could hurt business. If I cried myself to sleep at night and left with an ache in my heart, who was to know?

When going through something as emotionally damaging as a divorce, a person needs family support and I was no different. Maddie was as supportive as she could be, but it wasn't enough. My mother called inviting me to join them for dinner, and I eagerly accepted. It was the first time my parents extended an invitation that didn't include Richard. What a cause for celebration if they finally accepted my decision to get a divorce.

Rushing home from work, I threw all my dress clothes out on the bed. Several were discarded because they didn't fit. I couldn't seem to get rid of the extra pounds gained during pregnancy. Selecting a skirt with a loose fitting blouse that hid the snug waistband, and ran to shower and get ready. Madelyne helped with my make-up, and fixed my hair in a new, becoming style. When she finished with my makeover, I couldn't believe the difference. My hair was pulled back from my face, and left to trail down my back in wispy curls. Shadow and mascara was applied to accent my eyes, and color to my cheekbones and lips. I didn't look like the same person. My reflection showed an attractive young woman with a sensitive face, and large, expressive blue eyes.

"Wow," Maddie whistled, "who would have thought you had this hidden behind all that hair. You're really beautiful! If Richard saw you now, there's no way he'd let you get away." She nodded her head as she circled me, checking to make sure everything looked perfect. "Mmm-mmm. Can you tuck in your blouse? This outfit would look great with a wide belt to accentuate your waist." I tucked in a section of shirttail, and she immediately pulled it from my waistband. "You'd better wait until you've lost a few more pounds. Those maple bars you ate when you were pregnant have caught up with you," she admonished.

I dressed Matthew in a cute pair of Levi's with a matching shirt. He cooed and laughed as the shirt was smoothed over his fat little tummy. Smoothing the downy wisps of hair over his head, I kissed his chubby cheeks. "At least you don't have to worry about popping a button if you happen to eat too much," I told him as I tried to loosen the tight constraint of my waistband. "You're cute, chubby cheeks and all." Chucking him under the chin, I laughed at his delighted response. Waving his arms and kicking his feet, his eyes begged to be held and cuddled. I didn't hesitate, smothering his little face with kisses, and enjoying the moment before rushing out the door.

Mom greeted me, and took Matthew from my arms before I could ring the doorbell. "It's about time you got here," she chided. "Dinner's ready. Your father is waiting in the dining room."

"Since when is dad home before six?" Glancing at my watch to assure myself of the time, I was surprised. It was barely past five. For as long as I could remember she never served the evening meal before 6:30 P.M. Nerves tingled at the base of my neck.

"We wanted to discuss a few things with you, Nicole. We figured to have an early dinner so we could have a nice long talk. My, this little guy is sure growing. What are you feeding him that he's getting so fat?" She pulled off his hat and laughed at his great, big smile. The hard lines in her face relaxed and softened as she gazed at her grandson. When she bent over him, he made a grab for the necklace she always wore. Jerking the fine, gold chain out of his grasp, she dropped it under her blouse. "Out of sight, out of mind," she recited.

"What kind of things do you want to discuss?" I asked. Suspicion made me cautious, and I approached the dining room slowly. "Was it something you couldn't talk about over the phone?" I glanced at her questioningly, but she avoided my eyes.

"You'd better listen to your father," she said, "and don't start an argument with him. We're all very upset about this divorce, Nicole, and your father most of all." Stepping into the kitchen, she left me to face him alone.

He sat in his recliner with legs crossed and hands resting comfortably on the arms of the chair. A cynical smile curved his lips as he waited. His relaxed position showed a man completely at ease, but the look on his face hinted at something entirely opposite. There was a storm brewing behind those icy blue eyes that was about to be unleashed. "Where's my grandson?" he barked.

"Matthew's with mom and it's nice to see you, too," I retorted. Crossing the room, I surprised myself by placing a kiss on his cheek. I didn't know the last time I'd kissed my father, and the gesture shocked us both. It didn't change his attitude, however, and he regarded me with such cold contempt my feet shriveled in my shoes.

Rising slowly, he adjusted the sleeves of his suit jacket--which was always a danger sign. "Don't be insolent and don't try to placate me with a bogus display of affection." He closed the door silently before turning to face me with a sweeping gaze that took in my too-tight skirt, full blouse, make-up and hair. A prick of self-consciousness made me shift my weight nervously from one foot to the other. Ducking my head, I avoided his gaze just as I had when a child. A look of irritation hardened his eyes, and then the storm erupted.

"Look at you," he said scathingly, "made-up like its Halloween." He handed me a handkerchief, "Wipe that muck off your face," he ordered. We stood there for the longest time with my self-respect hanging in the balance. His hand remained in mid-air, extending a white handkerchief, which I refused to take. Shaking my head defiantly, I took a step toward the door.

"I thought we could have dinner without an altercation, but it seems we are destined to never see eye-to-eye. I'll say my good-byes to mother and then be on my way. . ." My next words were cut-off as he strode quickly to the door, barring my exit. Startled, I backed away looking frantically for another means of escape.

"You'd better listen, young lady, because I'll only say this once," he shouted. Pointing a finger, as if pronouncing judgement, his voice rose to a bellow, "You've been a black mark on me ever since you got married. I'm ashamed you're my daughter and wish there was something I could do to change it." I'd never stood up to my father before, but would not accept his verbal abuse any longer. Red-hot flames of resentment exploded in my brain. Richard's father, my father, Richard—-what right did they have to badger me like this—pushing me into a corner of defeat? A torrent of insults spewed from my mouth in retaliation for a lifetime of neglect.

"Don't tell me what to do, because I'm not afraid of you anymore. If you're ashamed to call me your daughter I'm not surprised, because you were never much of a father. You're . . ."

"Shut your fool mouth," he bellowed. Standing over me with nostrils flaring and his eyes like two angry, red orbs, I smiled. The similarity between him and a frustrated bull was almost comical. I wondered when his intimidation ceased to have an effect. He raised a hand to slap me, but I blocked him in self-defense.

"Take your best shot," I taunted.

"How dare you sashay into my home looking like a street walker, and then have the audacity to speak in such a manner. Is this what your friend, Madelyne, has taught you? I've heard enough about her from Richard," he gloated, "and now you're practicing to be just like her. But, she won't get much farther in this town." He smiled maliciously.

"What does that mean?" I asked. "Is that a threat? Is that how you're going to get back at me for divorcing Richard? Are you attacking Maddie? I knew you worked underhandedly at times, but I never took you for a crook. What you're doing is shady and dishonest. Go ahead and take your anger out on me, but leave her alone," I demanded. Laughing, he enjoyed his own private joke knowing that no matter what he planned, there was nothing I could do to stop him.

"How does it feel," he taunted, "knowing someone else is calling the shots. You had it made, Nicole, and everything was perfect, until you decided things had to be played out like some little kid's fairy tale. So what if Richard had a fling or two, it's to be expected. I'm giving you one last chance. Call off this divorce or never darken my doorstep again."

"I signed the divorce papers yesterday, and couldn't stop it now even if I wanted to. Richard doesn't love me and could care less about Matthew. We're all better off as things are and I refuse to allow your intimidation to scare me into changing my mind. And, if you don't want me here, why go to all the bother to invite us in the first place?" I shouted.

"Is that your final answer?" he asked calmly. His look of indifference tugged at my heart as a lump formed in the back of my throat. Swallowing convulsively, I blinked back the tears threatening to spill down my cheeks. Squaring my shoulders, I looked him straight in the eye.

"The divorce will be final in a few days and I'm not going to change my mind. Life is too short to be lived unhappily and both Richard and I have been miserable. He doesn't see beyond his next drink, and I want more from a marriage than he's able to give."

"You could be happy, just look at your mother," he begged. "She's an active woman with varied interests and no one ever hears her complain. Why can't you be like her?"

"She isn't happy, and if you took the time to notice, you'd see through the mask she wears to cover her pain. I don't want your kind of life for me or my son. Somewhere out there is a man that will love me and love him as a father. Matthew deserves that much and I'll find it for him somehow."

"Leave my house," he said with a note of finality, "and don't come around when things get tough asking for anything because you won't get it. From this moment on, you are no longer my daughter." He regarded me bitterly then turned away as if I no longer existed. I left my parent's home with a heavy heart. Holding Matthew close, I never felt more alone.

Chapter Nine

When I drove away from my parent's house, I was surprised to remain so calm. It wasn't until I pulled into my own driveway that things fell apart. As soon as the ignition was switched off, I began to shake. Then the tears came, and once they started, they wouldn't stop. When we didn't come in right away, Madelyne came to investigate. She found me gripping the steering wheel unaware of how long I'd been there. I'm thankful Matthew slept through it all because I was an emotional wreck. Maddie promptly took command, and helped me into the house. As she bustled about the kitchen preparing coffee and a bottle for Matthew, she chattered constantly about nothing at all. When the tears stopped, and the last vestige of my breakdown was wiped away, all the insecurities and emotional baggage of the last few months floated away. I fed Matthew his dinner; then let him nurse on a bottle. All the while I reminded myself that his wellbeing was dependent on me. Never would I allow my emotions to get out of control again. There was too much at stake, and I couldn't afford to lose any more than I already had.

Later, after the baby was sleeping peacefully for the night, I told Madelyne about the evening. Her eyes narrowed when I related all the things my father had said. It hurt, and I cried all over again.

"He said I've been a black mark against him, and he wished I'd never been born. What kind of father tells their own child such things?" Wiping my nose with a damp tissue, I kept my eyes fixed to a spot on the floor to avoid her concerned gaze. Conscience made me squirm until I told her the rest of the story. Raising my head so our eyes met, I blurted out the part I'd been holding back; the part that included her.

She was innocent, but would stand accused in his eyes because she was my friend.

"Maybe your father was just blowing off steam," she suggested. "Most parents don't picture a divorce in their child's future, and I'm sure he's just upset."

"It wasn't just about the divorce--there's more I haven't told you."

"Well. . .?" she asked with arms folded across her chest. Tapping one foot impatiently, she fixed me with a level stare. "Out with it and don't hold anything back. It's not the time to play cat and mouse so tell me everything I need to know. Did he threaten to take custody of Matthew or something? Because if he did, we'd better take whatever steps are necessary to protect you both."

She looked so sure of herself as she sat there, curled up on the end of the couch with a determined look on her face. It wasn't easy to tell her the rest.

"He didn't threaten Matthew or even ask to see him again."

"Then what? What are you holding back, Nicole?"

"My father never makes idle threats and there's always follow through of some kind." Picking at a piece of lint caught in the fabric of the chair, I refused to look in her direction.

Her intake of breath was almost inaudible, but I knew she finally understood. "He threatened me?" she asked. Stunned, her mouth made a little "oh" as this piece of news was absorbed. "But, why?" Her voice dropped to a whisper as she peered at me through frightened eyes. Her pallor turned ashen. She knew enough about my father to know he was someone to be feared when he was angry.

"I'm not sure why, but I do know Richard's been talking. Dad believes the Franklins', and will go to great lengths to remain on their good side. I think this whole thing is related to something mom let slip the other day."

"What was that?"

"It seems there was a contract drawn up at the time Richard and I married with terms dependent upon the durability of our marriage. Dad received a promotion, after all was said and done. The contract stipulated that the agreement became null and void if the marriage didn't last, and his anger stems from an empty pocketbook. It has nothing to do with you or me. He wants someone to dump on and," I motioned between us, "we're convenient."

"Oh, is that all," she breathed a sigh of relief. "For a minute there, you had me scared. If he's just looking for a scapegoat, then this entire thing will be over within a few days." In characteristic Maddie fashion, she was quick to avoid a problem. Sweep it under the carpet until forced to deal with whatever came next. Stretching, she grinned at the frightened look on my face. "Don't get uptight about things until they happen. He's your father, for Pete's sake. He certainly won't do anything to harm his own flesh and blood." Shrugging, she hugged a comforter around herself and flashed a reassuring smile. "I'm going to bed and suggest you do likewise. Things will look brighter in the morning." Madelyne was an excellent actress and skilled at hiding behind a charade of bravery. Her dark, luminous eyes revealed her true feelings as she turned away to hide the fear mirrored in them.

My father had always been decisive, and never left a job undone. It shouldn't have been a surprise that he acted so quickly, and within two days we began to feel the repercussions of his anger. Thank God, I was better prepared for it than Maddie, but it was still shocking to find how many people answered to Franklin money.

Wednesday started as a beautiful day with the sun shining bright, and birds swooping and diving after miniscule insects in the soft spring air. As I walked from my car into the office, I chuckled as two robins fought over the same worm. Spring was definitely in the air, and it brought a lift to your step and smile to your face. Humming to myself, I hung my jacket in place, turned on the coffee maker, unlocked the file cabinets, and removed the cover on the old *IBM* word processor. I'd no sooner seated myself, when the office intercom buzzed.

"Step into my office, please." Mr. Amsdale never asked anyone into his office and he usually wasn't so formal. Mildly curious, I had foolish hopes for a raise as I took a seat across from him.

Folding his hands on the desk, he took a moment to collect his thoughts. His expression didn't hint of a pleased employer, and thoughts of a raise popped like a balloon. "I'm letting you go, Nicole. You've made yourself somewhat of a pariah around town and I don't want any of the fallout to come down on me."

The Redemption of Madelyne

"Pariah?" I asked. "What do you mean by that?" The light came on with brilliant clarity—Amsdale was Franklin property. "I get it! You've been called either by my father or father-in-law and they've threatened you, isn't that right?"

"No, of course not," he fervently denied. A self-conscious cough escaped him as he gazed out the window to avoid looking at me. "It's like this, kid, and I'm giving it to you straight. I don't own this company, but manage it for the Franklins. It's actually subsidized by The Corporation, and is just one of its many secondary operations."

I felt like someone dumped a bucket of ice water over my head. I stared at him, hoping I'd heard wrong. "Do you mean they've been paying our wages, keeping track of our hours, and.. and.. every thing?" My voice tapered off to a squeak as I choked back my frustration. I refused to embarrass myself by breaking down in front of him. All of a sudden, the brightness went out of the day as my stomach did a slow swan dive to the floor.

"They know everything," he said. "In fact, the idea to have you clean the restrooms came from them. They wanted to humiliate you so you'd go back to your husband. Nobody expected you to accept the position, and no one was more surprised than I when you waltzed into the men's room and cleaned it so well it shone like a brand new penny. I'll tell you one thing; you've gained my respect, but unfortunately, worked yourself out of a job." Grinning, he wrinkled his nose like a rabbit, showing his teeth, and squinting his eyes. I assumed this was his 'I'm-helpless-to-do-anything-about-it' look, and it only infuriated me. Coming to his feet, he handed over my last paycheck, and attempted to shake my hand. "Hope there's no hard feelings."

I stared at his extended hand wanting nothing more than to slap the spastic smile off his face. Slamming both palms down on his desk, I leaned close to make sure he heard every word.

"You're a pig, Mr. Amsdale. In fact, you're a greasy, little toadie that answers to the Franklin beck-and-call and you ought to be ashamed. I worked like a dog for you and for what--a pink slip and a handshake? The least you could have done is be honest, but honesty isn't a valuable commodity, is it? It doesn't make my in-laws any money, so it's no wonder they'd have a slimy little twit like you doing their dirty work for them." Grabbing my pay envelope, I stormed out the door; threw my coat over one arm and my purse over the other. The final insult came when I withdrew my check and found it signed in Richard's recognizable scrawl. Calling him a few choice names under my breath, I charged into the nearest bank to cash it. As I took up the pen, I wrote a message of my own on the back.

"Are you sure you want to write that?" asked the shocked cashier. Her brows drew up so far they made perfect little triangles above her button eyes.

"That's right," I retorted, "and I'd like to say more, but propriety and the lack of space won't allow it." Crossing the two "t's" in butt with a flourish, I handed it over. She cashed the check, handling it reluctantly. Picking it up by one corner, she dropped it into the till as if it were something distasteful. If I hadn't been so mad, I would have laughed out loud.

Maddie got hers the next day. There was no reason for what they did to her other than sheer spite.

The following morning, I lingered in bed longer than usual enjoying the cozy cocoon of covers around me. Reluctant to leave the protective warmth, I took a few extra moments before throwing off the covers. Yawning lazily, I opened the curtain a fraction of an inch to peek out. My spirits sagged as I pulled it shut against a gray, leaden sky that threatened rain. So much for an early spring! Rising, I tiptoed across the room and pulled an old pair of sweats and a warm, but faded sweater from my dresser. What did it matter what I looked like? I wasn't going anywhere.

Madelyne was already dressed and looking like a million when I entered the kitchen. The aroma of fresh coffee filled the room and on the table sat a plate of warm cinnamon rolls. "Thought you might be hungry," she offered, "you didn't eat much last night." Waving the plate of rolls under my nose, she added, "They aren't like homemade or anything, just store bought, but they're good just the same; in fact, they're wonderful with morning coffee." Filling two huge mugs, she sat opposite me at the table. Neither of us was hungry, however, and only nibbled at the rolls out of polite consideration for the other.

"You didn't have to do this, you know." I motioned toward the coffee and the rolls, "but thanks anyway." Pouring milk into my coffee to cool it, I drank half of it in two swallows, burning my lip in the process.

"What are you going to do today?" she asked. Nervously smoothing the tablecloth, she studied the coffee in her cup and then the pattern in the wallpaper, trying to act like this was a day like any other.

"Oh, don't worry about me," I told her. "Matthew and I have a date to catch up on some TV and then maybe take a nap. I don't think I'll even get dressed, at least not any more than what I am. I'll take the day as a holiday and worry about tomorrow, well--tomorrow."

"Yeah, tomorrow will be good. There's no sense in rushing into anything." She stared at me for a moment and then took her dishes to the sink. Running water over them, she rinsed and then dried her hands. "Nicole," she said thoughtfully, "I'm really sorry about what happened yesterday and if there was anything I could do to change things, I would." Hanging her head so her hair swung forward, forming a covering about her like a Lady Godiva, she sighed. "I hope things change real soon, because I don't know how much more you can take. Richard's been acting like an absolute butt and..." As soon as she said the word butt, I exploded into hysterical laughter. Her head snapped up, staring at me in stunned silence. I laughed until tears rolled down my cheeks. "What did I say? What's so funny?" she sputtered with an indignant little shake of her head. "Honestly, Nicole," she scolded, "sometimes I worry about your sanity."

"I haven't gone off my rocker." Gaining control of myself, I wiped away tears of mirth. "It's just that when you said butt, it reminded me of something that happened yesterday." After telling her about the message I'd written to Richard on the back of my paycheck and the teller's reaction, she laughed, too. Laughter is great medicine, and we were both in pretty good spirits by the time she left for work. As soon as the door closed behind her Matthew woke hungry and ready to begin his day. I smiled to myself, at least there was one man in my life that was always eager to see me and always had a smile.

For the next hour or so, my mind was occupied with the care and feeding of the baby so I didn't have time to dwell on personal problems. After he'd been fed, bathed, and cuddled, he grew sleepy. He never missed his nap, and grew cranky if he didn't get it. Laying him down,

I kissed his cheek and placed an extra blanket over him. It was a chilly day and cold seemed to seep in under the doors and windows. The last thing I needed was for him to get sick. Tiptoeing from his room, I headed to the bathroom to rinse the tub and put things away from his bath. Bending over to pick up a towel, I caught a glimpse of my backside in the mirror, and laughed all over again. Oh boy! If Richard could see me now, what a story he'd have to tell. There'd be plenty to keep him talking for several days to come. Straightening, I spun around and studied my reflection with amusement. I still wore fluffy, pink bunny slippers with big ears and a tiny puffball at the heel for a tail. My sweats were old, faded, and sagged in the rear making my behind appear three sizes bigger than it was. Once upon a time my sweater looked good, but now sagged and bagged; stretched into a misshapen pullover. The hem had been yanked down to cover my stomach so many times it was permanently lopsided. My hair was uncombed and my face pale without makeup. I was certainly a sight for sore eyes, and the sorer the better. Finding a brush, I smoothed my hair and pulled it back into a ponytail. Satisfied with the result, I applied a scant amount of makeup so I wouldn't scare Matthew when he awoke. I wondered if Madelyne ever looked this bad and if so, when?

After straightening the bath, I wandered aimlessly around the house looking for something to do. Television wasn't interesting, I didn't want to clean anything, and the laundry had been done the day before. What did other unemployed women do to pass the time? Did they also fight the dull, empty ache that gnawed at your insides? Traveling from one room to the other, I decided to stave off depression by reading. Selecting a magazine, I curled up on the couch with a blanket over my legs. Maybe if I got comfortable enough, I could concentrate on the article instead of the nagging questions swirling around in my head. How was I to support my son and pay bills without a job? There was also that thing about food. A person needed to eat didn't they, and Matthew was still on formula. Opening the magazine, I settled on an article titled, "Living the Single Life." Reading through the first page without recalling a single word, I started over. I had just gotten through the second paragraph when Madelyne's car pulled into the driveway. Taking a quick glance at my watch, I knew she was too early for lunch

The Redemption of Madelyne

and too late for a morning coffee break. Something was wrong, and from the sound of her running steps, it was serious.

"Nicci, where are you?" she wailed as the door was thrown open. I barely had time to throw the blanket off my legs when she burst into the room. My jaw dropped--chin to chest. I had never seen Madelyne so distraught, and I'd known her since first grade. Her normally pale face was blood red and swollen from crying. Her eyes were shadowed and dark with pain. I stood up on shaky legs, but fell back onto the couch.

"What's wrong?" I asked in a quavery voice. Somebody must have died, and my first thought was Richard. Crossing the room in two steps, she threw herself down with her head in my lap. Crying bitterly, it took several minutes before she was able to speak. She needed to lean on someone else for a change and I prayed I wouldn't topple. Consoling her as a mother does her child, I stroked her hair and assured her that everything would be all right.

"They fired me," she wailed. Burying her face in my lap, she cried until exhausted. When the tears stopped, the wounded look in her eyes tore my heart out. It was obvious there was more to the story, but pressuring her for it would only compound the hurt.

I sat her on the couch and wrapped a blanket around her shoulders. "Sit right there until you warm up. Heavens, your hands are like ice. I'll fix you something hot to drink and when you're feeling better, we'll hash this thing out." Scurrying off to the kitchen, I heated the leftover coffee from breakfast, added sugar, but instead of milk poured in what was left in a bottle of Richard's Irish whiskey. The drink always relaxed him, and I figured the worst it would do was give her a slight hangover.

Rushing to the front room with her coffee, I shoved it into her hands. "Drink up," I ordered, "and don't come up for air until it's gone."

Taking a big drink, she fanned her mouth, gasping for breath. "What's in that stuff," she croaked. Choking, she took another swallow, then sat motionless for the longest time with eyes closed and nostrils flared. After a time, her cheeks regained some color, and her eyelids quit fluttering. Holding my breath, I waited until her chest expanded with a deep inhale.

"Oh thank God," I breathed, putting a hand to my chest, "I thought you were dead."

"Not hardly," she said, "just adjusting to the fire in my veins. "I don't know what you put in that stuff, but don't give me any more. My head's already spinning and if I stand, I know I'll be sick."

"At least your mind is off your troubles," I volunteered. Smiling apologetically, I held up the empty bottle of whiskey.

Her head fell back against the couch as if too heavy to hold up any longer. Tears fell from the corners of her eyes, and caught in her hair. "Can you tell me about it?" I asked.

She nodded and for a moment seemed to withdraw into herself. There was no way to shield herself from this inner pain. "They accused me of something I didn't do." Her voice was a lifeless monotone as she relived the nightmare. "You know there's three different departments at the network?"

"Yes, there's the office where I worked, the lab, and the modeling department where you work."

Yeah, well, me and one of the girls from the photo lab have become friends; she told me about an argument one of the girls was having with some of the crew. It seems she was depressed about it and needed some cheering up. She came in today wearing a lovely yellow dress and looked so pretty--so much like spring; I wanted to do something nice for her." Breaking down, she hid behind her hair as she cried. I couldn't help but cry too, as her pain touched a tender spot within me.

"What did you do?" I prompted. "Take your time and tell me everything."

"I only wanted to pay her a compliment and never meant to hurt anyone's feelings." Tears welled up in her eyes all over again and her face contorted into a mask of agony. Anger replaced the sympathy in my heart. Who in their right mind would accuse her of trying to hurt someone? Maddie went out of her way to help others. She rescued butterflies from mud puddles and cried over stray dogs and cats. It wasn't fair for a person to cause anyone this much pain.

"Go on," I encouraged softly.

"Well, I bought a package of muffins on my way to work. I figured if everyone in her department was arguing, maybe a muffin and some hot coffee would get their day off to a better start. I gave each of them a muffin and sent her card."

The Redemption of Madelyne

"What did the card say?"

"It said, "You look so nice in your pretty yellow dress." I meant it, but she took it all wrong. She thought someone was insulting her so she took the card to Mr. Amsdale. He called your father and posted the card in the main office, and taped it to the wall with a big sign that read, "Who wrote this?" As soon as I saw the sign I told him what I'd done, but he didn't give me a chance to explain. Instead, he told her I was a liar and enjoyed being mean to people. He told her I wasn't a nice person and should be avoided at all cost. She believed him and I was made to look like a fool, and the girl I thought was my friend, really wasn't. She was being nice to me in order to get information about you for Richard. Anyway, after I thought the worst was over, Mr. Amsdale called me into his office. He had the tape of the commercial we'd just finished sitting on his desk."

"Why did he have the film? Aren't they going to air it?"

"No. He held it up in front of me then took a pair of scissors and cut it into pieces. He said we were both troublemakers, and the only reason we were hired was because the Franklins wanted to keep tabs on us. He said I was too skinny to be a real model and that Mr. Franklin had a lot of connections and would see to it I never modeled again. I'll never forget the smile on his face," she shook her head, "or his smell or the beads of sweat on his forehead. He grabbed my arm when I stood to leave and laughed. He said that nobody believed anything I had to say. When I ran out the door none of the girls would even look at me as he shouted, "You're fired! Get out of my office. You'll never work in this town again.""

"I'm so sorry. . .if it weren't for me, you'd still be working. The only reason they fired you was to get back at me and it's a pretty lousy thing to do." Cursing the day Richard and all Franklin's were born, helpless anger ignited a flame of hate. "I'd fix it if I could, but how can I fight their power or influence?"

"I don't blame you, but do you think he was serious?" she asked. "Do you think Richard will stop me from getting another job like he did you?" Her question was stated without emotion. It was easy to see she had nothing more to give.

"I don't know--I mean--I hope he won't, but wouldn't put anything past him. They're accustomed to getting their own way, and will go to great lengths to get what they want." I shrugged, "It doesn't seem to matter who they step on."

Nodding her head, she looked away and whispered, "Oh." Accepting the news as if it were no more than what was expected, she turned to gaze out the window with an unreadable expression. Silence fell over the room so loud it roared in my ears. Life wasn't supposed to be this way. Madelyne always had the answers, but now looked to me for advice and strength I didn't have to give. When had our roles changed and where would I find the same nobleness of character she seemed to be born with? Pulling myself together, I shoved my sense of loss somewhere down, deep within me and came to her side to offer a shoulder to cry on. Somehow and from somewhere the answers would come.

Later that evening after Matthew had been fed and readied for bed, I looked in on Madelyne before turning in myself. Her room was dark, and she wasn't in bed. She stood at the window, silhouetted in moonlight with arms crossed over her chest, staring at the empty street below. Silent tears left glistening trails of silver on her cheeks. Closing the door as quietly as it opened, I went to my room and cried myself to sleep.

It's true what they say--things do look brighter in the morning and the answer to our problem seemed to leap out at me from the morning paper with glaring clarity. Normally, I didn't so much as glance at the headlines, but as I scanned through the paper looking at the want ads, one caught my attention. It was written in big, bold letters and highlighted in red. A new company was opening in a nearby city and was advertising for experienced help. I started to laugh; why hadn't I thought of it before? It all seemed so simple. There was no way Franklin money could possibly have influence so far away and there was absolutely no reason for Maddie or me to remain here any longer. We'd move and leave no forwarding address. What could be easier? The hard part would be convincing Madelyne to pack up and move on. A stab of regret at what I'd leave behind brought the sting of tears to my eyes, but I blinked them away. Tearing the article from the paper, I wrote down the phone number and business address and stuffed it into my purse. There was a lot to be done and little time to do it in.

Richard was more than happy to get his house back, but unwilling to wait until we moved out to take up permanent residence. He showed no consideration for either of us and brought his girlfriends' home at all hours. We learned to keep our bedrooms locked and our private baths posted as off-limits. The divorce was final, and he reserved the right to live as he chose in his own home.

Madelyne went around in a daze after losing her job and spoke very little. I worried about her, but figured she'd work things out in her own time. Besides, I was too busy fighting with Richard, packing our belongings, and making final arrangements to pay extra attention to her. We celebrated Matthew's first birthday, and it was close to Halloween by the time everything was finally settled. When we took a weekend and traveled to the city to find a place to rent, I was grateful my personal car had been selected for capacity and comfort instead of the smaller, sportier model I'd wanted. It was the only thing Richard did for me that was worth anything.

Madelyne perked up as we drove out of town. "I can't believe we're finally on our way," she commented as we passed the last city limits sign. Grinning, she removed the clasp from her hair and allowed it to blow in the wind. "With a city the size of Seattle, there's bound to be plenty of work for a model, and even if there isn't, I can always find work in an office." Humming along with the radio, I agreed.

"We both need jobs and the quicker-the-better. Our bank account is skimpy and we still have to pay rent, buy a few furnishings, and stock the place with groceries."

"And don't forget childcare," she reminded. Chucking Matthew under the chin, she added, "Poor little guy, he'll have to be with strangers for a while. I sure hope they love babies in Seattle."

"They will, because who could resist such a handsome guy," I teased. It was hard to joke about such a thing because I'd never left him with people I didn't know. I prayed we'd find everything we needed, and that a second trip wouldn't be necessary. We had to make our final move now, because we may never be financially stable again.

We stayed the weekend at Maddie's brother's place, and to say it was an interesting visit is an understatement. We never saw him, because he went to work late at night and returned home after we'd gone out for the day. There was always evidence of his going and coming by a trail of empty beer bottles and dirty glasses left between the kitchen, bathroom, and television. Madelyne communicated with him by leaving notes all over the house that he either ignored or wadded up and tossed on the floor.

She found a position our first day there and laughed as she told me how she got it. "I can't believe they gave me the job. All I did was walk in, sit down, and smile. The guy asked me if I typed and I said yes. Then he asked if I knew shorthand and I explained that I didn't. He said it didn't matter because I'd be a great decoration for the office. And get this--the whole time he's talking --not once did he take his eyes off my legs. Honestly, it's ridiculous how silly some men can be when faced by a pretty woman. For once, I didn't mind the stares because it got me what I wanted." Breathless after her narration, she flashed one of her spectacular smiles. Placing Matthew on her lap, she put a finger to her lips and pretended to be telling him a secret. "And there's more--I'll be making more money here than I did back home."

"That's wonderful! When do you start and please don't tell me Monday?" Squeezing my eyes shut, I peeked at her hoping we wouldn't have to stay any longer than necessary.

"Nope, I start in two weeks." Unable to keep the smug look off her face, she settled back with a cup of coffee and glanced questioningly at me. "Well, how did you do? Were you able to find anything?"

"Yes and no," I hedged. "I stopped at a diner not far from here to ask directions to this place." Pulling the article about the new company and its grand opening from my purse, I handed it to her. "I wanted to apply, but it's clear across town. The waitress suggested I check out the bulletin board in the foyer. She told me people sometimes post jobs or articles there for sale. I found a handwritten ad for a receptionist and called them immediately. I have an appointment for an interview in about an hour, but need you to watch Matthew. Will you?" I looked at her hopefully.

"Why are you still here? Get going and don't come back until you're a gainfully employed woman." Handing me a jacket, she escorted me to the door. "While you're gone, I'll ask around for places to rent. Maybe our luck will hold!"

Someone must have been looking out for us because things fell into place so perfectly it was as if it were prearranged. Using a map of the city, I found a little office tucked between two larger offices in a prominent building not far off Pike Street. Entering the smaller office, I was surprised to be greeted by a girl younger than myself who was obviously pregnant.

"Hi, can I help you?" she asked with a welcoming smile.

"I've come to apply for the job advertised on this slip of paper." Looking around at the plush office with leather chairs, soft carpeting, and satin drapes at the windows, I turned to leave. This couldn't be the right place.

"Hey, where are you going? I thought you wanted to put in an application for a job."

"You mean" I asked incredulously, "this is the right place?"

"It's the right place all right and if you get it, you'll wish you hadn't because you'll work your tail off. My name's Claudia, Claudia Powers," she said with real friendliness as she extended her hand. Giving her fingers a polite shake, I gawked around in honest surprise.

"I never thought a place like this would advertise for a receptionist by placing an ad on a bulletin board."

"Oh, that," she laughed, "was my idea. My father complains about some of the people that apply to "Help Wanted" ads found in the paper, so I decided to advertise in a different way. I put that one up, and it must have worked because here you are."

"Yeah," I said with my hopes shrinking, "here I am. Is your father here? Does he know about the ad?"

"He sure does and even though he didn't exactly approve, he didn't demand I take it down either. Now, let's get down to business. Can you type? Run errands? Write letters without someone telling you what to say?" I answered in the affirmative on all the questions except the one about running errands. After explaining that we had just moved to town, she shrugged it off as if it were unimportant. "You found us, so you can obviously read a map. You'll do fine. Let's go meet the boss."

I talked with her father for over an hour. It was an unusual meeting because he didn't ask the atypical interview questions, but asked more about my background. When I became teary-eyed at the mention of my ex-husband, he tactfully steered the conversation in another direction. I was thankful he'd never heard of Richard Franklin III and in fact, didn't know the town I hailed from. It was sheer providence that led me to his little office because he not only hired me, but also referred me to some friends that owned rental property. Based on his recommendation, I called them and they rented me a place without demanding a reference. By the time I left, I had a job as receptionist to Mr. John Powers: Attorney-at-Law, and a place to rent. All I had to do was go look at the place, pay a deposit, and move in.

"Wow," I told Claudia as I was leaving. Taking a tissue from the box on her desk, I wiped away grateful tears, "this can't be happening to me. You and your father have been so nice--I'd given up hope that people like you existed." Sniffling loudly, I blew my nose, embarrassed by such a show of emotion. I found it difficult to look her in the eye.

"Believe it or not, there are lots of people like us," she said with a chuckle. "Now, there's just one more thing. Didn't you say something about a baby? My cousin and his wife run a daycare out of a church not far from here. She's really good with kids, and in fact will be caring for mine when he or she is born," she said with a motherly pat to her very large tummy. "Here's the address. Why don't you go and talk to them? I can vouch for their credibility and so will my father."

By the time I returned to Madelyne's brother's apartment, I was exhausted, but happy. I had a job, a place to live, childcare for Matthew, and all we had to do was make the final move. I prayed there was money enough to cover all the expenses, and that Richard and his family wouldn't interfere.

Chapter Ten

The trip home was a joyous occasion, and even Matthew was caught up in the spirit of things by clapping his chubby hands and jabbering as if we understood every word. We sang silly songs, played 'slug bug' and even splurged by stopping for hamburgers on the way. Even though the miles were covered quickly, we still didn't get back to town until the wee hours on Monday morning. Pulling into the driveway, we both groaned and gave each other a here-we-go-again look. Richard was having another one of his all night parties and the house was ablaze with light. Our unexpected arrival put a damper on things, however, and several of his guests left in a hurry. Since I lived there, some assumed we were still married, and such was the mistake of his most recent girlfriend. She was among the first of the partygoers to make a hasty exit, and I shook my head as she scurried to the door apologizing all the way. She was the least of my worries. Falling into a vacant bed, I was asleep before my head hit the pillow.

I slept late the next morning and when I woke, took one look at the clock and jumped out of bed. Matthew should have been awake hours ago. Rushing to his crib, I found him asleep, but his cheeks were warm and one eye was matted shut. After making a call to his pediatrician, I dosed him with baby aspirin and changed his bottle from milk to juice. He soon went back to sleep and I got busy with our final arrangements. I was on the phone with the movers when Richard walked in.

"Hang up," he ordered.

"No, and don't tell me what to do," I retorted. Turning my back to continue my conversation, I found myself talking to air when the line was yanked out of the wall. "That's great, just great! I'm trying to make arrangements to move out of here and you disconnect the line. What next, Sherlock?"

"It's always such a pleasure to have a conversation with you, Nicole. Whatever happened to my cute little wife with the docile disposition?" he sneered. Reaching over, he pinched my behind so hard it brought tears to my eyes. "I guess you covered her up under a layer of fat, didn't you?" Crossing his arms over his chest, he waited to pounce on my next remark. I clamped my mouth shut and stared at him defiantly.

"Well, what do you want?" I finally asked.

"I overheard part of your conversation," he said as he took a seat at the table, "since when is any of this yours?" His proprietary gesture took in the entire house.

"It's just as much mine as it is yours," I snarled, "and I'm taking my half with me."

"Wrong again, my little wife," he teased, "I bought this house before we were married and according to law, that makes it all mine. When you leave this place, you'll go with what you came with. Oh, you can have the dishes and a few other odds-and-ends, but don't think for one minute that you're taking anything else because I won't let you."

"What about our wedding gifts, the furniture, and everything else? You don't really want the stuff, so why keep it?" Looking around at all the personal touches I'd added to make the house a home, I screamed at him in frustration. "Why are you doing this? What does it matter if I take a few things or not because you'll come out ahead no matter what? All I need is a few items to furnish a home and make it comfortable enough to live in. I want to make a home for our son, Richard, doesn't that matter to you?"

"Not at the moment." Leaning nonchalantly against the door casing, he grinned and stretched. "You'd better come up with a better plan because I'll never let anyone take anything away from me. I'm not going to start with you." Calling him every obscene name I'd ever heard, I threw a coffee cup at his head. It smashed against the wall as he stepped out of the room. He didn't turn around, but laughed, "Tut, tut, such temper. Is this what a few days in the city taught you?" The door closed with a whoosh behind him. Tears of helpless frustration burned my eyelids, but I refused to let them fall. I wouldn't let him win even if I had to leave with just the clothes on my back. Then so be it.

We would have left the same day, but something came up to delay us. When Matthew woke from his nap, he was burning with fever. His skin was hot and dry to the touch, and his lips chapped. Madelyne drove me to the emergency room where he was treated immediately for ear infection and flu. Richard refused to pay for a thing claiming child support was meant to pay for such emergencies and beyond that, his duty was done. I had to dip into money set aside for moving to pay for his prescriptions. The fever disappeared as quickly as it came and within two days he was much better, but my savings had dwindled rapidly. After paying for emergency room services and his medication, I had two hundred dollars less than when I'd started.

"Maybe it's a blessing we don't have to pay for a moving van," Maddie said brightly as we packed both her car and mine. All morning she'd valiantly tried to cheer up my dark mood, but I preferred to wallow in self-pity for a little while longer. "This way, we can travel light and save ourselves the time and trouble of loading and unloading furniture." The excited sparkle in her eyes almost brought a smile to my lips. I bit my cheek until the taste of blood filled my mouth, cutting off the temptation to smile in return.

"Yeah, sure, but where will we sleep and what will we sit on once we get there?" I despaired. "We don't have a chair, a lamp, a table, or even a decent sleeping bag."

"That may be true," she said, "but you'll have your freedom and what's more important? Remember, things can be replaced, but people can't. Just be glad you're getting away in time to start your life over because there's plenty of women that can't, or won't, and they live in misery all their lives. It's a heroic deed," she said expansively, "because you'll be saving Matthew from a life of disappointment and heartache." Waving one arm in a theatric gesture, she swept an imaginary cape about her as she bowed with her nose to the ground. She looked so silly, only a mannequin could have kept a straight face.

I hadn't thought of it quite like that and it encouraged me slightly, but the idea still rankled that everything I'd helped to build was being left behind. As a last resort, I approached my parents to plead for my old bedroom furniture. I was turned down flat--so much for family ties.

At last, everything was packed and we were set to go. Matthew's crib was the last thing stowed in the backseat of my car. I'd just closed my car door and stuck the key in the ignition when a car pulled up behind us with horn blaring. My mother waved me down and ran over to give me a quick hug. She stuffed a wad of bills in my hand along with a check large enough to cover my first month's rent.

"It's only a few hundred dollars, but it'll be enough to get you started. Regardless of what you think, I do care about you and Matthew. Now, get in that car and get going," she pushed me into the driver's seat and waved at Madelyne, "leave this town and don't look back. There's nothing left here for either of you. Call me once in a while, but never when your father's home."

"But, Mom," I shouted as I held the money up in one hand. "How will you explain it?"

Waving as she drove away, she yelled, "I'll tell him I went shopping." I waved as her car turned the corner and wondered if I'd ever see her again. Climbing back into the car, I started off with a heavy heart. Madelyne turned the stereo on as loud as it would go giving a thumb's up. It was time to shake the dust of this town off our feet--and the quicker the better.

Our trip into Seattle was uneventful and the rain that followed matched our mood. We took a wrong exit and got lost once, but easily found our way onto Highway 99 and then around a viaduct to Elliott Avenue. Following Elliott, we quickly ran into Magnolia and found the old mansion that had been renovated into apartments. The place looked much too grand for our pocketbooks in the light of day. After parking the cars in our designated spots, we unloaded our stuff and stood huddled together in the middle of the living room with our few meager possessions piled around us. Silence stilled our voices and it grew so quiet, we could hear each other breathe. It was Madelyne that finally broke the spell.

"Yeeahh!" She yelled, leaping into the air. She dropped to the floor in a graceful pirouette. "We're home. Can you believe it? This is the most exciting time in our lives and here we are standing around like two scared boobs. Come on, get with it--this is YOUR life, Nicole." Twirling around, she ran off to explore each room. We were surprised to find two spacious bedrooms, an updated kitchen with plenty of cupboards, and even a small pantry. I wondered if we'd ever have food enough to fill the cupboards let alone the many shelves in the pantry. My favorite spot in the apartment was a little bay window with a window seat facing the water. After inspecting every room, we selected our bedrooms and unpacked. The place looked even emptier after our things were stowed neatly behind cupboard doors and in closets. We cheered ourselves by going out to dinner at a nearby restaurant. By the time we returned, it was dark, but neither of us was tired. A radio provided music and occasional commentary as we played cards until we were so tired the spots on the cards appeared in triples.

Our landlady was a sweet little woman that took us under her wing as soon as her sharp eyes took in our situation. She came to collect the first month's rent the following morning and was instantly captivated by Matthew.

"Oh my," she clucked when she took in the empty rooms. Her shoes clicked on the tiles as she wandered down the hall. "This just will not do," she finally concluded.

"But, I have our rent payment. It's all here." Shoving a wad of bills into her hand, I almost collapsed with fear. What if she decided not to rent to us, where would we go?

"Yes, dear, I can see it is, but that's not what I meant. Two young ladies such as your selves just can't live like this. You need furniture—beds, a table, a few lamps, a couch. Goodness gracious, young people these days," she scolded, "just don't know how to plan ahead." Shaking her head, she placed a hand on her hips and shook a finger in our faces as she delivered a lecture on making provisions for our future by starting now. Maddie looked at me with brows raised to her hairline. I was just as shocked as she, and didn't have the slightest idea of how to respond or even if I should.

She finally ran out of breath and I heard Maddie echo my, "Yes, ma'am." What was there left to say? We stood there for a moment, eyeing each other and making decisions that would define the boundaries of our relationship. Her frown turned to surprised delight when Matthew came toddling from a bedroom. His little face lit up when he spotted a stranger in the room.

Running with a cookie extended in one hand, he jabbered away as if she understood his every word. Holding the mangled cookie out, he offered her a bite from what was left. She wasn't at all repelled by his cookie face, but scooped him up in her arms to plant a big smooch on his cheek. "What a darling," she cooed. Removing a giant key ring from her pocket for him to play with, she cross-examined us by firing questions in quick succession. "So, that's why you have no furniture," she said as our version of the story concluded. We told only what was necessary, leaving out the personal side allowing her to draw her own conclusions.

"We'll buy some furniture when we have the money, but for now, we'll get by with what we have." Madelyne didn't like the intrusion into our privacy and the icy tone in her voice proved it.

"Of course you will," she chirped. Placing Matthew back on the floor, she apologized for being so direct. "I'm sorry for sounding like the world's police--that's what my sons call it—I always make the mistake of trying to tell young people what to do with their lives. It's the mother in me, I guess," she said with a sigh. "My boys have always warned that I'd get into trouble some day with my bossiness and hope I haven't hurt your feelings. Now, this is what you can do. I don't know how much money's in your pocketbook, but I have a friend that owns a secondhand shop. It's not poor secondhand, mind you, but real nice stuff. Here's the address and tell her I sent you. She'll give you a good price on a bed and whatever else you can afford. After making your purchases, give me a call and I'll send one of my boys over with a pickup to move it for you. How's that for making amends?" She flashed a broad smile that spread across her plump cheeks. I couldn't refuse the offer, and returned a smile of thanks.

"You don't have to do this, but I sure appreciate it." Taking the card with the address and phone number written neatly on the back, I stuffed it into my pocket and walked her to the door. I was anxious for her to leave so we could get to a grocery store. Restaurant food was too expensive for our budget.

She left, but continued a string of advice as she went out the door. "Don't forget to check each stick of furniture for tears or burn holes. If you find any, ask for fifty percent off." I nodded politely, but couldn't believe we'd actually find used furniture without major flaws or damage.

The Redemption of Madelyne

"I'll bring over a few houseplants," she promised, "green, living things always make a house feel homey, and don't you agree?" she trilled.

"Of course," Maddie agreed, "a house wouldn't be a home without them." Holding the car door open, she helped Mrs. Perlman inside. We stood on the sidewalk waving as she sped off.

"Wow, do you suppose she's always like that?" Maddie asked as we watched the car come up over the sidewalk as she rounded a corner too sharply.

"I have a feeling she is," I answered, still breathless from her whirlwind visit.

"Does the sun ever shine around here?" she complained as we made our way back to the apartment. Wrapping a sweater around her shoulders, she followed me into the kitchen.

"What are you doing?" she yelped. "Don't rip up that address, we'll need it."

"Are you serious? Do you really think we'd find anything worth a dime at a junk dealer's?"

"Give me that." Yanking the card out of my hands, she smoothed out the wrinkles and read the address. "I think we should at least look. I've bought lots of stuff secondhand and have never been dissatisfied." I frowned at the suggestion, imagining a couch with lumps and sagging springs and a bed full of invisible, biting insects. A shiver of distaste ran down my spine.

"Yuck! The whole idea makes me sick. I can't imagine sleeping in a bed not knowing how many others have slept in it, too. Maddie, it's not safe."

"Safe?" she asked with a scowl so filled with disapproval, it scorched my cheeks. "It's a whole lot safer than sitting here in an empty house with nothing to sleep on except the hard floor. Get off your high horse, Nicole, and join the real world."

"I didn't realize you felt so strongly about it. If it's that important, let's get going. Maybe we'll find a good grocery store on the way."

"We might at that," she chuckled.

"What's so funny?"

"The look on your face when Mrs. Perlman said we could buy a used bed. It was priceless. I know you've led a pretty sheltered life, but a person would think you had never been in a used furniture store before."

"I haven't." Carrying Matthew on one hip, I locked the door behind us and led the way to the car. This time it was my turn to be amused.

The secondhand store was only a couple of miles from the apartment. We found it easily enough by following a map in the phone book; and when we stepped inside, I was surprised to find such an array of items. The store contained everything a person needed to setup a household. We looked for a couch first, and decided on a light green sofa that made out into a bed. The only thing wrong with it was some sun fading along the backrest. After making one purchase, the rest came easier. By afternoon, we'd bought two beds, one huge dresser with drawers enough to get lost in, a table with two chairs, three lamps, and four little end tables to place the lamps upon. Madelyne bought several throw pillows at a shop across the street. They were large enough to sit on and would add a splash of color to our otherwise, bland décor. Feeling good after making our selections at such frugal prices, I threw caution to the wind and bought a pair of lace curtains. They weren't new, had discolored from white to ivory, but still beautiful. The French lace would be just the right touch to accentuate the bay window. Juggling the furniture price tags, a lamp, and Matthew, I made my way to the cashier.

"Did you find everything you need, ma'am?" asked the young man behind the counter. His question was directed at me, but his eyes were glued on Maddie. She stood behind me, holding a matching lamp. "Here, let me help you with that," he said as he came around the counter to unload the lamp from her arms. Setting it on a desk, he didn't take his eyes off her as his fingers moved rapidly over an adding machine. Ripping the tape from the machine, he slapped it down in front of me. His attention was riveted on Maddie less than a second later.

"Would you mind holding this?" I handed the lamp and Matthew to the kid as I dug in my purse for the money. Counting out the correct change, I did a silent burn as "Sold" signs were placed on our purchases.

"Is somebody picking this stuff up for you or do you want it delivered?" he asked.

"Is there a charge for delivery?" I asked naively.

"It's twenty-five dollars to deliver anywhere within a twenty-five-mile radius and fifty dollars for anything over and we don't deliver out-of-town. Do you want me to deliver it for you, ma'am?" he shuffled his feet self-consciously and swallowed hard. His Adam's apple bobbed up and down, and his face turned scarlet when Madelyne flashed one of her spectacular smiles. Placing a hand on his arm, she played him like a fiddle.

"That much?" she asked. Her eyes widened in mock alarm as she gazed at him with a guileless expression. "It's so expensive. I was hoping to get better acquainted with your lovely town, with the right escort of course, but with things costing so much, I'll have to spend every spare minute working just to pay rent. Isn't there something you could do to lower the price?" As soon as she turned to gaze up at him with a helpless expression, the kid melted.

"Well, maybe I could borrow my old man's pickup," he gulped, "that is if it isn't very far away. He may not mind--too much." He didn't look very sure of himself, and was relieved when I asked to use the phone.

"Mrs. Perlman offered a means to move this stuff and I'm going to take her up on it." Dialing the number, I almost lost my nerve when the phone was answered. But, she took over the conversation just as she had earlier and before I knew it, arrangements were made for one of her boys to deliver our furniture before the store closed. I was still fuming when we left, and lit into Madelyne as soon as we got to the car.

"How could you flirt with that kid? It was embarrassing the way he fawned all over you and you eating it up as if it were candy. What got into you?"

"He deserved it," she snickered.

"What do you mean by that?" I snapped.

"The guy was rude and needed to be taught a lesson. His attention should have been on his paying customer and not on me; after all, I wasn't the one buying all that stuff. He should have helped you carry that lamp instead of ogling my legs."

"He called me ma'am." I said disconsolately. "That's the second time someone has called me, ma'am. Am I starting to look like a ma'am? I mean, do I look old?"

"No," she laughed, "you don't look old. But, you might think about dropping a pound or two. If you lost a few pounds and started doing something with your hair, and applying some make-up, nobody would ever call you ma'am again."

"Everybody gains a little weight after having a baby," I declared. "You're beginning to sound just like Richard. He said the same thing." Driving to a nearby grocery store in hurt silence, I wondered what other people saw when they looked at me. Madelyne was older than I by almost a full year, but I was the one they called, ma'am. It certainly put a dent in my ego.

At the store, we filled the cart with enough food to last a month along with all the staples. I added a couple packages of cookies and a half-gallon of ice cream. At the checkout counter, the boy asked politely, "Will that be all, ma'am?" As soon as the hated word was out of his mouth, I grabbed the cookies and the ice cream and handed them to Madelyne.

"Yes, that will be all and don't call me ma'am," I snapped.

"I'm sorry, ma'am, just doing my job," the boy mumbled.

"What do you want me to do with these?" Maddie asked.

"From this moment on, I'm on a diet and if I ever hear anyone call me ma'am again, I'll scream and make a complete idiot of myself."

"You mean, kind of like you're doing now?" she asked. Sauntering over to the freezer case, she replaced the ice cream, and gave the cookies to a passing clerk. "Touchy, touchy," she said as we rolled the loaded shopping cart to the car. "I hope you're not getting your period, because you're always such a whiner when your cycle comes around.

"I am not," I sputtered indignantly, "and that isn't any business of yours, Madelyne Hall." Stowing the last of the groceries in the trunk, she rolled her eyes at me and slammed the lid closed.

"I don't know what you're so embarrassed about because it isn't a big secret. Women have been having female problems for centuries, and the world isn't going to stop in shock because you're plagued with it, too. I even get a little witchy when it's my time." Grabbing the keys from my hand, she gave a weary sigh. "Come on, Nicole, we're both tired and hungry. Let's not bite each other's head off here in a cold parking lot. It'll be much more comfortable to fight in the warmth of our own home." Settling herself under the steering wheel, she waited for me to fasten the safety belt around Matthew before taking off. When we reached the apartment and saw our furniture being unloaded by two handsome men, our spirits soared. All thoughts of arguing vanished and we forgot to end the fight we almost had.

"Are you the younger or the older son?" Maddie sang out as soon as soon as the ignition was switched off. Bounding out of the car, she ran over to give instruction on the placement of the sofa. Our groceries were forgotten for a few minutes while the rest of our stuff was unloaded and placed in their appropriate rooms. Chatting as we worked, we learned quite a bit about Mrs. Claire Perlman and their relationship to her.

"We aren't Mama Perlman's sons, in fact, we aren't even related," the taller of the two explained.

"Yeah, no relationship at all, but she treats us as though we were. They have three boys of their own attending college somewhere back east, but it isn't enough for her. She takes in anybody under the age of forty mothering them as though they were her own. Micah and I only work for her husband, but feel more like family."

"Has she tried to lecture you yet?" the one called Micah asked with a glance toward me.

"If she hasn't, she will," said the other with a knowing roll of his eyes. "Don't take offense because it's just her way. At first, it made me downright mad, but now, if she doesn't light into me about one thing or another, I figure I've done something to hurt her feelings. By the way, my name's Andy and this is Micah."

"We're just a couple of her boys," Micah explained, "and she's really just a very nice lady. Be prepared, because she'll adopt you, too. She'll watch over the two, or I mean, three of you," he corrected himself when Matthew lifted his arms for him to pick up, "like an old mother hen." Looking at his watch, he handed Matthew to me and tapped the watch face, "We'd better get going. We promised Henry to come for dinner, and we're already thirty minutes late."

"Yeah, we'd better get gone," Andy agreed. Removing his cap, he turned to Maddie and delivered a smile as spectacular as her own. "It was sure nice meeting you ladies and if you ever want a tour of the town, you know, go out and see the sights, give me a call. I'd love to show you around and get better acquainted."

"Maybe I'll do that," she promised and walking them to the door, linked her arm in his. "I'd love to see Seattle and find out what it has to offer," she said meaningfully. "When you have some free time, give me a call." She placed the emphasis so there was no mistaking that she expected him to call her and not the other way around.

Elated over our new furniture, we rearranged things several times until satisfied with the way things looked. The placement of the pillows took more time than the arrangement of the furniture. Maddie went for a casual look, but placed them carefully so they provided a splash of color and brightened the front room considerably. When dusk fell and shadowed the corners of the room, we turned on the lamps. I couldn't have been more pleased with the feeling of warmth and welcome emanating from the place. It didn't look like the same cold apartment we'd moved into just the day before.

While I got Matthew ready for bed, Maddie prepared dinner. I was surprised to find candles on the table, napkins, and a small vase of silk flowers. "Just a few things I brought from home," she explained. "Now sit down and let's eat, I'm starving."

"What's this?" I asked as I lifted the glass to sniff its contents.

"Cola, and don't turn up your nose. We're sharing the bottle."

"You drink it." Placing the glass next to her plate, I poured myself a glass of water and added ice. "From now on, this is my drink of choice. I'm going to lose the weight I've gained if I have to cut off my head."

"You'd do better to lay off the maple bars and quit snacking," she teased.

"Done," I agreed. Clinking my glass against hers, we dug into the food she'd prepared. I was famished, and ate until ready to pop. I had never realized how good salad and fresh fruit could be.

The next week was busy and we both came home exhausted from our new jobs. Even though I hadn't met the owners of Matthew's daycare, he seemed happy, and the employees I spoke to all loved children. Things became more routine as the new wore off and a day-to-day sameness set in. Mrs. Perlman's visits provided minimal excitement. The only thing we looked forward to was a visit to the secondhand store to buy something new for the apartment. We were living in a vacuum with nothing to vary our daily existence. It was time for a change, and Madelyne was the first to break free from the confines of routine. At first it was subtle, and we hardly noticed the change snaking its way into our lives. But, once the doors were opened we were unable to close them again.

Chapter Eleven

Mrs. Perlman promised to bring over a few houseplants to brighten up the place so one small end table was left free of knick-knacks to set them on. I envisioned a tiny African violet or maybe an ivy or two, but the day she delivered them an entire forest filled the back of her car.

"My lovelies needed a nice, warm afternoon for their ride and they seemed to have enjoyed it. Look," she chirped, "not a single leaf wilted and not a single stem broken." Placing the palm of her hand under the broad leaf of one very large plant, she spread it out gently to show how strong and healthy it was. I nodded, but didn't have the slightest idea what I was looking at. The closest I'd ever been to a living plant was the grass under my feet or the occasional tree I stood under.

"You're not bringing all of them in here, are you?" My voice broke off with a surprised squeak because it was obvious that she did.

"Of course, dear," she said as she hurried past with her arms full. "You'd better grab a couple of them before the car heats up. They don't like full sun, you know."

"Oh, yeah, sure. . ." I mumbled. Carrying two plants that looked more like trees, I couldn't imagine where to put them. They were much too large for the kitchen and the only open space in the front room was for the TV we'd purchased the night before. It took all of five minutes to fill every open space in the apartment with every shade of green imaginable. As she placed each plant, turning it this way and then that so its best side showed, she clucked and cooed over them as if they were her children. She also kept up a continuous stream of instructions on their proper care and feeding.

"You have to feed a plant?" I asked incredulously.

"Why of course, dear," she responded, looking at me as if I were somewhat dense. "You have to eat, don't you?"

"Well, sure, but people require food for energy," I explained.

"Exactly, and plants need proper nutrition, too. Now this plant," she pointed to the leafy fern placed in a corner of the kitchen, "doesn't like sun and prefers a bath to a watering and this one," pointing to one with spikes for leaves, "likes sun, but not too much water. Are you listening, dear?" She looked at me with her head cocked, birdlike, to one side. It was no wonder she always reminded me of a sparrow. Her quick, jerky movements were never still and she talked nonstop as one might imagine a bird might. She wasn't more than five feet tall, had snow white hair pulled back loosely in a bun, wore sensible black leather pumps, and floral dresses. If there was an ideal of what grandmothers should look like, she was it. Even her eyes were quick to notice anything amiss, and look out if their soft brown color darkened to olive. She had a ferocious temper and didn't mind sharing it with whoever angered her. Even Henry, her husband, jumped when she barked and he stood almost a foot taller and was at least a hundred pounds heavier. She was a darling and I was very fond of her, but wasn't sure how to respond to her generosity.

"Well, I'd best be going," she said with her usual brusqueness, "some of my boys are coming for dinner tonight and I haven't been to the store yet." Brushing dirt from her fingers, her cheeks flooded with color as an idea came to her. "Why don't you and Madelyne come for dinner? It's about time the two of you started meeting young people your own age." Shaking a finger in my face, she warned, "You can't wallow in self-pity any longer and you aren't getting any younger. Matthew needs a father and you need a husband. Gracious, it's a wonder to me someone hasn't snatched you up by now. And don't lose any more weight dear," she admonished, "you're beginning to look a-might peak-ed." Grabbing her purse, she hugged me, kissed Matthew and trotted to the car. I stood on the sidewalk waving her off and winced as the car came up over the curb, almost wiping out a newspaper box. Helping Matthew toddle up the four steps to our apartment, I gazed about in helpless wonder. How could one-person care for so many plants unless they worked in a florist's shop?

Madelyne was thrilled with the splendor of all that leafy bounty, and thought the plants added a touch of class. "These are wonderful," she gushed, "maybe we can train this ivy to climb the wall in the kitchen. Have you watered them yet? What kind of food do you suppose a plant needs?" Wandering from plant to plant, she moved a couple of her favorites into her bedroom.

"Claire brought a spray bottle filled with some stuff to spray on their leaves, but I've forgotten what it's called. She promised to help until we know how to care for them."

"Don't include me in that," she stated. "I'll be responsible for the ones in my room, but not for any of the others." Looking around the room, she shook her head in disbelief at the splendid array of pots in every color imaginable filling our cramped apartment. "I don't want to be responsible if they die. Can you imagine the lecture we'll get when that happens?" Filling a pitcher, she watered a few that felt dry to the touch. Glancing at her watch, her eyes widened in alarm, "Oh for heaven's sake, I've only been home a few minutes and I'm already late. I've got to get changed."

"I thought we were picking up the TV tonight," I said. "Where are you going? You never mentioned any plans and dinner's in the oven." Trailing after her as she rushed from bedroom to the bath, I came to an abrupt halt when the bathroom door was slammed in my face.

"Since when do I have to check with you," she yelled over the sound of running water. Opening the door a fraction of an inch, she giggled, "I've got a date. He's taking me for dinner and then dancing, . . . and I've got to hurry so quit bugging me." The door closed, leaving me with my mouth hanging open. Raising a fist to beat on the door and demand to know who she was going with, I had second thoughts. I wasn't her mother and it certainly wasn't my responsibility to control her life or see that her date passed inspection. Besides, it wasn't really my concern, but plain-old jealousy. She had a date and as usual--I did not.

In the kitchen, the timer went off signaling the roast was done. I placed a cover over the cake I'd clumsily decorated celebrating four months in Seattle. The TV could be delivered and the cable was already turned on. My celebration would take place in front of the tube with a bottle of pop and a bag of chips. Dinner could wait until tomorrow.

Figuring her date was with Andy, I was mildly surprised she accepted a second. After their first, she'd come home declaring she'd never go out with him again. She thought he was boring and definitely not her type. It wasn't because he was a backseat Romeo either. He'd treated her like a princess, and hadn't offered to kiss her goodnight and she was insulted!

When she exited the bathroom, looking every bit the fashion model she wanted to be, I swallowed down a lump in my throat. Surely her excitement stemmed from the date itself, and not from what I feared. When the doorbell rang and she ran to answer, I squeezed my eyes shut and crossed my fingers. The floor fell out from under me when I heard the familiar, sensuous voice.

"Baby," he said, "you look great. Grab your coat and let's get flyin'. I'm in the mood to tear up the dance floor and have a little fun later, if you know what I mean." Pulling her close, he nuzzled her neck and they kissed noisily. The husky purr in her voice dropped my stomach to the floor. She only responded to one person like that. I should have known trouble would eventually find us. "Hey," Keith called, "come say hello. Nicci, where are you?"

Stepping from the kitchen into the hall, I held Matthew in my arms trying to sidestep Keith's unwelcome embrace. I shouldn't have bothered because he wrapped his arms around both of us kissing my cheek. "Wow," he admired. Taking Matthew, he spun me around. "Maybe I'm taking out the wrong girl. I don't know what you've done to yourself, but you look great. Maybe I'd better call up my old buddy Richard and have him come over and keep you company. He's in town, you know."

"Please," I cautioned, "don't bother. The less I see of him the better off we all are." Scowling at the suggestion, I took Matthew's hand and walked with him into the bedroom. It was best to leave before I said something Maddie would make me sorry for later.

As soon as the door shut behind them, I raced to the bathroom. Standing in front of a full-length mirror, I studied the reflection. My dark blonde hair, worn in the same style since high school, was pulled severely away from my face where it trailed down my back in one straight length. Blue eyes, framed by a fringe of light colored lashes, stared out of a delicate face. My face had matured along with my figure and I no longer looked like a high schooler. Brushing my fingertips along cheekbones I hadn't known I had, I was pleased with my appearance. I'd never have the Grecian, outright beauty of Madelyne, but was no ugly duckling either. Tossing towels to the floor and carelessly shoving cosmetics, perfumes, and other toiletries into piles, I searched frantically for the bathroom scales. It couldn't have been coincidence could it? What was it Mrs. Perlman had said? She'd told me not to lose any more weight and Keith had hinted that I looked good. Did that mean I'd lost a few pounds or was I just exceptionally pale due to lack of sun?

Charging from the bathroom to the kitchen, I went through every drawer and cupboard. Matthew, who was watching my reckless search, decided it must be a free-for-all. Getting into the act, and with great abandon, opened every forbidden cupboard and explored their contents to his heart's content. Pots and pans clanged against each other in a wonderful symphony until another drawer caught his attention. Leaving the shiny metal lids and flat-bottomed pans in a pile, he toddled over to the towel drawer. He was in the process of twirling a towel over his head to send it sailing across the room when I caught him.

"No, no," I chided, "these aren't Matthew's toys." Trading a towel for a stuffed polar bear, I picked him up and blew raspberries on his tummy until he laughed. Circling around with him in my arms, I finally spotted the bathroom scales. They were hidden under the cascading fronds of one of Mrs. Perlman's plants. Madelyne had used the scales to weigh the plant to be sure it didn't go over the decorative shelf's recommended weight of ten pounds. Placing it on the floor, I squealed with delight. Somehow, I'd lost all but two of the pounds I'd gained since being pregnant with Matthew.

Running to the bedroom, I threw open the closet doors. Stuffed way in the back was a box filled with all my old clothes. Wedging myself between the wall and door, I managed to drag it out with minimal damage to my back. The clothes on top were things I'd worn in high school. Trying a couple of them on, I was shocked at how childish they seemed. Had I really worn such ridiculous outfits? At the bottom were a couple of the dresses and pantsuits Richard had bought. When I put them on, my jaw dropped in astonishment. They fit just fine, but the styles were nothing more than expensive sleaze, and not the least bit tasteful. Clingy fabrics with plunging necklines and cutouts at the shoulders or lower back made me blush. Discarding each outfit, I was happy to put on my comfortable sweats. At the very bottom of the box I found the Bible Diane had given me so very long ago. I threw it into a dresser drawer, forgotten for the moment, and stuffed all the clothes back in the box and marked it "For Donation" in big black letters. With that done, I turned my attention to more important things needing my consideration.

Vanity made me eager for change and I planned a course of action as I fed Matthew his dinner. After he was down for the night, I pampered myself with a luxurious bubble bath. Wrapping up in the soft, terry robe I'd received as a gift from my parents and never worn, I curled up on the sofa to give myself a manicure. While the polish dried, I browsed through one of Madelyne's beauty magazines. I studied each glossy picture until finding a hairstyle that suited me. Ripping the advertisement from the magazine, I tried to imagine my face surrounded by that style. It was a pleasant picture and I smiled to myself. Tomorrow was a new day and change was definitely in the air, and not just for Madelyne.

The TV, delivered shortly after Maddie left, was turned to a movie. I settled down to watch but promptly went to sleep and didn't wake until hearing her come in. Her voice was raised in anger, and Keith was being his usual obnoxious self.

"I don't know what makes you so mad," he said. "All I'm suggesting is that you take advantage of having a college almost at your doorstep and take a couple classes." I could almost envision his innocent expression as he looked at her. Some people think poisonous snakes are innocent, too.

"It wasn't the suggestion that upset me," Madelyne responded, "it was what you said in front of all those people." The soft sounds of her crying made my ears strain to hear what variety of insult he'd used this time. "You said I was a poor conversationalist and needed to learn how to make small talk in order hold a man's interest."

I almost gagged. What man in his right mind would care what she talked about? Besides, Madelyne was one of the most intelligent people I knew and there were few subjects she couldn't converse on.

"You made me feel stupid and foolish, and you were flirting with those girls when you all laughed at me."

"They weren't laughing at you," he defended, "they thought you were amusing and laughed with you."

Fat chance!

"Don't get so emotional, I'm with you aren't I? I didn't make a date with any of them even though I could have." He sniffed self-righteously and it took great restraint to remain a silent listener behind the door. "Come on, baby, smile and show how much you love me," he cooed. That was enough for me. Stumbling around in the dark, I tightened the belt around my waist and made my presence known by turning on a lamp.

"Home so early?" I asked with a yawn. Blinking against the brightness produced by 100 watts, I wandered into the hall to look at them with feigned innocence.

"Waiting up?" Keith asked. "Maddie's a big girl and doesn't need a keeper," he added nastily.

That did it! The kid gloves came off and I let him have it right between the eyes. "She doesn't need a keeper until you come around and then she needs a guard dog and the marines to protect her from the likes of you. And whatever you're sniffing around for, you're not getting it tonight." Grabbing her arm, I tried to pull her into the kitchen, but she refused to go. She dug in her heels and wouldn't leave his side.

"Don't be crude, Nicole. Keith's right, I need to learn more about the world. Maybe I'll look into taking a class or two and it wouldn't hurt for you to expand your horizons either." Her gaze shifted to Keith, seeking his approval.

"How can you listen to anything he has to say? He's nothing more than a high school dropout that got lucky by landing a job with his best friend's parents. You're smarter than he is, Maddie, don't be taken in by him." Her eyes narrowed with anger and I knew her sympathies were with Keith.

"That was mean and uncalled for, Nicole. I want you to apologize, and right now."

"Don't waste your breath," Keith said angrily. "Richard already told me she's nothing more than a spiteful little witch with a sharp tongue. I always take that into consideration whenever I talk to her." The mocking smile on his lips dared me to deny the accusation.

My face felt hot and my lips pinched tightly together as I stormed out of the room. The argument was pointless. Until Maddie saw Keith for what he was, nothing would change.

The next morning as I rushed around getting Matthew ready for daycare and myself for work, I prepared for the argument I was sure to have with Maddie over the things I'd said the night before. But she surprised me. When she waltzed into the kitchen, looking like a ray of sunshine, she was all smiles and even hugged me impetuously. "It's a beautiful day, isn't it?" she sang. "I can't wait until my lunch hour. I'm going to enroll in a speech class and maybe English literature. Keith's so proud; he's ready to pop buttons. Do you know what he told me when he left?" I shrugged and shook my head dumbly. This certainly wasn't what I expected. She giggled girlishly and ducked her head with embarrassment. "He admitted that he loved me, but was scared of marriage, especially after what happened to Richard."

"What does that mean?" I snapped. "And what exactly happened to Richard that didn't also happen to me?" Her cheeks flamed red as she assured me there was no offense meant.

"Please don't be angry, Nicole. You're my best friend and I don't want anything to come between us, and that means Keith. I love him--you'll just have to accept that." Her dark, luminous eyes looked at me with such pleading, my anger evaporated as quickly as it came.

"I'm not angry and I'm happy for you," I said, "but don't ever expect me to apologize to Keith, because I won't. I don't like him, he doesn't like me, and I prefer to keep it that way." She nodded in agreement and left for a work with that same sappy expression on her face. I suspicioned Keith spent the night--leaving before I got up, but could never prove it. Maddie kept that part of her life secret resenting intrusions into her privacy.

I got home from work early that afternoon and decided to make a rush trip to the grocery store. Placing Matthew in the stroller, I decided to get some exercise, and took off at a brisk walk down the hill to the mall. On the way, I mulled over my plans for an improved self-image and vainly wondered if I looked as good as I felt. Stopping at an intersection to wait for the light to change, I was surprised to hear wolf-whistles coming from a flashy convertible. Looking behind me, to the right and then the left and finding no one, I realized the whistles were for me. Grinning to myself, I hurried across the street and straight into a beauty salon with a big poster in the window that advertised makeovers. It was now or never! After showing them the picture from the magazine, they went to work. The finished product was even better than I'd imagined. The pretty woman staring back at me in the mirror held no resemblance to the girl that had walked in. After the hair and makeup, I went into a clothing store and searched through the aisles until finding the perfect outfit. I bought two suits for work, one pair of shorts with a matching top, a pair of slacks with a silk blouse, and a dress with a miniskirt shorter than I'd ever worn before. The salesclerk talked me into it through sheer flattery. She must have been right, because nights spent at home came to an abrupt halt.

I didn't have to wait long to find out if my new look would bring attention. A familiar convertible was driving through the parking lot when I left the store.

"Hey gorgeous--want a ride?" Pulling alongside, the driver jumped out and introduced himself. "The name's Derek," he said as he shook my hand. His friendly gaze focused directly on my face and didn't wander over my body as Richard's had. When he introduced his friend I smiled openly. For some reason, I had no qualms about being picked up in a grocery store parking lot. They seemed the sort of guys you'd find living next door, or as your older brother's best friend. "This is Ken and we're attending Washington State this semester. I'd like to escort you home and take you out for dinner."

"Well, I don't know," I objected, "I'm not sure I like the idea of being picked up."

"This isn't a pickup," Ken denied with a charming smile. "Think of it as taxi service. You may not realize it, but that hill you walked down is steep, and will be difficult to climb pushing a stroller. We promise to take you straight home and will never bother you again if you'll promise to keep two lonely guys, far from home, company for one evening."

"Okay, one evening," I agreed, "but straight home or I'll scream my head off." Scrambling to stow my packages in the back along with Matthew's stroller, they seated me between them in the front seat, and within minutes pulled into the driveway. Madelyne stepped out onto the porch when the car parked behind hers. Derek lost his heart as soon as she flashed one of her fantastic smiles. He was out of the car and at her side before the car came to a full stop.

"Fickle, ain't he?" Ken joked. "Hope you don't mind my company because it looks like he'll be busy for a while." Derek and Maddie walked into the house, arm-in-arm, seeming to have forgotten about us.

"I'd love your company, and in fact prefer blondes to brunettes," I teased. "Now, since my chauffeur has disappeared, will you help unload my things?"

"Thought you'd never ask," he laughed. After the trunk was emptied and Maddie and I changed clothes, we drove over to Mrs. Perlman's. She agreed to baby-sit while we went out even though she lamented the fact we weren't in company of one of her "boys."

Ken and Derek were excellent company, and showed us both a good time. We went to dinner at a restaurant that was tasteful without being pretentious. While sipping an after dinner glass of Chablis, we argued about where to go dancing. A bar with live music had opened just a few blocks off college campus, and it didn't take much persuasion for them to talk us into going.

When we walked into the darkened room, the beat of the music, bright flashing lights, and gyrating bodies on the dance floor ignited a fire in me. I'd always loved to dance and the rhythm and new dance steps drew me like a moth to flame. In no time, I learned to duplicate the intricate steps and even threw in a few of my own. Ken sat a good share of the evening alone as I danced almost every set with a new partner. I was thrilled. For once the attention wasn't all for Madelyne.

"I need a breath of air," I gasped after dancing three in a row. Breathless, I fanned my face with a bar napkin and glanced at Ken to see if he took the hint.

"Do you want to step outside?" he asked. At my nod of agreement, he grabbed his drink and handed one to me. "We can finish our drinks and cool off, or we can heat things up a bit," he grinned lecherously, "it makes no difference to me." I followed him out the back door to the parking lot and leaned up against the car, sipping my drink and wondering what he meant. I didn't have to wait long to find out.

"Come here, baby," he sighed as he wrapped an arm around my waist. Pulling our bodies close together, he kissed me long and deep. At first, it was nice, but when his tongue grazed my lips, I stiffened and pulled away.

"What's the matter? Don't you want to get better acquainted?" The taste of his drink lingered on my lips and it nauseated me.

"Well, sure," I mumbled, "I'm just not ready for anything more serious than a casual date. I mean, we hardly know each other and here we are standing in a parking lot kissing like lovers. We ought to know each other better, that's all."

"Kissing like lovers?" he said sarcastically, "what's that supposed to mean? You're not trying to make me believe you didn't know what we were coming out here for, are you?" The skepticism on his face made my racing heart shrivel. The implied suggestion made it sound like I'd invited him to my bed or something.

"I'm not trying to make you believe anything." I spit. "I needed a breath of fresh air and now that I've had it, find the air to be a little chilly. I'm going back inside and then I want to go home." There wasn't anything left to say, and turned to leave with my head held high.

"Hey, wait a minute--maybe I misunderstood or maybe there was a faulty line of communication." He rested a hand on my arm without trying to restrain me. The look of remorse on his face made me hesitate long enough for him to explain. "Look, I didn't mean to get off on the wrong foot, but after seeing you flirt with all those guys and when you asked me to come out here, I guess I got the wrong idea."

"Do you often become insulting when a girl needs a breath of air?" I asked indignantly. "I figured since you didn't want to dance, and your friends did, what was the harm? It's not like we're an item or anything." Turning my back to him, I pretended to be studying the stars for a moment while deciding what to do next. Should I go back inside and demand to be taken home or make amends? I was almost sure Madelyne would know exactly what to do and what to say.

"I'm sorry," he said penitently as his hand rested on my bare shoulder. "If you'd look around, you'd see why a guy would get the wrong idea. We aren't alone in this parking lot. Look and see for yourself. Everybody comes back here to make out and get friendly after getting heated up on the dance floor. That's what I thought you wanted--you know--to get friendly." His hand trailed down my bare arm to my wrist. As he spoke, his eyes burned into mine with a hunger I'd seen before.

I stepped away from him, peering into the dark to see if what he said was true. My cheeks warmed when two rows over I spotted a couple wrapped around each other.

"I see what you mean," I said dryly, "but that's still no excuse for assuming this was just another cheap date. Either you don't think much of me or you have a low opinion of women in general. I think better of myself than to have a make-out session in the backseat of a car in a dark parking lot with someone I hardly know. Now, we've had a good time and I've met several of your friends, but now I want to go home."

"I hope we can go out again sometime," he said. Before I could object, he raised both hands in surrender and added, "Without any preconceived notions on my part. Won't you give me a second chance? Please?" The little boy look on his face brought a hint of a smile to the edge of my lips. He looked adorable with his hands stuffed in his pockets and pleading in his eyes. I couldn't help but forgive him. He scored a point when he said meaningfully, "I'd like to get to know you better, Nicole. You're different from most girls a guy meets at school. You're more real, more honest." My soft heart was completely taken in. It never occurred to me that loneliness and a deep-seated need to be loved had lowered my defenses. I decided to forgive him and hoped I wouldn't live to regret the decision.

Taking the arm he extended, we went back inside and rejoined Maddie and Derek at the table. They were getting along fine, as long as Derek kept his distance. It was clear she enjoyed his company, but wouldn't anticipate a romantic or long term relationship. That didn't seem to stop him from gazing at her in absolute adoration. He seemed willing to accept any scrap of affection she offered as long as he was allowed to sit in her presence for just a little while. She smiled with amused pleasure as if he were a nice diversion, but nothing to be taken seriously. Her heart belonged solely to Keith.

We had another drink, made polite conversation, danced a couple more times, and then called it an evening. Later, when we parted company at my door, Ken was the epitome of a gentleman.

"I hope you had a good time," he said as he guided me down the sidewalk with a touch on my elbow that was more a caress. "I really enjoyed myself and except for making the biggest gaffe of all time, think we hit it off pretty well." At the entrance to the apartment, he took hold of both my shoulders and pulled me close enough to place a brotherly kiss on my forehead. "How soon can I see you again?"

"I'm not sure," I hedged, "there's no sense in rushing into anything."

"You're not going to hold what happened earlier against me are you?" Even though his facial features expressed an innocent air of concern, his eyes burned with passion. He was sending two separate messages and the latter was the louder of the two. I'd seen the look before and it made me feel like a piece of meat on a hook.

"I'm not mad or anything," I said evasively, "it's just that I'm not ready for a relationship of any kind. Since my divorce. ."

"You're divorced?" he asked incredulously, "I thought you were just a girl that got caught, if you know what I mean."

"There you go again," I chided, "drawing conclusions before you know the entire story. Matthew's father, my ex-husband, also made assumptions about people and situations. The only difference between you and him was his power of manipulation to get what he wanted. I allowed him to manipulate me and I won't make the same mistake twice. I'm not ready for a relationship, but could use a friend. Will you be my friend?" Brushing his wrist with my fingertips, I studied the surprised expression on his face. It was obvious he wasn't ready to consider a girl as a friend.

"Yeah, sure," he stammered. "Look, I know we got off on the wrong foot and all...I'll come by on Saturday and if you want to go dancing, we'll go. Besides, all my friends saw us together this evening, and want a chance to make a fool of themselves over you. The least you can do is be obliging and make yourself available." His lips spread in a broad grin as if the whole idea were terribly funny. "Wait till you meet some of the girls," he added, "will they ever be jealous. Most of them have gone out of their way to be noticed by the guys you met tonight and here you are; Little Miss Innocence, able to wrap them around your finger after sharing just one little dance." Throwing back his head, he laughed as if it was a very good joke. I laughed too, although not as heartily, and to say I wasn't flattered would be a lie. But it was hard to tell whether he wanted me for a trophy or for a friend.

After our evening out, it was hard to return to a daily routine of going to work and then straight home. Maddie, being without commitments, took to Seattle's nightlife like she was born to it. Tired of boring evenings spent in front of the TV, she went out at every opportunity that presented itself. She became quite popular with the college crowd and was frequently invited to their parties. I was always invited to go along and often did. The thrill and excitement of being on the dance floor with a sensational partner beckoned, and nights out became every weekend. It was an addiction I couldn't break. I loved going out, and began to believe it was more important to be known by the bar and university crowd than to be known by my own son. On Friday's my heart thrummed with excited anticipation as I rushed home from work to get ready for a night out. I even excused my neglect of Matthew by convincing myself that after working hard all week I deserved a night to myself.

"Besides," I confided to Maddie one evening, "I'm a better mother than those girls with live-in boyfriends. At least Matthew won't be confused about who his father is, and he isn't being hurt by me going out once in a while. Besides, I always see to it that he's well taken care of." She should have slapped the pious look right off my face.

"I know you do, but don't you think he's left with a sitter an awful lot?" She gazed at me with frank honesty and her head tilted in question. "And as far as Matt knowing who his father is, I don't see how he could. Richard was never around enough to invoke much of a memory, and the guys you're seeing now aren't around long enough to leave a lasting impression."

"I've told you before; I'm not ready for a steady relationship. Before I think about settling down again, I want to play the field, get to know the person before making any commitments."

"How can you consider any of those guys capable of a real relationship when you're scared to death of being alone? Don't you think I know why you go out all the time? I know you too well, Nicole Franklin the Fourth," she teased. "It's okay to have a little fun as long as you realize that the dance floor and the bar scene isn't life. It's all pretense--none of its real and I sometimes wonder if the people in them know they are but shadows of their own imaginations. Sure, there's plenty of glitz and glamour, but keep it in the right perspective. What's real is what you have right here." She pulled Matthew onto her lap and wrapped her arms around him. Snuggling his little body close to her own she added with a slight tremble in her voice, "I'd give just about anything to have what you have. If I had a kid like Matthew, I'd never want to leave him with anyone." The sad look on her face caught me off guard. I knew Maddie wanted children, but never suspected she wasn't happy.

"Are you unhappy?" I asked. Touched by the look of sorrow on her face, I wanted our conversation to return to the lighthearted banter we usually engaged in. It was hard to be the life of the party and keep a smile on your face when you're on the verge of tears.

"I'm not unhappy, but I'm not happy either," she said as she rocked back and forth. "Sometimes, I wonder if I feel anything at all. The only time I am truly alive is when Keith is with me. Do you suppose I could be obsessed with him?" The direction of this conversation was disturbing and I wasn't ready to analyze her or myself.

"Maddie," I laughed, "what a thing to say. You're not obsessed with Keith, you're in love with him. There's a difference. Now, you can sit here feeling sorry and allow yourself to be all depressed because he didn't call this week, or you can get dressed, go out, and have a little fun. There's no point in spending the evening alone when in all likelihood, he's not alone and far from lonely." She gasped as a stricken look crossed her face.

"Do you think he's seeing someone else? I mean, he was before, but we're almost engaged. Keith loves me," she stated adamantly as if needing to convince herself of the validity of her own statement. "I've got to believe he loves me," she explained. Her expression wasn't a girl in love, but of a person in deep, personal pain. Holding Matthew, she carried him into the front room and sat rocking him for a very long time. As the sun went down, the darkened room filled with shadows as she hummed a lullaby someone must have once sung to her. When I left, closing the door firmly behind me, I congratulated myself on a life without entanglements or heartaches. At least when I spent an evening alone it was because I wanted to, and it was without regret.

Chapter Twelve

Time heals all wounds may be true, but for Maddie it took a visit from Keith. The day he flew in, she was sunk in deep depression and I was beginning to worry about her state of mind. For days all she did was cry, and had to stay home sick because of it. What a change when she spotted him coming up the walk.

"Keith," she cried. Running with hair streaming out behind her, she flung open the door and threw herself into his arms. "I've missed you so much," she said as she rained kisses all over his face. I choked on my coffee when I saw who it was that brought about such an abrupt change. I wondered what broom he flew in on and how quickly I could convince him to fly back out again.

"Well," he drawled as he came into the kitchen with an arm slung casually around her waist, "how's the little mother?" Taking Matthew from my lap, he lifted him up as if weighing a sack of potatoes. "He's getting too big to be sitting on laps," he told me and then to Matthew asked, "Aren't you?" Matthew grinned and nodded, always eager to please. Relief flooded his little face when he was placed safely back on his own two feet. "I'm taking Maddie out tonight--how about coming along?" Keith asked me. "First, we'll have dinner and then find a place for a few drinks and a little dancing. From everything I've heard, you love to dance, so how about it?"

A quick glance was exchanged between us. Madelyne only shrugged her shoulders; appearing as surprised as I was. "You've heard I like to dance? From whom? I would think you had better things to talk about than what I do for entertainment," I said sarcastically.

"Normally, I wouldn't take the slightest interest," he jeered, "and it's strictly out of courtesy I assure you. And as far as who I heard it from," he shrugged noncommittally, "Maddie must have mentioned it once or twice and I kind of picked up on it. If you don't want to go, that's fine with me because we'll have a great time with or without you." He grinned and shot a knowing wink at Madelyne as he smacked her on the rear. "Won't we," he said. Her cheeks turned crimson at the intimation, and I loathed him for being so vulgar as to broadcast the personal side of their relationship.

"In that case," I said sweetly, "I'd better come along just to be sure her honor remains intact." With that said, I flounced out of the room and headed straight for the phone. If we were going out, I needed to arrange a baby-sitter for Matthew. I called the daycare first, but they closed at ten. My second call was to Mrs. Perlman--she rarely turned down an opportunity to spoil Matthew.

"Hello dear," she chirped. "How are you and Madelyne doing? You're so busy any more that I rarely have the opportunity to visit with you. I'll be glad to watch the baby again, dear," she said, "but aren't you working an awful lot of late nights?"

"Well, it isn't exactly working," I stammered, "we're going out for dinner with friends, and then maybe a drink or two afterward." I usually used the excuse that I had to work late when we went out on Friday nights, but this time decided to be honest. It was doubtful she'd believe I had to work on a Saturday.

"Oh," she said curtly, "I see. In that case, I'd better keep him here overnight. I'll come over to get him so have his things ready in an hour." The friendly tone in her voice returned as she asked about the health of the plants she'd given me.

Eyeing the wilted leaves and stunted growth of the one next to me I lied, "Oh, they're just fine. Guess I'd better go water them. I'll talk to you when you get here," I said as I rang off. For the next few minutes, it was a frantic race to water each plant before she arrived. I couldn't remember the last time they'd had a drink and neither could Maddie, but Claire would know; she always did. I hid one plant in the closet because it had lost all but one leaf, and appeared dead. Keith just shook his head. He left a few minutes later, not wanting to be inspected by the infamous Mrs. Perlman.

"How are my lovelies," she trilled as Maddie opened the door to let her in. "Have you been watering and feeding them?"

I almost imagined the response from each plant as soon as they heard her voice. Valiantly they would lift their little heads, and stiffen weakened stems to appear strong and hearty. Eventually they would slump back into their pots, unable to retain the pretense any longer. Death threatened several with drowning while several others were cooked by the intense heat of the sun as it streamed through the windows. It was enough to make any self-respecting plant shrivel up its roots.

"Oh my goodness," Mrs. Perlman cried with hands to her cheeks, "you're killing them." Clucking and cooing over each of the sick and dying, she loaded up her car and took them home for some intensive first aid. If they had any chance at all, she was their only hope.

After the sickliest were placed carefully in the backseat of her car, she turned to appraise each of us with a stern eye. "Now girls," she began, "I wasn't born yesterday. I think you're spending too much time at a local hot spot instead of taking care of what's important. I don't know what your mother's would say, but shame and especially on you, Nicole, with a child to care for," she scolded. "You know I love little Matthew as if he were my own grandchild, but he needs to see more of his mother."

"Are you going to lecture me, too, little mama?" Keith joked as he came in through the back door. "The girls have listened to enough of your yammering and now it's time for us to get going. Are you coming or not?" he asked Maddie as he turned to leave.

Mrs. Perlman pulled herself up to her fullest height, and faced him with as much indignation as she could muster. "You are a cheeky young man and if you worked for my husband, I'd have you fired for your insolence. Madelyne, if this is the young man you've been pining away for, you have my pity." Scooping Matthew up in her arms, she marched out of the apartment with head held high. She wasn't just angry, but had been insulted on her own property.

Maddie reacted before I did. "How could you speak to her like that?" she asked Keith angrily. "Mrs. Perlman is a dear sweet lady and has done a lot for us. I think what you did is abominable." She turned to follow Claire, but Keith held her back.

"Hey," he said, "I was only kiddin' around. How was I supposed to know the old lady would take me seriously? Here," he smoothed her hair back, "I'll make it up to her. First thing tomorrow, I'll call her on the phone and apologize. Will that make you feel better?" She nodded, but folded her arms across her chest in a defiant posture.

"Do you promise?" she pleaded.

"You heard me say it, didn't you?" The smug look on his face was disgusting, and I should have refused to go with them. But, I didn't.

* * *

Going out became my primary reason for living. When on the dance floor, the beat of the music drowned out the lonely beat of my heart. The bar scene filled my ears with the sound of conversation, clinking glass, and laughter. The pounding music was in stark contrast to the lonely sounds of home where the walls move in on you when the silence is so intense you think you'll go crazy for want of another voice. The dance floor gave me an identity and for once, I wasn't mousey little Nicole Reese. I was an exciting woman that men wanted to be seen with. It didn't matter that a good part of me was buried under an exterior of phony materialism because worldly behavior was a sign of sophistication. Wasn't that what everybody said? Slowly, the barriers came down as other avenues of pleasure opened their doors. I continued to see Ken, because he was my means of gaining entrance into bars and other places without appearing tacky. After all, a lady doesn't go into a bar without an escort does she? But, after a while, it was more and more confusing to decide who was using who and in my search for acceptance and a place of belonging, Matthew was the one who paid the price.

"I'm going to be late again, tonight," I told the receptionist at Matthew's daycare. "I won't be able to pick him up until after ten. Can you keep him until then?" Twirling a lock of hair between my fingers, I listened to the girl's tiresome warning about children left in daycare for extended time periods. I'd heard the same lecture before, and it bored me.

"Yeah," I said as I smacked my gum, "you've told me this already. Anyway, it can't be helped. I have to work late and then run some errands." Isn't it funny how easy lying can be after telling the first, and then the second, and then the third, and then. . .?"

"I'll have to take it up with the manager," she said coldly. "We've had little Matt almost round-the-clock for two weeks and it's become a bit of a concern. Can I call you back?"

"Yeah, sure," I said as I rattled off the number. After setting up the answering machine, I hummed the latest rock song as I raced off for an early lunch. I wanted to give nature a little help by having my hair streaked. It had grown a lot over the last year and hung almost to my waist in one long curtain. Madelyne wasn't the only one to draw attention by the length of her hair.

"Nicole," Mr. Powers interrupted my headlong rush for the stairs. "Can you give me a minute?"

"Sure." I took a seat in his office facing him expectantly. He smiled kindly and spoke in a fatherly tone.

"I'm not entirely pleased with the quality of your work lately. You seem to rush through things and you're not putting the same concern into correcting your errors. I don't think I need to remind you that most of my correspondence eventually ends up on the desk of some judge. In my line of business accuracy in the written word is essential. Is there something wrong? You seem to hurry out of here every night--are you having a problem with childcare?"

"No," I ducked my head in shame. Feeling chastised, embarrassment flooded my cheeks. "I apologize," I confessed, "I've gotten lazy and didn't proofread the last few letters. I promise not to let it happen again."

"I hope not," he said with a chuckle. "It was pure coincidence that Claudia checked the outgoing mail and spied a typo in an address. She retyped each one, and they went out in the morning's mail, so no harm done. But, I can't count on my daughter coming by every afternoon to check the outgoing. I've got to rely on you, Nicole, that's why we hired you. Please," he said as he helped me to my feet, "be more careful." As soon as he closed the door after me, I knew our little talk was forgotten. He had a mountain of work to finish before his next case hit the court dockets and, thank God, he never held a grudge.

Guilt followed me all the way to the hair dressers, and I hoped the new color would revitalize my mood. It didn't! If I could have kicked myself for taking advantage of the kindnesses extended to me by John and Claudia Powers, I would have. By the time I returned to my desk

I was thoroughly chastened and vowed to never let it happen again. Every outgoing document was double checked as well as the envelopes and memos.

It was almost closing time when Matthew's daycare got in touch with me. The receptionist's voice coolly informed me that the manager wanted to meet. I could almost hear the "I told you so" in her voice as I agreed to speak with management as soon as I got there.

When I took a seat in the sparsely furnished office, I looked around at the hard metal chairs and bare wood floor. You'd think the people who ran the place could fork over enough dough for some decent chairs and a throw rug or two. The only warm spot in the entire room was a little alcove decorated with a hanging lamp, an overflowing toy box, a thick shag throw rug, several shelves of puzzles and games, and a picture on the wall of Jesus holding a little lamb. A soft voice invited me into the inner sanctum. When the receptionist showed me the way, I conjured up indignant anger. How dare these people tell me how to live my life? Who were they anyway? A bunch of religious fanatics that wouldn't know how to have a good time if their life depended on it? So what if they had provided excellent care of my son for the past seven months, there were other daycares weren't there?

"Please come in and be seated," the receptionist told me. "Mrs. Masters will be back in just a minute. She went to check on Matthew. He's been in the sickroom all day."

"Matthew is sick? Why didn't anyone tell me? Why wasn't I called?"

"We did call you," she declared, "I made the call myself. When I told you that he didn't appear well, you said I was imagining things and that he'd be fine after eating his lunch. He's been throwing up all afternoon, and is running a temperature. You should have known he was sick before you brought him."

Worry took the place of anger and I instantly deflated. The girl took great pleasure in knocking me down a peg, and I deserved it. Unable to sit still, I paced the room until the door labeled 'PRIVATE', in big, bold letters, swung open. When it did, I was absolutely astounded. I hadn't made the connection between the Mrs. Masters, manager of a daycare, and the Mrs. Masters I'd known since high school. The look of surprise was just as evident on Diane's face.

"Diane," I asked, "what are you doing in Seattle?"

"I guess I could ask you the same question," she said as she hugged me in greeting. "I never expected that Matthew Franklin was your son." Waving toward a chair, she pulled up a seat and we caught up on lost time. After a long explanation made short on how Diane and her husband ended up in Seattle, she sobered and put on her "it's time to face the music" face used to lecture negligent mothers.

"I couldn't be happier to find we have friends living in Seattle, but the reason I asked to see you was because of your son. This daycare is run through the church with me as manager, but we also provide counseling and parenting classes. We're quite concerned about the amount of time Matthew is left here. It's expected that we'll have a child for at least eight to ten hours a day, but never to the point where it's almost round-the-clock. Nicole, I know the Powers really well. John Powers is my mother-in-law's brother. I know the hours you work, and we need to settle on a reasonable length of time for necessary childcare. Is there a problem that some counseling could help with?"

"Oh, is that all?" I breathed a sigh of relief. "The receptionist said he was sick, and I was really worried there for a minute. Counseling isn't the answer. I've been busy lately, that's all." Diane studied my expression at length, and I squirmed under her scrutiny. Blinking, she looked away, busying herself by shuffling some papers on her desk.

"Were you really, Nicole? I mean, were you really worried? Because Matthew is sick, in fact, he's really sick and should be seen by a doctor. We've been pushing fluids on him all day, but we don't have the authority to take him for medical treatment." Glancing at me, her eyes narrowed keenly, "That right is restricted to the child's parents."

"Why are we sitting here if my son needs to see a doctor?" I asked. "Let me out of here so I can take him to the nearest hospital." Rising from my seat, I clutched my handbag in fear. I remembered the last time Matt was sick and how quickly his fever shot up. This time, I had no one to help me and his pediatrician was clear back home in Oregon. My mind scurried around frantically trying to think of doctor's names and where they might be found.

"Don't get hysterical," Diane stated calmly, "I took the liberty of calling my own doctor and asking his advice. I followed his instructions

The Redemption of Madelyne

to the letter. Here's my doctor's address and his number, so call and make an appointment before you leave. But, you can't bring Matthew back until he's been given a doctor's release. I don't know what kind of life you lead and have no intention of prying, but he needs you right now. He's a very sick little boy and keeps crying for his mama. Please Nicole," she pleaded as she gripped my arm tightly, "as one mother to another, don't leave him with another sitter until he's over whatever he has. Now, one last thing. Your hours for daycare are from seven-thirty to six, isn't that right?" At my nod of confirmation, she made a notation in an appointment book then closed it with a snap. I almost ran to keep up with her as she walked quickly to a temporary infirmary where Matthew lay in a crib. His cheeks were mottled red, and his eyes swollen. Heat radiated from him and he looked at me listlessly as he gave a feeble smile. I broke down and cried. I should have known he needed me, and shouldn't be told by strangers that he was sick. Bundling him up, I took him straight to the doctor's office. My heart broke when the doctor told me Matthew had contracted rubella. When I put him to bed that night, a red rash was already spreading across his chest and underarms. His throat was so sore he couldn't cry, but rasped, "Mama, Mommm, Mommm," over and over again. Huge alligator tears rolled down his little cheeks as he tossed in the warm bedding trying to cool his hot, aching body.

Neither Maddie nor I went to bed but kept vigil by his crib. I sat in a straight back chair at the head of his crib while she sat in the rocker at the foot. Angry at the way I'd neglected him, a wall of silence rose between us until she finally condescended to speak.

"How could we not notice that he was sick?" she whispered. "Didn't you know he was running a fever? I'm just as much at fault because I forgot to tell you that he wouldn't eat his dinner last night. I thought he was just being stubborn so he went to bed without it." Her eyes glittered in the subdued light. I was already crying tears of guilt, and didn't figure I could handle hers, too.

"It doesn't matter now," I said, trying to make myself feel better. "He's being taken care of, and I'll never let anything like this happen again. I've been so stupid," I confessed, "while congratulating myself on what a good mother I am, I forgot how much he depends on me.

I've been an absolute jerk and hope he'll forgive me." My tears wet his blankets as I straightened them around him for the hundredth time.

Falling into a fitful sleep, he tossed from one side to the other. His forehead remained hot, so I tried placing cool cloths over him. They heated up as fast as I could replace them. He'd only been resting a short time when he sat up and began to vomit. The stuff spewed from his mouth and nose with so much force it flew across the room and splattered on the wall. I didn't know how one little body could hold so much. When diarrhea cramped his tummy making it hard to keep a clean diaper on him, Maddie got scared. Grabbing the car keys, we ran for the car and rushed him to the nearest emergency room. His little body went limp before we got there. I was out of my mind, figuring he would die before medical help could be found.

The emergency room staff went to work as soon as we rushed inside. He was dehydrated and the fever continued to climb. It was only a matter of minutes before they hooked him up to an IV and began administering medication and necessary fluids through a needle in his arm. By three A.M. he was still feverish, but beginning to rest peacefully. Maddie called John Powers and Diane at the daycare to report that I wouldn't be in, and we watched in stunned silence when John and Claudia came into Matt's room with Diane close behind. The three of them immediately bowed their heads and began to pray. Since I didn't know what else to do, I prayed, too. In fact, I prayed fervently to a God I didn't know. I had doubted His existence until that very moment. I begged for the life of my son in exchange for my own. God answered my prayer, but not in the way I expected.

Matthew remained in guarded condition for the next few hours and then his prognosis changed to satisfactory. The fever disappeared all at once, and he sat up wanting a drink. We wiped grateful tears from our eyes when he drank a full bottle of juice. Mrs. Perlman sat with me while Madelyne went to work, and cried a river when Matthew grinned at her in recognition. The spots on his chest, face, and back remained for several days, but at least he was allowed to come home where I could care for him myself. That first evening, his fever went up and I frantically searched the apartment for the thermometer. My hands shook so bad when I found it, that it dropped to the floor and broke. There was another thermometer

The Redemption of Madelyne

that I'd used when Matthew was an infant, but didn't know if I could find it. Maddie helped search every drawer as we tore through the house looking for a needle in a haystack. When I searched through my own dresser, I found my Bible stuffed in the back corner of my sweater drawer, and underneath it the infant forehead thermometer. Shoving the Bible in among my sweaters, I slammed the drawer and made a mad dash for disinfectant. I was relieved when the red climbed to just a hair over 100 degrees and didn't go further. By bedtime his temperature was near normal.

Over the few days it took for Matthew to recover, I discovered the true meaning of the term, "fair weather friend". Ken called wanting to go out over the weekend.

"What's going on?" he asked, "I waited for you last Friday, but you never showed. How about meeting for a drink next Friday?"

"I don't think so, Ken. Matthew's sick and I can't leave him."

"What's the matter? Does he have the flu? It's been going around."

"No, it's much more serious than that. He contracted a form of measles and has been in the hospital. I haven't even gone to work so I could stay home and take care of him."

"Want some company?" he teased lecherously. "I could be there in five minutes."

"Don't make jokes," I said with an edge of impatience in my voice. I couldn't believe how insensitive the man was. "Matthew's still sick and needs me here. If you want to come over and keep me company, fine, but don't expect to stay longer than just a couple hours. We have a doctor's appointment later this afternoon."

"Hey, don't unload on me about the kid. It's not as if he's mine or anything and if he's that sick, maybe it's best I stay away. Is it catching?"

"Hopefully," I said caustically, "and since you were here last week, maybe you'll get lucky." I slammed the phone down hard enough to break an eardrum. Even Maddie's friends refused to come around for fear Matthew would infect them. The words of the late Henry Adams came to mind:

> *One friend in a lifetime is much;*
> *two are many; and*
> *three are barely possible.*

Madelyne remained faithful as was Mrs. Perlman, Diane, and Claudia Powers. Each did whatever they could to help. Maddie took care of Matt while I rested or ran necessary errands, Mrs. Perlman sent over meals to tempt his appetite (and ours), Claudia filled in at work for me, and Diane came over every day to share a comforting message she'd found in her daily devotions or just to visit. I was blessed to have such loyal friends. Matthew's good health was soon restored.

Summer weather turned hot, and we spent many days lazing at Alkai Beach. Matthew loved playing and digging in the sand while I sat nearby in the shade of an umbrella. Madelyne signed up for a class in Family Dynamics at the college, and got involved with a new group of friends. I often returned home from work to find our little apartment full and the refrigerator empty. I wasn't sure I liked this group of girls that spouted stuff about women's lib and sexual awareness as carelessly as if talking about the weather.

"What do you think," one asked as I came in from work one afternoon, and set a bag of groceries on the counter.

"Think about what," I asked as I dropped my keys into my purse.

"We were discussing the abortion issue," Maddie explained. "Some of us think it's a woman's right to choose just like our professor's been saying. But a couple of the girls think abortion is just another name for murder. What do you think?"

"Well," I considered the question for a moment while trying to come up with an answer that didn't sound like some platitude I'd heard somewhere, "if it's every woman's right to choose then I hope they opt for the child. Doesn't everyone have the right to life without the threat of bodily harm? Isn't that right protected by our elected officials? If we abhor the laws set forth to protect life aren't we setting a precedence that life is not valuable? If we mark our children for extinction and allow them to be exterminated, then we've sealed an alliance with men like Hitler or Lenin. I, for one, do not want to be linked with such monsters. Every child deserves the right of life," I stated emphatically. Taking an apple from the grocery bag for Matthew, I was surprised at the sudden silence. They asked the question and been supplied an answer, and it sounded pretty good to me.

The Redemption of Madelyne

"Gee, Nicole," Maddie said with a hint of awe in her voice, "I didn't know you felt so strongly about this issue. It sounds like you've taken a pretty firm stand against women's rights."

"Women may not have some of the same opportunities as men, but they may in time. It isn't an issue of who's right or wrong when a decision is made to abort a child; it's an issue of life and death. Everyone spouts the importance of equality for women but no one wants to consider the rights of the child. When is someone going to speak for the child?"

"The child," a cute blonde challenged, "is nothing more than a mass of cells and isn't even considered human until it's born. It's nothing more than a parasite that requires a host--a woman's uterus—in order to survive, and if a woman doesn't want her body used to support it, why should she? It's a violation of her rights!"

I stared at this girl dressed in an androgynous style and wearing a huge button blaring: Pro-Choice, as if she had suddenly metamorphosed into some kind of ogre. I couldn't think fast enough to come up with a viable response. What she said frightened me. It was a chilling thought that women would consider their own children as parasites and would want to destroy them with no more feeling than if they were a fly or a mosquito. Matthew wandered into the kitchen and I rushed over to scoop him up to protect him from this person. I didn't want her getting too close, and definitely didn't want her to touch him.

"Cookie," he demanded. Placing a cookie in his hand I ran out of the room with him in my arms. Their voices resumed in strident argument as soon as I left, but before I could find a place to hide out, the entire group followed me into the next room.

"When do you know a baby is a baby?" Maddie questioned. She wore a confused expression, and I wondered how much of the drivel she'd heard was actually believed.

"How do I know a baby is a baby?" Sitting Matthew on my lap, I brushed cookie crumbs from his sweatshirt and turned him to face her. "You were there when Matt was born and you've been here through the entire two and a half years of his life. How can you ask what a baby is?"

"I don't mean it that way," she said softly, "I mean, how does a woman feel when she's pregnant? When do you know it's a baby?"

All eyes were on me. Important decisions might be made based on my answer and spontaneity had never been one of my strong suits. I figured an answer based on experience would be best defended if challenged.

"I can't answer for all women, but I knew Matt was there before any doctor's exam or urine test." Hugging him until he squirmed to get away, I smiled with motherly pride. My eyes closed as I remembered carrying the secret of him close to my heart. "A woman knows," I said, "you sense something is different--something special. Something so wondrous you want to hold onto it for as long as possible."

"What hogwash," fumed the blonde. My eyes flew open and the tender moment vanished as she drew attention to herself. "Sure, she might have felt that way," she sneered with a dismissive gesture in my direction, "but what about all the women who don't? What about rape victims, or incest, or . . .or the health of the mother? What if the pregnancy just isn't at the right time in a person's life? Come on, girls, how many of you want to drop out of college to have a kid? Think about it! Your lives will be ruined, and so long to your future. Now let's get back to the reason we're meeting today. How many are attending the rally on Saturday, and who will volunteer to put a stop to the pro-lifers picketing the new clinic?" I was appalled when every hand shot up including Madelyne's.

Chapter Thirteen

It was hard to pinpoint when it began, but there was a definite difference in Madelyne. Her style of dress changed from tastefully becoming to short and even shorter. She'd never dressed to deliberately show off her feminine attributes, but these new friends encouraged a more popular style, and she happily complied. Now it was she who stayed out on weekends and most nights. I'm not saying I was at home all the time knitting or playing cards, but at least I knew where I'd be when I woke up in the morning. I'd learned my lesson! On occasions when I went out it became habit to be home before one. Maddie was having a good time, or so she said.

Mrs. Perlman worried as much as I did on those nights she didn't come home at all.

Along with change, comes differences in opinion. Some are to be expected when two adults share the same household, but one started as an argument over laundry. It ended with us almost parting company after a friendship of over eighteen years.

"Where are my blue shorts?" I demanded as I rummaged through the laundry basket. "Where are they? They're the perfect match to this blouse and I planned to wear them today. You picked up all the dirty clothes didn't you?"

"I don't know," Maddie retorted as she lugged in the last of the laundry. "I took it all to the laundromat, and if they're not in the basket, check the sack, maybe they're in there."

I searched again and didn't find them; in fact, most of my laundry wasn't in the basket or the sack. "Where are Matthew's things?" Looking through the clothes stuffed in the bag, it was obvious the only laundry done was her own. "Did you get the stuff out of the hamper?" I asked with an edge of impatience. Dumping all the clothes out of the canvas bag onto the bed, I tried not to lose patience.

"I took everything that was dirty," she said defensively. Tossing her head, ready to argue the point if necessary, she placed her hands on her hips and stuck her nose in the air. Obviously, prepared for battle. I'd seen the same look on her little blonde friend. Storming into the bathroom I opened the hamper and found it full. She hadn't bothered to gather any other laundry except her own. I was so mad I could have chewed nails and spit them at her.

"Look at this," I screeched with a finger pointing at the full hamper. "We decided a long time ago that whoever had laundry duty was responsible for gathering up all the dirty clothes. You didn't even bother to check."

"Why should I?" she spit, "when most of your clothes are usually left on the floor or wadded up in your closet. I'm not your mother, Nicole, and it's not my responsibility to pick up after you."

"Who asked you to pick up anything? All I expect is that you have the courtesy to take all the laundry instead of just your own," I yelled. Spying Matthew as he peeked around the door wide-eyed, I lowered my voice. "I don't know what's going on, but you are not the same girl I've known all my life. For the last month I've done all the housework, grocery shopping, cooking, and laundry without complaint. Today, for the first time in, I don't know how long, I ask you to help out and this is what I get. Well, thanks so much for your help Miss Hall." Stuffing all the dirty clothes into a pillowcase, I grabbed the detergent, my purse, and Matthew and headed for the door.

"I'm sorry, I didn't realize," she admitted as she took the pillowcase from me. "You don't have to go; I'll take the stuff over. It's the least I can do."

"I hope you don't forget to bring it back," I added.

Throwing the stuff down, she turned on me with venom. "Oh, let's play the little martyr, why don't we? Don't get sarcastic with me," she accused, "because I know the truth. It wasn't long ago that you were out until all hours of the night, and the only reason you've been sticking close to home is because you feel guilty because Matthew got sick. So

The Redemption of Madelyne

what if I forgot to do your laundry," she sneered, "it's not as if I haven't done plenty to help out in the past."

I wasn't prepared for a second onslaught, and stood there for a moment deciding whether to make peace or continue the war. "What's come over you?" I demanded, "Why are you shouting? If you don't want to do the laundry, then don't."

"Oh, that's right, act all self-righteous. Just remember, you're no better than me or any of my friends even though you think you are."

Shocked at the intensity of her anger, I hoped for an appropriate response that never materialized. We never argued like this, and I didn't know how to answer such a personal attack.

"You've always had so much, Nicole. When we were kids, you went to dance lessons while I delivered papers so I could buy clothes for school. Your parents sent you to camp for the summer; I worked at part-time jobs to help pay the bills. Even though your dad wasn't there for you, at least you had one." After making this announcement, she sailed out of the apartment with tears streaming down her cheeks.

Poor little Matthew watched her leave and turned to me, totally bewildered. "Aunt Maddie, have an owweee?" he asked.

"Yes, she has an owwee," I told him, "and mommy doesn't know how to fix it."

After the argument, our relationship was strained and she contemplated moving out. She left, but returned after a few days. We talked things over and I basically forgot about it. Things smoothed over until the next time the girls from her class came over for a meeting. This time I was lucky. Diane had come for a visit, and wasn't in the least put off by their intrusive questions. They listened to what she had to say, and were surprised at how conversant she was on the topic of abortion. I snickered under my breath when she shot down their every point leaving no opportunity to disagree.

It was a warm afternoon, and Diane and I were sitting outside watching the kids play. Diane's twins were almost four years older than Matthew, but the three of them had become inseparable. They were playing a game of chase and ran over to us out of breath.

"Drink," Matthew panted, gasping like a dying man on the desert.

"I'm thirsty," the twins sang in unison.

"Of course you are," Diane chuckled, "because monkey-see-monkey do." We led them into the kitchen for a cold drink and a snack. If we'd stayed outside just a little while longer maybe things wouldn't have gotten out of hand.

"I don't care what she says," the blonde bomber bellowed as we walked in the door, "how a woman chooses to dress is strictly her business. If a girl decides she doesn't want to wear a bra so what? It's no big deal! Bras were probably invented by a man who was terribly intimidated by the female anatomy. He wanted to hide the obvious by defeminizing a woman's body." She sounded so sanctimonious; it made me nauseous.

"You're half right," Diane commented as she sipped a glass of ice water as if conversations centered on women's underwear were common place. "The bra was patented by a man, but women actually invented them. Back in the Victorian Era women wore corsets that clearly defined the female breast. Even though the bra wasn't designed as we recognize it today until the latter part of the 1800's, women have been designing their own for years."

The little group looked at her in amazement. It wasn't that anybody was the slightest bit interested, but it was startling to find that the bra had such a long history. What was even weirder was that she knew so much about it.

"So, what's your point?" blondie asked bluntly. "Are you two going to join us and be liberated, or continue to accept your lowly, subservient station in life?"

This time it was Diane's turn to be amused. Setting her glass down, she managed to keep the twitching of her lips from turning into outright laughter. "I don't believe I'm lowly, and certainly not subservient--just setting the facts straight. A man did patent the bra; but he didn't actually invent it, that's all I'm saying."

"So, who was this guy anyway?" asked another one of the group.

"He was a French designer named Phippipe De Brassiere. He filed for a patent at the same time an American garment inventor did. Phippipe was granted the patent in 1930, and the name "Brassiere" was shortened to "bra" and that's my history lesson for today." Grinning at the shocked looks on their faces, she saluted them with her glass.

Maddie stared at Diane with a blank expression then turned to me, silently pleading for help. I became interested in a fly on the wall, and escaped her glance by staring intently as it crawled to the ceiling. Diane appeared to take some personal sense of pleasure in their obvious discomfort. Totally unconcerned, she seated herself comfortably on the sofa eyeing them over the rim of her glass.

"Did I say something wrong?" she asked innocently. "I certainly wouldn't want to offend anyone's delicate sensibilities by discussing such a.. ." she comically glanced both ways and then with a hand to the side of her mouth, whispered, "delicate subject."

"Diane, you're making fun of us," Maddie laughed. Her laughter alleviated the strained atmosphere.

"Is that true?" a girl with big blue eyes asked. "I mean, about the French inventor."

Instantly serious, Diane turned to study the girl for a moment before she answered. "It's one of those useless tidbits of information one picks up over time and to answer your question, yes, it's true. The man wasn't intimidated by women, but wanted to enhance that part of the female anatomy that's been admired by men for years. It was a good idea, and saved many women from having serious breast problems. I hope you've decided to keep yours on because women are more comfortable with one than without," she added softly.

"My, you're quite an expert on the subject aren't you? What other scrap of worthless information are you going to bestow upon us? Next, I suppose, you'll be telling us how to dress and what to think?" The Blonde Bomber stepped forward and plopped herself down on a floor pillow across from Diane. The gauntlet was thrown. Her eyes glittered in anxious anticipation to see if Diane would pick it up. We gathered in the cramped front room scrambling to find a place to sit. No one spoke, but threw nervous glances at the two women as tension between them prickled with electricity. I took a seat next to Diane offering a small semblance of support without really agreeing to anything. Maddie, torn between her new friends and the one's she'd known all her life, chose to sit on Diane's left. She might be confused, but would remain loyal to those she loved.

Calmly, Diane placed her glass on the coffee table and tucked up her legs to make herself comfortable. Her gaze swept over the little group and then came to rest on Blondie. My eyebrows lifted in surprise when she smiled warmly welcoming any questions the girl had.

"I don't think we've met," she said, "but my name is Diane Masters and those two," she nodded at the twins who were showing Matthew how to stuff a whole cookie in his mouth, "are my daughters." Extending her hand, she said earnestly, "I'm very pleased to meet you."

The girl didn't acknowledge Diane's offer of friendship, but glared with open hostility. "My name's Kathy and I am not here for a tea party. I'm a proud member of Women's Lib and a staunch supporter of pro-choice." Peering down her haughty nose, she dared anyone to try and top her.

Diane's eyes widened as if thoroughly impressed by the girl's honesty. "Wow, that's quite an introduction. I appreciate your openness."

"Yeah, whatever," Kathy glared. "Are you one of those pro-lifers or still undecided?"

"Oh I think I'm quite definite on the subject," Diane said with a smile. "I'm definitely certain I'm against abortion or any other means of destroying life." Audible gasps of disagreement went through the little group that made Maddie squirm in her seat. Obviously, Diane's answer was not the right one.

"Human life," Blondie scorned, "who's destroying human life? It isn't considered human until after it's born, everybody knows that. Life doesn't begin--really--until the ninth month when the fetus is expelled from the host and can survive without total dependence on her body." Nodding smugly, she folded her arms over her chest and sat back on the pillow with her back against the wall. All eyes were on Diane, waiting to pounce on her next response.

"Is that what they teach in school these days," she asked softly. She gazed at Kathy with pity in her eyes. "A child isn't an "it", a child is human from the moment of conception. There are pictures taken in the womb proving the stages of development. Have you seen them? Are you aware that a baby is almost fully formed by the eighth week of pregnancy? They have fingerprints by the third month and by the fifth, respond to sound. That means the child can hear the mother's voice and recognize it." Leaning forward, Diane was almost pleading with the girl to listen and understand. "In some rare instances, babies born prematurely in about the sixth month have survived. They are fully formed infants with an ability to respond to touch, sound, pain, hunger, and emotion just like you or I. How can you possibly believe a baby isn't human until after they are born? That's like saying people weren't 'human' from the beginning of our existence. We had to practice at it for a few thousand years, and be considered animals until some guy from the 19th century with a PH. D declared that we had evolved far enough to be called human. If that's what you believe, I feel very sorry for you because that isn't what God tells me."

"Well, you would say something like that," Blondie retorted. It's well known that people who profess to be Christians are against abortions just like they're against a woman making her own decisions. According to them," she turned to address her groupies, "women are slaves and men are the slave masters. In other words, they don't believe women should have rights."

"I'm afraid I'll have to correct you again," Diane interjected. "Women aren't to be treated poorly, but are to be respected as an equal in the home. We are to submit our will to our husband's and allow him to have authority over us by giving him our respect and devotion. There's a big difference between. . ."

"There's no difference that I can see," Blondie interrupted. "And we're not talking about marriage, we're talking about abortion and women's rights. It's all well and fine to sit in judgement of those seeking an abortion when you're happily married, and in a position to plan a family. But what about rape victims? What about their rights?"

Diane gazed into her eyes with tears in her own. "Oh," she said sadly, "I had no idea. Were you a victim? Is that why you're so angry?" Heads turned to Blondie with brows arched in shocked surprise. This was a juicy piece of news that no one had suspected.

"Of course not," she sputtered. An angry flush crept up her neck infusing her cheeks with red. "Are you trying to humiliate me or something?"

"No, please, I wouldn't do anything like that. I misunderstood and want to apologize." Diane's steady gaze never left Kathy's face. There was a look of intense sorrow in her eyes as she shifted her gaze to her children. "I'm sorry," she said simply.

"You haven't answered my question," Blondie reminded her. "What do you have to say about rape victims? Are they supposed to thank the attacker then forget about what happened? Are you one of those that believe the girl asked for it?" Her voice rose in pitch as she tried to pin Diane into a corner.

Sighing heavily, Diane's shoulders slumped for a moment as her attention was brought back from her musings to the present. "I don't believe victims of violent crimes should excuse their attacker, and wish laws were written to punish the attacker more severely. It's a travesty when a woman is assaulted, and even worse when it's a young girl or a child. A bad situation becomes worse if she becomes pregnant, but I still don't believe the baby should pay the price. I pray the unborn will be given a chance for life because I don't believe God makes mistakes. That innocent little life was placed here for a reason."

"Oh, isn't that just perfect," Kathy sneered. "The girl not only has to suffer having her body ravaged, but is supposed to raise the scumbag's kid, too?"

"I wouldn't expect the victim to raise the child unless she chose to. There's always adoption," Diane defended weakly.

"Adoption? That's always the answer you Pro-lifers give. Why should a girl allow herself to get big and fat for nine months, miss out on all the fun she could be having, just to have a strange man's kid?"

"It seems to me, in most instances, the girl has already had her fun and must face the consequence of her behavior. It isn't the child that made the decision to have casual sex, it was two consenting individuals that didn't have sense enough to use some form of contraception. Oh, don't get me wrong, I know there are cases where a girl is forced, but that's only one percent of all pregnancies. And, yes, I do believe that even rape victims should be encouraged to have their babies. They'll suffer enough without compounding their sense of guilt with the death of a child that even though conceived through a violent act, is still a part of them. Do you respect life?" she asked the group.

"Well of course, we do," snapped Blondie, "we're not heartless barbarians. We all want to be mothers someday."

"Then choose life," Diane pleaded, "your mother did."

"I've had it with you," Kathy exploded. "You've done nothing but antagonize me all afternoon and I'm not going to take it a minute longer." Coming to her feet, she threw the pillow at me and stomped out the door. Several girls followed, but two remained where they were. They were clearly confused by what they'd heard and looked at each other with puzzled expressions. Madelyne braved the question the rest of us were only thinking.

"But what about the impact on the mother's life; aren't her needs worth considering?"

Diane repeated her previous question. "Do you value life?"

"Of course, you know I do. I've always loved children, and want to have several someday."

"Then stop sitting on the fence. This is not an issue where you can say you value life, but only when convenient. You either do or you don't. The vast majority of all abortions are performed for social, not medical reasons. When we start making decisions on what child lives and what child dies, we're playing God and that isn't our place. Do you want the blood of an innocent baby on your hands? I certainly hope you don't, because once it's done, you'll never rid yourself of the burden of guilt. You'll carry it with you to the grave."

Chapter Fourteen

Kathy and her group stopped coming around after the debate with Diane. They moved their meetings to a local coffeehouse where the owners held the same philosophy and even advertised they were Pro-choice by placing a flier in an obscure corner of a window. I didn't miss them and found the grocery bill cut in half so it was just as well. Sooner or later I was bound to slip and call Kathy what my mind conjured up whenever her name was mentioned. I'm not sure she would appreciate being addressed as the Blonde Bomber or just plain Blondie, and I don't mean the singer.

Madelyne continued to see them, but some of their allure had dissipated even though she remained undecided on the issue of abortion. If I hadn't been certain about the issue before, I was after listening to Diane. She definitely scored a few points with me. A real friendship developed between us and she helped me get through some lonely nights when I might have chosen to go out just to hear the sound of another adult voice. She introduced me to Paul, her husband, and I decided that for a minister, he was okay. The three of us spent many evenings eating popcorn, drinking apple cider, and playing Monopoly. He had a passion for the game and loved playing banker. The two of them were a good influence, and helped me through some difficult times. Maddie joined us occasionally, but spent most of her free time either with Kathy and her group, or with Keith. He swooped back into her life, and filled her head with ideas that chilled me to the bone. I was in the kitchen with Matthew, baking a batch of cookies, when I overheard part of their conversation.

"This is your chance," he was saying, "and if you don't do it now, there may never be another one."

The Redemption of Madelyne

"But, how can I quit my job and return to modeling and especially when you're not even sure an agency will hire me? I have bills to pay, too, and can't expect Nicci to cover for me."

"Okay, so don't quit; at least not yet. Think of the opportunities, Madelyne. With your looks and your figure, you're a natural for this kind of photography."

"If you say so," she said hesitantly, "but who will take the pictures? I don't know any good photographers and what about clothes and make-up?"

"You let me worry about that. I've got it all worked out, and plan on taking a few pictures myself. As far as clothes, you won't need much and what's wrong with your makeup? Besides baby, no one's gonna' look at your clothes."

The hot cookie sheet almost dropped from my oven-mitted hand. I didn't like what he was insinuating, and hoped Maddie had sense enough to reject his offer. Unfortunately, she loved him, and would do anything to keep him happy. After he left, I tried to talk some sense into her, but it didn't seem to help.

"Mmmmmm, those smell good" she exclaimed when she came into the kitchen where Matthew and I were enjoying a glass of milk and a chocolate chip cookie. Taking a cup from the cupboard, she filled it with a little coffee and a lot of milk then helped herself. "I've been smelling these all evening and thought I'd drool all over myself before Keith left. I love chocolate chip and even more when I can dunk 'em." Giggling in the way she used to, she took a big bite and slurped her coffee noisily. Rolling her eyes, she let me know how much she enjoyed every bite. Matthew copied her example and slurped his milk, too.

"That's enough of that young man," I laughed. "You'll have milk all over you, the counter, and me." Grabbing a paper towel, I wiped chocolate from his face and washed up a few dribbles of milk. Matthew was three years old and quite the character. He loved showing off and imitated everything he saw. I had to be very careful about what I said or did because he picked up on things so quickly. It didn't take long to discover he'd learned something he shouldn't have because I'd get one of those phone calls from Diane. She'd call and chastise me for allowing him to hear foul language, and then warn me again about my responsibility as a parent. It was a constant learning experience, which sometimes left me red faced. I sent him off to play while we finished our coffee.

"Maddie, I don't mean to pry, but I couldn't help but overhear some of your conversation with Keith. You aren't seriously considering quitting your job are you?"

"Nope," she munched on a mouthful of cookie, "I'll hang onto my job until my modeling career takes off; if ever. After what happened back home, I'm not taking any chances. I want to be sure I have something to fall back on."

My mind scurried about trying to come up with a tactful way to ask a more personal question. I decided to follow her example and just be forthright. "You're not seriously going to model women's lingerie are you?"

"Sounds to me as if you overheard more than just a little bit," she said archly. Swallowing quickly, her eyes sparkled as her face brightened with excitement. "I've always wanted to be a model--you know that. If this is my last chance, I'll grab onto it with both hands. Keith says the lingerie market is hot right now and magazines are crying for models. Everything will be tastefully done. Even the most famous models are into lingerie right now," she explained. I can't wait to get started." Her beautiful, expressive eyes bored into mine. "Please be a little bit happy for me because I'm thrilled. Maybe it isn't too late for my dreams to come true."

"I want you to be happy," I concurred, "but don't want you to be used either. You're beautiful, and sometimes people take advantage of women like you."

"Now why would Keith try to use me? He loves me and is only looking out for my best interests. It isn't a secret that I've always wanted to model women's clothing, and he saw this as a chance for me to break into the field. I thought it was terribly sweet of him to find out so much about the industry." She had that dreamy look again and romantic thoughts of marriage were written all over her face.

"When will it get through to you? Keith doesn't want to get married and only comes around when he's been dumped by some other girl. Maddie, you're my best friend and one of the most intelligent women I know, but lately you haven't been using the brains God gave you. You're taking classes at the college, have a talent for accounting, and have a job where there's opportunity for you to advance. Why don't you take advantage of what's right in front of you?"

She laughed as she crossed her legs and flashed one of her spectacular smiles. "I am, and God, if there is one, has blessed me with a pretty face," she confessed. "I have an opportunity to use it, so I am."

"You're worth twice what Keith is," I told her, "and I hope it all works out just the way you want it to. But be prepared, and for heaven's sake, don't be taken in by a promise to have your face on the cover of some magazine because it may never happen."

"I know," she said sadly, "but if I don't give it a try, I'll always wonder. This may be the chance I've been waiting for."

Sighing, I shook my head impatiently. For somebody that was so smart, she certainly could be dumb.

For a while after our little talk, no mention was made of modeling and Keith disappeared--again. She was busy and finding it difficult to fit a job, two classes at the university, and several pro-choice meetings a week into seven twenty-four days. She seemed happy and since I was busy myself, little thought was put into the talk we'd had the night I baked cookies. Diane came over one Saturday to take Matthew and me on a picnic when, quite accidentally, I found out why Madelyne was so preoccupied.

"Are you ready," Diane asked as she hugged Matt on her way in the door. "It's a wonderful day and the kids will have a great time investigating all the tide pools. Maybe we'll find a few shells to add to your collection," she told the twins. The girls were dressed in Levis with matching jackets and looked like twin bookends. They were beautiful and adorable!

I was headed to the bedroom for Matthew's jacket when Maddie came rushing in the back. "Wait, don't go," she pleaded. I followed her to the kitchen wondering if there was a problem, and if so, what?

"We were just going to the beach for a few hours, do you want to come along," I asked.

"No, I can't," she said emphatically. "I was on my way to the rally to protest with the rest of the gang." She threw up her hands, "I chickened out."

"Well, I'm glad of that," Diane chuckled, "for a minute there you had me scared. I was afraid you were actually in support of that group of harridans you hang out with."

"Oh, I am," she defended, "I just don't want to go alone." She turned to me and begged, "Come with me. We haven't done anything together for quite a while, and I need you to come with me." With a sheepish expression, she traced the design in the carpet with her foot. The girl with all the answers was suddenly unsure of herself, and trying to hide the vivid shade of magenta infusing her cheeks. It was easy to talk-the-talk, but downright scary to go it alone.

"But, I promised Matthew a day at the beach. I can't very well change my mind at the last minute." It isn't that I didn't want to go, I did. I'd always been curious, but never had the nerve to attend a rally to find out why they protested in the first place.

Looking from one to the other, Diane decided that if Madelyne had someone to keep an eye on her, it would be less likely she'd get into trouble. "Look," she said, "there will be lots of days for you to go to the beach. Why don't you let Matthew go with us, while you go with Madelyne? That way we both win. You'll satisfy your curiosity, and I'll spend a glorious day having fun with the kids."

"Are you sure?"

"I wouldn't suggest it if I wasn't. Now scoot! We'll finish loading up, and be out of here in a jiffy."

"Okay," I agreed, "but one thing, Diane." She turned with brows raised in question. "How did you know I was curious about these rallies? I've never discussed it with you."

"Oh that," she laughed, "the expression on your face said it all. Now get going so we can get out of here."

Grabbing my purse and a jacket, I raced out the door behind Madelyne, and as an afterthought, stopped for my camera. Who knows, maybe there'd be something worth putting in a scrapbook. After kissing Matthew good-by, I ran to the car and within minutes was headed down the freeway to the university district. The rally was a big one, and took over several blocks along the boulevard.

"Are all these people here for the rally?" My head turned from one side to the other as I stared at the gathering crowd. I hadn't expected so many.

"I don't know where we're going to park." Maddie craned her neck to look behind us. There wasn't a parking place in sight. In fact, there was very little room to maneuver a bicycle let alone a car through the tight confines of the throng gathered on both sides of the street. We ended up parking far enough away that it was necessary to ride the bus back. We gathered from those seated near us that several busloads came in from nearby states to attend the rally. Many wanted to protest the U.S. Justice Department request to overturn Roe V Wade. A hearing about it had taken place recently. I had never heard of Thornburgh, and had no idea the case was going before the U.S. Supreme Court. A thrill of excitement went up my spine at the idea of being involved in something so totally American. Even though I was against abortion, it was nice to know so many had an interest in the political arena. Maddie's pro-choice group was in the throng somewhere, armed with pamphlets and placards, ready to support any clinic willing to provide abortions on demand.

"Are you ready to join the masses?" Maddie asked. We eyed the crowd speculatively and exchanged a glance of, its-now-or-never. Linking our arms together, we took the plunge and waded our way through the outer ring to squeeze into the center.

"Oh my—I don't believe this," Maddie breathed in shocked surprise. She had the advantage of height, while I had to peek over shoulders and around bodies to see what was going on. I stared in stunned silence. There in front of us was the Blonde Bomber and her sycophants. Each carried a poster boasting, "It's a Woman's Right to Choose. Support Pro-choice." They yelled and screamed at anyone who dared get past or through the tight protective circle formed around them. Anti-abortion foes stood silently around the perimeter with arms folded across their chests and wearing grim expressions. They also carried posters, which they waved in the air so those at a distance could see. There were pictures of aborted fetuses in various stages of development. My stomach rolled at the graphic images of the various tools and solutions used to extract the fetus from the womb. Those images will be burned in my mind forever. It was hard to believe anyone could see those pictures and still be an abortion advocate. I turned away and wretched when one of the posters was held right in front of me. Suddenly, I needed to hold my son just to feel his warm little body against mine. The urge to hold him, to assure myself that he was okay, was so great I started to cry; gasping for air between sobs. The rally with all the people, the noise, and activity ceased to be fun. I wanted nothing more than to go home and erase all of it from my mind. When I turned to find Madelyne, icy goosebumps skittered up my arms. They settled at the top of my head where prickles of dread sent nervous spasms along the muscles to my jaw. Pain tingled in my legs, the kind you get when you hit your funny bone, only I wasn't laughing.

"Maddie," I shouted over the tumult, "are you okay?" Grabbing her arm to pull her away, she didn't budge. She was rooted to the spot with eyes wide in horror--her skin a deathly shade of pale. When I followed the path of her gaze, my heart pounded painfully in my chest. I took an involuntary step backward. Coming toward us was an old man in a wheelchair with scraggly white hair and an unkempt beard. Stains blackened his chin and shirtfront; his bloodshot eyes honed in on Madelyne. His chair clicked ominously as it rolled along the sidewalk forcing bystanders to get out of his way.

"She's a worshiper of Molech," he screamed as he barreled toward us with a gnarled finger pointed at Maddie. "Look at her. She wears the blood of innocence upon her fingers," he chanted. No one tried to stop his advance and we were quickly surrounded by the curious. It was déjà vu; we'd been through this before. I looked around at the sea of faces hoping to find an offer of help, but we had become the sideshow they had come to see.

"I've seen you before," he shouted, "at another altar of Molech. Baby-killer," he screamed accusingly. Spittle flew from his mouth and dripped off his chin as he continued his tirade. Terror blinded me; my heart thundered in my chest. Gripping Maddie's arm, I edged away, but a wall of onlookers barred the exit.

The old man poked her in the side and grinned malevolently. "May you bear the mark of Satan and his minion Molech if you sacrifice the life inside of you." Poking her again, he laughed, showing blackened teeth and rotting gums. Maddie's eyes rolled back in her head as she collapsed in a dead faint.

"Help me," I screamed. Easing her to the sidewalk, I looked for someone willing to help. Kathy and her cohorts fought their way through the crowd and thankfully, helped get Maddie back on her feet. The old man disappeared just as he had before.

"What happened?" Kathy asked as she bathed Maddie's forehead with a damp paper towel. "Did she get too warm or something."

"I don't think so. There was this old man and he said horrible things, and we were so scared, and..." I broke down and to my embarrassment, began to cry. Kathy wrapped her arms around me to shield us from prying eyes.

"It's okay, Madelyne will be fine. She was just overwhelmed by it all, and fainted from the heat. You're babes in the woods when it comes to this sort of thing so I'm not surprised. You have to be careful in a crowd like this. Don't let yourselves become targets for every weirdo that comes out of the woodwork," she admonished. "Are you better?" she asked as she dabbed at my eyes with a tissue. "Can you get to your feet?" Nodding, I helped Madelyne to Kathy's car. She drove us home while one of her friends followed in Maddie's car. I appreciated the concern, but couldn't change my opinion about them. It was hard to like someone that spoke with a sneer, and looked down their nose on the world.

Home again, we took Madelyne to her room and made her lay down. She was pale and her eyes unfocused. When I took her a glass of water, she grabbed my arm as if afraid to be left alone. "How did he know?" she asked. "How did that old man know?"

"What are you talking about--what could he possibly know? He was a lunatic that scared us both half to death and that's all. Forget about it and try to get some rest. We'll be right outside if you need anything." Patting her shoulder, I turned off the light and left the room. Thankfully, it was almost time for Diane to bring Matthew home. I needed to talk to her.

"She'll be fine," Kathy assured me as she helped herself to a cookie from the cookie jar. "I've seen this happen before, in fact, the first rally Sherrie attended she threw up all over the car on the way home."

Sherrie smiled sheepishly, but threw Kathy a look of warning. "I wouldn't have gotten sick if you'd left when I asked. If you remember correctly, it was hotter than blazes and I was six weeks pregnant."

My head swiveled in Sherrie's direction. "You have a baby?" I asked, surprised that she volunteered such information.

"Not anymore," she said sarcastically. "I wasn't out of high school yet, and my parents would have killed me if they'd known. It was best for everyone that I had an abortion." A pensive expressive clouded her face for a moment, as if she were having second thoughts. "Yeah, it was for the best," she added with a nod. No wonder she was always the first to hold Matthew and loved playing with Diane's girls; she missed the child she should have had.

Standing in the kitchen with a dishtowel in my hand, I looked around at the commonplace trying to absorb this startling piece of information. Blinking furiously, my vision blurred as their voices drifted to me through the thick fog of my thoughts, and for that fraction of time, I saw and felt Sherrie's sense of loss.

"I'm sorry--I never suspected you carried such a burden," I whispered. Our eyes met for an instant as we shared a brief moment of culpability. Her face softened, and then hardened as she pushed the memory back into some obscure corner of her mind.

"It wasn't anything life-shattering. It was over and done with three years ago," she said casually. Waving away further discussion with a peremptory gesture, she added, "It was no big deal and it hardly bothers me at all. . .really." I wanted to hug her, or something to let her know I understood what she wasn't able to express, but the moment passed.

"Do you have anything cold to drink?" she asked with a brittle smile on her lips. Strolling into the kitchen, her features turned stony. It would be a very long time before anyone else would get a glimpse into her heart.

Diane pulled up and came into the kitchen with her arms full. Carrying a bag of their leftover lunch on one arm and Matthew on the other, the girls were left to bring up the rear. The four of them made quite a racket as they trooped in singing the chorus to another song she'd taught them. Even though they sang off key and at such a terrific volume it struck against the ears in ear-shattering, discordant harmony, it was music to my ears.

"Mommy," Matthew said excitedly as he pulled a small shell from his pocket, "see. . .see." I wanted to grab him in my arms and hold him there forever. I fought the impulse because there was no sense in alarming him. Kneeling down to admire each of the treasures he so proudly displayed, I loved him as I never had before. I couldn't imagine life without him, and almost cried when he wrapped his little arms around my neck to plant a wet kiss on my cheek. "I 'ove you," he sang. Hugging him tightly, I admired his brown wavy hair, dark eyes, and impish grin. He was becoming his own person and thank God, was kinder and more loving than either of his parents.

"Really?" Diane laughed, "if you missed him that much, you should have come along. We were only gone a few hours," she reminded. Emptying sand from each of the girls' shoes, she studied our faces for a moment. "Something's wrong, isn't it? That's why you're all acting so strange, something's happened to someone?" Glancing around, she took a quick inventory, putting a name to the face of each girl. "Maddie," she said as her eyes flew from one to the other of us, "where's Madelyne? Is she alright?"

"She's fine," Kathy said coolly. "But," she jabbed a finger toward me, "Nicole on the other hand, has been acting like somebody died ever since we left the rally."

"Well, somebody did, didn't they?" Diane asked pointedly. Kathy ignored the incrimination and feigning ignorance, continued her explanation.

"Madelyne fainted and Nicci thinks something's wrong with her."

"Maddie fainted?" Diane asked incredulously. "Maddie never faints and she's not the least bit squeamish. Where is she? Did someone take her to a doctor?" Opening the bedroom door, she breathed a sigh of relief when she found Madelyne asleep in her own bed. Closing the door gently, she put a finger to her lips. Motioning us into the front room, she handed each of the kids a cookie before sending them out to play. From the set of her jaw, she was terribly disturbed about something-- someone was in deep trouble. "Okay," she stated when she joined us, "what happened and why are you looking so guilty?" She faced the lot of us with hands on her hips while one foot tapped the floor impatiently.

"It was awful," I blurted out. "Maddie wasn't overcome with heat; it was that old man. Oh Diane," I wailed, "I had no idea and she didn't either."

"What old man? I'm confused. You went to an abortion rally and met an old man? Why would that upset Maddie?"

"I think we'd better all sit down because there's a lot that needs to be explained." I said. "It was more than just the old guy, it was because we'd seen him before and he singled Madelyne out then, too."

"Wait," Diane ordered, "start from the beginning because you lost me. How did the man know you and why would he single out Maddie?" We made ourselves comfortable, but I found it impossible to sit so remained standing. It was hard to appear calm and unruffled when my mind was busy conjuring up creepy images of old men. I could still hear the clicking wheels of the wheelchair and see the white wisps of his hair as it floated about his head as if electrified. The entire afternoon had been something out of a horror movie and I, admittedly, was frightened.

"We ran into him once before and quite by accident," I explained. "It was three or four years ago while we were Christmas shopping. We couldn't find a parking space so had to park a long way from the mall and, . . ." Everything came rushing out and ran together as I relived the memory of our first meeting with the old man. Diane frowned as she tried to follow the storyline. "Anyway," I continued, "we turned the corner and there he was. A bunch of people were picketing an abortion clinic that had just opened its doors, and he was one of them. He chased us down the sidewalk screaming about somebody named Molech. He said the doctor and all women who went into the clinic worshiped this Molech guy. He poked Maddie in the hip and told her not to be like the others. Today, there he was again, and he did the same thing. Only this time he accused Maddie of worshipping Molech and told her she was unclean. That's when she fainted," I explained, gasping to catch my breath. During the entire monologue, Diane remained silent, listening with eyes narrowed in thought; watching me pace the floor. The only change in her expression came when the name Molech was mentioned.

"Molech," she questioned, "are you sure that's what he said?"

"Quite sure," I said. "Who is this guy Molech and what does he have to do with anything?" I quit pacing, but held my arms across my chest protectively. Maddie might have been the one accused, but I felt threatened.

"Boy, you sure are worked up over nothing," Kathy interrupted. "He was a misguided old fart looking for attention. It's just like I told you before, the two of you looked like a good mark so you became his

The Redemption of Madelyne

target. I doubt that he remembered what you looked like five minutes after it happened." She shook her head in disgust that we were so naïve.

"But, he did recognize us. Don't ask me how I know, I just know. He told her he'd seen her before and that she was going to burn forever for her sins." Turning to Diane, I demanded, "Who or what is Molech? Do you know?"

"I know," she assured me, "but I'm not sure you want to hear the answer."

"Maybe she doesn't, but I do," Madelyne's soft voice interjected. "It was the most frightening thing I've ever experienced, and I need to know what he was talking about."

"Maddie," Sherrie demanded, "why are you out of bed? After what you went through today, the last thing you need is more stress." She tried to lead Madelyne back to bed, but she refused with a slight shake of her head. A glint of determination lit her eyes.

"I don't need to go to bed and the last thing I want is rest," she explained gently. Patting Sherrie's shoulder, she took a step forward and encouraged Diane to continue. "I'm not going to hide or be ignorant like an ostrich with its head in the sand. Please, help me to understand what he meant."

"If you're sure, then I'll do my best. Do you have a Bible?"

"A Bible?" Kathy sneered. "Now we're going to have a Bible study? Next, I suppose, we'll be having Sunday school complete with hymns and a preacher. For heaven's sake, just answer the question and be done with it."

"I am," she said coolly, "and it is for "Heaven's" sake, that I need a Bible. The answers are all within its covers."

"I have one," I volunteered, "but it will take a few minutes to find it. It's the same one you gave me." Rushing to my bedroom to search through drawers and closet, I found it buried in the back of my sweater drawer, right where I'd left it. When Diane took it from my hands, a look of reverence came over her face as her hands slid over the leather cover. A niggle of guilt stabbed my conscious that her gift hadn't been more appreciated.

"Let's see," she mumbled, "there's several references made to Molech all through the scriptures." Finally settling on one, she pointed at the page triumphantly, "Here it is—*Leviticus and the eighteenth chapter.* It says, *[Do not give any of your children as a sacrifice to Molech, for you must not profane the name of your God. I am the LORD.]* and again in Leviticus: *[I myself will turn against them and cut them off from the community, because they have defiled my sanctuary and profaned my holy name by giving their children to Molech.] Le 20:3*

We stared at her blankly, unable to make a connection. "Don't you get it," she asked, "Molech was a god worshipped in Biblical times by followers of the goddess Ashtoreth and the god Baal. People sacrificed their children to Molech by burning them on the altars or embedding their bodies, while still alive, in the walls of their homes. They believed Molech required a living sacrifice and thrived on the blood of innocent children." Her eyes filled with sorrow as her words wove images of the gruesome deaths of children in our minds.

"Oh please," Kathy jeered, "what does something written several thousand years ago have to do with today? Besides, you can't take it literally, because the Bible has many interpretations. And who seriously believes that book is the actual word of some god fabricated to satisfy some inner need to worship?"

We looked to Diane as our authority on the issue to see if she could dispute Kathy's accusation. "I'm not asking you to believe anything more than what your heart tells you is right. There are millions of people that believe and know through faith that the *Holy Bible* is the word of *God* handed down to man."

"It would figure that someone like yourself would believe in fairy tales. After all, you're a minister's wife, so you almost have to," she retorted. Such a lame response lowered her stature among her followers and she knew it. Casting a look at Diane that could have soured cottage cheese, Kathy's lips clamped together in obvious anger. She waited for an opportunity to turn the tide by appealing to our common sense. There were six of us, ignorant in the teachings of the Bible, and hanging expectantly on Diane's every word.

"There are many that believe the worship of Molech has been resurrected, but in a different form than the people of ancient times. Today we sacrifice our babies on an examination table instead of an altar, but with same result. The child is violently exterminated and all sign of their short existence destroyed."

Sherrie's cheeks paled, and her gaze dropped to the floor. Maddie put an arm around her shoulder and tried to comfort the girl, but she refused the gesture.

"What you're saying, then, is that abortion is an act of sacrificing our unborn to some unseen god that is a follower of Satan. Satan's goal is to destroy the innocent and to rid the earth of all good things." Sherrie wasn't asking a question, but making a statement, as if she knew.

Diane turned to her in surprise, "How did you make the connection? I never mentioned Satan or related one to the other."

"You didn't have to," she said. "My father is a Baptist minister, and I've listened to him preach all my life. Everything is sinful in his eyes and I quit hearing him years ago. I didn't realize how much I remembered until a moment ago. How can I ever find forgiveness for what I've done?" Wiping a tear from her cheek, she looked away, lost in the turbulence of her own thoughts.

"It'll be okay," Maddie told her as she gave her a sisterly hug. "We love you--and now you have to learn to love yourself by forgiving something done when you were still a kid."

Kathy smirked, "I can't believe you're listening to this. I don't know what pipe you've been smokin', but I've never heard of Molech before today and I doubt that anybody else has either. You're a fraud Diane Masters and these girls need to know it. What do you know of life? What makes you the expert? You're the daughter of a minister, grew up to marry a minister, and most of your life have lived with the protection of the church all around you. It's easy to sit here and preach at us when you've never experienced what we live on a daily basis. Life is crap, Diane, and stuff happens. If Sherrie had told her parents about the pregnancy, they would have thrown her out, and then where would she be? Well, answer me, Miss Know-It-All—where would she be now?"

"I'm not a prophet," Diane said, "but maybe she'd be better off than she is now. A person would have to be blind not to see the pain she lives with every day of her life. And how do you know her parents would have thrown her out? Maybe, if she had told them, her father would have forgiven her and been the pillar of strength she needed."

"Hah, fat chance. You really live in fantasyland if you believe that."

"I believe all things are possible with God," Diane defended, "because He is the foundation of faith and through Him, all things are possible."

"There you go again, using the Bible to excuse bad behavior. *If you repent of your sins, God is just to forgive us our sins*," she quoted.

"How did you know that line of scripture?" Diane asked, surprise evident in her tone. I had never heard it before, but knew as soon as she repeated it that it had to be scriptural. How indeed? Why didn't she believe what she obviously knew so well?

"You're not the only one to attend Sunday school," she retorted. "My mother sent me out the door every Sunday morning so she could entertain the latest boyfriend. It was a ritual at our house until I got old enough to know how pointless it was. Then I started planning my weekends elsewhere."

"I'm sorry things were so horrible for you," Diane sympathized.

"I never said it was horrible, it was a fact of life. I grew up fast and learned early what dear mommy was doing behind those closed doors, and in the backseat of one of her boyfriend's cars. It wasn't a memorable experience, and for years I wondered what was so exciting about the act of sex that kept people so riled up."

"Before, you denied being raped," Sherrie accused.

"I wasn't, but what about all the girls that have? Hey," she brightened, "maybe Miss-Know-It-All can enlighten us. What do you have to say about that?"

"I know it's against God and that it can be forgiven."

"I'm sure that's what all victims need to hear. First we tell them we're sorry they were abused, then we're sorry they got pregnant, but warn them to forgive their attacker because the Bible says so. Is that what you believe?" Snickering, she turned to those next to her to share a laugh. She continued to badger Diane, making fun of her and her beliefs until Maddie stepped in.

"Don't say anything more, I think we get the picture. Diane's entitled to her own beliefs just as you are, but don't belittle her just to make yourself look larger than life because right at this moment, you look pretty small."

"You're a fine one to be telling me what to say and when. What is it with you people? You want to tell the world how to live, but have no

The Redemption of Madelyne

answers for those poor souls that have been used purely for the pleasure of another. When you have an answer for them, let me know, because your words are useless until you can say something to that will wipe away the pain. What are you going to tell the girl that's been ravaged by an animal that calls himself a man and is now pregnant by him? Well, tell me," she shouted, "what are you going to say?"

Kathy's little speech got our attention and we glanced sheepishly at one another. It was a good question and not one of us had an answer. We turned to Diane, hoping she had a good comeback. She remained silent, staring at all of us as if she didn't know who we were. Then, her face began to breakup, moaning as if in deep pain. Startled, Maddie moved quickly to her side and wrapped her arms around her.

"Are you okay? Di, tell me what's wrong." For several minutes, Diane struggled to regain her composure. Choking back tears, she asked, "Where are my girls? Are they still outside?"

"They're in the bedroom watching cartoons with Matthew," I told her. She nodded and then stood facing Kathy. If any of us hoped for a confrontation between the two women, we were sadly disappointed. Diane's compassionate expression took in all of us as she gazed about the room.

"You have accused me of not knowing," she choked. "Well, I do know." Tears ran down her face in a river soaking the front of her blouse. None of us moved a muscle, we needed to hear whatever she had to say. "Rape is the most horrendous assault a woman can go through, and I ought to know because it happened to me." Her head dropped to her chest and her voice faded to a whisper. At her confession, startled gasps circled the room. Maddie moved to go to her, but I held her back.

"I was seventeen and a senior in high school. My mother warned me to come home early, but research for a term paper I was writing took longer than I thought. It was past nine when I left the library. I remember the song I was humming, and can still feel the soft evening breeze on my cheeks. A car pulled up alongside me and the guy asked if I needed a ride. I laughed and told him I didn't because I was already flying. I waved and turned to follow a shortcut through the park without looking back to see where he went. If I had, maybe I would have gotten away. Before I could react, there was running footsteps behind me before I was knocked off my feet. He clamped a hand over my mouth and dragged me into the bushes. I tried to fight him off, but he was so much heavier and his hands smelled like grease and I started to get sick. He hit me over and over again until I stopped moving."

I had never seen such a horrified expression on anyone before. Tears ran down my cheeks in sympathy. Maddie's eyes brimmed over and Sherrie stared at Diane in sympathy.

"Don't say any more," Kathy apologized, "I'm sorry, I really am." Shaking her head, her arrogance disappeared, her expression a study in misery. She couldn't meet Diane's haunted eyes.

"There's more," Diane told her, "and you're going to hear it so you know. Then, maybe you'll understand and will tell others. She continued even though Kathy shook her head.

"When he finished with me, he urinated on my dress and told me it was about time a good Christian girl learned how to be a woman and that my husband would thank him someday. I couldn't see him clearly because both eyes were swollen shut, but I recognized the voice. . .and if I ever hear it again, I won't be afraid to fight and do everything in my power to see him behind bars."

"I remember," Maddie interrupted, "your parents said you'd been in an accident. Nicci and I tried to come see you, but they wouldn't let us."

"That's right," I agreed, "you were out of school for a couple weeks and then came back and then was gone again. No one saw you for almost a year. We always wondered where you went because your parents didn't leave town."

"And there were bruises on your arms and one eye was covered with a bandage," remembered Maddie.

"You're both right," she said. Park security found me and rushed me to the hospital. I was beaten and hurt so badly that no one was allowed in to see me until some of the marks on my body healed. No medicine could mend the scars to my soul. Only God could do that! I went back to school and tried to put the entire thing behind me and then I discovered that I was pregnant. My parents sent me to live with my grandparents until the babies were born."

"Babies," I asked, "don't you mean baby?"

"No," she said sadly, "I meant what I said. The twins biological father is a rapist, but their father is my husband Paul. He helped me recover and showed me in God's word that hatred scars the soul while forgiveness heals. My girls have been such a gift," she said softly, "I like to think of them as God's way of giving back what I lost. They bless me every day with their love, their innocence, and sense of wonder."

"Aren't you afraid they may follow in the footsteps of their natural father?" someone asked.

"My daughters have been sanctified, given to *God* and I have faith that if we raise them to be moral and *God-fearing*, they will never know how they were conceived. I hope they never know such ugliness. *God* taught me to forgive and not take out my anger on the helpless life growing within me. It says in the book of Psalms:

For Thou didst form my inward parts; Thou didst weave me in my mother's womb. I will give thanks to thee, for I am fearfully and wonderfully made; wonderful are Thy works, and my soul knows it very well. My frame was not hidden from Thee, when I was made in secret, and skillfully wrought in the depths of the earth.

Life comes from God and He does not make mistakes. He knew us before we were born and knows every bone, fragment of muscle, and drop of blood composing our bodies. It isn't our right to decide who should live and who should die, and babies shouldn't pay the price for our sins. They are deserving of the life God gave them. Activists will fight to save a tree, or a field mouse, or an owl, or some recently discovered insect, all in the name of preservation, but no one is willing to provide the same protection to the weakest among us. God placed them in our care and we'll pay the price for ignoring their desperate cries. I know this is hard to hear, but we are to love our children and raise them up in the fear of the Lord. Uphold life and place great value upon it or we are lower than the animals because even they love their own."

"I can't argue with anything you've said, but what about the girl who isn't able to take care of a baby? Who is more responsible? Her or the father?" Kathy was clearly disturbed by Diane's confession, and felt great remorse for goading her so relentlessly.

"The responsibility belongs to us all. Why aren't we raising our daughters to be better decision makers and our sons to think with clear minds and not be led by hormones? We need to challenge doctors who perform abortions to come forward and tell the truth about what actually happens to the developing embryo when an abortion is performed. Will they confess that the child is literally severed limb from limb? Will they tell about the babies that are horribly poisoned with saline solutions? Will they dare to admit the child feels the pain and may even know they are dying? Will medical files finally reveal the result of abortion on the mothers? Every single day I praise God for my children and for my Christian parents. They were supportive, and helped me through a devastating time in my life. It hasn't been perfect, and it isn't forgotten. When the nightmares begin, and I relive that horrible night of my senior year, I know God is with me. He took that experience and turned it into something good. I have been blessed, and pray that if you haven't made up your mind, that God will make it up for you."

Chapter Fifteen

Diane's passionate plea touched us all, and even though Kathy didn't agree, she learned to respect her beliefs. We didn't hear much from Kathy for quite a while, and Diane was upset when she read an article in the paper about her. Kathy had become the spokesperson for a Pro-choice women's group. They planned to lobby congress for funds to pay the cost of abortions for women who couldn't afford one otherwise.

"It makes little sense because a prescription for birth control and a little foresight is a whole lot cheaper. People plan what they're going to wear, what they're going to eat, and how they're going to spend their day, but can't seem to plan for their own future. Advisors need to stress self-respect and abstention from sexual activity until young people are ready for the responsibility of a family. Girls must be discouraged from indulging in casual relationships that lower self-esteem and put their health at-risk," I declared after reading the same article.

"It isn't that easy—and many women don't know any better. They have no respect for themselves or their bodies and give sexual favors away as freely as water. It's what they've learned from TV, magazines, and their peers. We've got to enter their world in order to show them a different way of life," Diane responded.

"But what about the women who have another kid year after year just so they can stay on welfare?" I challenged. I'd just returned from the grocery store and was still fuming about somebody I'd seen there. It was payday and after work I'd rushed to the grocery store to pick up a few items for dinner. Since I was running late, I kept my purchases to a minimum in order to get through the "ten items or less" check-out. But, a young woman squeezed in a head of me. She had three kids with one on the way and a cart full of chips, soda pop, and candy. When the cashier gave the total, the woman pulled out a wad of coupons and a government credit card to pay for her purchases. I was disgusted and couldn't wait to tell Diane all about it. She listened, but didn't seem as upset as I wanted her to be.

"There but for the grace of God go I," she quoted. "That woman could have been any one of us, and I'm sure she didn't plan to raise a family on food stamps. You don't know her story and therefore you can't judge."

"But, she was pregnant," I protested. Diane's eyes widened and then narrowed. She had a way of putting a person in their place without saying a word.

"Okay, she was pregnant, Praise God! Were her children happy?"

"Well, yeah, they seemed to be."

"Were they clean? Were they well fed?"

"I suppose so." All of a sudden I didn't feel quite so self-righteous, in fact, my face warmed with embarrassment as I pictured the smile on the woman's face. She hadn't appeared wanton or cheap, and I remembered the hand placed at the small of her spine as she lifted the smallest of her brood. Her back hurt and her feet, too, probably, and there were lines of fatigue around her eyes. I hadn't even slowed down when driving past them as they walked away from the store.

"I get the point," I admitted "and promise not to jump to conclusions if it ever happens again."

"And it will, so I'll hold you to your promise." Walking me to the parking lot, she held onto Matthew while I stowed his things in the back. "I know you've cleaned up your act since our little talk a few months ago, but never forget your own weaknesses. You aren't above making mistakes and will many times in the future. Don't judge others for the same failures experienced in your life."

"I was married when Matthew was born and he has a father," I denied.

"That isn't what I was referring to," she said gently, "I meant that people, as a whole, will judge others severely for the same thing they themselves have done or thought about doing. Every day I remind myself that in God's eyes sin is sin, and not one thing we do is any worse than the other."

"I don't agree. I'm not the only one who believes babies shouldn't be brought up to live in poverty."

"Should they be aborted to save them from such a horrible life?"

"Well no, of course not, but. . ."

"Need I remind you that many great and talented people have rose above the poverty of their past to accomplish great and wondrous things to benefit mankind."

"You know what I mean, Diane. Women should be more careful, take precautions and. well...."

"I know what you said, but I'm not sure that's what you mean. Anyone can make a mistake. No one should be judged and labeled their entire life for making a poor decision. For some of us, that's how we learn," she added. "Forgiveness has to come from somewhere or we rob the soul of hope. Jesus forgives, and we must follow His example."

Before getting into the car, I turned to study her smiling expression. She always looked so serene, as if nothing in the world ever bothered her. I almost envied her peace of mind wishing to be more like her. "How did you get so wise?" I asked. Hugging her impulsively, I hopped in and turned the ignition.

"Wait," she cried as she waved me back, "Thanksgiving is next week, what are your plans?"

"Don't know yet," I shrugged, "Maddie and I haven't discussed it. Last year we stayed in town and ate at a restaurant, but this year I'd like to do something homier."

"My idea exactly," she laughed, "see if you can talk her into having dinner with us. We've invited a crowd and may need help with the clean-up." When I drove away, she stuck out her tongue and made a funny face. I caught a glimpse of her in my rear view mirror and laughed along with Matthew at how silly she looked. I was glad she was my friend.

Pulling into the driveway, I unbuckled Matthew and ran into the house to avoid getting soaked. A real downpour plunged the temperature to just above freezing--winter had arrived after all. Inside, I fumbled with the light switch so I could see to remove our jackets and then went to find Maddie. She was seated on the couch in the front room with all the lights off staring at a blank TV screen. Ever since the confrontation between Diane and Kathy, she remained subdued. She refused to see a doctor and I worried about her. The light in her eyes was gone, and there were gaunt hollows in her cheeks.

"Why are you sitting in the dark?" I asked. Snapping on a lamp, I told her about my day being sure to include Diane's invitation for Thanksgiving. She shrugged her shoulders hugging her knees to her chest.

"I don't care. Whatever you want to do is fine. I'm not feeling very thankful, but will go with you if that's what you decide."

"Have you heard from Keith, lately?" Any time I asked about him, I had to be careful. If she thought my questions were too personal or the least bit cutting, she became angry and wouldn't speak to me for days.

"No, and I can't understand why," she wailed. "Everything between us seemed great when he left."

"Well, maybe he'll call tomorrow." I tried to be encouraging, but wasn't as good at it as she was. She had been such a pillar of strength for me over the years and I wanted to be the same for her. I didn't understand the change. There was a lot to learn if I was ever to be as good a friend to Maddie as she had been to me.

Later in the evening, we made a big bowl of popcorn, a pitcher of sweet tea, and turned the TV to a movie. The movie was one we'd seen before so in between mouthfuls of buttery popcorn, we talked about how our lives had changed since moving to the city.

"Are you sorry we came or would you like to go home again?" I asked.

"I could never live in a small town again and wouldn't consider moving back. Everything is limited there, and the nearest shopping mall is fifty miles away. Besides, there are too many painful memories," she assured me. "What about you?"

"Not sure—maybe—if things were different."

"That's the problem, things don't change. There's another major difference between us. You're always hoping things will get better, while I'm sure they won't."

"But, you didn't used to think that way," I protested. "What happened to your sunny outlook? You had all the answers, you seemed so sure of yourself, and now..." I shrugged, allowing her to draw her own conclusion. "I'm worried about you, Maddie. You're my best friend and I know something is seriously wrong. Maybe you need a physical or maybe you need a shrink, but you've got to snap out of this mood you're in."

She glanced at me for a moment and then turned her attention back to the TV. "Yeah," she mumbled, "maybe I will see a shrink. Maybe he can explain why I have a brother in this town that never comes to see me or why my mother never calls."

"Have you called them?" I asked. "I know you phoned your brother once and left a message, but did you ever call back?"

"Nope. What would be the point? He told me there was little time in his busy schedule to entertain little sisters and that he didn't need a relationship with someone he hardly knows." My heart ached for her. Why did he refuse to acknowledge her existence?

"Look," I said, "even though he might feel that way doesn't mean everyone does. We love you and want you with us for as long as possible." She flashed a feeble smile that didn't quite reach her eyes.

"Can I ask a question?" At her nod of encouragement, I took a deep breath and plunged in. "A couple of months ago, we had an argument about the laundry."

She gave a blank look as she tried to remember. "What argument? Lately, I can't remember yesterday let alone two months ago. Why were we arguing and what's the big deal? We've had lots of arguments."

"Why we were arguing is unimportant, it's what you said. You talked about when we were kids and things you had to do that I didn't."

"Oh, that," she said with a gesture of indifference.

"Please," I begged, "at least give me a chance to defend myself."

"Well," she began, "things were different between us from the very start. Even in first grade, it was obvious your world was in complete contrast to my own. Your mother drove you to school and I walked. You went to dance class and hated it, while I envied your position and would have done anything to change places even for a day. Back then, I thought your parents were perfect. Now I know better, but wish your good luck would rub off on me. I thought they really cared when they ran your life for you. It wasn't until I was in junior high that it dawned on me how controlling they were. You always had so much and never went without. Your parents made sure you looked perfect, and was the ideal example of their prosperity and social standing. Even though your father wasn't around much, at least you knew who he was. I've never met mine! He divorced my mom before I was old enough to remember what he looked like."

"I'm sorry, I never knew you felt like this because you never said anything before."

"Well, now I have and let's change the subject. We can't change the past, but can do the best we know how to make the future better. That's why I want to be a model. I want to show the world I'm more than I was, and who knows, maybe my father will see my photographs and want to meet me someday."

No wonder she was so driven to be the best--to find acceptance. She had experienced so much rejection in her life. Tears of compassion stung my eyes and for the first time I was glad for the home my parents had provided me. All of a sudden, an idea formed in my mind. Maybe what she needed was a change of pace.

"Let's go home for Thanksgiving. We can leave Wednesday after work and be there before midnight. Even if we don't go to our respective homes, we can find a motel, look up some of our old friends, and eat a grand dinner at our favorite restaurant. It'll be fun!"

A sparkle lit her eyes as she thought over the suggestion. "Do you think my mom would want to see me?"

"We'll never know until we try. I don't know about you, but I'm calling home first thing in the morning. If my mother isn't receptive, I'll make arrangements for a motel. I wouldn't want to change your mind or anything, but wouldn't it be fun to go home for a few days? We can show off and tell everybody how well we're doing." Crossing my eyes, fingers, and toes, my attempted sarcasm wasn't lost on her sense of humor. She laughed and nodded her head in agreement.

"Yeah, for two wealthy young ladies, we sure live frugally." She looked around our tiny living quarters and laughed aloud. The musical sound was good to hear.

"Can we afford a motel room, our eats, and everything?" she asked with a look of alarm.

"I don't think we can afford not to and besides, it's about time Matthew met his grandparents. Don't you agree?"

We glanced toward the little body bundled in a blanket and asleep in his favorite chair. His baby face was becoming more grown-up--he was maturing faster than I could keep up. If he didn't meet the grandparents soon, it would be hard for him to form any kind of attachment.

The following morning, Maddie was up before me and on the phone when I wandered into the kitchen. A smile spread across her face as she spoke to her mother. It was obvious she was welcome to come home and the sooner the better.

"Can you believe it?" she asked when she ended the call. "Mom was actually glad to hear from me. She planned on coming to Seattle to find me if she didn't hear from me soon. But, the best news of all is she quit drinking. She says there hasn't been an ounce of alcohol in the house for over six months. It was hard to hang up because she started crying when she heard my voice." Grabbing Matthew, she tossed him in the air and spun him around. Laughing, she flashed one of her spectacular smiles, "We're going home," she said as she gave him a big bear hug.

Feeling confident, I dialed my parent's number with trembling fingers. After two years of silence I wondered if they would be receptive. We hadn't parted on the best of terms, and my father's final words rang in my ears as I waited for the call to go through. Would my mother be out of bed yet?

"Hello," a cheery voice said.

"Um, hi Mom. Is that you?" For a minute there I thought I'd misdialed because the voice wasn't familiar.

"Nicci," the voice screeched. "Nicci, oh Praise God, you finally called. Are you all right? Is Matthew okay? Are you well?" Running out of breath, she gasped for air before launching another excited, screaming assault against my ears. "When are you coming home? I really want to see you," she pleaded. Holding the receiver away, I stared at it in amazement. The person on the other end of the line couldn't be my mother. It had to be an imposter.

"Well, um--that's kind of what I'm calling about. We, that is Maddie and I, were thinking about coming home for Thanksgiving. Thought we'd better call first. I wouldn't want to barge in on you or anything or disrupt any plans." Drumming the table nervously, I dreaded the response.

"When can you leave?" she asked excitedly. "I hope you're planning to stay with us because your room is all ready. Things are a little different now and I think you'll be pleasantly surprised. We have so much to catch up on, and please stay as long as you like."

"We won't be able to spend more than two or three days because we have to get back for work, but will see you next Wednesday. Are you sure you want us? There's plenty of motels, and we can see each other for coffee or something if it's too big a hassle."

"Not on your life," she said, "your home is here with your family. We have plenty of room and a big yard for Matthew to play in. We'll teach him to build a snowman." Ringing off, I stood with the phone in my hand for the longest time. Was that really my mother? Since when did she go out in the snow? Did she even know how to build a snowman? I was tempted to call back just to reassure myself that the woman I had spoken with was really my mother.

Maddie came to life after contacting her mom, and looked forward to the holiday with great anticipation. She even called her estranged brother to ask if he was going home, too. His response was less than cordial, but it didn't dampen her spirits. Reuniting with family is wonderful even when there are ulterior motives. She planned to see Keith which was only icing on the cake. It wasn't that I didn't want her to have a good time, but I hoped Keith would be out of town—far away out of town.

The drive home was long, and the weather less than perfect. It rained most of the way turning to snow the closer we got to Portland. Twenty miles past the big city visibility worsened as blizzard conditions slowed traffic to a crawl delaying our arrival by several hours. By the time I pulled into Maddie's driveway and dropped her off, I was exhausted. The house was dark, but a light came on as soon as she opened the car door. Out of courtesy, I waited until her mother came to greet her before driving away. When I was finally on my way to my parents, my stomach twisted into knots. I'd forgotten to ask about my father. How would he react to my homecoming? It was after midnight and I didn't plan to wake them, but thought I'd at least drive by the house. Matthew and I would stay at a motel and come back in the morning. My eyes popped out of my head when I drove down our

The Redemption of Madelyne

familiar street and saw the house ablaze with light. As the car slowed, the front door opened and a figure ran into the street. I slammed on the brakes gaping in stunned surprise. Blinking the tired away, I peered through the snow and slap of the windshield wipers, positive that my eyes deceived me. Dressed in a bathrobe, my mother stood in the middle of the road grinning and waving as her hair whitened with snow. This woman had to be a figment of my exhausted imagination. She definitely was not my mother, and I twisted away when she ran to the car, threw open the door, and wrapped her arms around my neck.

"Mom," I asked stupidly, "is that you?" Laughing and crying all at once, her arms tightened in a strangle hold.

"Of course it's me," she laughed. "Who else runs out in the street on a stormy night just to welcome you home?" Stepping away from the car, she motioned for me to park in the driveway.

"You're getting soaked," I scolded, as she shivered in the cold. "Get back inside." Running through the slush and deepening drifts in slipper clad feet, she waited for me on the porch. When I joined her with Matthew asleep in my arms, she started to cry all over again. Pulling us inside, she took him from me to remove his coat and hat. Tears dripped from her cheeks as she sank into a rocking chair and crooned him back to sleep.

I stepped outside and checked the numbers on the house. Yes, I was at the right address, but this was certainly not my mother. This picture of grandmotherly concern was definitely not the woman I knew.

"Mom," I said hesitantly, "Your bathrobe is wet up to your knees and your feet are blue. Don't you think a change of clothes is in order?"

"Oh?" Surprised spread across her face. The snow on her head was melting. It dripped off her hair all over Matthew making him cry. He wasn't accustomed to having his sleep interrupted. "I'd better change," she said as if the thought just came to her. "I know you're tired, and your room is ready." She carried Matthew up the stairs, refusing to let me take him. When the door to my old bedroom opened, I was in for another shock. Nothing had been changed, painted, remodeled or anything. It was a startling moment--stepping back almost five years to the last time I'd slept there. My eyes widened at the only new addition.

"I brought in a trundle bed for Matthew because I figured you'd want him near you. I'll help you get settled then go to bed." She sloshed across the room, pulled back the blankets on both beds, and patted the pillows invitingly. Turning with a girlish giggle she clapped her hands excitedly. "Even if I go to bed, I doubt I'll sleep. I'm afraid if I close my eyes, you'll disappear just like you did a few years ago. But," she sighed with a wistful smile, "you're here now and we've got three glorious days to play catch up. There's so much to tell you," she said as she caressed my cheek. Shrugging away from her embrace, I dropped my purse and threw my coat over a chair.

"I'm really tired, mom, and Matthew needs to go back to bed. We'll talk in the morning."

"Of course," she said as she stepped out of the room. She blew me a kiss and closed the door.

"What was that about and who was that strange lady?" I asked Matthew. He stared at me owl eyed, fighting a losing battle to keep his eyes opened. When I dressed him in pajamas and tucked him in, his little body went limp with sleep. After brushing my teeth and washing my face, I curled up next to my son and cuddled him against me. Not because he needed my reassurance, but because I needed his. Staring into the darkness, my mind replayed everything my mother had said and done since we'd arrived. "It would figure," I told myself, "just when you know what to expect, somebody has to go and change the rules." My thoughts drifted, remembering and reliving life within these walls. When tiredness stole over me, fogging my mind and silencing the disturbing memories, I slept dreamlessly and soundlessly throughout the night.

Bright sunlight woke me and when I realized Matthew wasn't anywhere in the room, I jumped out of bed and ran to find him. "Matt," I called, "Matthew, where are you?"

Mother came flying out of the kitchen with an apron tied around her waist, "Don't worry," she whispered with a finger to her lips, "He's with me and we've been getting acquainted. I found out in a hurry," she laughed, "he doesn't like oatmeal." She pushed open the swinging kitchen door to reveal Matthew seated at the table with arms folded across his chest, and the same stubborn look on his face that his father often wore. A bowl of cereal was upended on the floor.

"Matthew," I scolded, "you know better than that." Rushing to find a rag to clean up the mess, my mother started to laugh.

"Don't worry about it," she said. Grabbing a fistful of paper towels, she wiped up the floor and grinned at Matthew. "I'm his grandma and should know his likes and dislikes. I should have listened when he tried to tell me he didn't like hot cereal."

"He's always grumpy when he hasn't had enough sleep," I explained. "I've never seen him do anything like this before."

"It's all right," she repeated, "no harm done." Her gaze came to rest on him as she opened the cupboard doors. "So, little man," she said, "what would you prefer?"

"Mom, you don't have to go to any trouble. He probably won't eat until later."

"Believe me," she said with a sad look on her face, "it's no trouble, and I'd love to fix anything he wants. After all, I only have three days to make up for all the time I've missed." The teary longing in her voice was as foreign to me as her actions, and I turned sharply in her direction. Her expression hid no sign of pretense, just open sincerity. Shifting my gaze to the window, a new car turned into the driveway.

My heart began to thump wildly in my chest. "Dad's home," I choked. "Um, how has he been?" What I really meant was how he felt about me coming home again, but was afraid to ask for fear of the answer. I didn't have to wait long to find out.

"So, our wayward daughter has come home." His deep voice held a hint of criticism, and his eyes were as cold as they'd been the last time I'd seen him. His gaze barely flicked over me as he turned his attention to Matthew. The hard glare of disappointment vanished as he smiled at my son with genuine gladness. "And," he said as he lifted Matthew in his arms, "this is my grandson. We'll be in the study, getting acquainted." Matthew waved bye-bye as his grandfather carried him out of the room.

"I'm glad to see he's had such a change of heart," I said sarcastically. "Maybe if I stayed away another ten years, he'd forget I ever existed."

"Don't jump to conclusions," my mother said soothingly. "Be patient with your father; the *Lord* isn't through working on him yet."

This time my jaw really did drop. I couldn't believe what she'd just said and doubted she believed it herself. So far, returning home had been full of surprises--like stepping into another world. The woman who called herself my mother was someone I didn't know and my father had somehow developed a heart? Even the house was different. Gone was the gleaming perfection I remembered. The furniture had signs of dust here and there, and the kitchen actually appeared used.

"Don't try to figure it out all at once," mother said as if reading my mind. "It would become too tiresome. Go get dressed and then if you're hungry, I'll fix some breakfast. My, you've turned into a beautiful young woman and I wasn't there to see it. Wow," her hand combed through my hair lovingly, "your hair is almost as long as Madelyne's. And you're so thin, goodness; you really do need something to eat." Retrieving a frying pan from the cupboard, she turned to ask, "Eggs and bacon?" I nodded, agreeing to the suggestion more out of curiosity than hunger. It wasn't like her to eat in the morning, and bacon never crossed her lips to my knowledge. We, obviously, had a lot to learn about each other.

Returning to my room to dress, I figured things would appear more normal after a long hot shower, but my surprises were far from over. Dressed in a becoming skirt and sweater, I was coming down the stairs when a strange noise caught my attention.

"Ka-thunk, -Ka-thunk,-Ka-thunk." My attention was drawn to the closed door of my father's study. What on earth was going on in there? Furtively, I stepped to the door to listen, and even tried peeking in the keyhole, but couldn't see a thing. The noise started again, seeming to thunder across the room and then recede, as if a herd of buffalo was charging about in a mad dash for freedom.

"Mother," I shouted. Running to the kitchen, I was brought up short when I spied what my mother was doing. She sat at the kitchen table with a pair of glasses perched on her nose. In front of her was a Bible opened to the book of Psalms which she'd been reading. This was too much! First last night, and then this morning, and then the noise, and now the Bible? I foolishly pointed toward the study door and then to her, mouthing words that wouldn't form themselves. Stammering like an idiot, I finally forced myself to ask, "What is going on here?"

She gazed at me with a benign expression. "Is something wrong, dear?"

"Dad, . . .in the study. . there's a strange noise."

"Oh, that," she said knowingly. "Come on, let's take a peek. I've been rather curious about it myself." Throwing wide the door, I actually fell to my knees. There on the floor on all fours was my stern, unyielding father. Riding on his back was an enthusiastic Matthew who seemed to enjoy the game of "horsey." Digging his heels into his grandpa's side, he urged his "horse" to gallop across the room again. When dad noticed our shocked expressions, his ears turned pink. Motioning for Matt to dismount, he pretended to be looking for something under his desk.

"Dropped my pen," he snapped. Matthew got down on all fours to help. When he bumped noses with his grandpa, there was no mistaking the smile on the man's face. He came to his feet and with a look, ordered us out of the room. Matthew's childish giggles followed us into the kitchen.

"Okay," I said. "This is just too bizarre, and you'd better start explaining before I lose my mind. What is going on around here?" I shrieked.

"It's all very exciting," Mom told me. "Sit down and I'll tell you all about it." Pouring us both a cup of coffee, she closed the Bible with a caress to its cover that reminded me of Diane. "Shortly after you moved, I was out shopping again," she said meaningfully, "when I ran into Diane's mother. She invited me to her home for a Bible study and luncheon. I was surprised at how many women attended, and found I even enjoyed myself. After that, I went every week. At first out of curiosity, and then because I wanted to learn more about what God had to tell me. When Elaine invited me to attend church with her, I jumped at the chance. He changed me, Nicole," she said with a rapturous expression, "the Lord Jesus came into my heart and changed everything. I don't get upset at your father and then spend money out of spite. I'm quite content with what I have; and more importantly, with who I was meant to be. I even hold a Bible study here on Wednesday afternoons and it's been well received by working moms. Jesus taught me to love with a mother's heart and to realize what a gift you've been to me. I'm so sorry," she wiped tears from her eyes, "for not being the mother you needed, but beg for a second chance." Her eyes bored into mine with such remorse that tears of compassion filled my own.

"There's a lot to get past," I mumbled.

"I realize the neglect of almost twenty-four years can't be forgiven overnight, but we can at least start off on a new path and in a new direction. All my faith has been placed in Jesus and I know we can become close like mothers and daughters are supposed to be. Didn't Jesus bring you here today? We prayed about it for over a year and He never starts a good work without bringing it to a fruitful conclusion." Her gentle smile held no cynicism, and I found myself smiling back. I'd always wanted an honest, open relationship with her. One that was based on love and mutual concern, and now it was being offered.

"I'm so proud of you." She stroked my hair as I often did Matthew's.

"What about dad?" I asked. "How does he feel about all the changes in your life?" My fingers shredded the edges of a napkin.

"Your father loves you, but is a very proud man. It's hard for him to admit he's been wrong, but he will," she said adamantly. "Be patient, God isn't through with him yet. He doesn't know it, but the entire congregation is praying for him. So he'll have no choice but to surrender to God's will." She shrugged matter-of-factly, "We can't rush things, because God works in His perfect time."

Mom planned to attend church later and encouraged me to go along, but I didn't want to spend my evening with a group of stuffy, old women all repenting of sins whether real or imagined. I declined, explaining that I wanted to visit some friends instead. She didn't try to change my mind, but promised to pray for me. In a weird kind of way, she reminded me of Mrs. Perlman.

Throughout the remainder of the afternoon, I helped bake pies, prepare stuffing, sort fresh cranberries for sauce, and dust and clean the best china. There was company coming tomorrow, but not the usual stuffy bunch from The Corporation. All the guests were from mother's church and weren't the least bit concerned with how much "things" cost. The only reason the special china would be used was because dad insisted on it. He kept Matthew occupied all day and even refused to let me bathe him come evening. When mom prepared to leave for church with her Bible clutched to her chest, he smiled indulgently.

"Have a good time," he said with a smirk.

"I will," she said. Pecking him on the cheek, she asked again if I would go with her.

"Nah, I'm going to call Madelyne and see how she's doing and then maybe look up some old friends. You know, just to say hello and catch up on old times."

"Have a good evening, and drive carefully," she warned.

After she left, I wandered around at loose ends. Dad still monopolized Matthew's attention. He sat on his grandpa's lap sharing a bowl of popcorn, his favorite snack, as they watched a Thanksgiving cartoon. Dad had never watched cartoons before and I was almost envious of the attention showered on my son. They barely glanced in my direction when I slipped out the door.

I drove to Madelyne's and was disappointed to find she was out. Her mother told me she had left an hour before with Keith. My heart sank when she spoke his name. This wasn't good news and would only burden Maddie with another severe bout of depression. I hoped the idea about modeling lingerie had been forgotten.

After driving through town a couple times, and then past the high school, I found myself parked across the street from an imposing building with a bright neon sign advertising "The Corporation." A flood of memories brought bitter tears. Even though I'd run from the truth in denial, this was what I'd come to see. The quiet hum of the heater reminded me of nights with Richard driving lonely country roads, and listening to the radio. My heart begged to see him again, just to know he was okay. Maybe, just maybe, I had loved him after all. I ducked down in my seat when a tall, dark-haired man came out of the building. Richard held the arm of a beautiful woman, helping her into the passenger seat of his sports car in the same way he used to help me. The sting of loss flooded through me all over again.

The next two days went by in a blur of activity. Thanksgiving was pleasant, the dinner wonderful, and the guests loads of fun. I couldn't remember my parent's house ever being filled with so much laughter. Dad really enjoyed himself when he discovered one of the husbands was a chess enthusiast. They entered into a very challenging game vowing to get together for future matches. They actually enjoyed each other's company. Richard's parents were invited, but did not make an appearance or even call to inquire about Matthew.

By late afternoon Saturday, it was time to pack up and return home. Parting company with my mother was difficult, and we both cried. We'd crossed many hurdles over the weekend with several more to go. She promised to call every week, and made me swear to let her know if there was anything we needed. Dad didn't hug me, but ordered me to call if anything came up. Reluctantly, he placed Matthew in the car seat. A suspicious moisture gathered in his eyes that he swore was allergies. I hummed along with the radio as I drove across town to pick-up Maddie.

"Did you have a good week-end?" I asked as we packed her stuff in the trunk. She didn't answer, but shrugged her shoulders indifferently. Hugging her mother, she patted her on the back.

"Don't cry, mom," she said comfortingly. "We'll be back for a visit in the summer." Her mother nodded but held onto her as if afraid to let go. Things had certainly changed in two years. "I'm afraid for you my girl," she kept saying.

"Don't worry," I reassured her, "she'll be fine."

Once settled in the car, Maddie remained silent for several miles and answered my inquiries with blank stares, heavy sighs, and sad looks. I figured Keith was behind her melancholy mood, so lapsed into thoughtful silence myself. Startled from my reverie, I jerked the wheel to the right, when she broke the silence.

"He wanted me to pose nude. The lingerie photos were pure porn. He never had any deals with reputable magazines. I've got the proofs taken this weekend and I look like a street walker. Do you think that's his opinion of me? Is that all I ever was to him? What am I to do now? I'm four months pregnant, and he refuses to take responsibility!"

Chapter Sixteen

"Are you sure?" I asked. "I mean...four months. Madelyne, how could you be so careless?" It was easy to point fingers when someone else's feet were held to the fire. "You should have known Keith wouldn't marry you, and if this is a ploy to force him to the altar, you should have known better."

"A ploy?" she said with a mirthless laugh. "I would never do anything like that. How could you believe I'd stoop to something so devious? I love him and thought he loved me, too. This was an accident...a mistake that should never have happened." I glanced sharply in her direction, hoping I didn't hear what her tone implied.

Staring out the window, she watched our fellow holiday travelers as they zoomed past leaving nothing behind but an icy breeze as they sped off into the night. "I wonder where they're going? Do you ever think about those who travel the same road you do?"

"It's never concerned me and certainly hasn't kept me up nights," I responded. "Why should something like that bother you?"

She sighed as if the weight of the world were on her shoulders. "I just wonder if anybody knows where they're going or what they're going to find once they get there?" Lapsing into thoughtful silence, she leaned her head back on the seat to take a nap. Turning down the radio, we drove for several miles with only the sound of tires rushing over pavement to disturb the ride. Becoming uncomfortable, she twisted around, drew her feet up under her, and then leaned the seat back. Her fingertips rested on her abdomen, drawing circles over a slight roundness.

"Do you think it knows?" Her voice was almost inaudible, and I had to lean close to hear what she said.

"What are talking about?" I asked impatiently. "I imagine everybody will know before long because it isn't something that can be kept secret." Disgust tinged my voice making my words sound harsher than intended. "You've always been such a dreamer, Maddie. It's time to come to your senses and look at the world with both eyes open. Before long there will be another person for you to be responsible for and you can't go chasing pipe dreams when you have a baby to care for." Anger furrowed my brow as I thought about all the change a baby brings. Could she afford the added expense? What about the medical bills? She should have thought about those things before getting into such a predicament, but what was done couldn't be undone.

"I know people will find out eventually, but that isn't my concern," she said softly. "I can feel it growing and moving, making room for itself inside my body. Does it sense or somehow know that I'm contemplating getting rid of it?"

As soon as the words were out of her mouth, a cold blast of Arctic air breathed down my neck. My hands gripped the steering wheel so hard I thought it would bend in two as I forced myself to take slow, steadying breaths.

"Don't make any rash decisions," I warned. "There's plenty of time to decide what's best and abortion isn't the answer. I'm sorry if I sound angry. I haven't lived an exactly pious life and shouldn't point fingers." Grasping at words and phrases I'd heard or read I rattled on, hoping to come up with something that would change her mind. "Think about the baby. It will be fun to have another little one around, and maybe yours will be a girl."

"Great," she said dryly. "Another child raised without a father or family to speak of. I wouldn't wish this life on anyone, least of all my own flesh and blood." She turned her face toward the door and was soon breathing deeply in sleep. I glanced at her profile as we passed under the streetlights along the freeway. A single tear streaked down the side of her cheek turning to silver under the artificial light. Hopefully, there would be another opportunity to discuss this situation because I needed time to prepare an argument convincing enough to change her mind.

When she woke she surprised me by picking up the conversation where we left off. "This thing growing inside me isn't a baby yet, it's just a bunch of cells. Kathy showed me all the evidence and even pictures. It isn't a baby until much later—-I think."

"That argument won't stand up in court," I protested, "and your own statement argues against it. What you feel moving inside of you is life, it isn't an inanimate object, or an amoeba, or a parasite. You can't pass if off as just a fetus, because that's just a word. Have you taken the time to look up the word fetus so you know what it means? Webster's defines it as a developing infant or an unborn child. Think about it Maddie, this life growing within you will love you unconditionally. He or she will never expect you to be anything more than what you are."

"I love it when you get emotional about things," she said with a satisfied air. "You make the most sense when your feelings are running high and you say what you really think. I know what you say is true, but also wonder if what Kathy says is true. Is it possible that your both right? I don't know," she said with mournful shake of her head. "For now, I'm going over my options. I promise you'll be the first to know when I make a decision."

"Good," I said with smug satisfaction, "I'll settle for that." If she was still thinking about what to do, there was plenty of time to present a good case and with Diane's help, how could we lose?

On Monday, we returned to work and for a little while, life was almost normal. Madelyne remained subdued, but didn't appear upset about her pregnancy; in fact, she frequently stopped whatever she was doing to place a palm over her abdomen. At those times, a poignant smile softened her expression as she cocked her head to the side, as if listening to some inner voice. The child was alive and revealing its presence in ways only she could recognize. I almost envied her. I never felt more powerful than when I carried Matthew under my heart. She never mentioned abortion again and I didn't ask. We were planning Christmas, and I didn't want anything to disrupt the holiday. Something should have told me that it wouldn't last. Maddie hadn't created the life she carried by herself. Keith had parental rights, too. Rights that were bestowed by the United States Supreme Court to have his say about the future of their child. It started innocently enough, but we never recognize the snake in the garden that hides its bite behind beautiful markings and poetic words.

"When shall we put up the tree?" I asked one evening. "The Christmas tree lot has some beautiful trees and if we bought one now, we could put it up over the weekend."

"That's a great idea," Maddie agreed. She sat opposite me at the table holding Matthew on her lap. A smile teased the corner of my mouth as I watched her. She'd taken over his care since Thanksgiving, and seemed eager to learn all she could about babies. I was sure she'd given up the idea of an abortion and if she hadn't, they couldn't be performed after four months, could they?

Setting Matt down, she cleared away our supper dishes and ran a sink full of hot, sudsy water. "Let's get a big one. I want a tree that fills this apartment and perfumes the air with pine. Let's buy lots of presents for everyone, make Christmas dinner here, and invite everybody we know. I'm in the mood to celebrate." Her face flushed with happiness and her eyes sparkled with life. I had never seen any woman look more beautiful than Maddie did at that moment.

"Don't move," I told her, "stay right where you are. We've got to take a picture of you so the baby will know what a beautiful mother she has." I ran to the bedroom and grabbed the camera off the dresser. Fumbling with the adjustments I'd never learned to use, I finally got it focused. Maddie stood in front of the sink with arms held loosely at her sides. A length of hair spilled over her shoulders curling down to her waist. She gazed into the camera's eye with one brow arched and a slight smile curving her lips with amused pleasure. After snapping two in quick succession, she made a face and made a grab for the camera. For the remainder of the evening Matthew and I became targets as she snapped pictures of us in what she called natural poses. I drew the line when she took a picture of Matthew as he got out of the tub. I wasn't sure about displaying my son's bare butt for the world to see even if she thought it was cute. He didn't seem to mind as he posed proudly with all of his male anatomy exposed. He reminded me so much of his father, I had to laugh.

"Let's get some clothes on before you catch cold." Giggling, he took off at a run as we chased him down to dress him in flannel sleepers. Afterward, he jumped onto the bed, grabbed his Teddy and his favorite storybook. We took turns reading until he fell asleep.

The Redemption of Madelyne

"He might be spoiled, but he's still a sweetheart," Maddie whispered as she closed the bedroom. "Do you think my baby will be as sweet as he is?"

"Of course," I assured her, "and even more so because she'll be yours. It's a wondrous gift to hold a child in your arms and a miracle to hold your own. I've always thought it a special gift from God made especially for women."

"Do you really believe in God?"

"Yeah, I think I do," I nodded, "because life doesn't have much meaning without belief in something. I like to think there's someone listening when no one else will. It's not like I pray or read the Bible or anything, but I'm hoping all that stuff about going to a heavenly place when you die isn't just lip service. It's got to be more than a nice story told so offering plates are full on Sunday morning."

"Yeah, I guess miracles have to come from somewhere, and heaven is as good a place as any. Well, I'm going to wash my hair and get ready for bed. I've been feeling tired lately and can't seem to get enough sleep."

"That's all part of being pregnant, so get used to it," I joked. "Think about it, Maddie. Next year you'll have your own child to plan Christmas for. It may not be the best timing, but we'll make it work, and I'll be there to help as much as possible."

"You're a good friend," she said as the bedroom door clicked shut. The remainder of my evening was spent planning where to setup the tree, and how to decorate the apartment so it looked as festive as possible. Last year's Christmas found both of us depressed and miserable, but this year promised another great beginning. I couldn't wait for the weekend. Come Friday, we planned to treat ourselves to dinner at Matt's favorite fast food restaurant and pick the tree up afterwards. That would leave Saturday free to decorate to our heart's content. Maybe I'd send out a few Christmas cards. As I climbed into bed, I crossed my fingers, and whispered a little prayer that nothing would interfere with our plans.

Everything was perfect until Thursday. Late that night the insistent ring of the phone woke us all. Maddie had a sudden change in plans.

"Keith called last night," she said with a sleepy yawn the following morning. "We talked for over three hours. and he'll be here sometime today so we can discuss what to do about our little problem." Patting the tiny bulge of her stomach, she winked at Matthew and grinned radiantly. "How would you like to be an uncle?"

Matthew set his glass on the table and flashed a milky grin. "Today?" he asked, which was a logical question because anything happening in his life had to be today because he never thought about tomorrow. It was his new word, and he responded to all questions in the same way.

"Not today," she responded with a tickle to his ribs, "but soon."

"Okay," he said. With that problem solved, his attention was brought back to breakfast. Sometimes his spoon wasn't enough and required a little help. I reminded him that spoons were to be used, not fists.

"So, Keith has reconsidered. Is he willing to be a father to the baby?" I asked skeptically. Something about the whole scenario didn't ring true.

"Well, he didn't in so many words," she hedged, "but I'm almost sure that's what he meant. He said there were several solutions we can discuss, but only one that actually makes sense. He wants me to think about the future, and how this child will fit into a family. What do you suppose he was getting at if he didn't mean for us to get together?"

"It certainly sounds like he's considering fatherhood, but be prepared for just about anything. And remember," I added gently, "a child needs the love of both parents and if one doesn't have it to give, then the child is better off without them."

"Like Richard?"

"Like Richard," I agreed.

Even though Madelyne didn't go, I tried to make Friday evening a festive affair for Matthew. We went to dinner and he ate carefully, using his spoon and fork and didn't cram food into his mouth with his fingers even once. Afterwards, we wandered around the Christmas tree lot going from tree to tree until he found one suitable. It wasn't perfect, but grand and stately in his eyes, and isn't Christmas for kids? The tree was tied to the roof of my car and we were on our way. He wanted to put up the tree as soon as we got home, but I explained it needed a long drink of water before coming into a warm house. He seemed to accept the explanation and went to bed without complaint.

"Tomorrow," I promised, "we'll decorate the tree and maybe go shopping for a Christmas present for grandma and grandpa." Since our

The Redemption of Madelyne

visit home, his favorite people were his grandparents. He talked to them almost daily and held long conversations with his grandpa on a toy telephone. Nodding sleepily, he curled his body around his Teddy and was soon sound asleep.

The day had been busy. The steady drone of the TV only made my head droop lower so I gave up the fight and went to bed. Sometime in the night, I was brought out of a sound sleep by Maddie's muffled sobs. Sitting up, I stared groggily at the clock and made out the luminescent hands positioned at three-thirty.

"She should be in bed," I mumbled to myself. Groping for a robe and slippers, I threw a blanket over my shoulders when I couldn't find either one. Just as my fingers reached for the doorknob, something in their conversation made me hesitate. I didn't mean to eavesdrop, and only intended to listen to her response, but suspicion kept my ear glued to the door.

"There's no point in sniveling about it, Madelyne, because truth is truth. Models don't have babies and that's a fact," Keith sneered. "My God, look at yourself! You look like you've gained ten pounds and your hips are the size of a Volkswagen. You don't expect an agency to take you on now, do you?"

"I haven't gained more than five pounds and I'm still wearing most of my regular clothes," she retorted. At least she was standing up for herself and putting up a semblance of defense against him. "Maybe I'd rather be a mother than a model. Feel my stomach, Keith, you can feel our baby moving and I know it's strong and healthy. Don't you want to see your own child?" Her soft voice pleaded with him, begging him to see the life growing within her as a human being. This was his child, and worthy of the home they could provide.

"You don't get it, do you?" Every word he spoke was a slap in the face meant to hurt and strip self-respect. "I don't want to marry a pregnant woman, and I certainly won't marry you. You're an embarrassment to me. A man in my position needs someone attractive, not somebody big enough to be their own airline. I'm telling you again, Madelyne, get rid of it. It will only bring trouble and look what's happened already. Do you want me to walk out that door and never come back?"

"No, please don't go. I love you," she sobbed brokenly, "you know I love you. How can you ask me to get rid of my own child?"

What he suggested was so loathsome that waves of hatred swept over me. I wanted to strike out at both of them. My fingers turned the doorknob, wanting to fling open the door to launch a physical attack. Surely an abortion was out of the question at this stage in her pregnancy, and I almost hated her for even considering such an idea.

"It isn't your child, yet," he threatened, "and you'd better do some serious thinking if you want our relationship to be anything more than it is. Keep in mind there are plenty of women eager to love me and be with me, if you know what I mean," he said evocatively. "But where am I? I'm with a woman that won't listen to reason." The sound of kissing made my ears ring and my stomach turn.

"Give me some time to think about it," she begged. "Are you serious about...about us? Will we really be married and have a family someday?"

"Sure baby," he lied. "Just not right now. . .we're not ready to be Mr. and Mrs. John Q. Public. I know I'm sure not! Come on, let's go to bed before we wake up that nosy friend of yours."

Shivering in the cold, I stood at the door praying she'd throw him out. My head felt hot and a dizzy sensation sent a message to my insides that turned them to mush. Making a quick dash to the bathroom, I kneeled with my head hanging over the toilet bowl as my stomach twisted time and time again. My brain refused to accept what I'd heard. People like us didn't get rid of our babies; we loved them and wanted them, didn't we? Maddie wanted her baby--of this I was sure, but how was I to convince her? Crawling back to bed, I lay in the dark shivering until sleep drew me into a horrible nightmare of old men, wheelchairs, and dead babies laid out in tidy rows that extended on as far as the eye could see.

Matthew and I spent all of Saturday decorating the tree, and the apartment. By the time we finished, we were exhausted. I went to bed at the same he did and slept until late Sunday morning. By Monday, my throat was raw and raspy, and fever turned my cheeks a vivid pink.

"You've got the flu, I'll bet," Maddie told me as she took my temperature for the third time. "Matthew will be better off at Diane's so

I'll drop him off on my way to work. You," she ordered with a point of her finger, "are to stay in bed, drink plenty of fluids, and get some rest. You look like you haven't slept in days. If you want or need anything, give me a call." She must have told just about everyone we knew that I was sick, because my day was far from restful.

"Hello," I croaked when the phone rang.

"Hello, dear, this is your mother. Madelyne told me you were sick. Do you need anything? Is it serious?"

"It's just the flu, Mom, and I'll be fine. I don't understand why she called and bothered you about it."

"She didn't call me, dear, I called you and she answered. It was early this morning, before seven. I guess you were still in bed and she forgot to tell you."

"You called me? Why?"

"Just to visit, and see how you're doing. I was hoping to talk you into coming home for Christmas."

"Mom, I'm not feeling very well, and this isn't a good time to talk."

"Of course, I understand. When you're feeling better, you call me so we can have a nice chat. Remember, I love you and am so proud of my girl." After ringing off, I marveled again at the change in her. I had lived in the city for almost two years without any contact with home, and now she wanted weekly updates and daily emails. Would wonders never cease?

My bed was moved to the couch with the TV for company. I turned the channel, took a sip of juice, and was prepared to take a nap when a tap at the door brought me bolt upright. Was it Keith?

"Hello," sang Mrs. Perlman. "Madelyne called and told me you were sick, poor dear. Oh, look at you, you look absolutely awful."

"You shouldn't have come here," I told her. Groaning inwardly, I wondered if Madelyne had informed every clerk at the grocery store and the mailman, too. "What if this is contagious?"

"Oh," she chirped, "I've had all my shots and doubt I'm going to catch any germs in the few minutes I'm here. Now, do you need anything? I'm on my way to the store and would be glad to get whatever you want." I started to get up, but she wouldn't hear of it. "Stay right where you are," she ordered. "I'll just take a peek in the fridge to see what you have on hand. Orange juice," she said emphatically, "that's what you need, and lots of it." Clucking to herself about the state of a plant left on the counter to drain from a recent over-watering, she waggled her fingers at me from the door. I'll be back soon, dear. Get some rest."

"That's what I've been trying to do," I moaned. Pulling the covers up over my head, the comforting warmth relaxed me and I was soon asleep. Matthew's hug and the clatter of dishes woke me a couple hours later.

"Hi," he said. "Mommy better?"

"Yeah, Mommy feels better." I struggled to sit up to see who was in the kitchen. It wasn't time for Madelyne to be home yet. Diane came in carrying a tray with a bowl of soup, and two cups of fragrant Chamomile tea. Pouring a bit of honey into the cups, she handed one to me.

"Sip it slowly because it's hot. Are you feeling any better?"

I took a sip and shrugged my shoulders. "Thanks," I said gratefully with a slight lift of my cup. "I've never had so much attention. Maybe I should get sick more often."

"Enjoy it while you can," she laughed. "Now, tell me, what's wrong and why do you look like you're about to cry. I know you're sick, but the flu isn't anything to cry over." I should have known there were no secrets with Diane. She had a sixth sense, and always seemed to know when things weren't right.

"It's Madelyne," I blurted out. "It's all so horrible. I don't know what to do about her but. . ."

I told her everything I knew about Maddie's pregnancy, and the conversation between her and Keith. Diane's only reaction to the information was a slight narrowing of the eyes when abortion was mentioned.

"Is Keith still in town?"

"I'm not sure, but I have reason to suspicion he spends his nights with her. I'd like to shoot him, and shake her until her teeth rattle. How can she possibly consider an abortion as far along as she is?" I wailed. "I hate her for it."

"She needs all the moral support we can give," Diane chided. "Madelyne's in a vulnerable position. She's torn between doing what's right and loving Keith so much she'll do almost anything he asks. Many young women, like Maddie, get caught in the same trap. They want to be loved so badly they'll accept any scrap thrown at them often ending up in abusive relationships. They frequently make decisions they regret. Sometimes it's because they're afraid of what people will say, and they don't want the stigma of "unwed mother," she said with her fingers making quotation marks in the air.

"But she's not fresh out of high school. She's twenty-four and should know better."

"I'm sure this wasn't part of her plans, and she believes Keith loves her enough to marry her. She's always needed someone to love her, to help her forget all the years of rejection."

"Keith is a total jerk. Why can't she can see that?"

"Love is blind," she reminded with a smile and a look that made my cheeks flame. Had things been much different between Richard and me? "Don't worry, I'll talk to her and won't give up until I get the message through. Nodding, I snuggled under the covers. Relief lifted a load of anxiety from my shoulders; Diane would take care of things. She always did.

"Madelyne and I have something in common," she added with unexpected coyness. "I'm three months pregnant and Paul is absolutely thrilled." If my throat hadn't been so sore, I would have cheered. We idled the afternoon away by looking at baby things in a catalog. When I dozed off, Diane snapped off the TV and read a couple stories to Matthew. I didn't wake until Mrs. Perlman returned.

"Look what I bought for you," she sang. Lifting one eyelid, I watched her quick, jerky movements as she rearranged a few things to make room for a very luxuriant plant. Dark green leaves streaked with purple, crimson, and grey grew out in thick profusion from a thick stem. The cascading fronds fell in graceful furls over the lattice support holding them. It was a beautiful plant and I wanted nothing more than for her to take it home because if it was left under my care, it would soon lose all of its leaves and wither away to a useless stick.

"Don't worry about this one," she chirped as she bent over to rearrange the leaves. "Leave it in full sun or put it in the shade—it won't matter. Give it a light dusting now and then and a rainwater bath. You can't hurt this plant dear, so don't be afraid of it."

"But, aren't you afraid it will die? I don't think you should leave it because my track record with living things isn't so good."

"Nonsense," she said with a flip of her fingers. "Well, I'd best be going. We're having some of the boys over for dinner, and I haven't started a thing." Bending over, she pecked me on the cheek then swooped out the door with a rustle of nylon and silk.

"Wow," Diane said breathlessly, "is she always like that? She's the most hyper-active person I know." I nodded in agreement.

We weren't able to speak to Maddie that night or the following evening either. We decided Christmas Day would be a good time because Keith wouldn't be around and there would be no stressful interruptions. Diane invited us to join her family for Christmas festivities, and since our work schedules didn't allow time enough to travel home, we jumped at the chance. We were to attend Christmas Eve services at her church the night before, and then come over in the morning for an early brunch, a gift exchange, and dinner. I went to the church service alone, because Keith came in for the evening. Maddie felt she needed to be with him.

The Christmas Eve service was beautiful. Music swelled from the throats of the choir filling the sanctuary with harmony. An organ accompanied them and if heaven sounded better, I'd need a truckload of tissues. Even Matthew sat in awe as we listened to the angelic voices of children as they sang, and then the more professional music of the adults. I wept real tears when Paul delivered a message that spoke of forgiveness. He said that Christ loved us so much that He gave his life and shed His own blood for people just like me. I'd never heard anything so moving. And to make the evening even more special, when we stepped out of the church flakes of snow swirled through the air, frosting every branch and shrub with crystalline beauty. I don't know who was more impressed—Matthew or me. We stood for a moment, just taking in the magic of the moment.

"Did you enjoy the service?" Diane asked when she came over to greet us.

"It was wonderful," I told her sincerely. "I've never heard anything that touched me deeply."

"It's the Christmas message," she said matter-of-factly, "and it's beautiful and more than just a nice story. Do you know what it means?"

"I guess so. Most churches say the same thing don't they? Is there a special meaning I should know about?"

"Jesus loves me," Matthew stated with all the exasperation a four-year-old can muster.

"That's right," Diane laughed, "but He loves everybody and that means you, too, Nicci. He died for all of us."

"Are you sure? Seems to me there are sins and then there are SINS."

"In His eyes they are all the same. Don't you read your Bible?"

"I guess not. I forgot about it." Making designs in the snow with the toe of my shoe, I avoided her gaze. The Bible had been a gift from her and I'd never even opened it.

"Go home and read the book of Luke. Pay special attention to chapters one through three. I promise you won't be bored. Well, I've got to light the candles for ten o'clock service. We'll see you tomorrow and Merry Christmas." Waving good-bye, she pointed to a passing light in the sky, "I wonder if that could be flying reindeer?" With a sly glance at Matthew, she marched inside, closing the door softly behind her.

Christmas Day was full of surprises. Mr. and Mrs. Perlman came over with gifts for each of us. I proudly showed off the plant she'd bought when I was sick.

"Look," I boasted, "there's not a single shriveled leaf, and it's still as strong as the day you gave it to me. In fact, I think it may even be healthier."

"Yes," she said with a nervous flutter of fingers to her lips. "I can see it's very healthy. What have you been doing with it, dear?"

"I've dusted it every week, gave it baths in the shower and fertilizer, too. I'm determined to keep this one alive." Beaming at the flourishing plant, I was surprised to hear her tittering laughter.

"You sweet thing, you," she chirped, "You've gone to all that effort for nothing. This plant will always look healthy, dear, because it's an imitation."

"But you said to dust and water it," I protested, "and I did what you told me."

"And you did such a good job," she praised, "I'm proud of your efforts even if they weren't warranted." I looked from one to the other of them and then to the plant. We all had a good laugh at my expense.

The real surprise came later; after we'd returned from Diane's full of turkey, stuffing, and pumpkin pie. All three of us were hunkered down on the floor playing with one of Matthew's new toys when someone knocked once and then walked in. My breath caught in my throat. My heart pounded so hard, I feared it would leap out of my chest.

"Richard," I gasped, "what are you doing here?" Coming to my feet, a hand automatically flew to smooth my hair and crumpled clothing.

"I brought a gift for my son," he said as if it was something he did every day. Lifting Matthew on one arm, he stared at him for a couple of tense seconds before putting him down. "Here you go, Tiger." He pulled a small gift wrapped box from his pocket and helped his son open it. Inside was a gold watch complete with engraving on the back. "You won't be able to wear this for a while, but when you do--think about your old man. See here," he pointed out the engraving to his son, "it says to Matthew from Dad. You'd best take good care of this watch because it's unlikely I'll buy you another." He slipped the band over Matt's arm where it dangled loosely. The watch was man-sized, and needed a much larger wrist. Satisfied with the token gift he'd given his son, he turned his attention to me.

"You're looking good, Nicole. Hope everything is going okay. I just wanted to stop by and give the kid something, and now I need to get going. Some friends are expecting me for a party, if I'm not too late," he said with a glance at the expensive Rolex on his wrist. When he left, I watched from the window as he lit a cigarette and then pulled a bottle from under the seat and drank deeply. It must have taken over half the bottle to give him courage enough to face his son.

"That really hurt, didn't it?" Madelyne asked as she came over to place an arm around my shoulders.

"Yes, it did, and I don't understand why." Blinking rapidly, I stubbornly refused to cry more tears over our broken relationship. "Will I ever stop caring about him?"

"Probably not," she said with a sigh. Leaning her head against mine, we watched him drive away.

Chapter Seventeen

Ken invited me out for New Year's Eve, and since Mrs. Perlman agreed to watch Matthew, I accepted. Maddie was excited about the evening because she had a new dress, and Keith was taking her out to dinner with dancing afterwards. Ken and I were to meet them at our favorite nightclub.

She wore a daring, black, satin gown that left the back open. It plunged down the front in a narrow slit to just between her breasts. Tiny rhinestones glittered in the fabric, and it moved as she did, changing shades with each step. The left side was split modestly to just below her hip. It was a stunning gown, but something about the way she looked bothered me.

"What happened to your waist?" I asked. Stepping closer, I examined the line of her body. Her ribs stood out under the fabric and the bones of her hips pulled the fabric taut over a concave stomach.

"I've been dieting," she said defensively. "Keith thinks I look great." She leaned into the mirror and studied the reflection of a face too thin, eyes too bright, and cheekbones too prominent. Her fingertips explored the lines of her face. "I'm a little thin, maybe, but everything is still intact including junior if that's what you're wondering."

"Promise me you'll quit this diet nonsense. A developing baby gets its nourishment from the mother and if you're not eating, the baby isn't either. You want a healthy child don't you?"

"It isn't really a baby yet," she corrected, "Kathy says it's just a fetus."

"That doesn't make it any less real," I snapped, "or any less your son or daughter, Madelyne. Don't play God with the life of your child."

"Don't get upset. I haven't planned anything for the moment. Let's just look forward to the evening." We didn't mention it again, but I watched her closely. She picked at her food, rarely eating more than a few bites. Hunger could be seen in her eyes, but still she refused to eat. Keith swore he loved her, but his devotion only lasted until another opportunity arose.

Our evening got off to a good start. We had a nice dinner with pleasant conversation, and took advantage of the warm evening air by walking the short distance to the nightclub. We ordered a couple drinks, and after two we were totally relaxed and ready to dance. When the beat of a favorite song began, I grabbed Ken's hand and pulled him to the dance floor. This was one I couldn't sit out. The rhythm of the heavy drumbeat brought a swing to my hips and forced my feet into an intricate dance step. Madelyne and Keith danced next to us and we were laughing, having a great time when a flash of something familiar caught my attention. Snapping my head around, there--right next to us, was Richard. He winked at the pretty woman he danced with and acknowledged us with a nod. The third finger of her left hand flashed as she threw her arms around him at the end of the dance. A huge engagement ring, about the size of the one he'd given me, demanded attention as it glittered from a diamond-studded setting.

When Richard came over to say hello, I moved closer to Ken, placing a hand on his thigh and the other on his arm in a gesture of ownership.

"Everybody having a good time?" he asked without taking his eyes off me.

"We always have a wonderful time," I said meaningfully. Gazing into Ken's eyes, I ignored his look of surprise.

"Great," Richard said. "I'd like you to meet Candy, my fiancée, but she just ducked into the little girl's room. We'll be around awhile, so maybe we'll catch you later." A look passed between Richard and Keith. It was obvious this little meeting had been arranged. There had to be at least a thousand different places Richard could have gone to for the evening, but somehow he ended up here and not two tables away. I was determined to show him it didn't matter.

"Want another drink," Ken asked. Usually, I stopped after three, but tonight was a time for celebration.

"Sure," I said with giggle, "and keep them coming." Snuggling closer, I grinned over the rim of my glass. "Let's dance the night away then see where it leads."

The Redemption of Madelyne

His eyebrows shot up in surprise. "Don't fool around like that," he said. "A guy gets ideas, and you know what I mean." We had another drink and then I had another and then another. With every round, I glanced to see if Richard was watching. I only wanted to make him jealous, to make him see me as a beautiful, desirable woman, but somehow things got out of hand.

"Kiss me like that again, baby," Ken whispered as we danced a slow one. When our lips met, I closed my eyes and saw Richard's face and felt Richard's arms around me. A tiny, annoying voice told me it was the alcohol, but I allowed passion to take full control. We had another drink and sat in a back booth, where our kissing became more passionate and our fingers itched to explore one another's bodies.

"Let's get out of here," he breathed. "I want to be totally alone with you. I've waited for this a long time." His words were music to my ears—words Richard used to say.

My head was dizzy as my feet stumbled their way to the door. I had to lean on Ken to make it to the car. At his apartment, we had another drink and he whispered all the things my hurting heart longed to hear. He held me in his arms. His hands explored, growing bolder, and I didn't try to stop what I knew would eventually take place. Leaning my dizzy head back on a pillow, I drank in his words of love.

Nausea woke me the next morning and I ran to the bathroom, gagging into the toilet bowl. My head pounded and my body felt like I'd suffered a severe beating sometime in the night. One glance in the mirror, and I was sick all over again. My eyes were ringed with mascara and my hair a rumpled mess. Grabbing a towel off a shelf to cover myself, I found my clothes tossed in a corner of the bedroom. With trembling fingers, I dressed quickly, biting my lips to hold back tears of remorse.

"Hey, want some breakfast?" Ken asked as he woke and sat up. "What's the hurry? Come back here, and let me show you a very good morning."

"No," I choked, "I want to go home."

"You're not bawling, are you?" Disgust was written on his face as he took in my tear-streaked face.

"Don't look at me like the guilt's all mine. You came here willingly enough, and you sure didn't seem to mind what happened afterwards."

Brushing a hand through his hair, he looked at me and shook his head. "Stop crying. . . I should have known. This was all about him, wasn't it?" Crying all the more, I shrugged my shoulders and wished I could disappear into the walls. I was grateful when he dressed, handed me my coat, and drove me straight home. He didn't offer to come in or even get out of the car when we pulled up in front of the apartments.

"See ya' around," he said as he dropped me off. We both knew our relationship, or what there was of it, had come to an abrupt end.

As he drove off down the street, I ran into the bathroom for a hot shower—and the hotter the better. Using a brush and strong soap, I scrubbed my entire body until my skin stung and my scalp burned. Would I ever rid myself of this dirty feeling? Would I ever feel wholesome enough to look my son in the eye?

Later, after dressing and making myself look as presentable as possible, I drove over to Mrs. Perlman's to retrieve Matthew. Even though I looked okay on the outside, things were far from normal on the inside. Another thought came to me during the drive to the Perlman's. Had Ken used any form of protection? I'd stopped taking birth control pills several months before because of some problems with my period. Did I dare call and ask him? Claire knew something was wrong as soon as I got out of the car.

"Tch, tch," she clucked as she waved a finger in my face. "Too much partying for you, I see. Come into the kitchen, and let me fix you something for your stomach. You'll feel better for it." Her Jewish accent was unmistakable as she lectured me about the effects of strong drink. She prepared a cup of the nastiest tea I'd ever tasted, and drank some right along with me. We both made sour faces as the stuff slipped down our throats. I had to admit the tarry stuff soothed my stomach, but did nothing to ease the emptiness inside.

Maddie wasn't in any better shape when she came in. She didn't speak, but flew past me to the bedroom where she threw herself across the bed, beating the pillow with her fists. I stood helplessly by, knowing any offer of help would be refused. She wasn't ready to deal with whatever was tearing her up.

Heartache and despair seemed to follow me throughout the remainder of the month. Poor Matthew--caught in the midst of all that silent pain.

He tiptoed around the house speaking in whispers. Emotions would surface at odd times leaving me drained and in tears at one time, and angry the next. For days I held my breath, hoping and praying my suspicions were incorrect. My cycle had never been regular--maybe I was off on the dates. But, after all my speeches about unwed mothers, and abortion, and how women should be more responsible, I found myself caught in an age-old predicament. The at-home pregnancy test was positive, and I had no choice but to admit I was as weak as those I condemned.

Circumstances for Madelyne didn't improve and seemed to mirror what I was going through. She was into her sixth month and beginning to show whether she wanted to or not. She wasn't any bigger around than a willow, but her middle was developing a roundness she'd never had before. When the phone rang, she ran to answer hoping it would be Keith. Otherwise, she showed little interest in things around her.

"I didn't get the promotion," she said woodenly the afternoon she came home early. "My boss was nice about it, but explained the position required a lot of travel. He didn't think it would be a good idea for me to leave a newborn for several days at a time." Her shoulders sagged as she dropped her purse and jacket onto the couch.

"I'm sorry. I know how much you wanted that job. Surely there will be others."

"Yeah," she said curtly, "but how long will I have to wait? How long will I continue to slog through life allowing things like this to happen to me?" Burying her face in her hands, her shoulders shook with the force of her sobs.

"Things will work out if we just give it enough time," I consoled as I patted her shoulder. The words sounded hollow, and I knew she didn't believe it any more than I did. Forcing a smile, she rose to her feet and patted her stomach.

"Does it show? I didn't think it showed much at all, but everybody at work knows."

"What does it matter? A pregnant woman is supposed to gain a few pounds and appear rounder, not like you just stepped out of Ethiopia. You'd better start eating or your baby may be born with problems." A little, worried frown creased her forehead as she covered her abdomen protectively.

"She or he will be alright, they just have to be. Guess I'd better call my mother and let her know she's going to be a grandma. I don't think she'd appreciate finding out after the fact," she sighed. Her comment made me think about my own mother. For the first time in my life we were developing a close relationship. Mom had admitted she was proud of me. Would she feel the same when I announced another baby was on the way with no father in sight?

Questions circled through my mind like vultures--over and over again. What would people say? Especially after I'd been so down on women having babies out of wedlock. How could I face my parents, and worse yet, Richard? What about Matthew and the stigma this could put on him? It wasn't fair! Men were never left holding the bag. This was baggage I'd carry for the rest of my life, and it could ruin everything. Once the decision was made, there was no turning back. I planned it perfectly so no one, not even Madelyne, would know. Work was no problem because I was due a personal day. A call was made to a clinic across town. I refused to think about the repercussions.

The place was small with discreet parking behind a square, cinder block building. A friendly receptionist greeted all the patients as they came in handing each a clipboard and a pen.

"Just a few questions, sweetie," she assured a frightened looking girl. "Don't worry, everything is strictly confidential." As I read through the admittance slip, I noted that several personal questions were voluntary. Omitting my date of birth, I wrote in a fictitious name and address. When Jennifer Jeffries was called, I didn't recognize the name until the nurse came over and asked if I was she.

Following the white clad figure, I kept my eyes on the floor, not daring to look to the right or to the left. She led me into a tiny cubicle where I was to undress, and get into a hospital gown and robe. A door separated the room from a larger room where there was a physician's examination table and an elevated tray of shiny, stainless steel, surgical instruments. My eyes skittered away from the table, finding interest in the pattern of tiles on the floor.

"Okay, sweetie," the nurse said. "Hop up on the table and get comfortable." Covering me with a warm blanket she made me as cozy as possible, and then took a syringe from the tray. "Just a little poke with something to relax you and in just a few minutes, it will all be over with." Flinching at the sting of the needle, I shut my eyes and tried to close my mind to what the nurse referred to as "the procedure." I didn't need the sedative because I was numb already.

"How's the patient doing today?" a cheerful male voice asked. "I'm Dr. Avery and we'll take very good care of you today. Can you take a big, deep breath for me? Good! I'm just going to examine you and there might be a slight feeling of pressure." Gripping the sides of the table, every muscle tensed at the intrusion into my body. "Um mmm," he said to himself. "Okay, another little stick, and it will soon be over. Are you a college student? What's your favorite subject?"

Didn't he get it? I wasn't in the mood to make small talk. Tears dripped down the sides of my face as I thought about the life being drained from my body. A poster on the ceiling of a kitten clinging to a branch seemed apropos'.

"Nurse," he said softly, "would you hand me the basin?" A basin? Was that the final remembrance of my baby? Would he or she be left in a basin to be thrown out; flushed down the sewer like yesterday's trash? Suddenly I wanted to see my child. I didn't want to go through with this—please God—stop! Twisting around on the table, I tried to sit up.

"Nurse," the doctor called.

"Don't look honey," she said in a soothing voice as she positioned herself so I couldn't see around her. Dabbing at the tears on my face, she smoothed my hair and talked about puppies, picnics, and life ahead; trying to get my mind off the syringe that sucked the remains of my baby's body from my womb. "Think about your future," she said brightly. "Put this behind you, and it will be as if it never happened. After all, everyone is permitted one mistake. You shouldn't pay for it for the rest of your life. You're a young and beautiful woman with plenty of good times ahead." I've never forgotten that nurse because she lied. In fact, the whole thing is one great big lie. There are some mistakes that you never get over, they haunt you--overshadowing future relationships and everything you do for the rest of your life. It chases you into the abyss and screams "Baby killer—murderer--worshipper of Molech. May the memory and blood of your unborn follow you to the grave."

Chapter Eighteen

There's no way to describe the emptiness--the overwhelming loss that a part of yourself is gone and is no more. Tears don't wash it away, and time won't take it away, because the heart never forgets. I didn't think I'd ever stop crying, but finally the tears dried, the sun came out, and my heart continued to beat--although with less fervor than before. If there had been a warning similar to some prepackaged items like:

> *Danger: Abortions are hazardous to your*
> *mental stability and peace of mind.*

Would I have gone through with it? Probably, because my own selfish desire took precedence over the needs of the innocent life within me. I was unwilling to face the consequences for a night of foolishness. All evidence of it was hidden under a doctor's knife. May God forgive me.

★ ★ ★

Four hours later I was back in my car, and on my way home. Tears blurred my vision several times--forcing me to pull over until the spasm of cramping passed. The doctor gave me a prescription for pain along with a sedative, but I needed to remain alert. There would be plenty of time for rest after I'd retrieved Matthew from daycare.

"Nicci," Madelyne gasped when I walked in the door. "You either got hit by a truck or you're really sick. I've never seen you so pale. Go straight to bed. I'll bring you something to eat after I've fed Matthew."

The Redemption of Madelyne

She helped me into a nightgown and robe, and if she noticed the Band-Aid on my arm from a recent blood test, she didn't say anything. I took two of the pink sedatives, and slept until late the next day.

"Feeling better," she asked when I stumbled out of the bedroom.

"Coffee," I mumbled.

"Sit down," she ordered. "Lie down on the couch and I'll bring you a cup. You look better, but not altogether like you should." My fingers trembled as I took the proffered cup, and was thankful she was there.

Monday found me shaky, but back at work. As far as anybody knew, I'd been sick with a violent strain of flu. For once I was grateful for the many varieties of the virus going around; a person could be sick several times over and never have the same strain. But Friday didn't find me any better, and I had to call in sick. It was all I could do to get out of bed to take care of Matthew. Out of desperation, I called the clinic and spoke to the nurse.

"Are you bleeding excessively? Say more than two pads every two hours?"

"No, in fact the bleeding has slowed to almost nothing. But, I'm still not feeling well. I don't sleep at night, and I can't turn off my brain." My voice sounded strained and quavered with the threat of renewed tears. "It goes over the same thing over and over again."

"Look hon, it sounds like you need more than a medical doctor. You're depressed, and need to see a mental health counselor. They can help you through this. Don't worry--many girls go through the same thing. Do you have a paper and pencil?" I obediently wrote down the name and phone number of a psychiatrist she recommended, and hung up feeling worse than I had before. On top of everything else I was going crazy. Putting aside all self-pity, I refused to let any of this affect Matthew. Taking up the shattered remains of my life, I forced myself to go on as usual. I developed coping mechanisms, burying repressed feelings in work. After a while, I appeared better on the outside, while inside I was a wreck.

Madelyne was feeling similar pressures, and coping as best she could. I didn't see how close she was to falling over the edge until it was too late.

"What should we do today?" she asked one Sunday morning. "There's a sale at the mall, do you want to go?"

"I'd rather stay home and curl up with a good book. Maybe get some laundry done, bake something, and fix a big dinner— I'm feeling rather domestic and want to just enjoy being home."

"Yeah," she agreed as if it were a brilliant idea, "maybe a day spent at home is a good idea. It's about time I called my mother, and maybe help you bake some chocolate chip cookies."

"Do you know what would be good for breakfast? I love maple bars." At the mention of the sweet roll, my mouth watered. The suggestion stirred a craving for the maple deliciousness.

"Make you a deal?" she challenged. "You bake a big batch of cookies later today, and I'll run to the store right now and buy a dozen maple bars. Maybe all those calories will put some of the fat back on your bones. You're beginning to look as skinny as me."

"Don't go to all that trouble; I can live without maple bars for breakfast."

"Course you can, but you've been sick and deserve a little pampering. Make a fresh pot, and I'll be back in a jif." The coffee wasn't through brewing when she returned with the doughnuts in one hand and the Sunday paper in the other.

"If they make the paper any heavier, . . ." she commented as she dropped it on the table. Pouring coffee, we helped ourselves to a roll and gave half of one to Matthew. One became two, and we ate most of the bag before I put them away.

"No more of those things," I said as I licked the sticky maple from my fingers. "I can already feel a lump in my stomach. They are good, but turn to lead as soon as you eat them." Hefting the laundry basket to take a load to the washer, I watched as Maddie prepared to do her nails. While they dried, she called her mother just to test the waters.

"Hello, Mom," she said. "Thought I'd better call and tell you the news. . .. No, I didn't get the promotion. No, I'm not getting married. . .. Mom, wait—would you just listen for a minute. I'm pregnant. The baby's due in three months and.. . .No, I didn't plan on waiting until after the baby was born to tell you. . .. I'm sorry if this disappoints you, but. . ... No, I'm not going to quit my job. Yeah, it was good to talk to you, too." Placing the phone in its cradle, she looked at me with a bleak expression.

The Redemption of Madelyne

"At least she didn't hang up, or scream, or yell. That shows promise," I said, trying to find the bright side.

"Seems nobody wants this baby but you and me, and I'm not so sure about me anymore. Maybe. . ."

"Don't even think about it because I know you'll regret it. Read your paper while I mix a batch of cookies. We'll console ourselves with a sugar high that'll last all week."

Turning the pages listlessly, she soon forgot the paper and paced the kitchen, twisting her hands and gazing out first one window and then across the room to the other. I couldn't tell her the truth about abortion unless I revealed the secret I kept hidden in my heart. Biting my tongue, I kept silent.

"Those cookies can wait, can't they?" she asked. "I need to get out of here. Let's go for a drive, get a Starbucks, or something before these walls close in on me. I need to think and do better when I'm driving. Come with me. You could do with some fresh air and so could Matthew."

We drove aimlessly at first; taking streets we'd never taken before just to see where they went. The mall parking lot was full so we didn't stop. Maddie wanted to explore some antique shops on the far side of town, but somehow we got all turned around, and ended up in an area that screamed poverty. There were derelicts hanging around on the street corners, and a few shabbily dressed women that I was sure were hookers. This wasn't where we needed to be and especially with Matthew in the backseat.

"Turn around, Madelyne. This part of town makes me nervous. Look at those tramps over there," I said as I covered Matthew's eyes, "somebody ought to come in here and wipe them all out. Can you imagine living like that?"

"Maybe—maybe not. I feel sorry for people who have no other choice than to settle for society's cast-offs." Suddenly a police car rushed past with lights flashing and sirens screaming. An ambulance was in hot pursuit, "Wow, what do you think happened? Looks like a crowd is gathering there by the cross roads---I hope there hasn't been an accident." Cautiously, she drove closer, and then pulled over and parked.

219

"What are you doing?" I asked angrily. "Do not get out of this car, Madelyne Hall, because I won't go with you. This place gives me the creeps. How do you know you won't get mugged?"

"I can think of worse things," she called as she ran over to join a small crowd gathered in front of the police car. Locking the doors, I refused to budge from the safety of the car.

She edged her way into the crowd then fell to her knees. When the crowd parted slightly, shifting position to make way for the ambulance technicians, Maddie could be seen kneeling on the ground. She held the head of a fallen pedestrian in her lap. Didn't she know better than to move an accident victim? Suddenly, a shockwave went through me; surely it wasn't who I thought it was. Locking my purse in the glove compartment, I eased myself out of the car gripping Mathew's hand so tightly, he cried out in pain. The closer we got the harder my heart pounded.

"Help him, please help him." Maddie's cries brought the ambulance attendants running to move the body of an old man onto a gurney. Wispy gray hair, caught by the wind, floated above his head. A matted, tangled beard covered his chin, hiding thin lips. A trickle of blood from the corner of his mouth stained his collar red. His clothes hung limply on a spare frame, now broken and bleeding. A wheelchair lay to the side of the street, mangled after being struck by an oncoming car. The frantic driver pleaded with the old man not to die.

Pointing a gnarled finger into Maddie's chest, the old man smiled weakly, showing black, tobacco stained teeth, "Look for the followers of Molech, they will come for you," he choked, "they'll find ya' the same way they found me." Maddie leaned closer, to hear his dying words. Her hair fell over his face and chest, shielding him from the morbidly curious. What he whispered to her in those final moments remained a secret that she never shared.

"Poor guy, probably didn't see what hit him," the attendant said as he closed the dead man's eyes. "Did you know him?"

"We've only seen him twice before in our lives," I said with a shake of my head. "He was at a street rally we attended, and he scared us both half to death."

"How did this happen?" Madelyne sobbed.

The Redemption of Madelyne

"He came from nowhere. Came out of the alleyway over there," the driver said, pointing to a dark side street sheltered on both sides by brick buildings. A dumpster sat prominently on the corner heaped to overflowing. "He charged out of there without looking and rolled," the driver continued, gesturing to the wheelchair, "right into my lane of traffic. He threw a bottle at my car. There, do you see my windshield?" he asked those around him. "Old man must have been drunk or something. The bottle shattered and cracked the window clear across my line of vision. I was on him before I could stop."

"We need to ask a few questions," the investigating officer interrupted. "Sir, can we have your name and address?"

"My name's Mobach, Dr. Mobach," the dark haired man answered with an air of self-importance. "My office is at the clinic around the corner."

"Abortionist you mean," hissed a voice behind me. Turning to see who spoke, I was taken aback by the expression of loathing on one young woman's face. Knowing she had my full attention, she explained, "The old man was a nutcase, but he wasn't suicidal. It wouldn't surprise me to find out the good doctor there ran him down deliberate."

"Surely you don't mean that?" I asked with disbelief.

"I most certainly do," she stated. Shifting a grocery sack from her arms to the handsome boy standing next to her, she continued talking in a lowered voice. "The old man hated abortionists, and spent a good share of his old age fighting against them in the only way he knew how. But, he wasn't always this way; he went off the deep-end after his daughter died."

"He had a daughter?" I asked. It was hard to believe that such a spooky old man actually had children.

"Well, actually, he had two daughters. The younger one, a pretty little thing named Corinne, got herself pregnant by a good-for-nothing when she was seventeen. She died under an abortionist's knife. The old man lost the use of his legs when he used his car as a battering ram to destroy the building where it was performed."

"Who would believe it?" I said with a choked cry. "How awful."

"Yeah, and after that, the older daughter blamed him for her sister's death and didn't want anything more to do with him. It was more than he could take. He lost it; started a real vendetta against all doctors that performed abortions imagining them to be demons. Guess this time, the demon got him."

"Does anyone know where the other daughter is?"

"Not that I'm aware of, but I do know she's still in the city. She shouldn't be too hard to find. Her name's Trina or Rena, or something like that. Well, I've stood here shooting off at the mouth longer than I should have and I've got to go. By the way, my name's Sylvia and this here's my boy Rueben. Thanks for listening, but we're leaving--we've seen enough trouble for one day." When she turned to leave, her chin was wobbling and her brown eyes filled with tears.

Maddie stared after the young woman as if she'd seen a ghost. "Kathy's real name is Katrina. She told me her father used to call her Trina and that she had a younger sister that died. And the doctor--his name is so similar to the very thing the old man hated." She stared in horror at the blood stains on her blouse. All color drained from her face as she gazed at me. Her troubled eyes pleaded for a reasonable explanation. Could it be true? Suspicion that the doctor deliberately hit the old man in order to kill him glittered in the eyes of those gathered near. Nothing could block the ugliness of what they had witnessed.

Was there a chance the old man tried to stop the doctor? Maybe the accident wasn't what it appeared. Mobach was well known, and his name was frequently in the paper. His clinic was famed for providing abortions on demand. All of a sudden I felt as sick as Madelyne looked. I knew the same thoughts were going through her head. Was it murder or suicide? For Madelyne, it was both.

Onlookers and motorists confirmed the doctor's story, and he was sent on his way after being cautioned that the accident would be investigated. Madelyne became hysterical and it took quite a while to calm her down. The old man was dead, but his legacy lived on. Both of us heard his dire warning of an ancient god called Molech. Were we destined to live out his prophetic malediction?

One of the ambulance technicians was concerned about Maddie's state of mind, and led her away from the grisly scene. Helping her into the car, he advised she see her obstetrician right away.

"She's had a tremendous shock and should be seen by her doctor-just to be on the safe side," he warned. Sending us on our way, he promised to call later to check on her condition.

Madelyne didn't say much on the way home, but kept her head down as if a weight were balanced between her shoulder blades. Every now and then, tears trickled off her nose into her lap. Would the Maddie I knew and loved like a sister ever be the same?

When we arrived home, she went to her room and stayed there the rest of the afternoon. It wasn't until evening darkened the windows, casting long shadows across the walls, that she burst through the bedroom door. The look on her face made me reach for the phone, thinking an intruder had somehow found their way inside.

"It's too dark in here," she cried. Snapping on first one light and then another, she turned on every lamp in the apartment, including a small light in her closet. Nervously, she paced the floor, jumping at every sound. "It's all so bizarre," she said in a high, strained voice.

"What's bizarre?" I asked softly. "Come over and sit down," I coaxed, "before you fall down."

"No," she said, waving me away with a flutter of her fingers. "I've got to figure this out. This whole thing is crazy. Somehow-- you, me, Diane, Kathy, the old man--we're all connected in some way. By some bizarre, twist of fate we," she pointed to both of us, "are doomed to live out this nightmare to the end."

"Nonsense," I soothed. "Your imagination is running away with itself. You've had a bad experience, you're pregnant, and you're not sleeping. It's only natural to think things are worse than they are-considering the circumstances. I've had a few bad dreams myself, but I'm not going to let it get the best of me. Life goes on, Madelyne, and you are not in any way responsible for that old man."

"Listen to me," she screamed in a high pitched voice. "We might have witnessed a murder, and nobody seems to care. And he knew, Nicci, he knew I was pregnant," she said as she shook a finger in my face. "He read my mind and seemed to know what I was thinking." Matthew came running from the kitchen with a half-eaten cookie in his hand. Coming to an abrupt halt in the doorway, he remained motionless, eyes rounded with fright. I moved to reassure him, and wasn't quick enough to catch Maddie when she collapsed in a heap. It took all my strength to get her from the floor to the couch. Placing a damp cloth on her forehead, I mopped her face until her eyes fluttered open. Exhausted, she slept, tossing and turning most of the night; muttering in her dreams as I sat the night-watch by her bedside.

By morning, my joints and neck were stiff, and the bags under my eyes were large enough to hide an elephant. After splashing my face with cold water, I made a pot of coffee then made a quick dash to the corner to buy a newspaper. It was spread out in front of me when she came into the kitchen. The obits had a small article about the crazy old man that visited abortion clinics harassing patients and doctors alike. His name had been James Polansky. He left one heir with no other family mentioned.

"What made him do it? Why was he down on abortion clinics and why did he roll into oncoming traffic? He must have known he would be killed," she said softly, her eyes large and questioning.

"The paper says he was mentally ill. Maybe he saw it as the only way to rid his soul of the demon or demons that haunted him. Maybe he was drunk, or maybe he was just a crazy old man that didn't know what he was doing. Whatever he was, you can't dwell on it. There was nothing we could have done to help him."

When she looked across the table at me, her eyes pleaded for something I didn't understand. She didn't speak; in fact, from that point on she rarely spoke at all. The next few weeks threw her into a rapid, downward spiral that only she could save herself from.

"Have a cup of coffee while I make you some breakfast," I offered. "How about bacon and eggs, or whatever sounds good to you." Opening the fridge, I found the eggs, bacon, bread and butter, and placed them on the counter. She looked away, showing no interest in food; and after a few sips of coffee went back to bed. She stayed home, refusing to go to work. When I returned late that afternoon, I knew Maddie was in trouble. The sheets showed spots of blood, and she was running a slight fever.

"You need to see a doctor," I begged. "Please get up and let me take you to the clinic." She gazed at me dispassionately and then rolled over.

"I'll be fine," she mumbled. "Leave me alone."

"Fine," I shouted, "ignore the needs of your child. If you don't care enough to do anything about it, I do. I'm calling Diane." Even though it sounded like a threat, it was really an act of desperation. Things hadn't been right with Madelyne for a very long time and it was time to admit we needed help.

Dialing Diane's number with trembling fingers, I prayed she'd be home and when she answered, I burst into tears. She was on our doorstep within twenty minutes.

"What's wrong and how can I help?" she asked. After explaining all that had happened, she knelt by the couch, encouraging me to kneel with her.

"What are we doing?" I asked, my voice a whisper as we knelt together. Was this some magical, mystic ritual she performed to make things better?

"We're going to pray for Madelyne, and then ask God to give me wisdom so I can talk to her." When she bent her head in prayer, I stared at the back of her head in astonishment. At a time like this she needed to pray? Maybe this was the secret—-maybe praying made everything right. Bowing my head, I joined Diane in prayer, begging for help, hardly daring to hope anyone heard.

"Amen," Diane whispered as she came to her feet. Her look of confidence was reassuring, and when she reached for my hand, I felt slightly comforted. We entered Maddie's room together. She lay listlessly in the rumpled bedding, flat on her back, staring at the ceiling.

"Get up, Madelyne," Diane ordered, "you need to see your doctor." Diane whisked the covers off and stood over the bed, ready to lift her if necessary.

"Don't try to carry her," I warned, "think about your own baby." That got a reaction from Madelyne, and she turned to study the thickening around Diane's waist. A feeble smile tipped the edge of her lips as she rolled to her side.

"I'm glad you're pregnant," she sighed, "someone needs to break the cycle. Besides, I can't see my doctor because I don't have one."

"You've never been to an obstetrician? Haven't you seen anybody?" Diane was more than shocked, and her expression showed it. "Haven't you been checked? How do you know the baby is healthy if you've never been to a doctor?"

"I know something is wrong," she said simply. "The baby stopped moving over a week ago." Turning with her back to us, she refused to listen to our arguments. Diane pleaded with her to get up so we could take her to the hospital, but she refused.

"If you won't listen to reason, then I have no other choice. Madelyne, I'm calling an ambulance and have you taken to the hospital." Diane's voice was firm and with a straightening of her shoulders, she marched from the room and headed for the phone. An ambulance was there within minutes and the choice ceased to be Maddie's. We followed in Diane's car, holding our breath, praying for the life of the baby.

As soon as she was rolled in the hospital doors, the attending physician took charge. We were politely asked to wait outside the examination room where we paced up and down the hall, our steps sounding hollow on the ceramic floor. We glanced up expectantly when the doctor reappeared over an hour later.

"Your friend will be fine, but I'm a little worried about the baby. The heart is strong, but there are signs of distress. How long has she been taking tranquilizers? Didn't her doctor warn her against taking drugs of any kind while pregnant?" He looked at me with a stern expression, as if I was to blame for her condition.

"I didn't know she was taking anything," I denied, flabbergasted at the very idea that Maddie would put anything stronger than an aspirin in her mouth.

"Sure," he said skeptically. Shaking his head, he jotted down a few notes on the clipboard he carried. "Get her to an obstetrician as soon as possible, and don't procrastinate. She didn't want me to do a pelvic, but suspect she's somewhere near the third trimester. Why you kids wait so long for medical help is beyond me." He didn't wait for a reply, but went down the hall without a backward glance.

Diane stayed until Maddie was tucked safely into bed and sleeping soundly. "I'll be back tomorrow and don't worry about work; I'll call in and explain the circumstances. I'm sure they'll understand." Giving me an impulsive hug, she cautioned, "Call if you need anything." I went to bed soon after she left, and was asleep before my head hit the pillow.

Bright sunshine streaming in the windows woke me the following morning, and I sat up with a start. Grabbing the clock off the nightstand, I was shocked to see it was already past nine. Throwing off the covers with my ears open for any sign of life, I hurried to wash, put on my make-up, and dress. Fifteen minutes later, I opened the door to Maddie's bedroom.

"Oh no," a hand flew to cover my mouth as if I'd uttered something obscene. Her bed was empty, and after a quick search of the apartment, it was obvious she was gone. Praying she went to see a doctor, I started making phone calls. She wasn't at work. Diane hadn't heard from her, and no one seemed to know where she might be. After getting Matthew up and dressed, I drove over to the Perlman's. There was a bad feeling in the pit of my stomach, urging me to drive faster and move quicker. It was imperative to find Maddie. By the time I arrived at the Perlman's door, I was shaking from head to toe and quite hysterical.

"I've got to find her," I repeated several times. "She's pregnant and might do something awful to herself or the baby. Please, take care of Matthew--I've got to find Madelyne."

"Of course I'll watch the boy, dear, but you can't drive in the shape you're in," Claire objected.

"Don't worry," a deep voice declared, "she won't be alone. I'll drive her anywhere she needs to go." One of Claire's "boys" came from the kitchen where he'd been installing new kitchen cabinets. Matthew ran to greet him, throwing his arms around his knees. The man threw Matt into the air and balanced him on one arm. I'd seen him around before, but couldn't remember his name.

Brushing sawdust from his jeans, he stuck out a hand and shook mine. "Name's Micah and I'll be your chauffeur for the day. Pulling a ring of keys from his pocket, he escorted me to his pickup. I was crying and hiccupping badly by the time he hit the overpass and sped down the off ramp. Within minutes, we were driving down familiar streets trying to spot Madelyne's car.

"Do you have any idea where she might have gone? Is there someone she might confide in? Come on, Nicci, think, there's got to be someone." Shifting gears, he gunned the engine as we went over a hill. He didn't slow until we passed a black and white a couple blocks ahead.

"There's only one," I hiccupped. "But, I can't imagine she'd go to her."

"Don't think for her, and don't try to rationalize her behavior because if she's as upset as you are, she's running on pure adrenalin. What's the address?" Glancing at me, he smiled and placed a comforting hand on my arm. "Don't worry, we'll find her."

"I don't know the address." Sniffling loudly, I reached in my purse for a tissue at the same time he pressed a clean, pressed handkerchief into my hand.

"Let me play the Good Samaritan just this once," he chuckled. "I've always wanted to meet you, but under different circumstances I assure you. Now, let's get back to our little problem. Do you know the name of this person?"

After blowing my nose and wiping my eyes, I nodded. "Her name's Kathy." In a flash of insight, I remembered my conversation with Sylvia. "Or maybe Katrina. . . yeah, that's it. Katrina Polansky is her name." Veering off the side of the road, he jumped out, leaving the door open as he sprinted to a phone booth. Tearing a page from the yellow book attached to the wall of the booth by a chain, he bounded back and took off with a roar. "It's in the university district and not far from here."

We turned the corner, flying down the next street searching for the correct address. I breathed a sigh of relief when we spotted Madelyne's car. Micah parked behind leaving little room between his front bumper and her rear bumper. When I slid off the seat, dropping to the ground, I flashed a grateful smile. "How can I ever thank you?"

"We'll worry about that later," he said. "Go check on your friend, and I'll wait right here. Don't hurry, because I'm in good company." Pulling a black, leather bound Bible from the glove compartment; he leaned against the door. Making himself comfortable, he was absorbed in his reading before my first knock at apartment 2B.

Chapter Nineteen

I rapped at the door, but doubted anyone heard. It sounded like World War III with voices raised in vehement objection to one who disagreed. Nothing made sense--everyone yelling and no one listening. The door opened of its own accord when I knocked a second time.

"Don't tell her it's okay, when it isn't," Sherrie argued. "She's too far along to even consider it, and I can't believe we're having this conversation." Placing an arm around Maddie's shoulders, Sherrie was urging her to leave. "Come with me, Madelyne. Let me take you home." The door banging against the wall caught their attention. Relief flooded her face. "Nicci, thank God, you're here. I've been trying to talk her into leaving, but she won't."

"What's going on Madelyne?" I asked. "Why are you here? Yesterday, the doctor made it quite clear that you needed bedrest. I've been worried sick; you need to come home with me now. We'll make an appointment, and get you to a doctor right away."

"You don't get it, do you?" asked a surly voice. "Madelyne is an adult and perfectly capable of making her own decisions. She doesn't need a nursemaid."

"Back off, Kathy," I said with a boldness I was far from feeling. "Madelyne needs a friend right now, someone who cares about her, and that doesn't include you."

"You don't think I care? I don't suppose you can see beyond that bigoted nose of yours," she yelled. Tears filled her eyes as she stepped over to Madelyne's side. "I care—more than I ever wanted to. She reminds me of someone I used to know," she said with a far-away look in her eyes. Kneeling in front of Madelyne, she peered into her face,

"I'll be here for you, just like I promised. Whether you do or don't, it makes no difference to me. You've got to do what's best for Maddie."

"What have you been telling her?" I demanded. "Have you been trying to convince her to have an abortion?"

"Not in so many words," Sherrie volunteered, "but they haven't discouraged it either. Madelyne claims there's something wrong with the baby. She says the baby hasn't moved for over a week and she's been spotting. Yesterday, the doctor told her the tranquilizers she's been taking may have affected the baby's development."

"It's true," Madelyne cried. Lifting her tear-stained face, my heart wrung with compassion. Her red-rimmed eyes were swollen, and her cheeks blotched with an unhealthy color. She shook like a wind-blown leaf--out of control.

"Don't do something you'll regret," I begged. "You admitted just yesterday that you haven't been to your own doctor. The one you saw yesterday told me the baby's heart is strong. This child will be born perfect in every way."

"Is that a guarantee?" Kathy asked, "and what about Madelyne? Will she be okay? She's only twenty-three or four weeks along. There's time for her to end this nightmare before it goes any further."

"What you're urging her to do wouldn't end a nightmare, but start one that never ends. Why are you so insistent that every pregnant girl have an abortion? Does it have something to do with a young girl named Corinne?"

The room went silent. Kathy's face flushed white, and her eyes shot daggers. A look of contempt--pure hate contorted her features as her gaze scoured over us. "So, you know about Corinne? Well, if you know about her, you may as well know the rest. Corinne got pregnant and when she realized she was in trouble, went to our father for help. He called her every name in the book and threatened to throw her out in the street. She begged him to change his mind, but he refused. She got so scared--she panicked and had an illegal abortion. Corinne bled to death, begging for our father's forgiveness while her life ebbed away. There was nothing I could do," she sobbed. "I held my little sister while she died knowing there was nothing I could do to help her." Covering her face with her hands, Kathy's entire body shook with great wracking sobs.

The Redemption of Madelyne

Moved to compassion, I reached to comfort her. She pushed me away shaking her head as if to clear the horrible images embedded there. She vowed, "If I can help it, no other girl will die the same death as Corinne. She would have been fine, perfectly fine, if the abortion had been performed in a hospital where medical help was available. I'll fight until my last breath to see that abortions are kept legal and safe."

"You're wrong," I choked. Furiously brushing away the tears blurring my vision, I knew my secret couldn't be kept any longer. "She wouldn't be perfect. She would've been scarred beyond repair for the rest of her life. An abortion doesn't leave a person untouched--it strips away moral decency and self-respect leaving behind an emptiness that will never be filled. You hurt every time a child cries, and your heart remains heavy. The soul longs for the sound of your child's voice, the touch of his hand, the music of their laughter. . .hearing them call you Mommy. You wake in the middle of the night drenched in sweat, but inside you're icy cold. Every day you relive the loss of that life growing inside you. Not once in a while, but over and over again. Don't you understand what I'm saying? A part of you dies-- leaving a sadness that shadows the rest of your life. You can beg to be forgiven--to have a second chance, but it's too late. . .too late." Even Kathy listened without the perpetual sneer on her face. I prayed they'd understand. Abortion isn't the answer to a problem because it brings a burden of guilt too heavy to bear. It is not a quick fix, but a nightmare relived every minute of your life. Fighting for control, I wiped my streaming eyes resolutely, directing my words to Madelyne. "I had an abortion." Gasps of shock echoed around me, making my eyes drop in shame. I had to concentrate, retain my focus, and make her change her mind. "It was the worst experience of my life and something I will regret until my dying breath. Maddie, I beg of you, don't abort your baby. Go to a doctor, and get the medical attention you need."

"I don't know," she moaned, "I'm so confused. I feel empty inside, as if it's already gone." Holding my breath, I prayed she'd make the right choice. "I'll wait for Keith," she decided, "he'll be back in a few days." My heart thumped wildly, beating in my chest with great joy. She was still undecided--or so I thought.

Keith made the appointment before I got home from work. He promised to stay with her and be there through the entire procedure. I'm still not sure how they convinced a doctor to do it, but she aborted her baby on a beautiful spring day that hinted of better things to come. Keith called my office late that afternoon and I knew something was wrong because his voice shook with panic. I could hear Maddie screaming in the background.

"Come home, please," Keith begged. "She just keeps screaming and screaming. The doctor said it would be okay, but she won't stop screaming." John Powers overheard the conversation and asked no questions. He hurried me out the door as he took the phone to call an ambulance. When I arrived at the hospital, the corridor outside Maddie's room was filled with Diane and her family, John Powers, Claire, and Micah. This time I knelt with them as they bowed their heads in prayer. We were still praying when the doctor cleared his throat to gain our attention."

"Um, excuse me," he said self-consciously. "I don't mean to interrupt, but is there a Keith James here?" Looking around vacantly, we were surprised Keith was nowhere to be found. In fact, I didn't remember seeing him when I arrived. "She's asking for him, but if he isn't here."

"Is she okay? Will she be all right?" Grabbing the doctor's arm, I looked at him anxiously.

"She'll be fine. Her main problem right now is in her mind. She had a late term abortion, against all medical advice, and claims to have heard the baby cry. The mind plays strange games sometimes, but also maintains a fragile balance between what is acceptable and what is unacceptable. She can't forgive herself, and somehow imagines an infant's cry. We sedated her heavily and hope to find her better by morning. She'll be here for a couple days, so please inform the desk who to notify."

"I can't tell her mother; she'd hate me for it. Other than that, there's no one else." I said.

"How could she do such a thing?" Mrs. Perlman leaned on Micah and wept for the child as if it had been her own. It was hard to understand. Not one of us knew what to say or do to console one another.

"I've got to go in there so she isn't alone when she wakes up," I told Diane. "How do I face her? What do I say?" We cried on each other's shoulders, me for the child I aborted and she for the lives of all discarded children. Bracing for the worst, I entered Madelyne's room prepared for another all night vigil. Micah sat with me through each long, lonely hour.

"Hope you don't mind," he whispered as he pulled a chair over next to me, "thought you could use some company. Paul took Diane home. She's a wreck and he was afraid of the effect of all this on their baby. John took Claire home, so that leaves you and me. If you'd rather be alone, I'll understand." His friendly smile warmed my heart. How could I refuse such an offer of real concern?

"Thanks," I answered honestly. "To tell you the truth, I'd welcome the company. Something tells me it's going to be until the wee hours." As the room darkened and the hour grew late, he squeezed my hand just to let me know he was still there. He leaned forward and bowed his head. Balancing elbows on knees, he stayed that way for a very long time, his lips moving every now and then in silent prayer. We blinked rapidly against a sudden infusion of light when the night nurse came to check Maddie.

"Would you like some coffee?" she asked. "There's a full carafe at the nurse's station with plenty of cups. Help yourself to whatever you want. Cream and sugar is on a cart down the hall." After taking Maddie's pulse and tapping on the IV bottle a couple of times, she left after dimming the overheads, but thoughtfully left a nightlight burning.

"Want a cup?" Stretching and twisting to get the blood flowing, he stepped out to get us some coffee and a sandwich. When he returned with his hands full, a Bible was tucked tightly under his arm. He opened it to a passage and read silently as he ate.

"What are you reading? I know it's the Bible and all, but what does it say?"

"I'm reading in the book of *Psalms*. Would you like me to read it for you?" Nodding in assent, I listened intently to the poetic words, and tears began all over again.

> *O Lord, do not rebuke me in your anger or*
> *discipline me in your wrath.*
> *Be merciful to me, Lord, for I am faint;*
> *O Lord, heal me, for my bones are in agony.*
> *My soul is in anguish.*

How long, O Lord, how long?
Turn, O Lord, and deliver me;
Save me because of your unfailing love. Psalm 6:1-4

"That sounds like a prayer—a prayer for Madelyne," I said in awe. "Do you think He heard? I mean, does He answer everybody's prayers?"

"All prayer, if sincere, is answered, but not always in the way we expect. God answers in His way and in His time. Would you like to pray for her?" Again I nodded and knelt with him on the cold, hospital floor. The words came haltingly, but my heart told me my prayer was heard.

Micah stayed through the night, but spent most of it in prayer. When he wasn't praying we talked--and he told me about himself and how he met the Perlman's. He left before daylight to go to work, but promised to be back later.

"Thanks." I walked him out to the parking lot, overwhelmed with gratefulness. Why did this man care so much?

"Thanks for what?" he asked.

"For everything," I gushed. "I've never known anyone like you. You're honest and sincere and have such a good heart; I don't understand why you care at all."

Kissing me on the forehead, he smiled tenderly as he pulled his jacket snugly over my shoulders. "I care because it's the human thing to do, and I selfishly have to admit, because I'd like to get to know you. Any woman that can raise a great kid like Matthew has got to be pretty special."

"No, no I'm not," I denied. Keeping my head down and face averted, I was ashamed to meet his gaze. "I'm not anything special."

"Let me decide, okay? I'll be back later and hang in there. The night is always darkest before the dawn." As he climbed in his pickup and drove off, I watched until the orange of his taillights faded from sight. What kind of man was it that quoted scripture, sat up all night praying for a woman he didn't know, and made me feel so totally alive? Hugging the jacket around me against the morning's chill, I breathed in the scent of him. A thrill of pleasure brought a smile to my lips. I was still smiling when the door to Maddie's room opened at my touch. She was sitting up, looking around wide-eyed, as if shocked to find a hospital room instead of familiar bedroom furnishings.

"How do you feel," I asked. Shrugging off the jacket, I hung it carefully on the back of a chair.

"Awful. My back hurts and I'm still cramping. A nurse brought me something for pain a little while ago. I don't want to feel. I don't want to feel anything ever again," she sighed and pulled the covers up to her chin. "Keith isn't here, is he?" It wasn't a question, but an answer to what she already knew. Turning her face to the wall, she closed her eyes and allowed the sedative to do its work. As she slept, I sat next to the bed holding her hand. I wondered why she did it? Was the need for love so great that she would sacrifice anything to obtain it? How sad because if that were true--in the obtaining, she destroyed the one thing she wanted most.

"How's the patient?" Micah asked when he returned. Placing a hand on my shoulder, he handed me a cup of coffee and one of Claire's huge sandwiches. "She was afraid you hadn't eaten all day," he explained.

Nibbling at the sandwich, I finally wrapped it back in the plastic wrap. "She slept all day and they've sedated her twice. When the drugs wore off the first time she got hysterical and started screaming for her baby. She insists on going home tomorrow. I don't know what to think."

"Looks like you need a break. Let's get out of here for a while. Matthew wants to see you anyway." We spent an hour at the Perlman's and then took Matthew out for dinner. The relationship between Micah and my son was obvious. Matt spent the entire time sitting on Micah's lap, and refused to go to bed until Micah read him a story and tucked him in. When it came time to return to the hospital, I almost didn't want to. I preferred to spend my evening with the two of them where a semblance of calm had been restored.

Micah dropped me off, and then went home for some much needed rest. Taking the elevator to the fourth floor, I was surprised to see the door to Madelyne's room swung wide open. I was even more surprised to find the room empty. The night nurse told me Maddie went against doctor's orders and checked herself out.

"I hope you find your friend," the nurse said as she escorted me to the elevator. "She's in pretty bad shape, and needs someone to help her over the rough spots. Get her to a shrink as soon as possible. If she doesn't work through this, she may never recover."

Before leaving the hospital, I placed a call to Claire, who in turn called Micah. My phone was already ringing when I arrived home.

"Did you find her? Is everything okay?" Micah asked anxiously when I answered.

"It's okay. She's here and sound asleep. I'll call if anything comes up."

"Can I come over later? Keep you company? Play a game of <u>Chutes and Ladders</u> with Matthew?"

"Sure, I'd like that. But, Micah. . .?"

"Yeah,"

"Don't feel obligated, okay?"

"It's no obligation, but I must warn you my motives aren't totally magnanimous. I want to see you again and am hoping to invite myself for dinner."

"Your invited," I giggled. "Get some sleep and I'll see you later."

Madelyne slept for a couple hours, long enough for me to run to the store and retrieve Matthew from the Perlman's. When he found out Micah was coming for dinner, he was ecstatic. He helped set the table, and even polished the silverware on the seat of his pants.

The sound of running water caught my attention. Opening the bedroom door a fraction of an inch, I peeked in to see if Maddie was still in bed. She wandered out of the bathroom carrying a glass of water.

"Can I get you anything? Dinner won't be for another hour or two, but I'd be glad to fix you some soup or something."

"No," she mumbled, shooing me off with a wave of her hand. Grabbing a bottle of pills off her nightstand, she shook two white tablets into her palm.

"Those are sedatives," I warned, "and should be one every six hours." Reaching for the bottle, I read the instructions on the label. There were five other bottles with similar instructions. All of them were a form of sedative, and it was obvious she had taken them before.

"I want to sleep," she complained. Placing her hands over her ears, she shook her head and squeezed her eyes shut. "It won't stop. At least when I'm sleeping the crying stops."

"What crying? Maddie, I don't want you to take any more of these pills," I said gesturing to all the half-full medicine bottles. "You're talking crazy and taking sedatives only muddles your thinking. I know things look pretty bleak right now, but it'll get better." She didn't respond or even look in my direction, but crawled back into bed. Her drug induced sleep lasted ten hours and when she woke, she swallowed some more. After three days of the same, I flushed the remaining medication down the toilet. I was afraid she'd overmedicate and never wake up.

Her body healed, but something inside never did. Over the following months, I watched her dwindle away. She used sedatives to go to sleep and uppers to wake up. Her skin lost its clear smoothness and took on the fragility of parchment. The lustrous color of her cinnamon hair faded to a dull brown. Her appetite dwindled to nothing, and the figure she'd been so proud of went from slender to skeletal almost overnight. She didn't sleep unless induced with drugs, and even then sleep wasn't restful. Nightmares made her cry out, rousing her at odd hours of the night. Several times she woke up screaming, imagining unspeakable things. Her world became a frightening place where she was constantly on the alert. Starting at every sound, she couldn't seem to take enough drugs to calm the war going on inside her head. Even a visit from her mother made little impression. We had to admit that the only person who could help Madelyne was Madelyne herself, but she wasn't willing.

Even when things looked the worst, Micah remained faithful. He sat up with me many nights, waiting for her to come home. We suspicioned she was buying drugs off the street, but couldn't prove it until she lost her job. The boss was tired of her coming to work stoned. She became a woman I didn't know. We begged her to see a psychiatrist--she refused and the downward spiral continued, plummeting faster to a point of no return. There was nothing we could do.

"Is she here?" Micah asked one evening as he came in the door. Lifting Matthew, he greeted him in their customary fashion. "Who loves you? I do and that's a fact."

"She's resting, I think. I'm worried--her behavior is more erratic. She has a bruise over one eye where she beat her head against the wall to stop the crying that only she can hear."

"Decisions need to be made," he said with a sad smile. "Have you called her mother? Something needs to be done before she hurts herself or someone else. That someone could be you, and there's Matthew to think about. You've bore this burden for too long. It's time someone else took over." Placing his arms around me, he enfolded me in a tight embrace. We'd been seeing each other for only a couple months, but I couldn't imagine life without him. I loved him so much it hurt.

"You go sit with her while I finish dinner. I know how to cook, believe it or not, as long as it doesn't have to be fancy. Let's see," he said as he poked his head in the refrigerator, "you've got hamburger, lettuce, tomato, and onion. I make a mean taco, and if you have the right seasonings, my own sauce." Leaving the kitchen to him and Matthew, I made my way into Maddie's room moving as quietly as possible. She slept, tossing from side to side and muttering to herself. Resuming my bedside vigil, I sat down with a sigh. Maybe tonight would be different. Maybe tonight she wouldn't wake up screaming. Maybe tonight the old Madelyne, my best friend, would fill the empty shell of this strange woman lying on the bed, and we would laugh like we used to. "And maybe," I said sarcastically to myself, "my car is a pumpkin and I'm Cinderella."

That night there was a change in her condition, but not necessarily for the better. When her eyes fluttered open, there was a deadly calm about her with no hysteria.

"It's time to put an end to all this," she stated matter-of-factly. "I can't follow my own thoughts anymore, and the crying never stops."

"It will if you let it." Micah stepped into the room with a dinner tray prepared for her. Stepping to her bedside, he whisked a napkin under her chin and bowed, "Dinner is served. Would madam like coffee with her meal or after?"

"Oh, after, of course," she said with a hint of smile. He balanced the tray against a hip as I unfolded a TV tray. We set up a makeshift table in her room so the meal could be shared together. She bowed her head as we did while Micah said the blessing.

God can't love me," she whispered to herself at the Amen. No one can love me."

"I love you, Aunt Maddie," Matthew told her. "Jesus loves you, too because He said so, didn't He?" He gazed innocently at Micah with absolute faith in God's love. I was humbled by the love my son showered on those around him. It was a glimpse into the true love of God.

"God loves you, Madelyne. That's a truth I am sure of," Micah assured her. "There isn't anything you've done that He can't forgive."

"We all love you," I echoed.

Throughout the meal, we kept a light banter going between us hoping Maddie would join in. She lapsed into another long silence. Tears filled her eyes as she looked about the room. A sweet, poignant expression crossed her face as her gaze came to rest on Matthew and then upon me. There was something eerie about it; as if she were saying good-bye. Micah sensed it and grabbed my Bible from the coffee table. After putting Matthew to bed, I joined him at Madelyne's bedside where he read aloud scripture after scripture. Words that spoke of God's love and faithfulness. There was an urgency in his voice as his fingers flipped through the pages until the passages he sought were found.

"God loves you Madelyne, do you hear me, *He* loves you as His own child. Listen to this, it's straight from the word of God."

> *Before I formed you in the womb I knew you, before you were born I set you apart, says the Lord. Jer 1:5*

"And,"...

> *The Lord is good, a refuge in times of trouble. He cares for you... Nahum 1:7*

"He can't care for me," she moaned, "I destroyed the child He gave me. I have committed the worst of sins. I murdered my own child. I heard my baby's cry and it haunts me. The sound of it is there when I wake in the morning and follows me throughout the day. It's the last thing I hear at night; distorting my dreams into terrifying images. The only way to drown it out is to drug myself. No, He can't love me, because I can't love me."

"You're wrong," he pleaded, "God doesn't measure sin as one being worse than the other. In His eyes, it's all the same. He promises that if we confess our sins, He will forgive us our sin."

"Not me," she said adamantly. "I've begged to be forgiven, but the voice is still there. I made the choice and will pay the consequences."

He stayed with her, reading from different sections of scripture until she finally fell into a fitful sleep.

When he joined me in the darkened kitchen and sat down at the table, I asked if everything he'd told Maddie applied to me. With a look of surprised delight, he knelt with me in prayer, and led me to Jesus. God's love covered all the hurt and pain in my heart, and healed the wounds of sin. When I raised my head after a prayer of thanksgiving, I was a new person. Micah's cheeks were wet with tears when he left that night.

"Thank you, Jesus," he prayed over and over. "I love you, Nicole, and am so grateful for such a merciful God. He led me to you and now He's led you to Him." When he left, he promised to call first thing in the morning. "Read your Bible," he advised, "God's word is a great healer."

Later, as I lay in bed reading from the Book of Psalms, I found it wasn't boring at all. The words touched something in my heart, and I rushed to the bedroom to share my joy with Madelyne. Her bed was empty and her car was gone. Bundling Matthew in a blanket, I drove the streets for over an hour, but never caught a glimpse of her. When we returned home, the phone was ringing with an ominous tone and I answered with a trembling hand. My heart ached and tears pricked my eyes. Somehow I knew.

"Madelyne, is that you?" I asked, trying to keep my voice as calm and level as possible.

"It's me," she said weakly. "I needed to call and explain so you would know why."

"Why what? No--you need to come home and go back to bed, Maddie. You're not well and you need medical help. Please, come home."

"I can't." She began to cry. Hammer beats of dread thumped in my chest. "I told you once before—we were connected. . .linked in some mysterious way. . that old man and me. He knew my secrets---he knew yours." Her voice tapered off to a whisper, and I could almost hear what she was thinking.

"Don't do anything foolish. If you can't drive, tell me where you are, and I'll come get you," I pleaded.

"Don't you get it," she cried brokenly, "can't you hear them?"

"Hear who? Madelyne, please, listen to me."

"Can't you hear them crying? I've heard them every night and every day since I allowed my baby to be taken. It's the sound of every baby—it's your baby, too," she hissed. "They never forgive, and there's only one way to stop it—only one way to atone for what I've done. I love you," she told me and then the phone went dead. It was the last time I spoke to my best friend.

★   ★   ★

Madelyne drove to the west side of town where the streets are lined with poverty and heartache etches the faces of the homeless. Driving at a high rate of speed, she rammed her car into the side of a cinder block building that sits on a street corner with an alleyway on one side and a dumpster on the other.

Micah met me at the hospital and wrapped his arms about my shoulders. "I'll be with you every step of the way. Go on in, she's asking for you."

When I entered the emergency room, I was surprised at how cold the room felt. Shiny steel and chrome circled the bed where she lay with so many tubes and monitors she was unrecognizable. I lifted a cold, limp hand and held it to my cheek for a moment.

"Maddie, . . .please wake up," I cried. Tears ran down my face, choking back the words I needed to say. "I love you, I need you, don't leave us." Her eyes fluttered open and she smiled in the old familiar way. Her gaze went beyond me, not seeing me at all.

"Can't you hear them?" she asked in a faint voice. "They aren't crying—they're singing. Do you think I've been forgiven? I pray *He* will forgive me, too. . ." and then with a shuddering breath, she was gone. She had finally found a way to quiet the voices from within.

So you are no longer a slave, but a daughter; and since you are a daughter, God has made you also an heir. Galations 4:7

Chapter Twenty

". . . and that's my story. As I said before, I'm not here to preach at anyone and if abortion is the choice you've made, I hope you've thought it through. Women need to know the possible repercussions of such a decision. Madelyne experienced post-abortion depression which led to suicidal thoughts. Those thoughts led to actions that resulted in her death. Approximately 60 percent of post-abortion women experience some aspect of this psychological disorder, but in varying degrees. I've fought my own battles with depression, and have grieved over the decision that ended the life of my child. We continue to use the technical jargon thrown at us by a "me first," society, but it doesn't change the facts. Fetus isn't just a word, but is a human being deserving of the same considerations that you expect for yourself. Scripture tells us that God knew us before we were formed in the womb and that He has a plan and a purpose for our lives. I want to assure each of you, that God doesn't make mistakes. I am not a mistake any more than you are, and our children are conceived for God's purpose." A restless stirring rippled through the audience. It was a signal to end her appeal and conclude the message she prayed had come through loud and clear.

"Okay, I'm getting off my soapbox, but thought you might be interested in hearing what happened to some of the people I've told you about. Micah and I got married two months after Maddie's death. We've been together ever since, and I can't imagine a day without him. Richard is in his third marriage, and recently committed himself into a drug rehab center. I pray he'll find someone he can love more than himself. The biggest surprise came within my own family. Even though

The Redemption of Madelyne

Maddie's death brought sorrow, it also brought salvation. My father came to know the Lord as did Madelyne's mother. Together, they run a counseling center for young women. My mother and father, along with Madelyne's mother Toni Hall, have been instrumental in bringing mental health professionals into the clinics so girls can get counseling as well as medical treatment.

On a sadder note, Keith was in a boating accident and drowned. He was twenty-eight.

Paul and Diane are still in the city, and he still pastors the same church. They outgrew themselves, however, and a new church building stands on an acre and a half, not including parking. She still runs a daycare, but now there are three facilities instead of one. They have five children, and the twins work with their mother in the daycare. Paul is a fine minister, and hopes their son will take over the ministry someday.

Matthew went totally against my mother's heart and grew up. For several years I was afraid to let go, afraid to let him wander far from home, but the strings had to be cut. It was an emotional time. Matthew had to follow the leadings of his own heart. He said his good-byes to Micah, the man he calls dad, and then to me over three years ago. He joined the service and now flies bombing missions in and out of Afghanistan. He's single and hopes to find the right girl someday. Mrs. Perlman sends him cookies, and thinks of him as one of her boys.

That about sums things up, but before closing, there's one more thing to add. Micah and I were blessed with an addition to our family that arrived shortly after our marriage. Some of you may remember the headlines about the baby found in a dumpster next to an abortion clinic. Micah and I adopted that baby and I'd like you to meet her."

A slender, young girl held the arm of her father as he led her onstage. Micah stood with a reassuring hand on her shoulder as she turned to face the audience. Audible gasps came from every direction. The girl gave a little shake of her head, as if unsure, and placed a hand at her temple, holding back waist length, cinnamon-red hair. Arching one brow, she surveyed the audience with interest as her lips curved into a smile of amused pleasure. She waved, flashing a spectacular smile that stunned the audience to silence. Nicole stepped to the girl's side and placed an arm around her shoulders. "This is our daughter, and her name is. . .Madelyne."

> *Who is a God like you, who pardons sin*
> *and forgives the transgression. . .*
> *You do not stay angry forever but*
> *delight to show mercy.*
> *You will again have compassion on us*
> *you will tread our sins underfoot. . .*
> *Micah 7:18-19*

Author's Note

Even though Madelyne and Nicole are fictitious characters, their stories are quite true. Both women had all the signs and symptoms of clinical depression that frequently results in suicide or self-inflicted injuries. Scientific and medical studies prove the reality of the link between the two. Women are definitely victims because they are led to believe the lie that an abortion will take care of a "problem" or fix a "mistake." They aren't told that the result of such a decision leaves emotional scars that can change the course of your life.

One study completed by the *British Medical Journal* that included a survey of American women, found that depression after an abortion lingers for several years. (Reardon et. al. 1) Their study was conducted in 2002 and supported by other medical professionals. "Researchers found that women who have abortions are at significantly greater risk of clinical depression than women who carry their babies to term." (Reardon) (Coleman, et al. 2002) that women who abort require more mental health treatments than women who deliver their babies. (Coleman etal 1) They studied the medical records of 173,000 women for four years to "follow their pregnancy outcomes." The results were not surprising. "Abortion was most strongly associated with higher rates of subsequent treatment for neurotic depression, bipolar disorder, adjustment reactions, and schizophrenic disorders."

A third study was conducted by researchers who looked at death records linked to Medi-Cal payments for abortions. The results should have been published on every pro-choice banner. They found that women who have had abortions are twice as likely to die within two years after the abortion. (Reardon 2) These women also have a high mortality rate over the eight years following an abortion.

A study conducted in Finland found that when comparing delivering women to those who abort, the women who chose abortion were 6.5 times more likely to commit suicide within one year. (Gissler & Reardon 1-2)

When will we stop believing the lie? If women would band together in support of "life" change will be a natural course of action. There is no room for hate or radical behavior. The doctors, nurses, and employees of abortion clinics need prayer—not condemnation. In attempting to help, to provide a service, they also have been led to believe the lie. Isn't that the ultimate goal of the evil one? If we can be persuaded to destroy the innocence within ourselves by aborting our babies, then evil wins.

According to *Idaho Vital Statistics 2013* there were 3,932,181 live births recorded in the United States. Of that number Idaho claimed 22,348 live births. The down side of this is the number of abortions performed during the same time period. Even though abortion rates are declining, the number is still disturbing. Keep in mind that the numbers are "reported" abortions. It does not include those that are self-induced and go unreported. The total number of legal abortions performed in the United States in the year 2011 was 730,322. In 2012 the number recorded in Idaho was 1,916 induced abortions. The number reported in 2013 was slightly less, but if compared to the total number of abortions performed in the US the numbers are still high.

"*The number of abortions reported in Idaho in 2013 was 1,794, a 6.4 percent decrease from the 1,916 reported in 2012. Abortions occurring in Idaho maybe to Idaho residents or non-residents. Of the 1,375 procedures performed in Idaho, 1,321 (96.0 percent) were to* residents of Idaho and 54 (4.0 percent) were to non-residents."

How incredibly sad. The methods are also recorded in the **_2013 Idaho Vital Statistics._** We've known about the methods for years, but choose to either ignore or pretend it isn't happening. The medical tools for ending the life of the developing embryo vary from suction, to dilation and suction, to intra-uterine saline solution to poisoning the developing fetus resulting in abortion, and including the non-surgical abortions induced through pills or other methods.

This information is not meant to condemn, but to inform. Scripture reminds us over and over again that we are not accidents, but formed by God for his good pleasure with a plan for life that is precious. Jesus loves you--warts and all.

The numbers reported center around Idaho because the author is from that particular state. Idaho's population is miniscule when compared to New York, California, Washington, Florida, and other more populated states. If the number of abortions were recorded for each state in the union the information would fill a book of its own. Help is available for anyone facing an unplanned pregnancy through any Prolife Hotline. (Reardon and Cougle)

"I, even I, am He who blot out your transgressions for My own sake;
And I will not remember your sins."
Isaiah 43:25

Works Cited

Coleman, Priscilla K, David C Reardon, Vincent M Rue, and Jesse Cougle. 2002. "State-Funded abortions versus deliveries: A comparison of outpatient mental health claims over 4 years." *American Journal of Orthopsychiatry* 141-152.

Gissler, M, and et al. 2005. "Injury deaths, suicides and homicides associated with pregnancy, Finland 1987-2000." *European J. Public Health* 459-463.

2015. "Idaho Vital Statistics." *Idaho Department of Health and Welfare.* Division of Public Health, Bureau of Vital Records and Health Statistics, April.

Reardon, D C, and J R Cougle. 2002. "Depression and unintended pregnancy in the National Longitudinal Survey of Youth: a cohort study." *British Medical Journal* 151-2.

Reardon, D C et. al. 2002. "Deaths Associated with Pregnancy Outcome: A Record Linkage Study of Low Income Women." *Southern Medical Journal* 834-841.

Printed in the United States
By Bookmasters